Unbent

If your mind is split, can your heart stay whole?

Courtney Shepard

Unbent

Unbalanced 2

COURTNEY SHEPARD

Unbent

This is a work of fiction. The characters, incidents, and dialogs in this book are of the author's imagination and are not to be construed as real. Any resemblance to actual events or persons, living or dead, is completely coincidental.

Published by CS Press
BC, Canada

~ * ~

First Edition

www.unbalancedseries.com

Version_1

*To the Flying Pigs...you know who you are, and I love you.
And to Diana, I miss your light every single day.*

Prologue

Before any record or construct of time…

The Master stood at the top of the Order's tallest tower and scanned his kingdom. The army stretched out below in every direction farther than he could see.

They would mobilize after the ritual, but he needed more power first. The vile creatures had not broken; they had healed faster than natural. Unlike the others, they had all that he coveted. True witches.

They made him…what is this feeling…? Fear?

How did such weak, fragile vessels contain what he worked so hard to achieve? His dark disciples held only a sliver of their original strength, but they gained small amounts through sacrifice. Though not one of their sacrifices contained a hint of what he sought, his disciples achieved traces more through the blood ritual.

But the females below had their *shakti*, their full spectrum of power, at their fingertips. No price was required of them to wield such vast wells of it. It was their magic, their *vyralis*, their birth-given gifts, and he would stop at nothing to harvest them.

The fires snuffed out across the land, and he descended the spiral tower steps. Upon entering the Grand Chamber, he noted the four females chained to the floor expressed nothing, their eyes shut.

"All attempts have failed, Master."

"Then kill them."

"Yes, Master," they spoke as one the way they often did.

Chapter One

Mere slumped against the door in the front seat of a moving car, while tears streamed down her face. There was nothing but searing, tearing, pulsating agony.

What happened to me? It had to be something awful for this much pain. Why can't I remember?

She couldn't pretend to be asleep forever, but from the instant she'd opened her eyes, all she could do was breathe and clench through the agony. A quiet buzz in the back of her mind prodded at her growing confusion. A sidelong glance had her gasping, the movement pulling at her skin and giving even more suffering, but she breathed relief to see, through her blurred vision, a woman driving. Blinking rapidly, Mere cleared the haze and the tears from her eyes.

White hair. Stiff posture. Heavy silence, but pulsing power. Avia? her gentle inner voice asked, attempting to soothe her confusion.

Of course, it's Avia, her darker voice snapped. *Who else is that stiff?*

Avia turned as Mere's gasp ended in pants. Her strange silver eyes narrowed a fraction before they relaxed.

Grunting through excruciating throbs, Mere dipped her chin, hoping to survey the damage and the source of her condition. It was easy to imagine what wreckage awaited her, but even that slight shift sent agony roaring through her.

Attempting to stifle her cry by biting her bruised, split lip backfired, and her scream burst forth unabated. The reverberation ricocheted in her head and throughout the confines of the vehicle, assaulting her already battered body as if the sound itself were solid fists.

Avia's only reaction was her fingers tightening on the steering wheel until her knuckles were white. "Stay calm—" The hollow voice was her sister's, but there was a note of command that had Mere fighting to obey.

Deep breath. Where are we? What happened?

The ground outside was wet. The sky was dark but lightening; dawn approached.

"What happened t-to-m-me?" Mere forced her words, squeaking

and rasping at the same time, through her throbbing throat to make just a wisp of struggling, tortured sound.

Shit...

Pain and confusion surrounded her, smothered her, and with each second, her fear transformed into terror. A fresh wave of tears escaped her lids and flowed over her cheeks.

Water, I need water. Water will heal me.

She called water to her skin and wounds to help heal and relieve her pain.

It didn't come.

Wait... I must be drained. Try harder. There...

An invisible film of water coated her skin.

Thank you.

"What happened to me?" Her voice sounded stronger.

"You're okay."

"I definitely disagree with that. Can't you see..." Mere said through gritted teeth.

"I mean, you're safe now."

Safe? Her darker voice scoffed. *No way.*

"I disagree with that, too." She paused, glancing out the window. "I take it we're not in Egypt anymore."

"No, not for days."

Despite the pain, Mere reeled from that news. *Days? How can it be days?*

She probed her memory, but thick, gray clouds billowed up and covered her mind—impossible to penetrate.

Was I drugged? Am I still drugged? She took another slow, prepping breath, then flipped open the visor mirror above. *Oh, my—*

One gulp to force the sudden, throat-obstructing lump down, then a swallow to ensure she could breathe before touching her hair's singed tips.

No, no, no... No.

Her once-long, wavy black hair was short, uneven, and curling below her ears. Her left eye was blood red, while the right was bruised and swollen. Caked blood crusted around her hairline, nose, the corners of her mouth, and on her neck.

How?

"What happened?"

Avia stared ahead, working the steering wheel with her grip.

"Avia?"

Is she ignoring me? Mere's angrier inner voice almost snarled.

Avia's slow blink begged for patience, and she said, "A lot has happened. But you should focus on healing right now. We have to get you to a safe place. We can't just keep running and hiding."

"I can heal and listen to you at the same time. The last thing I remember, I was under the pyramid...with Aron. We found some carvings, but I can't recall." She brushed her temple with her fingertips but flinched at the painful contact. It hurt to think, let alone move.

"The Order had you."

Mere's heart stuttered. "What?" Dropping her gaze to finally assess the damage, she flinched.

She wore a filthy trench coat that reeked of smoke. *Where are my clothes? Am I naked? Please, no...*

Her legs quivered and jumped from waning adrenaline, which caused cuts to open, stinging skin to stretch, and bones to shift. More tears leaked out. Glancing at her reflection, her tears smeared the soot on her face to resemble some wild warrior's tribal paint.

If only you were a warrior, little Guppy.

What did they do to me?

The list of injuries included burns, bruises, various cuts, and an ugly wound on her chest that throbbed, pulsed, and hurt more than everything else combined. The blackened skin surrounding the circular hole was jagged, peeled, and the pain stabbed right through her and out her back.

She gently touched the edge of the damaged flesh on her chest, gritting her teeth and flexing her legs in response to the pain.

Idiot. Of course, that's going to hurt.

Her skin was surface pain. The cuts and bruises went deeper, but she felt where those injuries ended. The broken ribs, she recognized those, and the bruised lungs and kidneys were familiar aches she'd received from past injuries, but there was still something worse; dense ice traced and coated her flesh and organs and all the lines of her body, cutting her as it froze her. The heavy pressure under its weight resembled slow, grinding glaciers.

"The Order took you from the pyramid."

Avia's voice snapped Mere out of her mental cascade.

"They had you until just a few hours ago...but you're safe now."

Mere's laugh was bitter-edged. *There's that word...* "Safe?" she breathed out with a mocking rasp.

Avia said nothing.

"Where are the others?"

Silence.

"Avia?" Mere snapped, the stonewalling from Avia stinging her almost more sharply than her injuries.

"We split up. They're on their way to a safe—a—house," Avia said, staring ahead.

With each heartbeat, Mere's panic increased. A ringing, growing louder and louder into a screech, pummeled her aching head. Her mind stuttered at the trespass. She couldn't stop the assault or control the chaos in her mind, so she shook—weak and powerless.

I am not powerless, her supportive voice encouraged.

Except when it counts, Guppy—when everyone you love needs you the most. Her dark voice reminded her of reality.

Not now. Water, first. Heal before anything else.

She summoned water, but it didn't come. *I must be too drained.* She pushed harder, drew another thin layer of moisture from the air and absorbed it into her stinging skin. It eased her panic a bit, but the pain persisted.

Avia stared ahead.

How does she come from a battle looking like that? Perfect, without a hair out of place, while I'm destroyed?

"Is anyone else hurt?" A pit yawned open inside Mere, and panic poured in. *Asha and Ivy…Aron.*

Tingling heat rippled through her at the thought of Aron, despite everything else currently consuming her.

Easy girl.

"Not like you," Avia said.

Of course. It's always me. I'm the one who gets shot. I'm the one who gets caught and tortured.

"What happened?" Mere asked.

Avia hesitated.

What is she hiding?

A lot, I bet. Even Mere's supportive voice questioned Avia's evasion.

Mere called more moisture from the air into her skin, soothing her injuries. She breathed out her relief. "Please, tell me."

The ice in her chest continued throbbing, but thanks to the water, it was bearable enough that she could focus on Avia.

Avia glanced over, then away.

Mere flinched when their gazes met for just a second. Avia's dark pupils were so large they almost overtook the white of her eyes, becoming pure black voids.

She raised her hand—

Jerking away, Mere slammed into the passenger door. Pain exploded through every molecule she was made of, and her vision flashed white, then to blackness, but she fought the surging oblivion. Her cry made her sob even harder for its weakness—for how pathetic it sounded.

No. No, her soft side wailed.

No! Be strong, her hard side scolded.

I'm trying.

Try harder.

"I'm not going to hurt you," Avia said, adjusting the mirror and lowering her hand to the wheel.

Mere breathed, drew in more moisture to soothe herself, and blinked, clearing the haze from her vision. It must have been some trick from the light in the car, because Avia's eyes were not demonic black voids. They were normal. Well, as normal as those gray eyes of hers could be. Wider now than usual, but normal-ish.

Calm down. You're spooked.

"Come on, Avia, why aren't you speaking? What aren't you telling me?"

"There was a fight with the Four at the Order. We barely made it out…And I am…processing."

"The Four?" Mere shuddered. The immortal gods the Order worshipped had terrified her beyond reason; beyond what fear had meant prior to first seeing them at Avia's cabin in Switzerland. Wow, was that only days ago?

"What happened? Where did you come from? Where's Aron? Are we meeting up with them?"

"Not right now."

"How come? What happened—?"

Cold prickled through her. *What's she hiding?* "Was it Aron? Did he betray me?"

"If he had, I believe it's fair to say Asha would've killed him."

"What?" Mere gasped. "No."

Avia whipped her head to meet Mere's panic. "If Aron had set you up, yes, she would've. And I would've helped."

Mere's heart hammered in her chest.

Avia's eyes narrowed as if she could hear its sprinting rhythm, her gaze searching. "Why that reaction? If Aron or *any* of them risk us, then we end them. We've already agreed to that."

"I trust him. I thought you did, too," Mere asked.

"I'm not sure we can trust anyone but each other."

"Avia, I said that before, and you told us to go with them. You convinced Asha when she was so worried."

"That was necessary at the time. Asha was ready to kill Clay, then we would've been—" Avia looked into the rearview.

Why is she being so cryptic? Ice prickled through Mere. "But we all made it, right?" Fearing the worst, she clenched for the answer she was frightened to hear.

"We all made it."

Mere's tight, clenched, fear unspooled just a touch, though there was no true relief. "Where are we going?"

"Somewhere safe—safer."

"And the others?"

"Miles has a network of places we can hide."

"The Master who got Asha out of the Order and told us we had to separate?"

Avia's grip squeezed; the leather squeaked under her clenched hands this time. Mere couldn't read her expression.

"What?" The heat from her burns returned, and she called for more water to soothe her. She had to work so hard to get the smallest bit.

"Apparently, that man, the one they call Master Miles, is our father."

Mere gaped at her before she scoffed, "Yeah, right. Very funny."

Avia faced her, and the lines at the corners of her mouth showed plainly that she wasn't joking.

Mere froze, plunged into fathomless, frozen water. Her mind and comprehension were white water spray and turmoil. "No way? How? Why didn't he tell us?"

"I don't know."

This news, along with everything else, was too shocking, so Mere shoved it behind her emotional dam to deal with later. "I'm in too much pain for that right now."

"You should see a doctor."

"Aron or Clay—aren't they all doctors, kind of..."

"Yes, but—"

"What?" Mere snapped, all her patience and composure breaking. "What's going on, Avia? Where are they?"

Avia pressed her lips together and checked the mirrors. "They're not where they're supposed to be—"

"What? Give me a straight answer." Mere wouldn't admit even to herself that she wished Aron was there—that she was more aware of his absence than she wanted to be.

But the pain...

I need more water. She could barely call a ripple. It must have been some battle for her to have such trouble conjuring it. Her power required a surge or a recharge. If she could find some natural water, she wouldn't have to work so hard. It would replenish her. Fill her tank.

Before Avia could answer, a tingle sped through Mere, and she almost gasped in relief. "Wait, stop. There's a small lake off the road…through the trees. I could really use a swim. Please? It will help me heal—and breathe."

Avia clenched the wheel.

"If you don't mind stopping?"

Avia relaxed her grip. "Of course not," she said, pulling over.

Mere reached for the door—

"Do you want company?"

Mere paused. The hesitation in Avia's voice made her sound unsure, almost frightened. Mere had heard nothing like it from her sister before.

"No, thank you. I have to—" How could she explain she wanted privacy to repair herself?

Something was off in her body and deeper…in her soul. Whatever it was, she would heal better alone.

"I need to do this by myself. But thank you. I appreciate it." And Mere did. Avia's usually cold and unapproachable vibe had faltered, exposing a vulnerability Mere hadn't seen yet. Avia dropped her shield, asking Mere if she wanted company. Letting her in for her sake. That offer hadn't come easy.

Avia grabbed a fancy leather backpack from behind the seat. "Here, take this."

The designer bag was oh, so different from Mere's old, torn piece of crap. Avia's probably cost a fortune, while Mere's came secondhand from a neighbor ten years ago—dark green, stained, and with a zipper that never fully closed.

But you used it.

So?

"I'll just be a few minutes."

Chapter Two

Aron hunched over the steering wheel, pressing the gas pedal into the floor. *How could I leave Mere? Why had I listened to Avia?*

Mere had become a *priority* since meeting her, and he'd walked away.

Why?

After the battle, outside the Order grounds, Avia told them all to go, and they'd obeyed without question.

But why?

Mere was severely hurt. He never should've left her that way, and yet he had.

From the instant he'd met Mere, there'd been a strong pull toward her. Hell, even before meeting her, seeing her for the first time across a snow-covered field in Switzerland, an invisible thread stretched across the distance and connected them—like a fishing line shot from her and hooked into his heart.

From the day he met her, he couldn't rationalize the impulse driving him to be with her and stay by her side. A force stronger than should be possible, he'd questioned it when it hit him—hard. His brothers experienced the same draw toward the sisters, yet they seemed to accept it better.

Only Cole resisted, and Aron understood why. After what they did to Anna, Cole wouldn't allow himself to fall for someone destined for tragedy. And the sisters—they were doomed.

The sheer number of Mere's injuries flashed in Aron's mind. He groaned at the awful pictures his brain conjured in his growing panic.

What is it that's driving me so hard even now? It could only be described as longing to make sure she was safe and protect her.

Even after she tried to kill us. I can't stop obsessing over her.

She'd come within seconds of taking them out. If Avia hadn't stopped her… After the battle with the Four, which Aron hadn't expected to survive, Mere attacked him and his brothers.

Once they'd crossed through the curtain beyond the Order's boundary and she could use her power, she'd attacked them, drowning them by forcing water into their lungs. He'd never experienced such helplessness. During his upbringing, the Masters suffocated him in the hopes it would trigger his aerashakti, but even then, it wasn't the utter weakness of drowning.

A quick glance at Rio, who watched him with that *un-Rio-like* heaviness. For every time Aron suffocated, they drowned Rio. Aron clenched his body to stop his shudder. And they burned Cole.

Avia had intervened. She'd stopped Mere but sent them away before he could object or think it through. Getting his brothers away to safety had been instinct, so he'd gone. But now that he'd had some time to recover, a compulsive urge to be with her had settled over him.

It was more than an impulse or knowledge he'd gained from a vision. The bond between them had to be unnatural. He could probably locate her even without Clay—their connection was that strong.

Was this what Clay went through in that Swiss meadow-turned-battlefield when Asha had dropped below ground with her sisters, leaving him? Aron now understood his brother's frantic reaction.

"Avia will be pissed we aren't listening to her," Rio said from the passenger seat.

"I don't care."

Rio's gaze had drilled into him since his brother had insisted on joining him and jumped into the car. When Aron dumped the others and informed them he was going after Mere, Asha and Ivy had shared a not-too-subtle glance of concern and distrust. They clearly hadn't approved of the plan, but Rio had assured everyone he'd accompany Aron and keep everything chill.

Asha, Clay, Ivy, and Cole were going to split up once they found another vehicle. Ivy and Cole would take Master Miles because of Ivy's incredible healing gifts, and he was in rough shape.

"Do you know where you're going?"

Aron barely heard Rio while he sorted through images and warnings in his head. *Where is she? Where did she go? Catch up to her before it's too late.*

"Yes, we just have to catch up.

"She said to give Mere space," Rio said.

"She's wrong. We shouldn't have split up." At his clipped voice, Aron wondered why he was so worked up.

"She tried to kill us—

Right, that could be it. Or— "She almost died," Aron snarled the words. "I want to make sure she's okay."

Calm down.

"If she's okay? Are you serious? She tried to drown us. I didn't get an *I'm okay* vibe from her, man."

"Did you see her?" Aron's stomach twisted in painful knots.

For one horrifying, life-shattering breath, Aron believed she was dead. Before the battle, when Clay carried Mere into the Grand Chamber, laying limp in his arms with her face bruised, her skin burned, and her body battered, his being broke apart, cleaved into two halves–grief and rage. The Order had spared her no torture. Time stopped. Every sound he'd heard in his life roared into his head in a pounding, rising cacophony until something in his chest cracked, then silence as if all sound was snuffed out. An echo was all that remained.

He couldn't move nor break his gaze away from her limp form cradled in Clay's arms. They'd killed her. In the pounding pause, grief and rage had exploded inside him. Emotions he'd rarely allowed himself overcame him until that was all he was. Electricity surged through him, igniting every cell with tight, controlled fury before Clay finally assured him that she lived.

Aron's stomach still churned with angry adrenaline at the memory.

Take it easy. Calm the fuck down.

Strong feelings were rare for him. He was a gifted liar and could act like anyone he chose. The affable brother just going along was simple enough to portray. Feigning emotions was no hardship for him, but to experience those things? Actual feelings? If they occurred, those were reserved for his brothers and his role as their protector.

But his desire for Mere was no act. That had not been part of his role. However, he wasn't stupid enough to fall into attraction's trap. The compulsion to be with her made him uncomfortable with its intensity. He was torn between concern and anger…or was that fear?

Admit it, tough guy. It's fear. Fear for her. Fear for us all.

After the battle with the Four, he'd carried her, unconscious, off the Order grounds. He laid her into one of the waiting vehicles, but after he turned away, her terrified cry had been a physical blow.

Whirling around, he'd glimpsed her standing with bared teeth and outstretched hands. Her eyes were wholly blue, and the only white visible were flecks of foam within the spinning, dark whirlpools. When he'd staggered one step toward her, ice-cold water flooded his lungs. Dropping to the ground, clawing at his throat, he fought to expand the shrinking pocket of air, but her water was too strong.

He clenched his jaw, grinding his teeth. If it hadn't been for Avia, he and his brothers would have died. Not even Asha's begging was able to stop Mere from drowning them.

She was so strong, and she'd almost killed them too quickly. She'd been pure wrath; nothing he could have done would have saved him or his brothers. It was humbling. He didn't wish to admit it, but he wasn't used to being powerless…or scared.

She was everything the Order warned them their enemies would be.

But she was also Mere.

Rio's hoarse cough snapped Aron out of his chaotic thoughts, and he glanced to the solemn stare awaiting him. His brother's scabbed throat now resembled Aron's scarred neck. While Rio's, Clay's, and Cole's wounds were fresh, his scars dated back through the years. Now, they would all carry the small reminders of their shared fight to breathe—to survive against the sisters.

No, not sisters, just Mere.

"I couldn't stop it." Rio's crooked finger stretched the collar of his shirt away from his throat. His laugh was sarcastic. "And I thought Asha and Avia were the scary ones."

"Have you ever tried that?" Aron asked.

"Drown someone by flooding their lungs? No."

"Will you try it now?"

"Of course—" Rio paused.

"What?" Aron swung his gaze to his brother.

"It would've taken a *lot* of power to do it, though, much more than I can summon. And to do it to all of us simultaneously and after that battle? How did she even have enough energy to stand up, let alone…"

"Put us down."

Rio rubbed his neck. "I guess they're all pretty scary."

He was right; it had been his biggest concern after witnessing Mere's massive wall of water in Switzerland. These women were frighteningly powerful, and Aron would ensure he and his brothers handled this the right way.

How could someone so tortured and drained the way Mere had been have enough left to take them out with such ease? The Masters had warned them. *Your enemies will be stronger. They will defeat you and destroy our world.*

"Their shakti is incredible," Aron said, infusing a bit of awe into his tone.

"Do the Masters really believe we can achieve their level?" Rio's tone was a mixture of doubt and awe.

He had to acknowledge the Order's fear. It was justified. Fear drove people to insane lengths. The Order would do whatever it took to destroy them. The ever-growing pit in his stomach, the urge to find her, and the surging emotions he couldn't control convinced him Mere's time was indeed running out.

Every minute since the sisters learned of the Order and their destiny to die in sacrifice, they lived under the shadow of their horrifying fate. Death and terror chased them everywhere they ran or hid, snarling and biting at their heels. He couldn't imagine the toll it must take to have that death hanging over their heads.

Nowhere was safe. If the sisters were together, the Four could track them, but even if they stayed apart, the Order would never stop searching for them. The Order's sole purpose was to kill the sisters. No matter how far they ventured, the Order would eventually discover them. They always did.

They'd managed to escape, but the sisters weren't safe. What about his brothers? Now that they openly betrayed the Order, there was no going back—no way to cover it up.

But Clay was never going to stay, not after Asha. When Aron caught Clay smuggling her into the dungeon, intent on saving her, it was clear Clay was no longer Order. No matter how hard Clay tried, he wouldn't be able to keep Asha alive.

And now Aron wondered about the rest of them.

How do we fit into the sisters' destiny? Will we be pivotal players, as the Order believes, or will we just be caught in the crossfire?

He sensed more doom on the horizon. Does the Order have some nefarious purpose? Worse than killing women for their power?

He and his brothers were lied to and manipulated their whole lives. They were raised to be weapons—the hunters searching for four others, never realizing they would be sisters rather than brothers. But the revelation was more than that. Their gender wasn't the issue. When Aron saw Mere for the first time, escaping that burning cabin, there'd been an overwhelming desire to help, not attack. Aron understood Clay's motivation to leave the Order for Asha. To risk it all for her.

How had they gotten it so wrong? Why would the Order and Four risk keeping us alive? They had to suspect there was a possibility of them pairing up, especially with how compelled they'd been to join the sisters. Just spotting Mere across a battlefield stirred in him the urge to join her and fight with her.

Prickles stung Aron's skin, and while focused on the road, a vision flickered in his mind. He drove on, but his body flexed, and he realized what was happening. His heart pounded as if he were running his fifth mile at top pace.

His visions, usually an almost black-out flash, now played behind his eyes rather than in front. He could see the road while the vision played out. It came to him in a wave of knowledge, understanding, and sensation, accompanying the visual flashes without affecting his other senses.

The prickle on his skin was the only warning before the pictures flashed together. *Aron strode along an Order hallway. He was cold, but he was never cold. He moved—no, glided—in slow motion with eerie quietness. His brothers, as always, were with him.*

Turning the corner, the reflection in the shining obsidian wall made Aron's mouth go dry and his speeding heart stutter to a halt. In a swift glance, he caught a glimpse of the Four's ominous black robes; the hooded and usually black, empty voids showed his face and the cold but familiar faces of his brothers standing behind him. Time stopped, and the air froze into crackling frost.

The vision came and went so fast he wasn't sure what he saw. But he could have sworn—

"Are you prepared to face her if they aren't happy to see us?"

Rio's question jarred Aron, returning him to the present. Visions weren't new for him. Even though it had been fleeting, its clarity and strength *were* new.

What he'd just witnessed left a cold pit in his stomach, but he couldn't dig into that right now, he had to focus on what awaited them when they caught up to Mere and Avia.

Not that he wouldn't be dissecting what he just witnessed when he had a chance to think.

"It won't come to that," he said.

"If you say so," Rio scoffed but continued staring at him. "You're not yourself, man."

"Damn it, I know," Aron gritted out.

"Dude, what are we doing?" Rio asked. His voice was stern with an unfamiliar edge. A warning. Strange to come from Rio. "I'm not here to chase Avia, though that does sound like fun."

Aron shot him a glare.

"Without the Master or the sisters here…to hear…" Rio quirked his lips to a half smile, though his expression showed no humor. "What do you think? Honestly. Do you believe we have a chance of helping them? Clay was compromised; we got him out, but we're all out now. Are we really going to betray the Order? What do you see for us?"

Aron frowned, the vision he just had, their reflections, flashed in his mind. How was he supposed to answer that?

Chapter Three

Heath sat in the Grand Chamber on the gilded chair beside his father's throne.

Get your head in the game.

His father was dead. Miles escaped alive. He'd survived the knife wound. But that didn't mean he was still alive. *Miles.* His brother, once heir to the Grand Master's throne, now Order traitor.

Heath had seen some truly shocking things, but Miles betraying the Order topped the list.

He wouldn't be able to save Miles when the Four found him, and Heath was torn over it because Miles had saved him from Asha. Heath knew the only reason he lived was because of Miles's emphatic demand no one hurt him.

Now what?

As if in answer, the chamber doors opened.

He hitched his breath as the man in billowing black robes, identical to his own, strode into the chamber. The breath and strength left Heath. He rose, then dropped to his knees. This was Archive Master Iacomus. He'd been the Archive's Master for decades, long before his father rose to Grand Master. But with a smack of shock, Heath realized he hadn't aged in almost fifty years, with the same tall body, ebony hair, and dark plum-colored, eyes.

The ageless man glanced around. He had the same dark aura of power, tinted and edged in purple Heath remembered from childhood.

The memory came unbidden. Five-year-old Heath searched for Miles, who was hiding somewhere during a rare and whimsical game of Hide and Seek. After counting to one hundred, Heath ventured into the hallway and discovered the archives door, permanently locked, was open.

Fear gripped him, imagining where his brother might have gone. The archives had always been off-limits, and so Heath raced down the spiral stone staircase, his heart pounding with the knowledge they'd face punishment if caught.

He had to find Miles before they were discovered. Creeping silently, he reached the bottom of the shining, black stairs. He jumped when the torches magically leaped to life as if to announce his presence.

"Traitor," he mumbled at the bright beacons. He hurried out of their light.

The Archives were an underground lair of locked rooms, storage, and a secret level of the enormous library above, with various workrooms and laboratories stocked with equipment for their experiments. He remembered the basic layout because of the quick tour and warning he and Miles had received. They'd never been allowed below since.

Moving through the wide hallway, he scanned the walls of built-in and packed bookshelves, storing texts, historical scrolls, and records. A large roaring fire was dancing erratically in the huge fireplace built into the wall on the left. Tables and chairs for study sat on rich carpets, the only ones he'd ever seen in the Order. He hurried to the other side of the library, leading to the lab and work rooms. The library's rich, decor changed to cold, sparse, and clinical once he passed the far archway and doors.

Where is Miles?

At the far end of the hallway, in the last room, there was movement within—not movement, shadows. *Miles.* Heath almost shouted, but the way his brother stood, Heath recognized something was wrong.

Miles was frozen. Terrified. If something scared his brother this much, Heath would probably wet himself. So, gaze aimed at the ground, he shuffled to his brother.

Don't look, don't—

Heath shuffled toward his brother. When he saw Miles' shoes, he reached out and grabbed his arm. He tugged, and Miles, frozen stiff, finally shifted and followed.

Out of the lab hallway, Heath shoved him forward. The dread of curiosity was too intense, and he couldn't stop himself from one quick glance behind him. Even now, the memory was hazy.

Four women, in separate barred-but-open cells, were chained to the wall, with blood dripping from their arms. A fire blazed in the room, causing the motionless figures' shadows to dance eerily.

A hooded figure in each cell gripped a dagger. They turned their heads together, and Heath's bladder released. Warmth soaked his pants and ran down his leg. His very first glimpse of the Four.

Another man watched from outside the cells, his hood off and purple-tinted eyes almost glowing. Heath jumped and dragged Miles with him, and they ran up the steps.

He'd never seen him after that. The next day, his father rose to Grand Master and said the previous Grand Master had abdicated.

Heath remembered him from all those years ago. The terrifying childhood memory he had forgotten but returned upon seeing him now. Miles, his fearless brother's terror, the Four, and the alchemist were all present during a harmless game of Hide and Seek.

"What happened here?" The man's voice was deep, dark, oily

ooze.

Heath shrank inside and shuddered at his presence and the power that thrummed off him. He couldn't speak. All thoughts beyond recognition had flown from his mind.

"Answer me."

With great strain, Heath answered. "T-they came. They were here. The sisters." He forced his voice to steady and to carry something of command in it. "We had them. But the fire one, she was—she killed the Grand Master."

Purple eyes narrowed and slid to where Asha had been standing when she shot his father, then to the empty throne. "How did they get here?"

"Master Miles and the brothers brought them through." Heath walked off the dais, unable to remember what this man's true title was, but Archives Master for an ageless man seemed underwhelming.

"You may call me Iacomus," the man stated, almost reading his thoughts.

"Do you believe your brother has betrayed us?"

"Yes." Heath had to answer honestly. *What else could I believe?*

He had so many questions. Who was this ageless man? Where did he come from? What did he want? But barely above cowering, he couldn't voice the questions. One did not question this man.

He was merely a small animal in the grips of a predator, trying to speak. "It's shocking, actually. The elemental sisters are his daughters."

"Really?" Those purple eyes gripped him, but Heath suspected Iacomus wasn't surprised at all by the revelation. "The one hand we cannot control—fate. Destiny."

"The Four arrived. They were about to take their sacrifice—"

The Archive Master's eyes narrowed. "On whose authority was the sacrifice to begin?"

"Authority?" Heath asked. "The Grand Master was eager for it."

"I see. Continue."

"It seems the brothers paired with the sisters are a more formidable threat than we feared. With the brothers' help, the sisters succeeded in achieving something new, and our Lords retreated."

"New?"

"The sisters were losing, but when Asha touched Clay, her pyroshakti returned." Heath's skin still tingled from the heat of her flames.

"*Her* power?" He swiveled his head, scanning for evidence. "Her fire burned in this chamber?"

He would find no scorch marks marred the chamber.

"Yes," Heath said. "They all joined hands. A light beamed from them, holding the Four. I didn't think it was possible. But—"

"Interesting," the ageless man said, returning his gaze to the same spot on the floor. "Let me guess, the air element failed to rise to the challenge."

Heath cocked his head. "Yes, you are correct. She fell from their chain. No light came from her."

Iacomus's lips tightened.

"But Aron replaced her, and a white light beamed from him and the three sisters."

Iacomus' head whipped around. "Pardon?" His voice was low, quiet, and cold enough to freeze Heath.

"Yes. They hit the Four with a combined light."

He tap-tapped his staff to the floor. Scanning around, he said, "Everything remains solid. What happened to the Four?"

"They disappeared as if they disintegrated."

Iacomus raised his head. "We have suffered a loss but not defeat. And we have also achieved a victory. You will be Grand Master."

Heath bowed to the oldest amongst their Order, not a Master, or a priest, or a General, but the Alchemist. He would make a much more formidable Grand Master than Heath would, but it seemed the tide wasn't rolling that way. "The Four returned and named me thus. Will you be a Master and stand by my side?"

Iacomus cocked his head, his purple gaze raking him up and down. "At such a pivotal time, I suppose I must."

Heath bowed.

"I have much to do. Events have been set in motion. The truth will be explained to you once I return." Iacomus left the room.

Unnerved by his reflex submission to a man he barely remembered, Heath was now the leader of the Order, and he was relieved to know there was another at the helm—another who could run the show while he checked into other things.

What did Iacomus mean by the truth?

Chapter Four

Mere left Avia in the vehicle by the road. She drew in the sweet, moist air and stumbled into the forest. Sharp debris poked and scratched her bare feet before wet leaves, moss, and mud followed, coating and soothing them in mulch bandages.

She hobbled through the woods, probing at the holes in her memory.

Darkness…gray roiling clouds….

What happened to me?

The last thing she remembered was being shot with a dart and losing consciousness under the pyramid—days ago, according to Avia. Her shudder tugged and triggered more pain. A prisoner at the Order for days with no memory, only her injuries as evidence. *Surreal.*

Approaching the edge of the small, calm lake, in desperate anticipation, she could already feel relief. Removing the blackened, bloodstained coat, she let the cool air caress her burns before walking into the inky depths. The water on her skin was rain after a drought, heaven after hell—everything needed to smother her pain, and she was a sponge drawing it inside her.

"Yes." Her appreciative word escaped with her breath, and she dragged it out. Her overwhelming pain eased, escaping with her voice and finally leaving her.

Diving into the pond's welcome embrace and propelling herself into the darkness, she absorbed the cool water to heal her. Her drained power refilled. Sometimes it was that easy. Touching or submerging in naturally formed water recharged her. Hell, even if she'd never had a drop of vyralis, her birth-given-gift over water, a swim in this pond would still recharge her soul. But on the rarest occasions, if she used too much, only time would help. *Vyralis.* They'd learned the word from Ivy, who'd read it in her handler's journal. It meant vital aura, and it was perfect because water was vital, and it was her aura.

According to Father Bennett's journal, Mere was born aquavyr until her test, then she became aquashakti. By reaching her power's full potential, her vyralis transformed to shakti.

Swimming along the lake bottom, she relished the touch of the waterweeds brushing and stroking her battered body with a familiar, comforting tickle. She blew out the remaining air from her lungs and sank like a stone. Soft mud squished between her toes, and she gazed up at the surface.

Stay here. How did Nimue become the Lady of her lake?

You can't, Guppy.

But—

She was arguing with herself, so that must mean any lingering shock had worn off. Because similar to her extreme emotions, the voices in her head were also volatile and opposing. Often opposites, her two sides argued inside her mind. She convinced herself one voice was her heart and one her head. They rarely agreed; like the proverbial angel and devil on her shoulders, hard versus soft, strong versus weak, they argue-whispered constantly, prodding her into opposing actions.

When her lungs strained for air, she finally pushed off the lake floor to swim up. Breaking the surface, she took a full breath of the night air.

She floated onto her back and stared at the giant pillowy moon against a blanket of stars.

What did they do to me? Why can't I remember?

It's probably for the best.

If she was imprisoned inside the Order, and Avia couldn't tell her what happened, how would Mere ever figure it out?

Her obscured mind thrashed and roiled but gave her nothing.

She'd remember eventually. *Right? Maybe?*

Though black, undulating clouds covered her memory, the missing details were there, just behind the obstruction.

Don't try so hard. She shut her eyes.

"You will beg for death."

She gasped. The voice was familiar but unclear. Her memory *was* there, but the harder she probed, the further it slipped away.

Her ability to be strong, to hold it together, and stay positive, was tenuous and temporary. She usually had to work to portray it. It was the same with optimism. She had to force it—to a point—then she'd inevitably break and have to rebuild. It wasn't real. It was a façade.

You're the façade, Guppy.

She was always frightened, even before the Four immortal gods obsessed with her sacrifice had appeared. And though she worked hard at her power, it was all she had. Being a bright and positive person was part of her strategy to keep her darkness buried inside. It didn't always work. And after all this, it would take her entire will to keep the sunshine and optimism up. Because underneath it all, she was consumed with guilt and self-hate.

Inside, she believed she was nothing—just water. That water made her something, sure, but the Order wanted to kill her for it and take it.

Right now, she was worse—empty. She was a fragile, decorative vase, cracked into a thousand pieces, barely holding its shape the second before it shatters. Her strength and courage leaked out through all those cracks. She shook with the effort to keep the building pressure of tears inside and behind her eyes.

Let them go; free yourself. You are alone. No one will see. There's no danger here. Avia is just a shout away. You are safe. A cold, bitter laugh tripped over her lips at that thought.

Safe? Will I ever be safe?

No.

She descended below the surface, sinking into the dark water. The muffled sounds soothed her.

Her tears escaped, released to mingle in the lake, adding to its depth as she sank. When the last of her air bubbled out between her lips, she came to rest upon the lake's bottom. The soft, sediment could have been a pillowy bed for how it comforted her. While the water should have been too dark, the moon was brighter than a spotlight, giving her the ability to see clearly.

Silence under the water flowed into her, quieting everything, even her battling voices of doubt, giving way to a calmness that told her the answers would come. They had to.

From a great distance, in the dark recesses of her mind, her screams echoed. Her instinct to cut off her mind was reflexive she had to fight just to investigate the sounds and follow the trail to where it led.

She'd trained her mind along with her gift since she was a child. At the mercy of expansive emotional swings and reactions, Father Austen had worried her moods would trigger her power without her intention. Suffering the vast spectrum between joy and rage, calm and terror, she constantly had to shove all that mess behind a dam she built in her mind. Only training with a mental barricade could keep her feelings from interfering.

She trapped those overwhelming, swinging feelings behind her dam, and the water rose higher, so she had to build her dam to match. The water churned behind that fragile concrete wall with sprays and drips, making it through the cracks or splashed over the top, but the vast collection of her emotions stayed behind that dam so she could live and function.

What was crazy was how often her dam sprang a leak, threatening to weaken and destroy the entire structure, and risk unleashing everything onto her—crushing her. If she was going to hold it together and not melt into a blubbering mess, she needed to get herself under control.

Damn, she hated how easily she cried. She wanted to be tough, not a weepy child.

I was hurt and tortured.

You need to be stronger, Guppy, her hard side sneered.

I'm trying.

Hearing her screams flipped her stomach upside down and triggered a pounding ache in her head.

I don't want to know what made me scream like that.

You must. It's important. Ignorance isn't bliss. You know better. Knowledge is everything.

I don't want to know. Running from her pain and terror was a better idea if she was going to maintain her denial, but the not knowing…

She'd been naked except for that coat, burned, hurt…and for her to figure it out, to remember, she'd have to search inside herself and dive into the ripping, roiling water behind her dam.

The temptation to leave it alone was equal to her desire to know, for going in there could release everything and drown her.

It wasn't your fault.

Leave me alone.

One day or the other, you'll have to face it, Gup.

In her mind, standing on her dam's edge, the water's white caps danced and dipped while the deep water rolled and churned as if giant whirlpools fought to spin in opposite directions, never fully forming, thrashing, and spinning the water.

Up and out in a perfect dive had her slipping in and swimming straight down. Memories, regrets, and trauma swirled around her, but her purpose was her lost memory. She wasn't here to relive the past.

Her screams grew louder the further she dove. The sound, it was… *No…*

She hesitated.

Be strong.

She couldn't see anything but dark water, though there were shapes and movement within. The trapped, angry currents battered and tossed her…

Come on.

There's nothing there. It's blocked.

Wait.

"You will not die yet, but you will welcome death when we are finished with you."

The voice was slow and cold—like a recording running low on batteries. She understood the words, but the voice was too strange and demonic.

She searched and probed, but nothing more came. Swimming for the surface, she ignored all the currents tugging at her, trying to drag her back, all her denial and pain.

No. I don't have time for that. Will I ever remember?

Forget it, Guppy You're alive. That's what matters.

She wasn't going to allow this or those monsters to break her. This would motivate her, and she would use that to destroy them.

Yeah, right.

Rising from the bottom of the lake she'd never be the enchantress of, she drew air into her lungs and propelled herself to shore.

Avia's waiting.

Exiting the water, a throb drew her gaze to the still-aching wound in her chest. The skin hadn't healed at all.

How had it happened? It was a strange shape. She imagined being stabbed in the chest with a red-hot fire poker…burning, impaling, and branding all at once. The thought sent shivers through her.

It was inflamed and hot to the touch. No matter how dirty the lake might be, water never infected her. It cleansed her, always. Healed her. But this wasn't looking good.

She ignored the discarded trench coat and picked up the pack Avia had given her. Their most basic training required that they always have a small stockpile of gear or a go-bag within reach. Her air sister was nothing if not the prepared type.

Avia's fancy cashmere sweaters, blouses, and sleek pants were folded with meticulous care inside the pack. Mere couldn't help the slight curve up of her lips. You could tell a lot about a person by how they packed a bag. For example, embarrassing though it might be, she didn't pack; she stuffed things into whatever receptacle she had available. Garbage bags had made more than one appearance as her go-bag because at least they were waterproof.

Something similar to mild jealousy tickled her into pre-annoyance. Fabrics like cashmere and silk had rarely touched her skin. Not quite the dress-up type, she preferred swimsuits, shorts, T-shirts, and hoodies, yet with her sister's luxurious items, she could try them out.

She dressed in Avia's gray slacks and a black 'V'-neck cashmere sweater. There was also a pair of black ankle boots; unfortunately, they had heels. At least they weren't too high, and they were solid.

With a guilty glance to where she couldn't see the road beyond the cover of trees, she explored the rest of the bag. And found a thick stack of bills wrapped with an elastic band stashed in one of the inside pockets—and passports…plural. The first passport was Avia's but with the name Amelia Carter.

Fake passports?

I knew it. Well, she didn't know, but she'd suspected. *She's got to be a little bit sketchy. I bet Asha has one, too.*

But how would she know? Without a past together, her sisters were practically strangers. After a lifetime of separation, they'd only spent one night together before the Order appeared the next day. They'd fought for their lives, separated into pairs, and fled.

Mere opened another passport and choked before a small giggle escaped her.

The photo was of Avia, but she wore a black wig with blue contact lenses. No one would ever question if the passport was Mere's because she and her sisters were identical—*other than* their hair and eye color.

Other than… So, not identical…Mere rolled her eyes at herself. But close enough.

A travel-sized first aid kit was stuffed inside the pack's front pocket. Rummaging through the waterproof kit, she found a large bandage to cover her wound. She applied it carefully.

Why does it still hurt so much?

But the pain wasn't worse than the fear of the unknown and her blank past.

Avia better fill me in. I will piece the rest together. We will survive. Be strong.

A flash of the Four pushed into her mind.

She shuddered.

Be stronger.

Chapter Five

When Mere returned to the road, Avia waited beside the SUV, rigid as usual.

Geez, she couldn't relax if she tried.

"Are you okay?" Avia asked without breaking her gaze from the hill in the distance.

Mere shrugged. "The water helped. I can move better now. But I think some areas will take longer to heal."

Avia faced her. Her eyes narrowed, and her mouth hardened just a bit. But for what Mere had witnessed of her air sister, that was equivalent to a full-blown tantrum.

Mere's muscles clenched in response, then her shoulders fell, and her body loosened. Not from anything good, but because she was tired of…everything. "What is it now?"

"They're not where they're supposed to be," Avia said with a low voice and shut her eyes in a long blink.

If she could show emotion, Mere would guess this was Avia's anger. "Who?"

"Aron and Rio."

Something akin to excitement rippled through Mere. Heat warmed her skin, her heart kicked up its rhythm, and her nerves tightened. "Where are they supposed to be?"

"They will be *here* shortly."

Another burst of heat and a light prickle ran along her skin. Yep, she was pleased by that. "Why did we separate in the first place?"

"I won't get into the details, but after we left the grounds and the sparks of our power returned, you attacked the brothers by filling their lungs with water. You almost killed them."

Avia's hand shot out without her even turning her head and grabbed Mere's elbow when her legs buckled. All the air left her. She might have accused Avia of using her element on her, with the speed all oxygen abandoned her, but it was her own panicked response.

"Why? Why would I do that? I mean, *how* would I even do that?"

"I wouldn't know how it works for you."

A flash of Aron's bulging, fear-filled eyes. "They're coming here? Now?"

"Isn't that what you wanted?" Avia asked quietly.

"I don't *know*, Avia," Mere snapped at her very cryptic sister. "I don't know much right now. And honestly, you're not being helpful. Tell me what happened."

Avia's rigid posture eased a bit.

"Okay. The important points. We had to connect with the brothers to access and use our elements on the Order grounds. Sort of like how Asha was only able to strike the Four when she and Clay connected at the cabin. But even with access, we were far weaker than we should've been. I told you Master Miles is our father. The Grand Master tried to kill him, but Asha killed the Grand Master. We faced the Four, and with the brother's help, managed to get away." Avia spoke like she was reading from a list. Her eyes were vacant and far away, never leaving the road.

As headlights came over the hill, Mere stiffened. "That's—?"

"If we don't speak with them, I fear they will keep coming after us until we do. Aron didn't want to leave you."

Something warm and cozy unfurled in Mere's stomach.

Avia finally turned to her. Her gaze was momentarily cold before the approaching car drew her focus away. "Despite their questionable histories or allegiance, I believe, for now, we need them for our survival."

Despite Avia's clear concern, Mere was relieved by her sister's words. Hearing her say that, though it was obvious she disliked admitting it, was more important than it should be. There'd been an instinct to trust Aron, but had it just been her desire? They'd been together at the pyramids when she'd been taken, and the way it sounded, Asha wasn't entirely convinced of the brothers' good intentions either. But if Avia was, Mere could hold on to that.

She'd grown close to Aron. She trusted him from the instant he touched her hand and that shock had flowed through her, introducing her to his presence and his air element. Not a shock in an unpleasant way, but a full-body zing through her blood that spoke of power, destiny…everything.

Her attraction to him made her quiver and her mouth go dry, but that wasn't the main reason she wanted to see him. Despite any doubts now, something meaningful had grown between them. Whether Aron chose to acknowledge it or not, they had a connection that was almost physical. She'd felt safe with him, and though Avia was no slouch, for some reason, Mere wanted Aron.

She groaned. The woman she was and the woman she wanted to be hated herself for such an old-fashioned desire tied to a feeling of safety. But she'd been alone for so long. Father Austen, being her guardian didn't really count… *Shit.* Her heart twanged painfully at her dismissal. He'd been a companion and teacher, but she so badly wanted a partner—someone to lean on, to share this horror and… And she couldn't be with her sisters.

"Well then, let's play this cool, okay?" Mere suggested, rolling her shoulders and straightening her posture to portray strength she didn't have.

The tiny drop of Avia's chin was barely a movement.

~ * ~

"Are you sure about this, man?" Rio asked.

Aron didn't bother to answer. They crested the next hill, and he spotted Mere standing with Avia beside the truck parked on the shoulder. The cord in his chest thickened, and heat blew through him. *Shit. Such a physical response could not be trusted.*

"There they are," Rio said. "Last chance to change your mind."

Aron didn't break his focus from the dark-haired figure ahead. "No way. Have you changed your mind about coming along?"

Rio shrugged. "No, not really. I just want you to be prepared. I know she's cute, but she could easily take a chunk out of us."

"I won't leave her," Aron said, his words clipped. "I'm prepared."

Rio's expression grew serious.

Avia and Mere's vehicle was ahead, and they turned. Aron stopped the car behind theirs.

He flung open his door and got out. *She's okay.* He took a long breath.

Avia stepped in front of Mere becoming a protective barrier. "I told you she needed space."

"And what does *she* say?" His voice came out much colder than he wanted.

Get in the game.

"*I say* hello." Mere shifted around to stand beside Avia and whispered, "I said *cool*."

Tension flared and sparked in the silence. Aron glared at Avia, but she refused to budge.

Mere glanced at Avia, then rolling her eyes to the sky, waved to get his attention. But she already had it, even while he stared at her sister.

"Forgive Avia; she's just being protective. Of course, she is, after all that happened." Mere gestured to herself.

His tension ratcheted up as he swept a gaze over her. Some healing had occurred, but not enough. He forced himself to portray ease. Even after the torture she'd endured, she was the most beautiful woman he'd ever seen.

Calm down, animal.

Strangely, Mere appeared more at ease than Avia. A glance at Rio, whose raised eyebrow also displayed his surprise, proved Mere's demeanor had caught them both off guard.

"Hello," Rio said to her with a wink. "You seem…better."

"Yes, I'm not sure what happened, but I'm healing after a swim."

When they caught up, Aron wasn't entirely sure if he'd end up fighting Mere, which had him tied up in knots. To find her in this calm state was more than a relief.

"Mere," he finally whispered when he was calm enough to speak.

She flinched.

He brought up his hands in a gesture of supplication at her horrified expression.

Her gaze darted to Rio, then to Aron. She stepped across the tense divide, her fingers reaching for his neck.

He clenched.

Tears welled in her eyes.

What did I do? Why's she crying?

Her tears glistened on her lashes and slid down her face. His gaze locked on them—at the sorrow evident in her eyes. A knot twisted in his stomach, filling him, stretching him. Her sadness triggered a physical ache.

But he froze when her fingers inched near his neck. His body roared with fire and fear. She could kill him with a thought.

That must be why his physical response to her proximity was so acute. Fear of her power. Nothing more.

Trembling, delicate fingers stopped so close, the heat from her skin ignited something deep inside him.

He swallowed. Still, the tears leaked and streamed.

"I—I am so sorry." She withdrew her hand, her attention swinging to Rio. Her face crumpled, and her shoulders hunched. "I don't know how I could do something so horrible to you all. It's unforgivable. And you were trying to help us…*help* me."

Aron wanted to take her in his arms and hold her until she smiled. Her tears, her sadness, were tugging and tearing at him in such an unpleasant way. He frowned. "I don't blame you. None of us do, not after what you went through."

Rio smiled at her–his attempt to ease her guilt.

It had been her rage and terror taking her revenge on them, but now, painfully aware of what she was capable of was sobering and terrifying. "I would like to speak with you alone." Aron didn't miss her glance shift to Avia. "Only if you're comfortable," he added quickly, forcing notes of softness and concern into his tone.

Mere pointed to the woods. "There's a little lake just through there."

"I'll be right here, Mere," Avia said.

"I'll be right here, Aron," Rio said, grinning at Avia.

Avia's eyes narrowed, but she refused to look at Rio.

Mere headed toward the woods. Aron followed.

Avia asked Rio, "Why must you mock me?" But their voices faded before Rio's response reached him.

Rio seemed to enjoy goading Avia. Aron wasn't sure it was wise. If Aron was stiff, Avia was steel.

Mere stopped at the water's edge before facing him.

"Mere?" he whispered.

Her smile was tentative, but her anticipation tingled through the cord between them.

He hadn't been ready for that. "Are you okay?"

"Not really, are you?"

"Better now that I know you're safe."

Her tentative smile grew, though it was forced and fake. "What happened, Aron? We were together under that pyramid, then…what?"

"Do you remember Trigger, the dig director?"

"Yes," she hesitated, tilting her head. "Why?"

"The Order must have stationed him there, and I—I messed up. I was too distracted. He shot us with tranquilizers." He dropped his head. "I'm so sorry." He was ashamed that his focus on the confined tunnel and cave caused him to miss the man's approach.

"No, don't be. Was it your responsibility to be clued into the set-up? Or that someone was coming? If you're at fault, so am I."

"I should've seen it."

"What do you mean seen it?"

"I should have known the Order would come."

"You said, *seen* it."

Shit.

He averted his gaze, his stomach squeezing. "Trigger shot us both with a sedative. When I woke, you were gone. I went straight to Ivy. I hoped she could locate you." A muscle flexed in his jaw. "But she couldn't. The Order had you hidden behind the Curtain."

"Curtain?"

"The Order resides behind the Curtain. It's a barrier that hides a natural reflection of this world."

"What? I don't—" She frowned. "Like a parallel world? That's crazy."

He just stared at her. Her bruised face. Her swollen, bloodshot eyes. He took an involuntary step forward. "Yes, I guess it is."

Mere chuckled. But her laugh sounded hollow and forced like her smile. He understood. She had to work to portray her resilience.

She lifted her chin, frowning. "So, what now?"

After all she'd been through, he expected her to be more affected by the torture, the terror, the damage. The way she'd acted after the battle at the Order... Her reaction had been violent. She'd been ruthless vengeance. But he understood it. It made sense. Now, she was almost the same as before they took her. He studied her, perplexed. After being a prisoner and tortured, anyone would've been on high alert and defensive, but now she acted like it never happened. Other than her fake optimism, she seemed almost at ease, and that was highly unnerving.

Why had she attacked them? What's changed?

"We must find a way to defeat them. Running and hiding aren't good enough. Until the Order is destroyed, you and your sisters will never be safe." He didn't enjoy shattering her humor, even if it *was* an act.

"I suppose that's the problem. I'm alive and free, but never free from them. Do you have any tips on how I deal with this?" Her expression evoked an authentic plea. She was seriously asking for his help.

He was speechless at her open vulnerability.

"I mean, come on. Have you met my sisters? Asha? She could probably take them all on single-handedly. She's a super-powered, super-trained fire warrior. Avia's so badass, it radiates off her like..." She smirked. "Lightning. And Ivy's so solid and brave. Her strength isn't just physical, oh and hello, she heals."

He frowned.

Exasperated, she ran her fingers through her now shorter hair. When she reached the singed, jagged ends, the agony that flitted across her face was so blatant. He realized with absolute shock she couldn't hide her constantly shifting emotions when they displayed themselves so clearly on her face.

Her honesty and transparency were so refreshing that after the initial shock, he drank it up, thirsty for her authentic openness after the desert of hardened souls he usually encountered.

Her sisters were playing the same game he and his brothers were. But Mere wasn't. She was pure. Her open, trusting nature caused warmth to breathe through him.

And he remembered. She'd played spy to hide her fear, making her mission a game. The innocence of that was so stark compared to his dark deeds and the man he was.

I'm a complete asshole.

Then they'd taken her…and hurt her. That warmth froze and soured.

Something too big cracked inside him. It had sharp edges, slicing and cutting him as it opened him wide.

"My sisters seem ready for all this. They were prepared for it. I mean, of course, they were. And I was, too, I guess. But I think I'm the only one struggling. They're instant heroes—rising to challenge after challenge and looking hot doing it." A hollow laugh escaped before her trembling lips formed a shaky smile. "Here, I'm falling apart. Barely keeping it together."

"Mere—

"I was shot in Switzerland, taken hostage, tortured, and worse, I can't recall what they did."

"And maybe that's why you feel this way," he said. "You've suffered so much already."

And she'll only suffer more.

She took a long, slow breath. "What did you need privacy for?" she asked, stepping toward him.

He shivered at her expression; her wide eyes, flickering blue fire, and her hair shorter now only made them more prominent, more hypnotic, he matched her step.

He swallowed the lump in his throat. "I wanted to check on you, make sure you were okay…under control…and to gauge whether you might try to attack us again."

Chapter Six

A yawning void of embarrassment opened in Mere's stomach. She hadn't expected a declaration of love or a passionate, injury-healing kiss from Aron when he'd asked for privacy, but maybe, she'd hoped for it. Even with all the horror and fear, she'd wanted him since their first meeting, but to her increasing frustration, he didn't reciprocate.

But this? So jarred by his statement, she recoiled. "I said I was sorry for that."

"You did, yes. But you must understand. You were ruthless. Asha couldn't get through to you. You were in a trance of some kind, which is a concern for all of us. If someone can pull your strings—?"

She raised her hand to stop him. "Wait a minute. *My* strings? Who's the Order soldier here?"

"I am no mere soldier." His voice was colder and harder than frozen steel.

She stiffened and gaped at him. The hairs on her arm stood, and prickles stung her skin. Taking an involuntary step away, she swung her gaze to the road where Avia waited with Rio. Mere couldn't see her sister.

Aron's face blanched and his eyes widened. "I'm sorry." He reached out but halted. "That was an automatic response. I shouldn't have said that—"

"*You* are the Order member, not me. *You* need to earn my trust, not the other way around."

"You are so strong, we—

"If I'm safe from you, you're safe from me. There's no one controlling me. I don't know why I attacked you; I assume it was shock because, in case you forgot, they fucked me up." Her breath hitched.

"Mere…"

"Let's go back." She spun toward the road, devastated that the romantic reunion she'd hoped for hadn't happened.

Emerging from the forest and approaching the cars, Rio and Avia stood apart but rigid. Mere's gaze shot back and forth. Silent tension stretched between them, taut as a rubber band.

What did we miss?

"What's going on over here?" she asked, dismissing her temper and forcing light humor into her voice.

"Nothing," they snapped at the same time.

"Uh-huh." Mere glanced at Aron, who should've been amused but wasn't.

He was stiff, with a cold, distant expression.

"What now?" Mere asked them all. "I've had my swim and feel a bit better. Except for this…" She tugged the 'V' of her sweater.

Aron flinched when she exposed the bandage and more bruised, inflamed flesh surrounding it.

Avia turned away as if the sight of her injury made her want to gag.

Mere had to work to keep the pain of Avia's revulsion from coming out in fresh tears. "Yeah—it's gross underneath. I can say goodbye to low necklines for a while. This will scar for sure…"

"We should keep moving, but that needs to be checked out," Aron said.

She wasn't sure what she expected, but more warmth from him definitely. She'd experienced the most frightening, painful experience a person could endure, yet he was only concerned about his brothers.

Instant shame was ice-cold water in her veins.

You almost killed them, Guppy.

He'd asked if she was okay first, after all.

What more do you want?

I want him—

Foolish fish.

"We should go," he said. "We're in the open."

"No chance we won and this is over?" Mere asked, naïve hope soaking her tone.

"No," both Avia and Aron said.

"If the Order stands…the Order stands," Rio said with an inappropriate smirk.

"Then what do we do? Where do we go?" Mere asked Avia since they'd been heading somewhere.

"We go somewhere safe and plan our next steps," Aron answered.

Mere stifled her defeated chuckle. "Where's that?"

"Nowhere," Avia snapped, returning to their SUV. She jerked her chin. Mere obeyed the summons and crossed to the passenger door.

Aron and Rio's gazes met.

Mere watched unspoken communication pass between them as she opened her door.

"We were heading to one of my places near here," Avia said.

"Well, that's convenient," Rio said, moving to their SUV.

"It's more than convenient. I suspected we might need a hideout in the general area. I've been preparing for a long time."

"Preparing for what?" Mere asked, awed and breathless.

"Trouble."

Mere frowned, got into the car with Avia, and they sped away.

The silence between them was weighted and awkward.

"So, Aron can see the future?" Mere asked.

Avia tilted her head in acknowledgment.

Mere would've preferred a verbal answer. "And you?" she prodded.

Avia checked her mirrors. "I don't seem to have the clarity and accuracy Aron does."

Mere frowned. "You can't mean he has more power?"

"With this aspect, maybe, yes. I used to see more...clearly...I think, but now the visions get muddled. Or they're there but blurred beyond recognition with the volume too soft to hear. The harder I reach for understanding, the further it drifts. Everything's all tangled up and obscured. But there are answers if only I could see them."

"That sounds brutal."

"It's maddening."

Mere made a sound between a snort and scoff. "Like my memory. It's all there, just out of my reach. Just behind some fog and noise."

Avia glanced over. Their gazes met, and Mere could've sworn there was something in her eyes, something she'd never seen. *Fear?* The rest of her face remained blank. "There was a time I saw you, Asha, and Ivy. I was young. When you and Ivy showed up at my place, I remembered seeing you." She took a breath that hitched, and the pause that followed was full of unknown meaning. "I searched for daily markers indicating I was going a certain way, following the right path. But then something changed, and I can't see the clear paths anymore. Just flashes. Old flashes, new ones, and they're almost impossible to link together."

"What do you think that means?"

"I made a mistake somewhere—I'm not sure what I did, but I must fix it."

"You think *you* did something?"

"It's the only thing that weakened rather than strengthened."

Mere frowned. "And Aron's getting stronger?"

"The way he warned us to get off the road suggests that either his is growing or is just being more vocal about it," Avia said.

"You mean you can't see the future, but Aron can?" Mere asked, doubting Aron could possibly have more than her sister.

"It's not seeing the future exactly. If his gifts are the same as mine, it's more like seeing pathways and options of possible futures.

Sometimes, based on fast logical observations, or understanding predictive behavior and outcomes, pathways unroll before me, showing what will happen. Sometimes, it's something more, and the paths that appear the clearest, brightest, or loudest are usually correct. But not always, and events and details may shift or change it. Anything, big or small, can scramble all the paths, and has, frequently."

Avia had never spoken so many words in Mere's presence. Her voice carried an ethereal, breathy, and comforting quality that made Mere want to relax, maybe even sleep. "So, you don't know what's going to happen?"

"No, not anymore. But I did see once, so I take *déjà vu* seriously. I interpret certain awareness and recognition to be part of that forgotten future hidden behind the fog and blur."

"Okay?"

"I had an unnatural reaction to a property about a five or six-hour drive from here, so I purchased it. Aron's right. Even without specifics, we need to get off this road, and that includes driving. We're still too close to the Order. Asha and Ivy are going to a safe house Miles has arranged in the opposite direction."

Mere turned to her sister. "What about the brothers and their loyalty? Have you seen an ending for us?"

Avia's firm, "No," came too quickly and too sharply.

Mere wondered if that was a lie.

"Even with all this, all you went through, what we just survived, I'm filtering through our options, our pathways. Blurry as they are, I hope to see clearly, the way I once did—even just a flash. Because sometimes it's the quick flashes that mean the most."

Mere frowned, unsure how to respond when electric prickles ran over her skin. Static filled her ears, and her heart stuttered before it slammed into her chest and stopped. A spasm in the atmosphere vibrated and shimmered ahead, interrupting any thoughts or responses.

She swung around, grunting from her injuries being tested.

"Did you feel that?" Avia and Mere said together just before a sharp whistle pierced the silent dawn, triggering a memory from a past battle in a Swiss meadow. Avia sucked in her breath at the sound—their only warning.

Missile.

No.

The rocket flipped the SUV upon impact.

Mere called water to surround and protect them inside the explosion, dousing the flames. One of the first things Mere trained for was an automatic response to any attack. Her water-cocoon came on instinct. She just had to call one drop of water from the air, and she could expand it to a tsunami-sized wave. Here and now, despite her flickering, waning aquashakti, her fear managed to surge her wells enough to protect her and her sister. Like a mother lifting a car off her child, Mere had always seen the effect her emotions had on her power.

She reached for Avia just as the whirlpool formed, and the vehicle tore and broke around them. Thankfully, she was able to push all the tearing, thrashing metal from their water-protected bodies.

They rolled together, free from the wreckage, and when they hit the ground, they splashed apart, and the water vanished. Mere had to release Avia after the first of a series of skin-tearing bounces, adding more pain on top of her torture-healing frame.

Oof. Landing to one side of the road, the burning, scraping agony overwhelmed everything until she was all pain once more. *Breathe. Get up.*

She searched for Avia as she struggled to stand. Despite uncontrollable agony, Mere managed to rise. Her heavy body struggled upright on shaking legs.

Where had that rocket come from? The road was deserted.

Avia lay unmoving on the ground, strapped into part of the car seat, cradling her thighs and lower back. A car sped up behind her.

Mere stumbled toward her sister to make sure she breathed.

Please...

Static humming filled the air. The Four stood before her.

No.

Terror washed over her.

The Four shimmered and shook, then flashed, but they raised their skeletal, vapor fingers, and the speeding engine sound behind her changed. She glanced quickly over her shoulder for a glimpse. It was Aron and Rio, but their SUV was in the air, flipping through the air.

No.

She faced the Four.

Avia hadn't moved.

Mere was alone. She only had one option. Fight.

How?

Buy time.

I can't fight them.

You must.

But... I can't...

Fight!

Mere called her water, and it rose from the ground. It came slowly. With her urgent need, it shouldn't be so hard. She couldn't be that drained even with what she'd just done. She pushed harder. But her chest burned and ached. Her water rose higher, but it moved too slowly. *Something's wrong with my power.*

A strangely familiar laugh came from the Four.

Had she heard it before? She was imagining it. She had to be.

Together, the Four took one step toward her, then another.

Her wave vanished. Dissolved.

What?

Footsteps from behind her were coming up fast. *Please let it be Aron and Rio.* She needed help. There was no way she could do this alone. She needed Avia.

The Four flickered like static then vanished.

But before she could breathe relief—what had appeared behind them. *Oh my—no.*

Rows and rows of hooded men in black armor waited on the road.

The soldiers marched toward them—Avia.

Where did they come from? How did they just appear?

"Avia?" Mere's weak voice broke. "Avia?" she tried to shout.

She called another wave up from the ground, but it also rose too slowly. Forcing it to race along the highway toward the soldiers, it crested high and swept them away.

How can I be so drained? The battle was hours ago. I went for a swim. Now, already empty?

The air crackled, and more soldiers appeared, marching in formation, replacing those she'd washed away.

"Avia," Rio yelled, sprinting past her to where Avia lay motionless.

Aron skidded to a stop beside Mere, assault rifle up. He opened fire, providing Rio cover while Mere kept scanning the road.

Ahead, Rio cut Avia's seat belt with a large knife Mere hadn't seen before. In a swift, fluid motion, he swung his gun behind him, picked Avia up, and ran over with her.

"It's okay," Rio said to Mere, gently laying Avia down. He removed his jacket and placed it under her head in a makeshift pillow. "She's breathing."

Mere released a breath and didn't miss the way Rio looked at her sister and brushed her hair from her face before he stood.

Aron sent waves of air into the lines of men, shoving them back, holding off their approach.

"I'm drained," she shouted at Aron over the roar of his wind, still not quite understanding why.

She searched the area with all her senses.

"They're coming. Go, now. Run," Aron shouted, sending out more air shields to hold the Order soldiers off.

"Protect Avia! I'll be right back!" Mere bolted into the forest, sprinting through the trees.

Branches scraped her face as she ran, but she searched for a creek or pond…a damn puddle would probably do. Aron and Rio wouldn't be able to fight off those forces alone. If Avia was out, then it was up to her. Mere had to charge up and return fast.

Tingles tickled her just under her skin.

A creek…

Sprinting deeper into the trees, she barreled through the uneven terrain, the branches reaching for her with sharp claws and hooks.

Just ahead.

Collapsing into the shallow stream, she panted with frantic breath. Her stores were refilled, like pouring water into a glass. She only prayed it lasted longer this time. Spinning, about to bolt for the road, movement caught her eye.

A twig snapped, and the sound cracked in the stillness.

Shit.

Sensing a presence, she peered into the trees as another snap came from behind. "I don't have time for this," she shouted.

"Time is all I have," a low, flesh-freezing voice said.

Her courage faltered, and she shook at the lethality of that voice.

Be brave.

It's just one man.

Is it ever just one man?

A chorus of quiet clicks came from all around her, proving numerous unseen assassins loaded their guns. She tipped her head in acknowledgment to herself. *No.* It was never just one man. Her stomach roiled. Darts flew toward her from all directions, activating her instinct to call the creek, and water surrounded her in a frothing, circular shield, protecting her.

Before she could breathe relief, a hand shoved through the water and gripped her arm, then another and another. She was trapped inside a swords-in-the-lady magic trick, where they held her from every angle.

Her being screamed in disgust at the contact. Sheer terror froze the water around her, and thick ice immobilized the hands clutching her. Wedged in, she twisted away to free herself.

Frozen fingers released her shoulder and clawed at her throat. A dagger-shaped ice shard with a sharp jagged edge appeared in her hand. Slicing the hand squeezing her throat, she jerked as warm blood sprayed her face, and a black and purple fluid oozed out with the dripping blood.

She forced ice spears to shoot from the barrier around her, turning the ice from shield into weapon. Waiting, she counted ten seconds of silence, then let the ice fall. Strange purple mist covered the ground, swirling around her.

Avia.

She sucked in her breath and bolted for the road. Minutes later, she stepped up beside Aron, who continued to hold the army at bay with wind.

Impressive.

She called another wave and worked harder to speed it up the road toward the marching army, but it was still a struggle. Her body chilled to ice with her sudden panic. What had happened to change her power? *Something they did at the Order?*

Turning to Aron in confusion and fear, she noticed beads of sweat on his forehead and his fingers clenched into claws. There was a strange crackle, then, with his hands spasming wildly, light shot toward the soldiers.

What?

When his eyes met hers, they were wide and awed. But the corners of his lips lifted ever so slowly.

"Was that…?"

"Yes," he breathed with reverence. "Lightning."

He clapped his hands, rubbed them together like Mr. Miyagi, then pulled them apart. Sparking electricity connected his palms and wound through his fingers. He stretched the lightning between them before facing his palms out and fired long golden bolts. Unlike Avia's white lightning, Aron's was gold.

A prickle between her shoulder blades crawled up her neck. Mere turned to the forest. A figure stood watching. Her core liquified with terror as if she beheld death before her. Only had the Four evoked such fear. The shadow of his hood hid his face, but there was a faint purple glow where his eyes should've been.

A midnight aura pulsed around him, growing and stretching. The trees and shrubs around him withered and died. The growing void killed while it spread. She couldn't look away.

"Holy shit, bro," Rio cheered.

Spell broken, she spun to face the battle.

"Get the car," Aron said, pride bordering on arrogance shining in his eyes and heavy in his tone.

Rio rose from his crouch and handed her some kind of assault rifle. She took it in her shaking hands, and he flipped a switch near the trigger. "Aim high," he said. "I'll be right back."

He whirled, then sprinted away.

With one hand, Aron used the wind to hold the soldiers; with the other, he continued to fire lightning at the ranks, dropping them like toys. Mere was too rattled by the man in the forest to catch up to what was happening. Thank goodness, they handled it without her aid.

There was a screech and a hum, and Rio was there with the smashed-up but thankfully intact SUV.

Aron summoned Mere with a jerk of his head. "Get in. We have to move now."

Avia moaned and stood.

Mere gasped in relief. *Thank you.*

On shaky legs, Avia whipped her head to the edge of the woods where the man…had stood. He was gone. Was he one of the Four? *No.* They felt different. Terrifying also, but…different somehow.

"We have to go," Avia croaked, echoing Aron. A gash over her left eye bled steadily. Rio moved to help Avia into the car, but she straightened. "I'm fine."

"You need at least six stitches, ma'am," Rio stated, clearly expecting pushback.

"It can wait until we get there."

"Then let's go," Rio shouted at Aron, who dropped the roaring wind and finally jumped in.

Rio sped off in a skidding spin, and they raced away from a marching army before Aron's door was shut.

"Get off the road, now," Aron said.

Rio swerved onto the shoulder over a ditch that was thankfully on an incline and into an open field, flooring it at top speed. A beat later, a missile hit the road.

Mere turned. "How?"

"I deflected it," Aron said.

Approval and gratitude were in Rio's expression when he glanced at Aron.

"But they're gone. How are they gone?" she asked, more shocked by their disappearance than their appearance.

"They do that," Rio said.

Chapter Seven

Heath stood before the dais in the Grand Chamber, studying his father's throne.

How could it be mine?

The ancient alchemist, Iacomus, had summoned him as he'd said he would.

No one summons the Grand Master, yet he calls me like an underling.

Heath would try to emit more strength this time He had no doubt Iacomus only tolerated him and would rather have Miles be his Grand Master. Heath would've opted for that, too, but he could play a loyal subject willing to do whatever was commanded. Hell, he'd done it his whole life.

He only remained the Grand Master because Iacomus allowed it. If Iacomus wanted the role, he would have it, and the Four would probably prefer it, too.

Power respected power, but Heath couldn't help his cower in the ageless man's presence.

The doors swung open, and the air in the room chilled.

His bow was involuntary.

Iacomus swept in and halted before him. A shrewd, purple-eyed gaze raked him up and down. The perusal emptied Heath as if those violet eyes scooped all life and meaning from him, leaving nothing but his withered shell.

"Grand Master," Iacomus said in a voice so cold it made Heath shiver. He had a strange accent he couldn't place.

Old. Ancient.

"Yes," Heath forced bravado and met those dark eyes.

Iacomus was remarkably beautiful. Heath could admit it, even within his fearsome presence. He was danger and darkness personified, an unholy demon, a fallen angel turned to violence and rage.

Heath swallowed and glanced away from Iacomus but caught the scowl forming on the man's face before he broke eye contact.

Man?

A man who hasn't aged a day in more than fifty years. They could all alter their appearance, but this wasn't the same. This man was unchanged.

"I have returned for your inauguration," Iacomus said.

Heath scanned the room.

"Not the pageantry you expected? This is the private initiation just for Grand Masters upon their ascension. The Four would usually take care of this, but they're occupied, and I wanted to handle this one personally." His pause was heavy with anticipation. Did he want a response?

Heath gave nothing but open obedience and waited.

"I expected your brother to be here. He had such a dark soul, even at a young age. But we must adapt and move forward. We are at a pivotal crossroads a millennia in the making. This is not the time for vacant leadership."

Pangs of regret hammered Heath. Miles had been the one destined to rule. Not him.

"For now, you are here, and we must continue. There's much for you to learn and see. Let's go."

Dread chilled Heath's veins, but he held his shiver inside. Iacomus believed him a coward already, but noticing Heath's reaction would be even more humiliating than any bowing and scraping he could do.

The air crackled, and Iacomus's robes vanished, replaced by a black tailored suit. "I suggest you change. We're climbing."

Heath bowed and rose, sweeping his robe over his arm, revealing plain pants and a wool sweater the brothers had given him as a gift one year. It was black knit, similar to the ones they wore. He laid his robe over his previous chair. He wasn't ready to sit on the Grand Master's throne while this man stood before him.

Iacomus spun, and the doors opened on his approach. Heath had to push himself to keep up with the alchemist's long strides. To the end of the long hallway and out the side door, Iacomus led him through the grounds toward the rear of the vast property. After minutes of walking in silence, he finally spoke. "As the new Grand Master, it is time you understood the true mission and your duty."

True mission and duty.

"You thought you understood it all. How would you be here at the top if you were not the most informed? That is true to a degree, but it is time for you to rise higher. One more level of access and information. Like the Order, let's start at the beginning."

Heath bowed his head in acknowledgment and deference.

"There was a sliver of time before the Curtain. The Order was once the Order of Alchemists. The hierarchy consisted of a Grand Master and Four Masters."

Heath frowned. *Four? Not two?*

"Together, through study and practice, they reached untold levels of power and control, but as is the way with such things, they coveted more. Achieving immortality and harnessing the strength and essence of the natural elements became their obsession."

They finally reached the black obsidian wall bordering the grounds, and Iacomus touched the stone. It shimmered and transformed, rolling open, revealing an archway to land beyond.

Heath had never left the Order grounds other than to go through the Curtain on the other side where the world lay.

"Why do you hesitate?" Iacomus asked.

Heath had stopped, unsure. "What is this?"

"Our realm." Iacomus went through.

Heath followed. "Our *realm*?"

"You'll see."

Heath shivered, passing through the archway. A black tower stood beyond a forest of black trees. Did the forest block the tower? How had he never seen this before?

Inside the tower, the stairs spiraled up.

Iacomus shot Heath a dark glance, proving he was an unfortunate mouse and Iacomus, the cat, toying with him before chowing down.

As they climbed, Iacomus spoke, and his deep, rhythmic voice sounded even more ancient, a voice that had spoken through the ages and carried history within it. "The Order grew in might and reach. They conquered nations, subjugated kings, then slowly began to enslave everyone else. Men were taken for soldiers, but the women, too weak to fight, were used for labor and study."

Study.

"As our rule expanded, true mastery of the elements eluded us. We had the magic but lacked the strength. There were occurrences where we gained minute amounts, but only with one common thread: blood. There was no strength without death. And yet, even with blood, any strength we gained never lasted.

"We learned our power increased far more with female sacrifice. So, we took scores of women, for they were more potent. But it was still not enough.

"Then the break we needed arrived when under an eclipse and alignment of the planets, the first elemental sisters were born, and they approached the unholy Masters of the Order, greedy for more. The sisters' goal was to destroy us. But the Masters took them first, and behold, their natural gifts over the elements was what the Order had always coveted. Finally, here it was, born into these…*unfortunate* vessels." Iacomus's sneer sent cold chills shivering into Heath's bones.

"When all the tests and torture had failed to transmit any true power to us, the Masters prepared one last attempt to harness it. A ritual was designed to force them into their raw elemental forms, gaining their shakti before they were sacrificed.

"The Grand Master stood on the dais in the Grand Chamber watching his Masters try everything to draw out the elemental sisters' raw form, for once the females were dead, if they had not achieved a transfer, their gifts would be lost."

Heath barely breathed during Iacomus's speech.

"Within the ritual, each one transformed into their raw element before one of the Masters stabbed them in the chest."

"The first sacrifice," Heath said, adding awe into his tone.

"Yes. The first and only one of its kind."

"We have performed many—"

"Yes, many, and many of those were not the elemental sisters. You must be aware. The Order's history of sacrificing any women with strength—there are occurrences when the Order sacrificed women who weren't even related, let alone the sisters. Just females growing in influence—"

"That is our mission. There are different kinds of power."

Iacomus paused his ascent, then resumed the climb with a scoff. "As those first elemental sisters died, much shaped our future roles, our limitations, but also our imminent success.

"With the first elemental sisters' final breath, a shockwave blasted out and rolled over the planet, and a copy of the world was created with a Curtain separating this new realm from the living realm. The Order was forever trapped behind the Curtain while the world thrived beyond, just out of reach."

Heath frowned. "But I've never been here." He panted. They'd climbed high but weren't even halfway up. "I was told the Curtain or Cloak on the Order was an ancient spell to hide and protect our operations from interference."

The scathing scan from Iacomus withered him. The alchemist continued, "Behind the Curtain, we rule nothing. Our empire went from everything to nothing. Our land, empty and segregated from humanity, the world—our prey beyond our reach. The magic from that first sacrifice trapped us here. Those females..." His voice oozed hate, rage, and vengeance.

Heath waited for more.

"The force that blasted from the sisters with their death hit the Masters first, standing before them, they were caught in the shockwave and obliterated. Those Masters became the Four. Their bodies vaporized with such force that they melted into the building, fusing with the stone itself, transforming the structure into something living yet not."

50

Understanding dawned on Heath.

"Have you noticed how the stone drinks blood? How it shakes with anger or pleasure? The Masters' bodies, separated from their dark souls, became the living Order, and their souls, shrouded in the stolen shakti of the original sacrifice, became the Four. They'd absorbed the elemental energy from the dying sisters."

Though Heath still climbed, he could almost see the events as if he witnessed them.

"The Four, like the first wave of the Order's army, can pass through the Curtain, but only temporarily, and they begin to weaken once they're on the other side."

Heath hadn't known that. Did Miles?

"That is the reason for you and all our mortal gatekeepers. The Grand Master hunts the sisters, yes, but also, keeps the world outside working on our agenda while we continue our search for a way to bring down the Curtain." Finally, they reached the top of the tower. "The Curtain is just a doorway to another world—a copy of what lies outside. There's nothing here but us." Iacomus opened the door to a circular room with a large, primitive telescope with multiple lenses, brass casings and apparatus.

What?

"They are waiting…anxiously." Iacomus gestured for him to peer into the telescope.

Heath pressed his eye to the cold metal and recoiled, gasping, but quickly swallowed his horror.

He checked again but couldn't grasp what he saw. Impossible.

It was a nightmare. What he first mistook for charred earth, along the distant horizon spread out as far as the view from the tower could see, was hordes of soldiers. He searched past the telescope at the stain and spread of the masses.

"That is the Order's true force. They cannot take the world until the barrier is gone" Iacomus said.

Heath didn't understand. "Our soldiers cross through often."

"Only the soldiers who were in the Order building during that first sacrifice can cross through the Curtain–the first wave. Those out there; they can't even approach it."

With his eye still to the telescope, Heath asked, "What will you do?"

"Break the barrier. Take back what was once ours. Soon, we will have an opportunity. These sisters will be ours. With every sacrifice and death, the sisters have grown more powerful. They have finally reached levels high enough to destroy the barrier; we will succeed and unleash ourselves on the world.”

"How do you know all this?” Heath suspected, but Iacomus had to say it aloud so the horrible truth couldn’t be blamed on implication, imagination, or insanity.

Iacomus frowned, “Come now, Heath. You must have guessed. I am the Grand Master who gained true immortality during the First Sacrifice. I stood upon the dais and the exploding wave took me too; however, while I gained control over all the elements, the strength was minimal. I achieved the most basic abilities, but it was only a drop of what I *could* have.”

"How do we achieve this?”

"The brothers have an important role to play.”

Chapter Eight

Even with the waning adrenaline, the tension in the truck was solid. Mere remembered how it had been when they first met the brothers in Avia's cabin.

"We need to find another car and separate. They found us too quickly," Aron said, his face tight.

Avia stiffened. "Yes, but I'd hoped…two of us, maybe…"

Mere's stomach sank. They couldn't all be together, *fine,* but like Avia, she wished that at least two of them could stay united without fear the Four could track them. The reality that they must all be separated—must face their trials alone, added a whole new layer of terror.

"I think we all did," Rio said.

"We can't risk staying together. They could still be tracking us—planning to attack," Aron said, staring ahead.

Mere bit her lip. "We celebrated too soon." All gazes turned to her. Okay, so maybe she was the only one who'd been celebrating.

Aron took out his phone, pressed a button, and held it to his ear. "They hit us—the Four too. We're fine, but they must have tracked us because—yes. You will have to tell them to split up." He paused, listening. "Figure it out," he snapped.

Rio raised his eyebrows at Aron, echoing Mere's reaction. Who was this guy? He wasn't the same sweet man she'd fallen for on their trip to Egypt.

"They'll also be finding separate modes of travel," Aron ground the words out.

"Great," Rio said, glancing over his shoulder at Avia. "I need to inspect that cut. I wasn't joking when I said you need stitches."

Mere's chest squeezed under invisible pressure.

This is too much. I can't catch up.

Just breathe.

"Mere and I can go to a motel in the town coming up, and you and Avia can go to her place," Aron suggested.

"You don't think they'll check the town?" Mere asked.

"Doubtful, but I'll see it coming if they do."

"You will?" Avia asked.

"Yes," Aron replied.

"Switch it up," Rio said. "Avia needs attention. Do you want to go to the hospital?" he asked, holding her gaze in the mirror.

Avia didn't answer.

"Then *we'll* go to the motel, and you guys can go on to her place.

Fine with you?"

"Fine with me," Avia answered.

Rio jerked the wheel, and crossed the highway, to take the upcoming exit.

"You'll have to find a car after we drop you," Aron said.

"Rio can steal one," Avia whispered as if speaking to herself.

There was a strange lilt to her voice Mere hadn't heard before.

"You bet I can." Rio grinned, meeting Avia's gaze in the rearview mirror.

What's up with that? If Mere hadn't believed Avia lacked the ability, she would've thought Avia and Rio shared an inside joke.

"So, let me guess. Another cabin in the woods?" Rio asked, humor in his voice and his expression.

How could his smile be so genuine and teasing, considering what they'd just escaped?

But despite its inappropriateness, it was contagious, and even with Mere's current predicament, she smiled a bit. His tone alone chilled the atmosphere a smidge.

"In the woods, yes. Cabin, no," Avia remarked, easing away the bandage Rio had given her to check if the blood still flowed, before returning it to forehead. "I don't visit this one. I don't like the way it…breathes. I loved my cabins in Switzerland. But this one…I just—it doesn't feel good."

Silence followed her statement.

Aron twisted around, and Mere met his gaze. Even Rio glanced over his shoulder.

Avia had hit her head. Could that be why she spoke so…openly, casually, and so unlike her. It was conversational. The first Mere had heard from her sister since they met. Even on that first night, while they'd all drank wine and talked, Avia had barely spoken, answering direct questions in one or two words, constantly shifting the conversation away from herself.

"Maybe you should hurry," Mere said to Rio. If Avia had a concussion or something worse, could Rio and Aron help with that?

"Oh?" Rio coaxed. "And why did you love that place over this one?"

Rather than concern over her uncharacteristic sharing, he was amused by it and encouraged her to keep talking. He must have picked up on that open tone, too. Maybe his questions could get Avia to share more about herself.

Cold had been the wrong descriptor for her sister. *Protected.* Iron armored…maybe.

"I always felt love at my cabins. Being there was living inside a hug." Avia raised her other hand to touch her temple. "But I only experienced fear and pain at this place, the one you're going to."

Rio's smile faded, as did Mere's.

"Considering you and I are injured, the atmosphere of pain makes sense I suppose." Avia paused, and it was so heavy, so altering, and unnerving that the world seemed to hold its breath with her. Fates changed, and destiny wavered in that suspension. "And I suppose we all have enough fear…"

Heavy stillness echoed in the aftermath of her words.

"I've only been there once to inspect and sign papers. Though other people have visited since then."

"Who?" Mere asked. Pushing past the ominous words and warning, it was new for Avia to speak this way, and Mere enjoyed it. So, like Rio, she hoped to keep it going.

"Ghost hunters."

"Are you serious?" Mere gaped.

"No." Avia's lips curved up the slightest bit. "But you should've seen your face."

Aron smirked, and Rio's mouth dropped open, evoking his stunned expression. He quickly recovered, grinning and winking at Mere.

"Wow, you got me." She smiled, unable to stop her admiration from bubbling out. "Nice one."

Avia's smile grew; it was still small, but to Mere, Avia's face had transformed into a shining beacon brighter than the sun.

"No, but seriously, I have staff who come monthly to maintain it and keep it stocked with supplies."

Seeing Avia so relaxed comforted Mere enough that her fear-frozen shell began to thaw.

"It's good to see you smile," Avia whispered.

A tug pulsed in Mere's chest. "Same here."

Silence returned and settled between them. Aron twisted in the passenger seat. "Did you see?" he asked Avia.

Her lips tightened, and with that, her lightness vanished. "See what?"

"The lightning," Aron said.

Avia's eyes widened. "Did you create lightning?"

"I did," Aron said.

Aron frowned at Avia. "You aren't pleased."

"I'm not sure I am."

Poor Aron. Wanting to comfort him, Mere had to fight the urge to reach out and touch him. Aron had recoiled, furrowing his brow as if Avia's words had physical impact. "Why not, another weapon, stronger—" Aron asked.

"To possibly use against us," Avia said.

"What?" Rio asked sharply.

Avia's back to herself.

"Really, Avia?" Rio frowned at her sister's reflection. "I was the one who had to pry *you* off my brother while you were shooting lightning through his chest."

The air inside the vehicle thickened, crackled, and could've sparked with the sudden tension.

"What?" Mere croaked.

That tension solidified.

"Leave it, Rio," Aron growled.

"Please, tell me what happened," Mere said to Avia.

Avia stared at her lap. "At the Order, Clay and Asha joined hands, then Asha used her power, weak though it was. And I needed mine." Avia met Mere's gaze. Her pupils had grown large and eerie. "So strange not to have it. Wasn't it?"

"I don't remember."

Almost distracted now, Avia responded, "Right. Having no spark at all… It was…" She hunched her shoulders. "It was awful, foreign, so I reached for Aron, who stood beside me. He was air, so I assumed he'd give me access to my own. And yes, he had a spark, but it was *his* spark.

"Without mine inside me, I behaved like a starving woman who falls upon a feast, a drowning person clamoring for rescue. I'm ashamed. I lost control. What was left in place of my spark, that emptiness, a void, whatever it was, acted alone, searching for his element, then more of it, mining into Aron, trying to take it. I had to wrestle for control, but I couldn't get it. I was locked onto him. Then lightning blasted through Aron." Avia paused. "I thought I'd killed him."

Mere frowned. Avia without control was a sobering thought. Her shooting lightning through Aron and killing him made Mere's stomach drop.

"Rio broke the connection, and I was able to release Aron. With Rio and I connected, I had access and control."

Mere didn't fancy the sound of any of that.

"I'm sorry for what I did." Avia's voice was robotic coldness once more.

Aron turned to Avia, who lifted her chin, still holding pressure to stop the bleeding near her hairline. "I don't blame you," he said. "You

56

were searching for a lifeline to your abilities. I was the logical generator."

"Just you weren't," Avia stared at him, her focus unwavering.

"No. Rio was." Aron swiveled to face Mere.

"Show me," she asked. She didn't care if it was too bold a request, but she had to see how hurt he was.

Aron tugged down the neck of his sweater. He showed Mere the wound over his chest. It was healing but the damage was raw and awful.

"We're almost there," Mere said as the town lights glowed ahead in the distance. The words had formed on her lips while she studied his ravaged chest.

She glanced at Avia, hoping there was nothing in her expression that showed her shock, but Avia only stared at the damage she'd done to Aron. She was pale, though her face was like stone.

Rio's gaze returned to the rearview, but Avia refused to meet it. "How long are we going to do this back-and-forth trust dance?"

"Until we're sure," Avia mumbled.

"How can you not be sure?" he asked.

Was that a note of hurt in his voice? *Poor Rio, if he's half as emotional as I am, then Avia's going to destroy him.*

Like she almost destroyed Aron. He's okay.

Aron frowned at Avia, his expression hard. Shivers rolled through Mere's at the cold anger in that expression.

"You are Order," Avia snapped, almost defensively.

"Were," Rio shot back at her. "Not anymore. We're working with you."

Listening to Rio's anger and Avia displaying her distrust even after the battles they'd fought together proved how stupid Mere had been. Shame washed over her once more. She'd wanted to play stupid spy games after Asha had been kidnapped and tortured.

You were scared, Guppy.

I'm always scared.

Denial had been her dear friend, *but damn.* It was time to get her head in the game. If her damaged body wasn't enough to shake her out of it, witnessing the tense exchange between Aron and Avia did.

With this conversation, Avia told her they had no choice but to go with the brothers; however, trusting them might still be an ongoing mission.

The only reason they risked it was because, according to Avia, the brothers had helped them survive.

Twice.

Though, Mere only remembered the one time at Avia's cabin when the brothers had broken them from the Four's trance. A loop of vicious sacrifice and murder committed by the Four and the Order played in her mind as if she'd witnessed each one. Aron had just touched her, and the Four's hold shattered.

At the town's edge, Rio found a travel motel. Mere glanced at Avia, who furrowed her brow and wrinkled her nose at the shabby, wooden two-story building.

Mere almost laughed at the snobbish gesture. For some reason, it eased a bit of her panic to see such a princess-like reaction from her usually blank sister.

"We'll be just a minute," Aron said. He and Rio got out and walked to the office, whispering while they strolled nonchalantly.

Mere watched them. "Avia, tell me this is a good idea."

"I can't. I'm sorry. But, this is our only option. The other is to go at it alone. And we can't do that."

No. Mere couldn't imagine running alone. At least she wasn't so scared with Aron around. He was intelligent, determined, and had a confident grasp of what he was doing and what was happening.

"At least Aron is a layer of protection and knowledge," Avia said, her attempt at reassurance.

She removed paper and a pen from her bag and sketched a rough map while telling her everything she needed about the road to her house, gate, and grounds. Mere hugged Avia whether she wanted it or not, and Avia awkwardly patted her on her back in return.

"Are you going to be okay?" Mere asked, realizing she'd made everything about her, and Avia was still bleeding and staying here with Rio.

"Yes," Avia said, with a sharp nod, but Mere understood the underlying meaning within. *I can handle myself, but can you?*

Mere squared her shoulders. *I have to try.*

Rio returned with Aron and helped her sister out of the car, taking her bag with him. He led her along the line of doors and stopped.

"Will she be okay?" Mere asked Aron as she slid into the front seat.

"He has all the supplies he'll need to treat her injuries, and there'll be enough for you."

That wasn't what she meant. Nervous prickles rose to her skin, but when his gaze met hers, warmth flowed through her.

"Buckle up," he said.

A shiver ran up her spine, but it was the good kind. *No shit.*

Chapter Nine

They crept into the forested foothills away from the small town, split by the northern highway. "Take the next turn-off ahead," Mere said, glancing up from Avia's notes.

The charcoal-colored clouds kept the morning from truly waking and shrouded the day under the shadow of a dark, heavy storm. The winding road bumped and roughened to dirt as they drove on and on and on. Eventually, they approached a shabby, old cattle gate. She reached for her seatbelt buckle, but Aron brushed her hand to stop her. His touch sent that familiar zap and heat racing through her, but he recoiled as if she'd burned him.

What kind of reaction is that?

"It's okay, I got it," he said without meeting her gaze.

She swallowed and pushed away her far different reaction to such a quick touch.

He got out and walked to the gate. Once there, he opened the padlock and it swung open on strong but rusty, screeching hinges. Returning, he drove through and got out to lock it behind them.

"Looks like it's about another ten minutes' drive to the house," she said. "It's not a small property."

The dirt road was rough and not welcoming, as Avia had warned, but Mere gasped when they drove around the bend coming out of thick forest.

Aron whistled.

"How is there a house like this way out here, in the middle of nowhere?" But she grinned. "I get the ghost hunters thing now."

"Agreed. Do you think it could be haunted?" he asked in a conspiratorial tone. He was trying to lighten the mood the same way he had in Egypt, playing spy with her. But sheesh, with this place's vibe he just scared her.

"I really hope not. I can't handle any more malevolent forces."

He sobered. "Right. Me neither."

The large Victorian house had seen some things. The weathered exterior proved its age, but it stood solid and timeless. Nestled along the banks of a small, private lake, the forest grew around the house as if it was a closing fist, trying to drag it within and hide it even more from the world.

Some dark history radiated from it. She understood Avia's dread. Darkness coiled and swirled everywhere.

"Something happened here." Aron raised his eyebrows.

"Yes, Avia said she didn't want to know. A possibly haunted house is one thing. But the reality of terrible deeds is another, I guess?"

"I disagree. Knowledge is power. It surprises me that Avia would choose ignorance."

"Yeah, you're right." Not wanting information wasn't the type of person Avia was at all. That was more Mere's thing.

Then she understood. Of course, Avia was informed; she just didn't tell *her*.

Aron's expression showed he understood it, too.

She's protecting me.

Had she withheld the truth because she thought Mere couldn't handle it?

Regardless, Mere preferred not to know.

Just Avia buying and never returning said so much. She was willing to spend untold amounts of money on the possibility that they might need it. More understanding hit Mere. Avia's visions, if that was what she called them, were probably more of a sure thing than she'd let on.

A gravel pathway led around the rear of the house, where an overgrown and neglected garden pressed into the eastern side. A large wooden deck extended from the side door to wooden stairs and a walkway leading to the small lake. Under the moody sky, the water was black and churning in the building storm.

"A caretaker lives a ten-minute drive past the shed up there." Mere pointed to a hill to the right with a rickety, worn, old structure.

That information should've been more comforting.

She found the key under the flowerpot, according to the notes. "Got it."

Aron faced the lake, silent and staring, as she unlocked the door.

"You, okay?" she asked.

"Yes. You?"

"That's hard to answer. But I'm fine. I mean. Better."

His smile was designed to comfort and encourage, but he stopped her before she walked in. "Let me." That smile shifted into something harder, colder, and he slipped into the dark opening of what was quite possibly a haunted house. Minutes later, he returned. "All clear," he said, picking up their bags.

Inside, the house was a familiar horror movie setting. Through the large kitchen, they found three floors of dark, dusty, opulent rooms filled with sheet-covered furniture.

"We should check in with the others. Make sure they're okay," Mere said, her heartbeat pounding.

60

"Yes," he said, pulling out his cell phone.

Mere gaped at the enormous house around her. Avia had bought this on a whim. *Shit. Why am I so out of everyone's league?* She was a child among adults.

~ * ~

Aron shut off his phone and slipped it into his pocket. "Cole and Ivy are fine. They're on the road and will drive through the night. Master Miles is hanging on. Clay and Asha are okay, too."

He announced the summary of the calls while Mere continued to stare in awe at the dining room and the living room across the large front hall, but even her wonderment couldn't calm the storm inside him.

"Avia said she has everything we need—a medical bag and some nonperishable food in the pantry." The lights worked, and she flipped the switch before going through the swinging door to the kitchen.

In her absence, the room crackled. He sucked in a deep breath, then released it. Golden sparks flared in the corners of the ceiling and floor and at his fingertips.

She'd been tortured. They escaped. She'd attacked him and his brothers. She didn't remember what happened. The Order attacked.

I conjured lightning.

He was roiling more than he could ever remember. Only the time during that one test came close to the surging emotions blasting past his usual ironclad composure. He held himself together—always. Whatever was required, he could be. Aloof or loveable, he could play any role to believable perfection.

But right now, he couldn't get himself together.

He never lost control, but he was spinning. Was it his aerashakti? Did this wild panic come with his lightning? Because if it did, he wasn't sure it was worth it. He clenched his fist and brought it to his face, admiring the connecting sparks flashing into barbed wire.

Yes, the lighting had finally come. When he'd feared the worst, when his air had weakened, and he couldn't hold the soldiers on the road off any longer, it had come.

Mere had emerged from the forest to stand by his side. A tingle had raced through him, similar to the zap when he first touched her, and sometimes still. It shot through him from his extremities, racing into his core. It grew to a shock and thumped hard in his chest. She'd swung her gaze to him as if she'd heard it.

Her smile was hesitant but brave. His chest constricted, remembering her expression while full-blown terror hit him. He didn't have enough left to protect her from the Order—protect any of them.

He'd raised his hands toward the army, praying Mere had

replenished her wells, but he'd flushed with heat as electricity raced from his core to his fingers, and sparks crackled to bolts and fired.

"Was that?" Her voice had been hushed but clear.

"Yes," he'd breathed while his chest tightened, and he floated with charged energy.

He clapped his palms, rubbed them together, then pulled them apart. Sparking bands connected his hands. He stretched the lightning between them before turning his palms out and firing long, flashing spears.

Finally.

Lighting had been his goal from the first time he watched Avia in battle. Lightning as an air power had surprised him. He believed his wind was his minor ability compared to his ability to see future events.

But then, on that field in Switzerland, everything had changed. Not only had what the Order lied to them about been revealed, but also Mere and their instant connection, frightening in its strength. Then just recovering from his reaction to the black-haired beauty that was Mere, Avia began shooting lightning like damn Zeus reborn…and Aron was confident he would have that upon his own ascension.

The sisters had shown him and his brothers what they were capable of, and they marveled at the gifts that awaited them once they passed their tests and achieved shakti. Being the first elemental brothers, they had no way to predict what skills would come to them, but by meeting the sisters, they'd gotten a picture of their future.

Though Cole could control fire, Asha's incredible strength proved Cole's pyroshakti would eventually conjure fire without a spark. Clay's healing talent would grow, and his control over earth. Rio would be able to call water from the air and expand it to untold amounts, and Avia had lightning.

One prodding question remained. Why had he never seen it? Not once in all his visions, blurry and fragmented as they were, had he ever seen himself with lightning. But then, he'd never seen the sisters either. Clay had seen Asha in his dreams, so why had Aron, the one who could see the future, never seen any of them? Not even Mere.

But now he had it. Lightning.

Did I pass my test?

Surely, he would be aware if he'd had the test meant to trigger his shakti, let alone passed it. Much to Miles's and the Order's fury, he and his brothers had yet to face the tests that would unlock their potential. Miles and the Grand Master had done everything they could imagine to trigger them without success. It couldn't have just happened, could it?

Usually, when Aron was drained, it took a substantial rest before he was recharged. And he'd been nearly drained, then he'd had a new sparking force within him and vast wells of it. Even after fighting the army, blasting them away with bolt after bolt, he brimmed with it.

The sparking light was there, ready at his fingertips, and he should probably make sure it wouldn't burst out while he was so volatile.

"Mere?" he called. "I'll just be outside for a minute."

Storming out the front door, he stalked toward the lake, where the dark water frothed, stirring whitecaps.

Burning electricity stretched his skin, so he shot his arms in front of him. Long, strobing streaks of lightning fired across the lake. Raising his arms to avoid touching the water, he expelled the crackling bolts. The urge to bellow built in his chest. What if Mere heard him?

Who cares?

So he roared. With it came release, and unshed tears stung his eyes. The scene flashed before him. Clay carrying Mere, burned, beaten, lifeless…into the Grand Chamber.

Never in his life had Aron been so powerless, so frightened, so guilty. He'd seen his brothers within death's grasp many times. After all the Order put them through, they'd come to the brink often, but the Order wanted them alive; they wouldn't intentionally kill them. He and his brothers could survive, suffer, yes, but survive, they always did. The Order wanted the sisters dead.

And they'd done it. Mere was gone.

He'd *thought* she was gone. And he hadn't been right since.

She's alive. Right now, she's alive. She's here with you. Safe.

But for how long?

He used each finger to test his aim and precision. After only minutes, he didn't need his hands—just thinking what he wanted and where, sent the lighting to its mark.

Panting, he closed his fists and his eyes, and the sparks and all light vanished. This was too much. He couldn't deny whatever his test was, he'd passed it, but how?

His skin thrummed with electricity.

You have too much power.

But less than Avia.

He shook his head, trying to clear it. His aerashakti and the test could wait. Take care of Mere. Turning, he stopped short. She stood by the open door, eyes wide, watching him.

Frightened.

As he walked toward her, she rolled her shoulders and held out her hand.

Fearless.

He clenched with sorrow at her trusting, open act of support. He didn't deserve it. Because even with his new clearer sight, he wouldn't be able to save her. Every vision he'd seen of the future since first meeting the sisters at Avia's cabin showed their death.

Chapter Ten

Aron removed the sheets covering two intricately carved chairs and the dining table, revealing an almost mirror-like gleam on the dark oak surface.

Mere dropped the large red bag, bulging with medical supplies, onto the table. It resembled something an army medic might carry.

Tight tension stretched between them, so solid, it drew him to her and swallowed the air in the room.

Spinning one of the chairs to face the other, he sat. He opened the bag and rummaged through it.

Coming around the table, she joined him. "Nothing's broken," she said.

"That's good, but I want to be sure," he said, adding notes of concern and humor into his voice, but they fell flat.

The sparking energy between them prevented him from even forcing a smile. Their knees were less than an inch from touching, and the tingles in his skin reached for her.

"What's bothering you the most?" he asked.

"My lack of memory."

"I meant physically."

Her smile was hesitant, and she pulled off her sweater with shaking hands. "This." Tugging down the already low neck of her black tank top, she peeled off a corner of the bandage.

He flinched but froze. The wound was angry, red, and infected. Black lines webbed out from the injury as if dark poison leaked through her veins about an inch from the source. "What did that to you?"

"I don't know."

His frown deepened.

"The swim should have healed it—not completely, maybe, but much more than this. I've never had a cut or scrape that water didn't heal. It seems to be getting worse."

He took out some ointments, bandages, and a small bottle. Studying the first aid kit's contents, he sensed her gaze was on him. Heat and heaviness gave her away.

"You seem so different. Is it because I hurt you and your brothers?"

He paused in his preparations. "No."

"Are you angry—"

"I thought they killed you." The sparking tension in the room grew even worse, and the air stopped.

"A-Aron, are you doing this?" She gasped. "I-I can't breathe."
What am I doing?

He tore his gaze from her wound to meet her wide, panicked eyes. Her hands were at her throat. The air flowed again, fresh and light, through the room. "I'm so sorry." He shifted forward. *What the hell is wrong with me?*

"Are you all right?" He reached out but stopped, not wanting to touch her like that. *Just take care of her injuries.*

"Yes, I'm okay," she panted, her hand on her chest.

"I'm sorry. You're right. I'm not myself. It's just—I thought you were dead. Then I thought you were going to kill my brothers…and me." Just before he could brush her wound with an alcohol swab, she jerked back.

"Wait. Sorry. I think it might be better for me to try a bath. I could be drained after everything. Maybe that pond did cause some infection, though that's never been the case before; maybe a fresh, clean water bath will be exactly what I need."

He fought his unease at seeing a flash of fear in her eyes. "What about the impact from the car after the missile? That was—"

"I'm fine. I was able to cushion it."

"Okay, if that's what you want." He met her gaze, showing her with his expression she had nothing to be afraid of. *Your reflection in the obsidian stone of the Order. Your face within the black hood. My brothers beside me.* "Whatever you need."

Just because you saw a flash doesn't mean anything.

Sure, it doesn't.

She rose but halted. "Do you need help with your injuries?"

He unfolded, stood, pulled off his sweater, and showed her his injury. "How does it look? I can barely feel it now."

"Much better," she whispered, her voice had grown softer.

"I'll find something to eat."

Her gaze darted around, but she didn't leave.

"There has to be a nice bathtub somewhere in this place," he said, trying for a light tone.

Her gaze searched around, never landing anywhere.

Oh. Solid ice inside his chest melted. "Do you want me to come with you?"

The relief in her eyes. "So lame, right? But—"

"Say no more." He forced the most soothing expression he could onto his face.

"Ghosts." Her laugh sounded hollow.

~ * ~

Mere avoided his gaze, and her cheeks heated. Aron stood to accompany her, and she almost stumbled, tripping over her feet. She didn't believe in ghosts but was too scared to explore alone.

Blaming her longtime love of horror movies paired with the spooky energy of the place, she walked with him in search of a bathtub.

Down the hallway off the main foyer were various rooms: a library, a living room, and some kind of billiard room with an adjoining bar. *Wow.*

"Are we in a game of Clue? This place is insane," she said, hoping her chatter might lighten anything or everything as they searched.

He cracked a smile. "Seems so."

The last door at the end opened to a lavish suite with an enormous ensuite bathroom decorated with marble, brass, tall windows, and skylights.

"Damn, Avia." She chuckled, her hand covering her laugh.

The bathroom boggled her mind. Shining white marble tiles led to an infinity pool, reaching a far bank of windows overlooking the churning lake. A cream-colored couch with a stack of fluffy towels atop stood beside a full-length antique mirror.

"Well, that'll do." He crossed into the room.

"It reminds me of those ancient Roman baths, where multiple people would bathe together."

He raised his eyebrow. "Multiple people?"

His voice was low, and the sound rolled into her, vibrating through her. She lifted her hands, palms out. "Not my thing, but to each their own."

His laugh was quiet. He went to the faucet and turned it on full blast. "Start with full hot, right?"

"With a tub this size, absolutely."

As he squatted, she noticed the gun holstered at his back. She tried to laugh with him and be casual, but it was too hard.

Rushing water pouring into the tub broke the silence.

He stood and faced her. "Are you sure you're okay, Mere?" The expression was so serious that more heat flowed through her, but he was just concerned. His gaze drifted from her face to where the wound still throbbed, then to her face.

All her attempts to keep everything inside were at risk just staring into his eyes.

Her breaking point was so near. On the verge of collapse, she was that cracked vase again, barely holding herself together. His concern was going to tear her apart.

Unsure how they came to be standing so close, he lifted his hand slowly to her cheek. The movement was careful and deliberate, giving her plenty of time to move away and avoid his touch.

She must have gone to him because he stood near the faucet at the tub's edge.

The second his thumb brushed her skin, her tears escaped. Then she was surrounded by him. In his arms.

He squeezed her tighter, and the vase fell into pieces. She'd held it together too long, but in his arms, she felt safe, and that triggered her release. He smelled of fresh morning storms. And the scent soothed her. Healed her. How was that possible? She took a long, slow breath of him, and heat coiled within her.

She forced herself to look anywhere but his intense eyes.

A laugh puffed out of her at the inch of water in the tub.

Sneaking a glance at him, his intensity had softened, and light humor coated his concern. "You'll be waiting until tomorrow."

She snapped her fingers to fill the tub, but nothing happened.

No.

Once more, she tried calling for her power to fill the tub. *Nothing.* Her knees buckled, weak.

How?

He took her weight as her legs gave out. "Hey, what is it?"

"The water. M-my aqua-aqua-whatever it's called. It's not coming."

He half-carried her to the couch. "You're too drained."

Frowning, she sat. "I can't be. Not for such a small thing. Not for this long."

"It hasn't been long."

"It has for me. Healing is one thing, but filling a tub? Unless I'm beyond drained, I should be able to use it in fifteen minutes, thirty at the very most."

Her spark thrummed inside her, but she was having trouble accessing it.

Getting to her feet on shaking legs, she turned both palms to the tub. The water level began to rise. "This is wrong, wrong. It's too hard." Sweat formed on her brow, and her hands shook with effort. Cold agony seared her chest as if she'd been stabbed with an icicle. She choked, and her legs gave out, but he was there to keep her knees from crashing to the ground.

"What the hell? Are you okay?" His face was pale and hard.

"My aquashakti is gone." She stood, turned her palms out, aimed at the tub, and screamed inside for it. It was there; it just wouldn't respond. She pushed, pulled, and urged it to come, calling it to her. The water rose slowly until the tub was full.

"It's okay. It's working now." She brushed away the blood from under her nose and rinsed her fingers in the water before he saw.

"Are you okay?"

She frowned. "Maybe if I soak…I'll heal, and it'll return."

"I'm sure it will." But his false tone wasn't fooling her.

She had to work at the smile she gave him, full of nervous butterflies. She gave him that fake, '*I'll be fine. I'm tough, just give me some privacy*' expression.

His lips pursed like he didn't believe her. "Enjoy your bath."

She acknowledged his ability to read her by tilting her head to him.

But when he crossed the threshold, she panicked. "Wait. Can you leave it open?" She tried to smile once more but couldn't. "Just in case."

With the door open a crack, he left her to heal in privacy.

Okay, recharge, then we can make a plan. He's okay. I'm okay. They're all okay.

She took off her clothes and stood in front of the mirror. Her reflection was far worse than she was prepared for. The bruises were dark and ugly even after her swim in the pond. Taking in all the damage, a quiet buzz hummed in her head. She expected to be much further along in the healing process.

But the black wound drew her gaze, and she flinched, disgusted—dark veins spread about an inch out from the source.

Yikes.

She moved to the tub's edge and swept down the warm marble steps into the tub. The soft and silken water stroked her skin as she stepped down, and the water climbed higher over her body. She indulged herself the way an ancient goddess or queen would, walking naked into a vast bath the size of an indoor pool.

It had taken so much effort to fill. The agony burning her chest frightened her, but she was stoking her denial too hard right now. She drew in the warmth and relished this opulent experience, submerging until the water covered her shoulders.

Below the surface, her body wasn't healing. Her power wasn't refilling.

What's going on?

She peered at her wound. A little wisp of dark blood leaked into the water.

Mere shifted forward, trying to see it better.

The blood didn't dissipate; it twitched, and she jerked, splashing back in horror. It darkened and grew. Her heart stopped beating, and her skin iced over. The blood stretched into a shimmering black thread, reaching the bottom of the tub.

It stuck there, anchored, then split, and another line shot to the surface. Then, another speared from the surface to the tub's bottom. She recoiled, dread pouring into her. The inky threads solidified into thick cords.

Get out! Now!

Reaching for the tub's edge, she was halted by a cord wrapping around her ankle, then another around her wrist, and pulling her under.

Surging up, she cried out, "Help! Aron!" She managed to gasp out the words before she was dragged beneath a second time.

The dark strands kept stretching, growing, filling the tub. Forming a web, crisscrossing in the water, the strange cords pinned her to the marble bottom of the tub.

Her breath whooshed out as the bindings coiled around her chest, under her breasts, with enough force to wind her.

No! No, no, no. Am I going to drown?

Bound and trapped underwater, she could barely see through the black webbing, spreading viciously, darkening the water. Everything grew murky...

Or is that my vision? Am I passing out?

Though she struggled, the panic she expected didn't come. Her movement caused the bands to tighten, coiling around her thighs, ankles, and neck. Desperately needed air leaked out of her.

She squeezed her eyes shut.

The cell was cold and dark. The Four were there. One of them came forward and touched her chest.

No!

She fought away, but he stabbed through her flesh and froze her heart.

Hands reached for her. She jerked underwater, recoiling from what wasn't there. Burning fire lanced through her, and the last of her air escaped.

Terror of those hands. More so of them than drowning.

But they grasped the cord around her neck while she twisted and thrashed.

Aron?

No, it wasn't him. Without air, she couldn't call for help—a hooded figure. Skeletal, vapor hands but solid, wrapped around her neck.

No! Please, no.

The Four. Was this the torture she'd blocked coming back?

She screamed underwater.

This isn't real. This can't be.

The figure lowered his dark-hooded void, his hands around her throat, squeezing.

Stars flashed in the pulsing darkness.

I'm drowning.

But the coils gave a bit. They lost their iron strength around her throat, then her chest, and relief flooded her.

Blind, she surged from the water and stood sputtering, gasping for air. The strange restraints shattered into sharp splinters, sliding down her body with the water.

"A-Aron?" She'd been on the verge of dying, and her sight was slowly returning.

"Mere." He collapsed to his hands and knees in the water before her.

Standing and still panting, she cupped the water, lifting and studying the fibers with a texture of thin, splintered stones.

He was on his knees, breathing harder than she was. He looked up, meeting her gaze, and she was inside his panic, his fear. He'd saved her.

Chapter Eleven

Without thinking, Mere reached for Aron. She gripped his shoulder like a lifeline and pulled him up to stand with her. She gravitated into him; thankfully, he wrapped his arms around her.

She calmed, absorbing such sublime peace and comfort.

"I think I saw The Four torturing me," she said when she could finally speak.

"You're okay. I've got you."

Just being in his arms brought the security she'd yearned for, but even while relishing it, she faced its futility. He couldn't give her what she needed. No one could. Something very bad had happened in the tub. Whatever it was, she didn't want to face it.

It had been terrifying, being that powerless— *No, Guppy. You're not powerless.*

Dread, prophecy, or instinct—didn't matter which, but something told her, like that buzzing in her mind, she wouldn't survive much longer.

They were thigh-deep in the water. She was naked and stretched against his soaking and fully clothed body. He panted from the exertion it took to save her, yet his embrace—this was exactly what she needed.

She'd been tortured and terrified, hunted and captured, and yet right now, before she died, she wanted *him*. And she hoped he felt half of what she did. There'd been long, heated looks, more physical contact than necessary, and of course, that electrical charge that fired through her when they touched. But he'd stopped it last time.

She tilted her face up, and he dipped his down as if her thoughts brought them together.

Lust, hot and aching, unfurled low inside her.

Danger be damned.

Just before their lips met, her breath hitched. *Yes.*

On contact, shocks flew through her, melting her into molten liquid.

Oh, yes.

His lips were warm, light air on hers. There was hesitation in his kiss, but her desire came out in a soft, urging moan. In response, his lips became solid heat and passion on hers, sweeping her into head-spinning oblivion. Holding her to him, he was the strength she lacked, and she fell into him. She forgot everything but his mouth on hers, kissing her slow and gentle but devouring in the most perfect, burning way.

She arched into him, pulsing as he opened his mouth, and his tongue swept over hers. She met it with hers, and the silken stroke flooded her with fire. Releasing a soft moan, she gripped him harder.

He cupped her bottom, drawing her so close nothing could separate them, and she pressed along the clear evidence of his desire, her aching need only increasing.

Trying to get to his skin, she tugged at his soaking wet sweater, tracing her hands over a muscle-rippled stomach beneath.

He flinched at the contact.

No.

He paused, breathing hard, fast, still.

Not again.

"Mere, I can't. I'm sorry."

"Don't be." The burning passion wasn't fading, but she was almost sick with desire *and* the sting of rejection. Had she ever been so exposed in her life?

"What happened?"

"I don't know… My blood… I think…"

He moved to turn away, but she gripped his arm.

"Wait, I…" She stared at him, forcing all her longing, desire, and need onto her face. "You may not want this…or me—I thought you did. But I don't care that I was hurt or I just almost drowned. It doesn't have to mean anything. I'm not asking for any commitment. I just—"

She wasn't used to asking or making the first move. Men usually took care of that awkwardness. In embarrassment, she dropped her gaze from his searching one.

His fingertips were so gentle on her chin when he lifted it. His expression was heavy and severe, but there was desire there.

"How could you think I don't want you?"

Her shoulders sagged with relief. "You have rejected me at every opportunity. When we were in Egypt, you walked away. I threw myself at you. I put effort into that seduction, and after one kiss, you just left me on that balcony."

His lips curled in a flash of a small smile. "You have no idea how difficult that was for me, Mere. You were–*are* so beautiful, but it wasn't appropriate, despite my unfathomable desire for you. We'd just met."

Fire roiled low in her body. "You've never had a one-night stand?"

"We could never have something so trivial–or keep it to one night."

His sure words took her aback. "What?"

"I know you feel it, too. It's too intense." His hard focus fell to her mouth, and that fire flared. "Whatever's between us and the others, too, it's more than attraction. It's too strong. Just fighting it is difficult. What happens if we give in?"

He's attracted to me.

"Yes, of course, I feel it. And I like it. I hoped you would, too. What happens if we give in? What do you think happens? We experience something good in all this horror, even if it is only momentary and forced." At his frown, she hurried to add, "Didn't you just imply that?"

"I don't know. But, yes, even with everything happening, I want you."

His gaze burned so hot into her flesh that she was going to self-combust.

"I don't know if it's the right thing to do," he said.

Stung and humiliated by his rejection, the flames inside her chilled. If he was into her, why wouldn't he act on it? She twisted her mouth to the side, her face growing warm. "Fine. I thought it could just be sex." She shrugged, hoping she portrayed casual ease.

He went rigid, his mouth forming a thin line.

And now you're begging for it, Guppy? Where's your self-respect?

So, what? I could die tomorrow.

An unreadable expression flickered across his face. "You really think it would just be sex between us?"

That heavy fluttering inside returned, and she went molten as his dark gray eyes met hers, and lightning forked across his pupils.

He was correct; there was too much destiny between them for it ever to be *just* sex. And hell, maybe that was why she pursued him the way she did. She'd had great sex but never a true connection.

"No, maybe not," she said as more tingling anticipation spread through her.

"It would be grotesque to take advantage. You were abducted. You aren't even fully healed from their torture—"

"And yet I was hoping for a pleasant distraction from—"

"A pleasant distraction?" His gaze fell to her mouth, and his jaw flexed. He was so still.

She burned under his tugging, hypnotic gaze. Emboldened by the lust in his eyes, she took his hand, brushing her thumb over his rough, callused palm.

His breath hitched.

With their fingers entwined, so naturally, so comfortably, a softer pleasure rippled through her. Though her mind continued to fear the unknown, she needed this—this level of desire—this distraction—right now, she needed him more than anything. Deep down, it wasn't just the diversion she was after. From their first meeting, when he first touched her, she'd lusted for him more than any surfer or lifeguard in her past. And it hadn't been just a little bit more.

Tilting her face up at the same time he lowered his, she brushed her lips over his with feather-light hesitation. Unsure and tentative, she prayed he'd kiss her the way he just had. *Yes.*

She craved him the same way her body and soul yearned for water.

Closing his eyes, his soft lips held a restrained urgency on the brink of consuming her. His hand in hers flexed, his thumb stroked across her knuckles, while his other arm remained motionless at his side.

His lips were so gentle on hers. She could've wept with all that was unsaid but there in the way he kissed her. But his *stillness*, he seemed to be holding himself on some invisible leash. A small moan escaped her at his sweet longing.

Her arch was involuntary. He opened his eyes, their gazes met, and the fierce need in his took her breath away. She paused their kiss, breathless, even with the slow, tender intensity, but kept her eyes on his as she took their joined hands and brought them up between them. She kissed his palm, then placed it over her breast.

The sound he made was something between a groan and a growl, and he broke through some invisible restraint. He grasped the back of her head, pulling her into another smoldering kiss, and he unleashed himself. His mouth took hers harder this time, and the impact was everything: hot and shaking, flowing and filling, flutters of excitement and rightness.

Oh my— Yes.

Fire roared from her core; her primal response was immediate, radiating through her. His touch ignited a fire inside her that had never burned with such heat. Everything she suffered, fear for her sisters, the Order, and the Four, faded. Desire consumed her mind and senses.

His kiss became urgent, hard, and overwhelming. She yanked at his soaking clothes. In one motion, he dragged his sweater over his head and dropped it into the full tub.

He lifted her, and she wrapped her legs around his waist. With one arm holding her up and the other fisted in her hair, he carried her out of the bathtub, their lips ravenous for each other.

Setting her on her feet before the cream couch, he took one of the fluffy towels and offered it to her. She was too busy staring at the man's torso. *Damn.*

That had been under his clothes this whole time. She knew he was fit, and she'd grazed those abs, but seeing him soaking wet in jeans had her licking her lips and ignoring the towel. She covered the distance, her gaze meeting his, while she reached for his pants.

Almost dizzy from his expression and the need in his gaze, she trembled... They no longer needed words between them.

Lightning forked in Aron's dark irises, and he leaned in, their lips meeting this time without hesitation.

He finally kissed her the way she imagined in her naughtiest fantasies, and she allowed herself to relish the freedom and the intensity. Melting into liquid, her body rocked and flowed. She was a wave of pure desire with no control or containment. As he kissed her, her thirst for him increased. An attraction at this level was brand new and far, far too much for her. But she would not run away from it, or fear it.

Her heart beat so loudly that no logical thought other than her hunger for him could take hold.

Impatient, she ripped at his belt and opened his jeans. Removing his lips from her throat, he stepped out of his remaining clothes. The silence, so thick with need, hung between them, but he paused, asking her permission, giving her a chance to stop him, to say no.

As if.

Inhaling his scent, she thought of billowing clouds and impending lightning. Her body rolled and quaked with electric vibrations as he cupped her face gently in his hands and kissed her. But the building passion was getting too much; she needed him now. This was far more intense and shattering than she expected, and they were only at light foreplay.

"I have wanted you since I first saw you across that field, laughing in our faces, standing before an army."

Sizzling fire surged in her at the passion blazing in his eyes.

Holding her gaze, his fingers traced her cheek and his thumb her jaw. His touch weakened her legs so thoroughly she dropped to the couch. He crawled forward, guiding her to lay atop the cushions, and hovered over her, his perusal taking her in.

She shivered.

Yes.

The hesitation before their lips crashed together in perfect harmony was sweeter than fresh morning dew in spring. He traced his fingers from her cheek to neck, to shoulder. Stroking past her breast, he caressed the swell then her waist, hip and over her stomach setting off a trail of invisible sparks along the way.

He was everywhere, in the air all around her, even in the air she breathed into her lungs.

What was that?

Not now.

She ignored the one dark tint spoiling his pure energy, and throwing her head back, she abandoned herself to the pleasure flooding and consuming her body and soul. He settled between her legs, sending more fire racing through her blood, heating it to the brink of boiling.

But when he slid a finger inside her at the same time he grazed his teeth along her neck, she exploded. Rocking with her climax, she spasmed with fierce pleasure, and she groaned and writhed against him.

Oh my—. Yes.

"Aron." His name was a plea, a gasp, a prayer.

She throbbed for more of him. Roving her hands over his physique, she traced rippling muscle and skin, smooth and scarred on the way down.

She couldn't stop her groan of excitement when she brushed the warm, hard length of him. He was perfect, ready, and she needed him now.

Tugging at his shoulders, arching for more, she gasped. "Aron, please, now."

He slowly raised his head. His eyes were dark, heavy-lidded, and hungry.

Yes, yes, yes.

The intensity in his stare brought her to the brink. Had she ever wanted anything more?

Reaching up, she dragged him to her. His gaze traveled over her, studying every inch of her. His eyes paused and narrowed, staring at her chest.

No. Please.

She guided his face to meet hers and lifted her chin.

Now. Please now.

He flexed his jaw, and they stared at one another. The same level of passion reflected in his gaze must be flashing in hers.

"Aron," she said with pure ecstasy on her lips.

"Mere." Her name from his mouth—the way it rolled over her, vibrating into her over her bare skin had her cry out, and as she twitched with the building release, he thrust forward, entering and filling her at the exact moment he crashed his mouth to hers in a searing, spinning, kiss that swept her away.

Oh, yes.

The orgasm that had started with the sound of her name on his lips rocked through her. It soared higher and stronger, flowing through. She broke their kiss, and her cry burst from her with her shattering release.

Spiraling and panting, she floated in the most exquisite ecstasy she'd ever experienced in her life.

Then, Aron began to move.

~ * ~

Aron lunged for Mere. Her blue irises were spinning like whirlpools, covering the pupils. The sight of those eyes, her curves, combined with the sound of her heart and breath flipped a switch inside him.

Yes

He had to have her…and there was sudden ferocity in his need. Sliding an arm under her arching and bending to take her mouth harder and hungrier this time, he surged forward.

Gasping together, then ending on a moan, their bodies became one. He stopped. The air burst from his lungs. She was soft, warm, silk beneath him, surrounding him. She brought more than pleasure; the connection, the completeness, burned straight to his chest.

Her pure energy called him—controlled him. They were a flawless fit. Electricity stirred, then fired every sensor inside him.

She flexed around him, vibrating as she cried out. He memorized her face while she climaxed. Everything, the sensations, the pleasure, and Mere were too intense. Gritting his teeth, he held himself behind rigid walls, preventing the surging need from threatening his control. He could have followed her over the edge, too, but that wouldn't do.

Shit.

He had to move. She gripped him with magnificent perfection, and he tried to go slow, but desire forced him on faster. She met each thrust, tilting her hips, and their pace increased, crashing back and forth like a tide in synch. Their power mixed and joined until she pulsed with her second climax.

Their rhythm was unspoken but somehow known. He couldn't stop; desire and need pushed him faster and harder until he reached a precipice. She cried out; her delicate muscles jerked and fluttered once more. He hesitated at the edge, looming over, questioning everything before he dove off headfirst into the abyss.

Electricity shot through his veins, and pleasure exploded through him in ecstasy, wilder and stronger than a raging tornado.

Breathing ragged and propped on his elbows, he stared into her sapphire eyes. The way they spun around her small pupils drew him so far into their depths that he could have drowned. Dropping his chin, he brushed his mouth over her parted, perfect lips. He kissed her lightly, caressing his thumb over her cheek.

78

It's never been like that.

After containing himself within his walls, keeping himself in check his entire life, one encounter with this woman had him smashing them all to rubble, ready to hand her his soul. Okay, maybe two encounters. That made him pause. He opened his eyes and studied the slight smile on her bruised face. It had barely healed after her ordeal. And that injury on her chest, he was worried about the dark, inky veins spreading from the wound. It had to be some kind of infection.

Anger replaced the euphoric tornado, and fury tore through him. His anger triggered sparks to flash in the far corners of the ceiling.

Whoa, easy. Breathe. Why am I so unhinged? It's okay. She's okay. Breathe.

As they lay breathless and panting, entwined on the couch, the room flashed brighter than midday.

He sat up, instantly alert, but it was no emergency. White strobes lit and filled the sky outside.

Shifting, she also sat up.

"It's okay," he said. "It's just some lightning."

Her eyes widened as she stared through the skylight then the bank of windows. He reclined with his arms folded beneath his head and studied her.

She wore a small smile of wonder. "Some?"

Wow, the way her eyes sparkled and her half smile was both enthusiasm and hesitation in the gentle curve, lighting him up inside. She was so beautiful.

The bruises and damage on her soft curves sent another clench of rage through him, at the Order, the lies, everything she'd suffered… and would still suffer.

I will not let the Order take her from me.

Breathless passion hovered between them while his thoughts and fears darted like sharp fragments through his mind, leaving blood and pain behind.

The Order will have her. The Order will kill her.

No.

Or you will.

You will lose her no matter what.

Anger reared within him. So much for his calm, collected persona.

Fight with her.

He'd never intended to make love to her—not ever—because there was no hope for her or her sisters. He'd seen it.

But now…

There was no hope for him either.

~ * ~

Mere gazed out the large windows at the most lightning she'd ever seen in her life. *This is nuts.* Raising her eyebrows in wonder at Aron, she was surprised to see his eyes shut and his mouth a tight line.

Their connection had been earth-shattering…*for her.*

Just sex. Yeah, sure.

Just be cool.

"Let's go outside," she said, smiling at the wonder he'd created.

He blinked, and when their eyes met, he smiled in return. It warmed her more than she wanted to admit.

Grabbing the towels, then passing one to him, she dried off and dressed. He wrapped the towel around his waist, and she stifled a smile when he glanced pointedly at his pile of wet clothes in a heap.

"I'll just grab some clothes from my pack." He brushed his fingers through his hair, and she had to stop herself from licking her lips while gawking at his flexed arm and mussed hair.

Biting her lip to keep from giggling, she followed him out the door and to the kitchen, her gaze glued to his towel-covered butt while he strode ahead. She was in that euphoric haze caused by fantastic sex with a new guy that she was really into. That rare ecstasy before reality and disappointment knocks you tumbling from your pedestal of joy and lust.

Come on, Guppy, get in the game. This is serious, you flighty bitch.

But she had said it earlier with everything that had happened and was maybe going to happen, why shouldn't she take joy and lust if she could?

He dressed in jeans and a black knit sweater in the dining room where he'd left his pack. With his hand outstretched and a wink to her, they went out the side door they'd first entered.

Whoa.

She halted just outside, and they stood under the sky filled with hundreds of flashing lightning bolts. They arced down from above. "I've never seen anything like this. It's a bit scary—sort of an end-of-the-world, wrath-of-God display."

"It won't hurt us." His smile was kind—soothing.

"How do you know?"

"I just do."

"You did this?" she asked, almost breathless. "I had no idea you could—"

"If I did this, you did that." He pointed. In the dark, she could

80

barely make it out.

The lake was one giant whirlpool slowly rotating.

Prickling panic covered her body. She automatically gripped his arm. *What?* "I can't feel that."

"Really?" He angled his head to study her, his eyes flashing with the lightning's reflection.

"I should feel that; I should have sensed it forming." The bathtub and her struggling power burst from her passion fog, and more questions raced into her head. *What happened back there?* "Something is messing with my aquashakti." She said the word slowly, still getting used to it.

"What was that in the tub?" His flashing eyes drilled into her, but his questioning tone was hesitant and unsure. She'd met the serious and confident Aron. There was also his playful persona that she'd enjoyed in Cairo, but she hadn't met this worried and unsure Aron. "I think it was my blood," she murmured, the weight of the revelation settling upon her with a heavy pulse, shifting the peace and joyous mood to the harsh reality of their situation. Her situation.

They fell silent and stared at lightning.

Damn. That didn't last long.

Chapter Twelve

After a few more minutes of strained, heavy reflection, gazing at the continuous lightning display, Mere became concerned. *This isn't great.* She swung her gaze to Aron. "Is this going to give away our location?"

"I was just thinking the same thing." The second he finished the sentence, the lightning stopped.

"Oh," she said. "Nice. That was easy."

"I didn't do anything." He frowned.

"Well, it's a good thing it stopped, right?"

His smile didn't quite reach his eyes. The lake still churned behind her. She did her best to ignore it.

"Can you stop that?" he asked.

Having reached for it the instant he pointed it out, she couldn't connect to it. She had no control over that water, and she wasn't ready to face what that could mean. How could she tell him when she couldn't admit it to herself?

You're losing your power.

Thanks. I said I wasn't ready.

Denial won't help, Guppy.

He glanced toward the house. Maybe he regretted asking her to stop it since she couldn't. "We should make something to eat then get some rest before we move on. There's some soup in the pantry. We can call Master Miles first if you want to ask him about what happened."

Okay. So, he's shifting into some kind of caretaker mode.

She flushed with cozy warmth. His effort to take care of her was comforting under the circumstances. No one, not even Father Austen, had made her feel as safe as Aron did. Father Austen would've scolded her for her girlish desires. Self-reliance, defense, and offense were the foundations of her training.

Never need anyone.

Inside the kitchen, Aron put the soup in the pot and heated it on the stove. He pulled out his phone and dialed some numbers before turning on the speaker. "Cole, get the Master."

"Hold on," Cole's rough, rasping voice sounded like low, distant thunder.

"Aron?" asked another hoarse voice, but this one from weakness. Before Aron and Rio had shown up, Avia said that the Master had been stabbed in the heart just hours before. Being awake and talking was a testament to Ivy's healing ability.

"Something's wrong," Aron said.

Mere blinked at him, shocked by the unrestrained anger in his voice.

"What happened?" the Master asked.

"My power drained—fast." She jumped in. "Even after recharging, it drained almost immediately. I'm struggling to refill it, and the wound on my chest… It hurts when I—"

"What wound?"

"I have a puncture."

"With dark…almost black veins spreading from it," Aron added.

"Dark veins?" The Master's tone was stiff, carrying a note of dishonesty she picked up on.

He knows something.

Aron's face tightened; he must have sensed it too.

Silence for a beat, then another.

"What is it?" he snapped. "I will accept no more secrets or lies from you."

"Mere," Master Miles said and coughed. His breath wheezed, but he continued. "They've marked you. I'm so sorry. I assume with Asha's escape from the Order, they wouldn't want to risk losing you." He coughed. "Brace yourself. It is grave."

"We know that." Aron ground out the words with an intensity she hadn't heard from him before. "The black fucking veins paint a pretty clear picture. What does it mean?"

She swung her gaze to Aron. He stiffened under her surprised perusal, but such anger from him wasn't a pleasant display. She'd never seen that from him.

"Your aquashakti is tainted." Miles's voice had lowered. Her father's voice, she supposed. It was awkward that they hadn't addressed that, but it didn't seem as important as everything else they were discussing.

What was she supposed to say? *Hey, Dad, your former cult buddies took me hostage, tortured me, and are getting ready to hunt and kill me?*

It was rather alarming that the man who'd arrived badly beaten with the brothers and helped Asha escape the Order was their father.

It was too freaking much.

No one had ever looked like less of a father to her. Well, other than that dude by the road.

Mere, focus.

Her father continued. "Your power will change and fade while the mark consumes you. It will eventually disappear until you can't access it, but your spark will remain until the Order is ready. They will bend you to their will."

"What?" Terror filled her.

Sour rage poured in, pushing every other emotion out. The violation—how dare they? The Order took her, broke her, corrupted her. Her element was her identity. She was nothing without it. Her emotional dam bulged, and the building pressure behind it pounded harder with every grief and fear, insecurity and trauma. It all rocked and crashed against her faulty foundation—her restraint and control. Her dam took it all, but this new development? Could it take this, too? A large crack raced from the bottom of her ever-leaking walls to the top, allowing more water to spray and run out. *Hold it back*. Keep it together. More brick, more scaffolding. *Hold it together*. She couldn't speak. If she opened her mouth, she'd scream or cry. Or throw a tantrum, and she had to hold everything together. And if one tear escaped, her vase would shatter and her dam collapse. *Always hold it back*.

"You have been marked, Mere—corrupted," Miles said. "Your power will weaken; then it will weaken you. It will begin to fight you until you march yourself to the Order."

"It already has," she whispered, finally able to speak. Curling her hands to fists at her sides, her chest throbbed until she couldn't breathe. She fought to keep her tears behind her eyes. *Be stronger*.

"It tried to kill her." Aron gripped the edge of the table, bending to say the words into the phone's speaker.

"What?" The Master's voice was now sharp, clear, and stronger.

"Whatever just happened to her almost killed her." Aron offered his hand in invitation to partake in the conversation, but she reeled.

Deep down, her power was failing, but she'd hoped she was just drained or scared, not that the Order had done something to her.

"How strange?" Master's words came out slowly. "That seems counterproductive."

"Seems?" Aron's voice vibrated, and it rolled over her body with light but physical pressure. "I would say very. How do you explain it?"

"It would be very old magic," Miles said. "And magic isn't always precise—"

"No, it was more than that—a black web of some sort. It was strangling her." Aron finally broke his focus on the phone and met her gaze. "When I grabbed it off her throat, it moved like something with a pulse. It moved, gripped, and wanted to end her. It was alive." His eyes were communicating something to her she couldn't read.

"Sentient?" the Master asked with doubt. "I don't know how that could be."

The pounding water behind her dam churned, rolling and surging. She forced more bricks, more mortar, higher, and thicker. *Hold on.* Water slushed over the top, then was staunched by the last fragments of her resolve.

"Why would magic want me dead?" she asked, finally finding her voice.

"This is Order magic; everything they are is dedicated to hating you and your sisters. I couldn't tell you why or how, but that is not how it is intended to work. With the mark, the Four may be able to find you even now, but once your aquashakti is gone, you will flash like a beacon, and they will locate you. You won't be able to hide; once they have you, you will lead them to the others. You'll have no way to defend yourself. The Order will have total control over you."

She clenched her fists. *They will bend you to their will. My power in the Order's hands? They will find me, then my sisters.* She vibrated with fury and terror.

Aron's grip squeezed the phone so hard she expected crunching sounds any second. "I'll be with her."

She wished his brave statement made her feel better, but it didn't.

"Do you really believe you can stand against the Four?" Miles asked.

Prickles crept along her skin. Had she picked up the slightest note of reverence in Miles's voice?

"I will if it comes to that." Aron ground out his stiff words. "How do we fix it?"

"You will not be able to fix it." A heavy pause followed. "I'm very sorry, Mere."

"I don't accept that," Aron snapped.

"Well, other than defeating the Order, there is nothing you can do," Miles barked.

The last of the fight just whooshed out of her, and he turned to her as if he heard it leave her body. He locked her gaze with his, searching her face with an unknown intensity. It was too much. All of it. Too. Much.

Before learning of her destiny to die in sacrifice, she met her sisters for the first time. The horror of their future, death by sacrifice, came with the joy of discovering a new, very much needed family. But due to that impending doom, she had to run from her sisters while her terrifying destiny closed in too fast. *It's not fair.*

"We have to do something," Aron said, not breaking the hold his stare had on her. He might not be ready to give up…

But me…?

Guppy? Be strong.

She stepped away, finally dropping her head. The cord between her and Aron tightened as if he tugged on it, hoping for a response from her. She couldn't stop her sadness and fear from speeding like an electric current toward him in response. Fear and… despair. *Resignation.* It was her state of mind. She was just being honest.

"There has to be a way to stop it. To protect her," Aron continued, and that connection tugged for her to look at him, to engage with him.

"There isn't." Master Miles had calmed, but he was still impatient. "Not that I know of."

Aron waited, watching her, like he wanted her to say something. "So, her power will disappear, then they'll come?" he prompted. He held out his hand to her. To comfort her? To hold her?

Master Miles said nothing. She tilted her head, not understanding what Aron wanted.

"Help her," Aron said—more than a plea—a command.

"I'll try to think of something."

"Call me when you find a way." Aron hung up. He met her gaze and said, "Avia. Let's call Avia." He dialed some more numbers.

Chapter Thirteen

While the phone rang, Aron thought of how Mere's blood had solidified and pinned her underwater. Just before, he'd been overcome with an urgency to see her even though she was bathing. No vision told him that was happening.

He'd been hovering outside the door when she'd gasped his name. Her shout had been so quick, he wouldn't have heard it if he hadn't been at the door perving out. Would she have died if he hadn't had such an urge to disturb her healing peace?

He was shaken that his rudeness, his inexplicable desire, had saved her. Now, he didn't want to let her out of his sight, yet he hated the pull and passion that had him pawing at her like a horny teenager.

Like an animal, he'd conceded to his lust and approached the bathroom. Only half aware of himself, he rushed to the tub's edge, horrified to find her trapped underwater by thick bands of the flexible rocky substance resembling black sea coral. Her pale face and stillness had him jumping in, going for the cord wrapped around her neck.

He'd yanked and tore at the sinewy binding. As he stretched and choked it, the life stuttered and left it, transforming the living cord into rocky splinters.

Then she'd been free, staring at him, eyes wide, mouth parted, and looking so surprised. She reached for him only a second before he lunged for her. All the world disappeared except for her. Her touching him and him touching her.

It wasn't normal or natural. Something eternal was at play far bigger than base lust and attraction. His feelings for her grew daily, hourly, but he didn't want to love someone he would lose.

Fuck. He shut his eyes while the phone rang on speaker.

"Hey. You made it," Rio's voice came over the line.

"Yes. How's Avia?" Mere asked. Did her voice sound different?

She's tired. She's frightened. Relax.

"Her perfect glowering self. You want to talk to her?"

"Yes," she and Aron said at once.

"What's wrong?" Avia's voice was tight.

"Miles says the Order marked me." Mere dropped to one of the chairs.

"What does that mean?" Avia bit out the words.

The only color on Mere's face was the purple circles under her hollow eyes. With little enthusiasm, she said, "My power's compromised, and it will fade to nothing. He said they'll find me then all of you. I'm so sorry about this."

Aron was struck by her monotone and expressionless face.

"Are you okay?" Avia's voice was hushed.

"Obviously not," Mere snapped with a bit more energy.

Aron stayed quiet, hoping Avia would jump in and tell them what to do.

She didn't. Since they'd called Master Miles, Aron had watched Mere's emotions swing from joy to fear to rage and now to resignation. Her transparency was a gift, but the resignation concerned him.

After she finished describing what happened and what Miles said, the pause grew heavier with each second.

"Avia?" Aron asked. "Do you have anything?"

"No. I haven't seen this. Rio and I will search the Vatican scrolls and books we got from the archives in Rome. Maybe there's answers in there."

"I will send you photos of the pyramid carvings Mere and I got before she was taken," he said.

Mere glanced at him.

"Good. And call me the second anything *else* happens," Avia said.

"I will," Aron said, his eyes on Mere. He prayed Avia would find out more, or maybe Master Miles would figure it out—

"I'd forgotten about those carvings under the pyramids." Mere's mouth twisted to the side, then she shrugged. The hopelessness in the gesture cracked a fragile barrier inside him. He didn't want to think about what that barrier protected.

He served the soup and crackers. He observed while they ate, watching as she scarfed down her bowl so fast that he offered her his before he was half-finished.

She passed on it. Her weary expression grew exhausted, and her lids fluttered. "Why can't I remember what happened to me?"

"I'm not sure," he said gently. "It could be what the Order did or a result of the trauma you suffered. You should rest now."

He stood, escorting her to the large bedroom, and waited in the doorway until she'd climbed under the covers fully clothed. "How are you holding up?" he asked stupidly.

"I'm okay. I guess. As the outside starts to feel better, the inside feels worse. But we will figure a way out of this, right?" She tried to put forth a bold front, but he saw through it.

He offered a warm smile, hoping it gave her a sliver of comfort, and turned to leave, determined to do anything and everything to help her.

"Wait, I hope you're going to join me."

Thank you. "Of course. I'll clean up, and then I'll be in."

"Can you please leave the lights on…?"

He opened the door wide, then returned to the large, modern, steel kitchen and went to the gigantic fridge, pulling it open to peruse. Inside, there were twenty bottles of Champagne.

Hmm?

He took the pot and bowls to the sink. Flipping on the hot water, he reached for the soap, but the water filling the sink…the sound… He gazed into the suds.

The vision came on. *He was underwater, searching.*

Darting his gaze around, he tried to find her, but it was too dark; he couldn't see anything.

She'd been under way too long. The panic gripping his chest squeezed the last air bubble from his lungs.

Gasping for more air, he fought the dipping waves. They were too strong to stay on the surface, so he dove under, swimming, searching, reaching.

She's gone.

No.

No one could survive this long.

No!

He was Cole then because he stared at Ivy with such terror and hopelessness. *Her eyes were white voids, and as if in a trance, she touched her hand to his face before she went rigid.*

Through Cole's eyes, Aron stared helplessly at the sky. *The rocky walls stretched so high they had to be in the deepest gorge.*

Cole shut his eyes, calling Ivy's name while he held her rock-solid form. And when he opened his eyes, Aron had moved from Cole to Clay.

From the driver's seat, Clay gazed out the open passenger window. Asha was in the foreground, smiling at him. She pointed to the dormant volcano behind her.

A flash forward of a parking lot and a hike before he followed Asha into a cave. She winked at him from over her shoulder, but there were flames in her eyes. Another flash and Clay knelt beside her on the ground, cradling her head. His hand was on her cheek. He was horrified by her wide, white eyes.

Aron jerked and dropped the pot he'd been holding. He squatted and caught it before it hit the floor, but when he stood again, he jolted at the full, almost overflowing sink. His visions had been faster and more precise, not obstructing his other senses. But whatever had just happened was something different—time had passed while he was in a trance.

He washed the dishes quickly and swept the perimeter of the house. The security system was good enough, and he was thankful for what he hoped would be at least a few hours of solid sleep.

He returned to the bedroom. Mere was asleep, her breathing even. She needed rest, and so did he.

He stood over the bed, watching her. The scent in the room was morning rain and fresh dew on grass. Light but alluring, it strengthened and tugged at the cord connecting them.

A vision hit him from nowhere, and he flinched and palmed the wall to stay steady as terror shrouded his body. *Mere stood on the dais at the Order, eyes inky hollow voids and dark veins covering her bare arms, throat, and face. A Master with violet eyes stood beside her.*

No.

She gave a frightened whimper, breaking him from his vision. Aron's cold heart cracked. Even though she slept, her brows were furrowed, her mouth a firm line, and her jaw almost grinding.

She's scared and aware she's being hunted.

With his gaze never leaving her face, Aron stretched out on the bed beside her. Sleeping *with* women wasn't new for him, but he'd never slept *beside* a woman.

She lay on her side, facing away from him. Her scent and warmth pulled at him until his face was in her hair, and his arm itched to cover her.

He fell asleep, battling his arm and hand to stay put.

Mist billowed around Aron, clouding his vision before it cleared, revealing the Grand Chamber doors that opened at his approach. Entering, then falling to his knees, he bowed his head to the Masters, who waited with grim expressions.

The Master with purple-hued eyes raised his staff and tapped it twice on the mirrored, obsidian floor, mumbling incoherent words.

A frigid wind blew through the room. The floor rippled, transforming into smooth, shining tar, and a shimmering onyx pedestal rose, forming a strange altar. The Master slammed his staff to the floor once more, and the formation hardened into stone with a grinding crunch.

"Bring her."

An unconscious Mere was dragged between two soldiers. Her head hung forward—her hair covered her face.

No.

The soldiers tossed her onto the altar. Iron shackles clamped around her wrists and ankles.

Aron struggled on his knees, but he was held immobile. He couldn't look away from Mere on the altar.

The Master had changed in that dreamlike way; he shifted into Master Miles, then to the mysterious purple-eyed one, then Heath, then someone Aron didn't recognize. The Master struck the floor three times, and dense mist billowed from where his staff met the floor. Mere began to squirm and fight.

One of the Four appeared at her side and brought the knife to her right forearm. It shuddered as it cut a long, shallow slice.

Her blood flowed onto the altar, and the building shivered; the floor below his knees undulated.

The mist surged forward and swallowed Aron. Her scream echoed with heart-rending misery but hushed as if he'd been transported far away. The fog pricked and stung his skin like venomous needles. He fought it, blowing with his wind, but nothing worked.

A violent tug from his chest sucked the air from his lungs. Suffocation was nothing new to him, but this torture was far worse. The mist burned and stabbed him, too. Agony consumed him. He thrashed, yelling at the Masters to stop, but the cloud squeezed him, jerking and ripping him from his body. The mist was killing him.

After a sharp shock of pain, he couldn't breathe, speak, or feel anything. His fear for Mere waned. Everything vanished.

An anguished cry echoed in the vast chamber.

Mere yanked at the obsidian restraints trapping her arms above her head. Blood leaked from many minor cuts on her forearms into rivulets and channels carved on the altar.

He longed for her, his hand reaching out instinctively, but she recoiled.

From the moment he met her, this had been his true goal. Taking her. Having her. The urge grew stronger within him.

Do it.

As if propelled from something deep inside, he bolted forward so swiftly he blurred. Sweeping closer, he lowered his face to loom just above her. Tears ran free. Cocking his head, he touched one and stroked it over her skin before inspecting the wetness on his fingertip.

Take her.

Beside her...his reflection...on the obsidian floor.

He flinched. Shocked, he didn't recognize himself. There was something different...wrong. A hood with an empty void overlapped him and covered his head, but he was there underneath. He gripped a knife, and there was a loose, shadowy sleeve and a skeletal hand melding with his.

His face shifted. He was there, but his eyes were inky voids, hollow, empty holes—his face full of hate; then his reflection was Rio, Clay, then Cole before he shifted into himself.

Mere gasped, and her face blurred and melded into Avia's, Asha's, and Ivy's before it returned to the one he loved.

Her eyes were wide and terrified, but her head lolled back and forth as sobs wracked her. The knife was against her throat, and he thrummed with ugly urges that weren't his. The fear in her eyes became something harder, angry. "No. You can't," she whispered.

He stared at her pale, smooth skin. Just another rivulet. He flicked his wrist and cut. The red bead that bloomed stirred him at his core. His escaping moan was more animal than human, and he caught her blood with his finger.

Licking it, it filled his empty carcass with heat and substance; there was life in it, and there was life in him because of it.

Bleed her more.

He wanted to run his tongue along the cuts his knife made, drinking her potent life from the source of all.

She sobbed on the altar, flinching and fighting him with every cut he made.

The longer she bleeds, the stronger I will be.

As her blood flowed onto the altar, he made another cut, but this time, the shrouded sleeve and arm of the other had become his own. The reflection in the shining surface—true aerashakti and complete. I am finally whole.

Electricity burned his palm, and he reached for his sword, tracing the hilt.

"Not yet. We need the others first."

Who said that?

Was it Rio, Cole, or Clay? Or the Grand Master? Aron couldn't identify the voice.

No one commands me.

Mere whimpered, still tugging at the chains.

Grinding his teeth, steel sang, and he drew his weapon from its sheath.

"Not yet." The shout came from the dais.

No one!

The sword glittered as he spun it around, lifted it above her heart, plunged it down, and stabbed her in the chest.

Shocked, sapphire eyes bulged, and blood sputtered from her mouth. Her blood. Their blood.

The Grand Chamber shook as if awakening. The room inhaled and exhaled. It breathed. Waiting…

Impatient.

More of her precious blood dripped from the altar, pooling beneath her on the floor, it drained away, sucked up by the building that craved it.

The floor slurped her blood.

Aron leered at the sword glowing with her raw, limitless, elemental power, drawing in her essence like a deep breath. The connection between Aron and the Order solidified. They became one.

Without another glance at the altar and the dead body on top, he waited. The Masters rose and bowed.

This is what you must do.

Aron gasped, jerking up in the bed beside Mere.

No.

Chapter Fourteen

Heath sat in the seat beside the throne. What was Iacomus up to?

The doors opened, and Shane, the Order's human general, bowed before he walked forward with long strides. The torches flickered as if he'd moved them with his motion. Stopping before the dais, he bent again.

"Grand Master." Shane's voice was hushed.

"Let's take this discussion to my office." Heath started to rise.

The torches danced when the doors opened. Iacomus strode in. "Ahh, Heath."

"I'm off to a meeting," Heath said, hoping he conveyed enough authority that he would be able to escape.

"No need. Conduct your meeting here." Iacomus chose the chair on the other side of the throne and sat, swinging his purple-hued gaze to Heath. "I would be included in your plotting."

Shane's face neither blanched nor twitched, not even a breath at the uncomfortable display between the new Master and himself, the Grand Master.

But Heath flinched at the word plotting. "You believe me to be plotting?" He scoffed.

Iacomus studied him in silence. Under that icy stare, a chill crawled across Heath's skin, so cold his flesh could melt away.

"I don't understand, Master," Heath said, dropping his chin. "Will you speak plainly?"

Without answering, Iacomus slowly shifted his gaze, brimming with calculation and judgment, to Shane.

Heath wiped a sheen of sweat from his forehead, his heart hammering. Iacomus's suspicion unnerved him. Was it because of Miles's betrayal? Guilt by familial association?

Probably.

"What was your mission?" Iacomus asked the Order general.

"This is Shane. He is our general and the Master of our human assassins." Heath gave the introduction like he was conducting a tour, a small dose of shame at his submissiveness in front of Shane. "Shane, this is Master Iacomus, our former Master of Archives."

Shane gave Iacomus a deeper bow. To his credit, he gave no sign of anything untoward. Nothing ruffled Shane. A valuable quality in his fellow man. Even if he had been behind the Curtain since he was a child, Heath more than admired his composure.

"Master." Another perfect bow. "My mission is to find the

sisters."

"And you are here to give a report."

"I have a lead," Shane said.

"Assemble and send a team," Heath commanded.

Shane bowed once more, then spun and marched out. The doors shut behind him.

Heath regretted his role as Grand Master. Dealing with Iacomus was far worse than anything his father had thrown at him—evil fuck that he was.

"What are you planning?" Heath finally asked the question burning since their first meeting. Hell, he'd be almost grateful if Iacomus took over.

Where is Miles? What is he doing?

Iacomus's icy gaze focused on him, but this time, Heath didn't meet it, keeping his attention on the table.

"All the years you have had access to the brothers, and they failed to reach shakti. Just days beyond the Curtain in the company of the sisters, and Aron achieves it?"

Heath's eyes widened. *What?* "Is that true? What does that mean?"

"We wait while the Four ready themselves. Then we will move. But before that, all four brothers must ascend."

Heath frowned. "I am not clear on what your appearance now means to us and the cause."

"Well, of course you're not clear, Heath, I haven't told you anything." Iacomus rose. "I expect to receive all communications from Shane and any others tracking the sisters. In fact, I will be included in all future meetings."

"What are your plans for Master Miles?" Because they *would* find the sisters, and they'd be sacrificed. Why did the sisters have to be Emma and Miles's daughters?

Heath never wanted to sympathize with Miles, but how could he not? If Heath had been with Emma and had children... Heath shook himself. *Why the hell are you thinking about her? Now? Are you crazy?*

He'd lost his father and brother in one day. His father had been a half-mad, rabid dog; Heath cared little that he was gone. But his brother? Miles had been his only companion, and yet Heath wasn't sure about the void his absence left. Miles had been a bully, but they were family.

Iacomus paused on his way to the edge of the stage. "Well, that depends on what Miles has done."

"He took the sisters and left us."

Iacomus turned. "Yes, he did. What do you have in mind for Order traitors?"

Damn. "For this level of betrayal? Only death would meet it."

Iacomus carried on. "Agreed. I will return."

From where? Heath had to stop himself from asking.

Follow?

Yes.

Heading out a moment after Iacomus, Heath had a good idea of the destination. Where else would he go? He approached the door to the archives, and as he opened it, a shadow of that day returned. That game of Hide and Seek that had him fetching Miles from a horrifying display that still lurked foggy in his mind.

Had Heath ever returned? No. He had no need. The library up on the main floor fulfilled all his needs. Maybe laziness kept him from the study required to seek archives, but as someone whom the Four named Grand Master he should care a little about what happened down there.

It hit Heath then that Iacomus could have been at the Order all these years, in the archives the whole time. *Doing what?*

Torches sprang to life on his descent, giving a warning to anyone below. At the bottom of the stairs, he took two steps, and his foot hit something a second before his face smacked into an invisible barrier. He couldn't move forward.

The open library lay ahead with no visible obstruction, but there was a barrier blocking him. Sliding his foot along the width of the room, he tested the barricade while brushing his hands over the solid, smooth surface the way a mime would.

A spell. *A mini Curtain?* Iacomus had strange power Heath didn't understand. Was this some kind of protection? The man was up to something and going to lengths to hide it from Heath. He shrugged, partly relieved he didn't stumble across some violent event in the lab.

He backed up and ascended the stairs.

~ * ~

Mere's breath puffed out in clouds in the icy cell. She sat up on the metal slab.

No.

The Four were with her inside the room. The cell became a raging, burning inferno. An oven ready to cook her alive.

Shuffling away from the heat, her gaze darted around the room.

Flashing, shocking light covered her in an electric web, jerking her on the slab with such violence, her spine bent... She was going to snap.

Her scream was shrill and piercing.

"Just kill me," she cried out.

Out of the fire came a voice of many overlapping as one, an echo, ancient and cold. "You remember us, don't you?"

The flames parted, and the Four stepped closer.

Aron raised his translucent, smoky hand toward her. No. Was it really him? How?

How could he be here? How could he do this to me?

"No, no, please," she cried out. "No, no, no." She cringed away. Her revulsion and terror thrummed out of her.

His expression surged with fury at her rejection, and he lunged forward, grasped her around the throat, then squeezed.

Struggling in his grip, she clawed at his hand.

Lifting and shaking her as if she were a rag doll, he brought her up to his face and whispered, "You will die, but not yet. When we are through with you, you will greet death gratefully." Then he tossed her onto the slab.

"Leave us alone, please," she pleaded.

A bitter laugh escaped him, and she crawled toward the wall of fire surrounding her. Blowing Cole's flames back, Aron grabbed her leg and dragged her away. Shackles floated up, clamped around her neck, wrists, and feet, anchoring her to the metal shelf. "Though you may seek it, you will not die yet."

Her heart beat fast and frantic.

He leered at her, gripping her neck and pinning her.

Trailing his fingers down her throat to the source, he stopped over her heart.

No.

He pierced her skin and pushed his finger into her chest.

A scream erupted from her tight lips, but he didn't stop. He stabbed through her flesh, through the bone to her heart. The vibrating organ stuttered under his fingertips.

"Please just let me die," she whispered through clenched teeth.

And when he pierced her heart, her cry bulged in her ears. Her heart's wild rhythm spasmed then stopped.

With a quiet crunch, her heart hardened into ice. Purple veins spread from the black hole on her chest, covering her body, and she twitched on the slab.

Laughter rose and built, surrounding her in a painful swarm. Such a low, creepy laugh wasn't an expression of joy or glee. It was nasty, the sound of bullies and mockery. Her wail, which grew along in retaliation, was her pure expression of outrage and suffering.

Like flickering, fluorescent lights, her splintered mind shook. An image of Aron and his brothers wearing black robes and surrounded by flames strobed, flashing too bright and too terrible in her mind.

Black walls surrounded her. Despair overwhelmed her.

Hissing through clenched teeth at the pain, sharp blades sliced her arms. A blurry filter overlapped her reality, and lifting her arms, bloody wounds covered them in crisscross cuts.

Her gasp choked out when more fire encircled her. There was nowhere to run, and she couldn't use her water to fight. The burn was too intense, and her spark was snuffed out.

I can't take this. Death would be better than this pain...

Her skin bubbled, blistered.

Kill me now.

"Not yet."

Please, it hurts too much.

"Soon enough."

The blazing inferno puffed out. Silence. Her sisters, parents, Father Austen— Images flew through her mind. Like a loose film reel— spinning and flapping in the dark—it projected snippets of her life, dreams, and nightmares to play before her at random.

A lightning flash filled an oily night sky. Marina and Joy, her childhood best friends, laughed as they swung on the school swing set together. Sunbeams shone through tree branches, and Mere had to shield her eyes with her hand.

Her mind struggled to follow the trail as more flashes overtook the others. A tidal wave bigger than a mountain cradled her, the size of a mere speck, within.

I can control it all, yet I am nothing to it.

Her heart broke as she watched a houseboat sink into dark water.

She awoke, her heart hammering in her chest, tears rolling down her face in a steady stream, soaking her pillow.

Her breath hitched before she realized the arm over her waist and body behind her belonged to Aron. His presence soothed her panting to slow and her tears to cease.

She rolled over as slowly and gently as she could without disturbing him. Studying his face, relaxed in sleep, he looked younger.

The dream fog subsided, and prickles stung her skin, raising the hair on the back of her neck. It was only a nightmare or her subconscious warning her against sex with a man this hot—this dangerous…

But it was so real.

Closing her eyes on her way back to sleep, her last thought was clear. She'd ask Avia about it tomorrow.

Chapter Fifteen

The next morning, Mere glanced out the patio doors as she passed through the living room, and movement caught her attention. Last night was still a bit fuzzy, like a morning after partying too hard. But she remembered the important points. Near-death bath time, mind-blowing sex, the mark. *Shit.*

Sleeping with Aron had rocked her more than she could have imagined. It had almost been too much. The force and intensity of their connection had only upped the already frantic stakes, which was probably why he'd fought it. But she didn't regret it; in fact, she was hoping they could do it some more. But first, she had to clear the air.

A bright flash outside.

Aron?

Last night's nightmare returned to her. Terrifying dreams stalked her every time she slept, but they were always the same. The day of her test, her birthday, the houseboat. But last night, her nightmare had new elements. Tightness stretched across her chest, wrapping around her back, squeezing her lungs until her breath came out in sharp puffs. Her hands shook as she pressed her chest, drawing thin wisps of breath through her shrinking airway.

It had to be some terrible premonition.

Be strong. Tell him, Guppy.

How will he take it?

Tell him your fear. She couldn't hang with denial anymore and had to face her frightening situation. Since last night, being unsure and wary of him, she couldn't shake the suspicion that she was being maneuvered. If she lost her power, she needed her head on straight because flailing with fear, trust issues, and trauma wasn't getting her anywhere.

It was just a nightmare.

You don't know that, Guppy

Of course, it was.

Find Aron.

She left the house, wandered over the uneven patio and walkway leading to the dock and the lake. The small, rickety structure was ancient, and the swimming raft anchored about a hundred yards from the shore held a collection of geese atop it, cloud bathing and gossiping together in the morning gloom.

"This place isn't nearly as spooky during the day as it is at night," she said, watching the lightning bolt fly across the lake and disappear.

Aron turned. His smile didn't reach his eyes.

"You're making that look easy," she said, trying for a light mood despite her inner turmoil.

He dropped his hand, but a hint of tension was in his voice when he said, "Yes. I suppose. Thanks."

His enthusiasm had waned since yesterday.

"That's a good thing, isn't it?"

He approached, and though the same pull tugged at her, something was unsettling about his silhouette, the way he moved. His gait was a hunter's, approaching his prey.

Get a grip.

A phantom cloak appeared around him like a shadow, then it was gone. For quicker than a split second, she could've sworn his figure stuttered and transformed into one of the Four.

It's my imagination—my fear. It had to be. *I'm too stressed.*

He halted less than a foot in front of her. Part of her wanted him to hold her the way he had yesterday, the way he'd soothed her. His presence, his proximity, his touch had given her the soothing comfort she needed. Another small part of her was frightened to be so vulnerable with him after her nightmare. It had been terrifying.

She closed the distance between them, and as if reading her mind, he opened his arms and folded them around her.

The cocoon of warmth sunk deep into her frozen core…

Her frozen soul…

Her frozen heart.

Aron…

His finger, a skeleton's misty finger, stabbed her chest, and pierced her heart.

She stiffened. *Wait.*

His arms tightened around her in response, and…*it…all…came…back.*

Please, no.

"You will die, but not yet. When we are through with you, you will greet death gratefully." It *was* Aron's voice. She remembered him. The world around her dissolved, and she was in the Order cell, in their dungeon.

No!

She jerked and fought his embrace.

He held on.

No!

She thrashed in his iron hold. "Stop," she gasped.

And he dropped his arms.

She shuffled, staggering away—

He reached for her, confusion on his face.

Her legs buckled. "Don't touch me."

As if she'd struck him, he froze. "Mere?"

"No." She tried to stand but couldn't get her legs to work.

No, No, No. Could it be? No. It can't be.

You just saw it, Guppy.

Could it be a trick?

Wasn't that the way? *He hurts me, but I search for a way out, a way it didn't happen.*

Pathetic.

Was it really Aron?

Yes.

No. Impossible.

He was one of the Four, and he tortured you.

"What happened?" His face paled.

Her heart hammered. "Give me the keys."

He didn't hesitate, taking the keys from his pocket and tossing them to her. She snagged them from the air, even with her hands shaking so badly.

"Your phone."

"Mere, please, don't go. We need to talk. What happened? We have to trust each other."

"Give me your phone."

He stepped forward, holding it out, but she couldn't stop her stiffening recoil at his approach.

Turning his palms up and out, he squatted, placed it on the ground, and stepped away.

She finally stood, but her legs wobbled.

"I won't stop you. Just tell me what happened."

His words were a plea, but she couldn't deny the brutal truth. Her memory had returned, and he was a villain.

She ran for the truck, her hands trembling as she started the engine, his betrayal screaming through her mind. A second later, she sped up the driveway.

She fumbled with the phone while trying to stay on the dirt road. They didn't have another vehicle, and other than the forced pause at the gate up the road, he wouldn't be able to catch or follow her. Holding up the phone, she scanned the latest calls. It showed a couple coming from and going to R.

She pressed the return call button, and Rio answered. Trying not to tip him off that anything was wrong, she made her voice light and fake.

"Hey, Rio, can I speak with Avia, please?"

"Of course. Is everything okay?"

"Yeah," she snorted. "Totally, just need to ask her something."

Avia was on the line a second later. "Are you okay—"

"I *remember*. Move away from Rio right now. I need you to hear this without him nearby."

Avia mumbled something then a door closed. "I sent him outside. You remember what happened at the Order?"

"Yes, everything. I know why I attacked them."

Avia just waited.

Mere went cold, and she slammed the brakes. "You fucking know, don't you?"

"Know what, Mere?"

Mere glanced in the rearview at the empty dirt road behind her and accelerated. "The brothers are the Four," she panted in her panic.

"No, they aren't."

"Avia, listen to me. I saw it. They were at the Order. It was Aron. He tortured me. You have to get away from Rio. Alone is better. I promise you."

"Take a breath."

"No!"

"Mere!" The force in Avia's voice had her pausing. "Take a breath. And another."

Mere's iron grip loosened, and she took two deep breaths. A slight calm soothed the raging panic's white-hot edge.

"Tell me what you remember," Avia said.

"I just did."

"Tell me everything, exactly."

"It was Aron who hurt me. He and his brothers, Rio, Clay, and Cole, were all in my cell—all of them. But Aron stabbed me…with his finger. He caused the wound in my chest and whatever is happening to my power. This mark."

"Are you sure about that?"

"Yes."

"Rio only left my side momentarily. Clay and Cole never left Asha or Ivy. But after you were taken, perhaps Aron could have done something." Avia sounded unconvinced. "What do you want to do?"

Mere wanted Avia to tell *her* what to do. "I'm leaving. I'll stay in a motel…or I'll hide."

"No! Mere. Please. Listen. I need you to stay with Aron."

"What? No way." Mere still hadn't reached the gate.

"You must. Right now, you are at the most risk among us all."

"You want me to stay with him? After what I just told you?" Mere's chest throbbed, and ice spread through her, triggered by her devastation and terror.

"It's hard to explain."

"You better try, because I just told you he tortured me. What's there to explain?"

"Okay, calm down. What else do you remember?"

Mere checked the mirrors. Aron wasn't following her.

Her memory had returned, but a small part of her wished it hadn't.

She was back in the cell, and they came through the flames. When the Four appeared, one of them lifted her… *wait*, it hadn't been Aron. It had been Cole.

There was no face in the hood at first; then Cole's face appeared, then Aron's. "I don't know, I'm not sure. Their faces shifted."

"What do you mean shifted?"

"In the hood—the one in the front—its face shifted from Cole to Aron. I think Cole started the fire and first picked me up, but his face changed."

"His face—"

"Cole lifted me, and when he brought me closer, he—he shifted into Aron."

"As if the Four knew your connection was to Aron, not Cole."

"Maybe it wasn't him. Shit, I don't know."

"Mere, you need to breathe," Avia said.

"Could Aron have set me up?" The words came out so much meeker than she'd intended.

"At first, Asha was convinced he had." Avia's voice was gentler as if she added the softness intentionally.

Though it still came off wooden, Mere appreciated her effort. "What changed her mind?"

"I'm not sure it was. But Aron's actions at the Order convinced me he cared for you. Do you remember that part or just the torture?"

"He fought against the Four. He held my hand." Mere swung her head to the house.

"Yes."

"That was enough to earn your trust?"

"That's not a yes or no answer. I don't trust them, not yet—not completely. But I don't think Aron set you up. Without them, the Four would have had us twice over by now."

Aron's bulging, panicked eyes flashed as he fell, drowning. "I hurt them."

"Now we know why."

She'd almost killed him. Asha's tear-streaked, frantic face flashed before her, begging her to stop.

Mere saw Cole's face glaring at her before it melded into Aron's. "Why must I stay with him?"

"I told you the paths I see are muffled. It's true, but I still see some things. And right now, as you are driving—I assume you're still driving—all paths lead to your death, then ours, then everyone's."

"I beg your *fucking pardon?*"

"I see many things shifting all the time, yet this is clear; you leave him, they catch you, then everyone dies."

"Well, holy shit!" Mere slammed the brakes as the gate appeared. "No. Nobody's dying."

I am not letting anything happen to my sisters or...

"Mere."

"Avia, I don't think I can stay with him." Her tone shifted from assertive to pleading, a note of uncertainty creeping in.

"I believe you're safer with him. Would you rather I see if Rio will come? Maybe it will be okay with him?" Avia trailed off.

"What? No," Mere snapped.

What is Avia even suggesting? I'm sure Rio wouldn't want that, either.

"In that case, promise me you won't leave the property. Not until I give the all-clear and we have a safe place."

Mere stared at the locked gate. The combination was scrawled on the paper she'd stuffed in the cupholder... Then, looking up into the rearview at the road behind her, she pivoted her gaze between the gate and road until her decision was made.

She swallowed. "Okay. If this the only option I have."

"There's the caretaker," Avia said. "You could go to Mr. Prince's place."

Mere had somehow chilled, and her heart was beating normally. "Yeah, maybe, but I will keep Aron's phone and stay in contact. If you don't hear from me, I don't know...fry Rio and run."

"I will question Rio a bit more, and I'll call Ivy and Asha to warn them. Remember, it's to the Order's advantage if we doubt the brothers," Avia said.

Mere desperately hoped this was true. She couldn't bear the thought of Aron as her enemy.

"With them, we stand a better chance," Avia said. "The first time the Four appeared to us, we were frozen by visions, and we couldn't strike a blow against them. Just by touching the brothers, that loop was broken, and we could fight."

Mere shuddered. "I remember." The utter helplessness of that moment had stayed close to the top of her panic pile.

"We couldn't use our power on the Order grounds until we made contact with them."

Maybe Avia was trying to be reassuring, but the matter-of-fact way she reminded Mere how much they'd needed the brothers scared her more.

"Fine, maybe the brothers aren't the Four, but they must be connected somehow. They share a similar energy. Not to mention they wore their faces. Warn Ivy and Asha of that." Mere looked at the gate. *Don't run. Face it.*

"I am searching for a safe path." Avia sounded calm, and her words were gentle. Nothing about Avia's vibe was this soft or pleasant, so she must be trying hard to coax Mere to return.

Hearing that was enough. It had to be bad if she was going to such lengths. Mere backed the truck up. "Fine. I'll call you in an hour."

She hung up and dropped the phone into her lap, then sped down the road to get answers.

From the beginning, she'd known Aron meant something big to her. That was still true. But now, she wasn't sure if it was for her salvation or destruction.

Avia said they had a better chance with the brothers. And sure, Mere and her sisters could take the brothers on easily and win, but they couldn't take the Four.

Of the two, Aron or the Four, the Four were scarier. But this was still terrifying.

Be strong.

You can do this: act the spy, be Asha.

Mere filled herself with warrior strength and bravado she didn't have and lifted her chin. *Play this right and get your answers; yours and your sisters' lives depend on it.*

Decision made. She parked the truck, got out, and went inside Avia's haunted house.

Chapter Sixteen

Aron watched the truck speed away up the dirt road.

Mere's running.

"Fuck!" In his panicked fury, he released a gust of concentrated wind. It shot out, bent, and snapped the giant cedar beside the dock to crash into the lake. Lightning crackling and coiling around him, he spun, heading into the house.

What made her run? What changed?

His hooded reflection in black obsidian… Mere bleeding on an Order altar.

No. He gripped his forehead and the top of his head as if he could pull the dark images out of his mind. Pacing in front of the windows, he was a caged panther, watching the bend in the dirt road where she'd vanished. He grabbed another encrypted satellite phone. *Who do I call? What do I do?* She'd been so frightened; had she somehow read his mind, seen what he refused to acknowledge?

As she'd bolted from the house, panic and horror clear on her face, the urge to chase after her had bordered on compulsion. The only thing that stopped him was the realization that he couldn't come back from that. Sprinting after her, all raged up and chasing the car like the fucking Terminator would've been unhinged. Even now, he had to fight against the need to chase her.

That terror in her eyes had hit and winded him as if it were a physical blow. There was not much he hated more than Mere with that expression. Fear at that level reminded him of the tangled doe he'd discovered when he was a child. A fence's sharp razor wire had wrapped around her neck. He wanted to help her, free her, but at his approach, she struggled more and more frantically, choking and cutting herself.

Her terror-widened eyes had been rolling when he finally gave up and moved away, but it was too late. In her panic, she'd cut something vital, and Aron, young and guilt-ridden, watched the poor doe bleed out before him.

Her fear of him had pushed her to her death.

That memory coming to him now was far too ominous not to shake him to his core.

He moved to the front door, unable to stop himself from going after her. They were still too close to the Order. They could find her…

At the sound of the returning truck, he stopped mid-reach for the doorknob.

She's coming.

Relief flooded him, and he dropped into a chair.

No such luck that a ghost had scared her into fleeing. The way she'd looked at him. It had something to do with him. He had done something.

Mere sobbing on an onyx altar—cutting her—

No. It was just a horrible nightmare.

A few moments later, she walked in, fear, trepidation, and anguish in every inch of her, though she tried to hide it with a tight posture and elevated chin.

Did she have any idea how brave she was?

"Mere." He prayed his voice was soothing and didn't give away the fear gusting through him.

"Aron." She lifted her chin a fraction higher.

"What can I do?" he asked, surprised the notes of tenderness were already in his voice, and he didn't have to add them.

"You can slide me your weapons." She wouldn't meet his gaze.

He didn't hesitate again, disarming himself and laying the knives and guns on the coffee table. Her eyes widened while she bit her lower lip.

Backing up, he put long steps between him and the coffee table so she could approach and take them. She kept the distance between them without having to move the pile of weapons.

The silence grew and spread.

She picked up a pistol, and he noted the slightest confidence boost it gave her. After weighing, gripping, and studying it, she waved the weapon at him, indicating he should return to the chair in front of the rear window beside the piano.

"Tell me what happened. Why did you run? If we can talk honestly—"

She scoffed, repeating him with far too much sarcasm in her tone. "Honestly?"

At least she was speaking to him. Even if she pointed his gun at him, it was something. But what could have changed? Why had she run the way she did? Would she tell him?

"Okay, you first, then. Have you seen anything about me or this mark in your visions?"

Bleeding on a black altar from the cuts he made... Her black veins, leading to her black eyes, empty, standing on the Grand Chamber dais...

You'll make everything worse. "No."

Her eyes narrowed. "Are you lying to me?"

Shit.

108

Be honest with her. He raised his hands. "I'm sorry. Yes, I'm lying to you. But not for the reason you probably think. I'm trying to protect you."

She scoffed but still wouldn't meet his eyes. "Protect me? When you believe knowledge is power?"

"You implied you'd prefer not knowing something if it might add to your fear."

Her pursed lips had him holding his breath.

"Tell me what you saw." The gun shook in her outstretched hand, but she aimed it at him.

Just start with the vision. "You stood beside a man I don't know on the Grand Chamber stage; the veins had reached your face, and your eyes were black."

He sensed vibrations, and she pulled his phone from her pocket.

She read out the number.

"That's Cole," he said, his hands still up.

"Ivy," she said before she answered the phone. "Hello?"

Her stony expression slipped into a smile. For a second, she was happy, and he saw it so clearly on her face. She was no spy, and to further illustrate his observation, she turned away, leaving him and the gun in her hand forgotten.

He could've unarmed her, grabbed the pile of weapons, or just walked out the door—

And there we go.

She spun, her eyebrows up, realizing she was supposed to be watching him. "I'm questioning him now." There was a pause, and her mouth quirked. "Yeah, I'll tell him."

She listened, and her cheeks flushed. The woman showed him absolutely everything, and he adored her for it. The open vulnerability he had never been safe enough to allow himself to feel.

"So, you say. Thanks, though. I should get to it." She laughed.

And her joy hit him with force. The warmth in him chilled until his core was ice cold. *She is too good for this world—for this hell she is living in.* He hated to admit he couldn't protect her and couldn't save her.

Laughing again, she said, "Love you too, Ivy. Talk soon."

He watched her force away the love, humor, and all the joy, and reacquaint herself with the fight before her... all around her... the impossible destiny weighing on her.

Fucking brutal.

That was hard to watch.

As her face mastered interrogation mode, the phone rang again. She read out the last four digits. "Clay's number?" she asked.

Aron bowed his head in quick acknowledgment. She held the gun like she would a finger, requesting he give her a minute. If he weren't so frightened she might run away from him, he'd be bemused by her behavior.

She answered the call. "Asha?" There was a lengthy pause while she listened to Asha. "Avia said we can't. There's no way of knowing how far apart we need to stay. They're in the town about fifty miles away." Now, she laughed. "Ivy said the same thing. But I think she was joking." Pause. "I'll tell him." Her gaze flickered to his for a brief meeting then darted away. "Yes. I love you too, Asha." Pause. "Talk soon."

She turned, mastering her face faster this time. Asha probably gave her some tips on how to play it. Her expression was the blankest and least transparent she'd ever given him. Icy air filled his lungs and spread through him over her guarded glance.

"Tell me what?" He didn't want to smile or send any message she might misinterpret, so he tried to maintain his expressionless mask.

He wasn't going to force concern into his voice or features; he was going to be…well, honest as he could be.

"Oh, yeah. They both said to remind you they have your brothers in case anything happens to me."

"I'll keep that in mind."

A vision flashed, and he flinched. *Mere stood before an army of Order soldiers. Her arms raised, her dark veined face staring at him. Her black eyes were empty, but he touched her cheek, and she shivered.*

Faster than it had come, his vision vanished.

Fuck. What the hell was that? We need to fix that mark.

Her face shifted. She lowered her lids and tightened her lips. Her resolve locked in as if she armored up, preparing for something frightening. Was she scared of him?

"So, you've seen this mark take me over?"

"In more ways than one. I'm sorry."

She shut her eyes and shook her head hard as if she could shake the tears off. Unable to stop himself, he stepped closer. Her eyes flew open and hardened, and her hand was steady, holding the gun pointed at his chest.

He backed up two steps. "That doesn't mean we give up."

She lifted her chin and rolled her shoulders. "Well, of course. Why should I give up? Why should I keep trying?" She glanced at the gun and lowered it then studied the floor before his feet. "Thank you for telling me the truth. I guess it's my turn. My memory returned. It just came to me—in a flash. While we were hugging." She waved the gun to the dock where they'd been standing.

He stiffened. It was the flatness of her tone. "Okay?" Why would that have her fleeing him? Was it what she'd done to him and his brothers?

"While I was at the Order, the Four came to my cell." She pulled down her sweater to show the bandage and black veins, now spreading over her chest and shoulders. "It was *no mere soldier* who did this to me."

The words that slipped out by the pond. *I am no mere soldier. What? No.*

His eyes narrowed. "What are you saying?"

"I remember. *You* did this to me."

The emotion in her voice broke his heart but also stirred his rage. *What have they done?* "No. Impossible."

She clenched her fists, and her eyes flashed. *Be calm.*

His blunt answer provoked her, and she shot a wide-eyed glance at his pile of weapons on the coffee table. "I'll tell you what happened, and you can deny it all you want, but it won't change it. The Four came through the wall. They set the cell on fire—they were near enough for me to see under their hoods—the faces there. It was you—

No.

"—your brothers."

He kept still as a statue, not wanting to frighten her. If he exploded right now—*breathe. She's talking to you. Breathe. She returned. It was a trick. Breathe.*

"It's impossible. It wasn't me. It wasn't us."

She stiffened. "Then how do you explain what I saw?"

She couldn't believe it completely, or she wouldn't be there.

"How could you see me at the Order when I was under the pyramid? When I woke, I went to Ivy. Cole was there. Clay was with Asha, and Rio was with Avia. They stayed with your sisters. You were taken from me." He gritted his teeth to keep his voice calm and steady. "They took you." Every muscle in his body flexed with his words.

She hesitated. "I saw you, Aron, *your* face in that hood. I stared into your eyes as you pierced my flesh with your finger."

Needles pricked his skin. He'd only known fear such as this twice before, but if he reacted wrong, everything could fall apart. *Keep it together. Stay calm.* He closed his eyes and breathed, calming his heart and his voice to soothe. "They made you see what they wanted you to see."

"You said I would beg for death. It was your voice. Your laugh."

No.

He dragged his fingers through his hair. *Breath. Fucking, breathe.* "It wasn't real. They're trying to create discord and mistrust between us, to make us enemies." He paced in front of the window.

"How is that possible?"

"The Masters and priests can change their appearance, not completely, but magic can shift features. So, the Four would be able to."

"And you."

He stopped pacing. "What?"

"Just now, your face changed, and it was more than your expression. When I told you what I saw, your face went expressionless, cold, with nothing in your eyes. You're not who I thought you were."

Fear roared through him, but he kept his features from reacting. His practiced mask never showed any emotion, just a blank expression, and he wore it now while ice raced through his veins and stabbed every inch of him. It was far safer to show no emotion than react the way he felt.

"How do you think I've changed?"

She stared at the carpet, not sparing him more than a glance since her return. "Before, when we were in Egypt, you were chill. You've become so…intense. You're more and more like Avia every day."

"Perhaps I am because I've reached aerashakti. The visions come with such clarity and frequency now, but they're overwhelming. Imagine the sun's always in my eyes—too bright. The squints and scowls are by-products. I am filtering through visions and messages, but I have to admit, it's been difficult to adjust."

She narrowed her eyes. "How do you expect me to feel? I was in that cell. And you and your brothers came through the wall. You tortured me. You were the Four."

He clenched his jaw. "It was an illusion. It wasn't us."

"I saw you." Her voice was a plea.

His cracked heart broke apart. "I'm not doubting what you saw. But…do you truly believe that after getting to know me, I could do that to you?"

She dropped her head.

Mere laid on an altar, sobs wracking her while she bled from multiple cuts.

No. Stop showing me that.

"I don't know. But I did see your faces shift. Your face changed. First you were Cole, then you were you." She met his gaze. He could finally see it in her eyes. Her frown relaxed with the doubt she desperately wanted to believe.

"Maybe the Order manipulated me— It worked." Her voice

wavered. "It broke me."

The room chilled until her breath came out in clouds. Horror rocked him. It was what she'd been trying to tell him. "That's why you won't look at me. When you say I frighten you, it's because you saw *me* hurting you." Even if he could convince her it wasn't him, how would she ever not see him as the one who tortured her?

She said nothing, her gaze still on the floor.

His shoulders sagged. "Oh, Mere…"

What could he say?

"Aron?"

He glanced up, bracing himself for her to exile him.

"I'm terrified. Of the Order. Of…you. Yet, against all reason, against all odds, I'm safer with you than I would be out there alone or here alone." She shuddered. "I will work with you because Avia says I must for everyone's safety. I'll try my best."

He once again flooded with relief. She'd stay. Under the pounding weight of what she revealed, he stood. His legs shook, and he almost stumbled to the door. "I'll give you space."

As he opened the door to go outside, her voice halted him. It was gentle, pleading, and full of harshly fractured innocence. "You weren't there, were you? Tell me one more time it wasn't you."

"I swear on my life. I swear on my brothers' lives, I didn't hurt you. I couldn't, and I never will."

She lay motionless on the black altar. New living shakti thrummed through him. He relished the taste of her blood. He'd had to taste her power, and it was impossibly more and far stronger than he'd imagined in the millennia he'd waited for her.

He left the house, striding for the lake.

Liar.

Chapter Seventeen

From the door, Aron's heavy, longing gaze swept over Mere, causing heat to spread through her before he left, striding out.

She had difficulty looking at him. But that last glance had regrettably melted something in her.

They'd spoken, and despite everything, she was somewhat proud of her straightforward and mature approach. It was better than playing games. They couldn't afford to waste time or energy being suspicious. He'd been emphatic in his denial, and though she was scared, she believed Avia when she said the others hadn't left her sisters. Aron was right; it was exactly the sort of thing the Order would do.

Walking to the window, she watched Aron retreat to the lake. Just the sight of him had her legs weakening. *Why? This man, these men are so clearly dangerous. Why didn't I see what Asha was warning us about?*

You were too into him.

Aron stood in a black robe. His face twisted in hate. She shook her head, hoping to clear the memory away.

What Aron had said made sense.

There was no denying the pain when his face appeared within the hood's void. Recognition had been an extra jolt of anguish. And the hate on his face fired another spear into her.

Her head grew so light she thought she might faint. Sitting and dropping her head between her legs, her chest constricted while she took long, deep breaths.

How can you still feel something for him?

I don't.

You better not.

The room stopped spinning, so she rose and snuck over to the window. Unseeing and lost in thought, she called on her element to form a water sphere in her hand. It didn't come. She stared at her hand and pushed, but searing, icy pain burned her chest, so she gave up.

Aron reached the edge of the dock and sank to his knees.

At the door, she had her hand on the knob before she realized what she was doing.

She was going to him. The cord between them tugged at her.

Did he hurt her? She wasn't sure, but she didn't think so.

Did it feel like he did? Yes.

Did that make being with him hard? Yes.

Do I have a choice? No.

She hesitated at the end of the walkway behind him. "Are you okay?"

His body went still. "Why would you ask me that? I should be asking you that."

"I don't know. You seem—?"

"They did it on purpose. They want you to fear me." He stood and turned.

The memory of his hateful expression burned in her mind.

She shifted her focus away before their gazes met.

"And they succeeded," he said.

He was right. They had.

"There are so many paths, but I can't figure out which path will be ours."

"Avia told me that when she had too many options, usually she found the brighter, clearer one, the right one. If that makes sense."

"It does. Thank you," he said.

She wouldn't meet his eyes and kept her gaze no higher than his knees. "I'm going to try."

"I wish you didn't have to work to try. I can stay nearby without crossing your path. I can be a shadow, and you'll never see me."

She warmed at his offer. "I think the bath proved keeping you close is better for my health."

Her cheeks burned at the memory of their lovemaking, and she darted a glance at him and away.

His jaw flexed, and he turned to the water. "We need to focus on the mark. Can you tell me anything about how it happened?"

"I can tell you exactly how." She took a breath. "I was shackled to a metal cot of some sort. You used your bony, skeletal finger to stab me here." Her hand shook, pointing to the area.

He took a step, but she was relieved he left enough space between them that he didn't crowd her.

"The pain was so cold, it burned, and I think you touched my heart. My being seized. Then that was it," she said.

"I'm so sorry, Mere."

She bit her lower lip. "It's taking my power. How much time do I have left?"

"I have an idea."

She lifted her head and finally, since remembering what happened, met his storm-gray eyes. "You do?"

~ * ~

The ice in Aron's chest thawed. Mere finally looked at him.

Yes.

As she spoke of how he'd hurt her, a vision came over him. What she described was so clear, he could've been there. He shuddered at that fleeting thought.

He could even see her misery and her helplessness against their attack.

When she finished, the vision setting shifted from a dark Order cell to Mere, lying on the couch in the house behind them. He hovered over her, and with his finger at her wound, he sent light into her, cleansing the poison from her veins.

Was it possible?

If the wound on her chest was the source, and it was poison, they had to flush it out. He shut his eyes. "I have an idea."

She met his gaze. "You do?"

"I don't know if it'll work, but my power might help."

She stared at him. He kept the eye contact going, holding her gaze captive, and it was progress—there was already so much progress.

Thank you.

Again, he was blown away by her trusting nature, and though he was thrilled it allowed him to return to her side, anyone so open was at serious risk.

"I think I can use my aerashakti to cure you." He took out his other phone, and her eyes narrowed. Palms out, he gave her a reassuring smile. "No more secrets. I have other phones and weapons. You can keep the one you have. I'm going to call Avia and ask her advice; whether she thinks it will work. Why don't you call Ivy?"

She turned and headed for the house. That had gone so much better than he thought it would. The ice around her was already melting.

He dialed Rio. "It's me. Is Avia there? Put me on video."

"Okay," Rio said. "Avia's coming."

A minute later, Mere returned with the other phone, speaking to Ivy. "Aron said he has an idea." The phone screen showed a video call with Ivy in front and Cole and Master Miles standing behind her.

"Mere has Ivy, Cole, and Master Miles on another line. We have to cure that mark," Aron said.

"How?" Avia asked.

"I'm not sure my idea will work, but it may be worth a try. I had a flash. I saw how it was done, and with the intense draw toward Mere, what if my lightning, turned down to a gentle light, could burn it out?"

"That's a hell of a what-if," Rio said.

But Avia's brow furrowed. "Do you have that kind of control?"

"Lightning?" Master Miles asked. His eyes were wide a second before he recovered.

116

Aron realized he was still unaware he had reached shakti. "Yes. I don't know how it happened exactly, but I have lightning and much more replenishable power."

"I must know how," Miles insisted.

"How is not important. Not right now," Aron snapped. "What do you think, Ivy?"

Ivy appeared doubtful. "You think you can send lightning through her veins?"

He straightened, crossing his arms across his chest. "Yes."

"Can you test it first?" Ivy asked.

Aron went to the lawn and returned with a handful of leaves. Showing them a small wet one, he touched the edge. A glowing thread, thin as the veins, traced the lines of the leaf perfectly. Not one slip-up. He held it to both the phones' cameras.

Ivy pursed her lips, her eyes widening. "That is perfect control. I'm impressed."

Cole's smile was barely there, but for him, it was the equivalent of a normal person's grin. "How long have you had the lightning?"

"Yesterday."

"Shit, I guess it pays to be an overachiever," Rio said.

And for a split second, all six of them, even Avia, smiled—all but Miles, whose mouth formed a tight line.

Aron reached for his phone. "Okay, I need to focus. We'll call you when it's done. One of you let Clay and Asha know what we're doing."

Ivy bit her lip, and her smile flickered. "Be careful."

"Yes," Avia said. Her expression gave away nothing, but her voice was harder than usual. Not as flat.

"Call us after," Rio said and waved.

The screens went black.

They had to heal the mark. What he had seen couldn't be their path. It couldn't be. "What do you think? Should we try?"

Mere shrugged, and he frowned at the gesture. It was too casual for the situation. She should be terrified at what he proposed or, at the very least, unnerved.

Just because she wasn't outwardly quaking didn't mean she wasn't scared. Maybe because he was, he just expected the same from her.

Every new vision haunted him because they were all unacceptable. "Let's go inside."

He had to mark her—this time with his light.

In the bright sitting room, he lifted the sheet off an oversized couch he'd seen her lying on in his vision. *Check.* The storm had cleared, and the sun beamed in through the skylight, hitting the couch.

She sat, and he knelt on the ground beside her.

"Do you think this can work?" Her tone was casual.

He frowned again. "I do. When I was checking your wound last night, I felt something from your injury. A small tug, sort of magnetic. Maybe it means I should do something."

She took off her sweater, revealing a black lacy bra. He flinched and froze at how far the veins had spread across her torso. They'd reached her belly button.

"Lay back."

She reclined, shutting her eyes. Her muscles were so tense. "I'm trusting you way more than I should," she said through clenched teeth.

"I know. We can call Ivy or Asha, and they can be witnesses, if you want?"

She opened her eyes. Her gaze flicked to his and away so fast. "I appreciate that. I do, but you said you need to focus."

"If it would make you more comfortable…?"

"You giving me that option helps. Go ahead, and let's get this over with. I assume it's going to hurt."

His chest thumped, and he gave her an uncalled pitying expression. "Yes, I imagine so. Probably a hell of a lot." His lips couldn't form the smile he attempted to help ease her fear. "Okay, then, here goes."

The heat pumping from her wound was hotter than the air in Hades. *Not good.*

With his hand hovering over her, he trailed his finger down to the black wound—the source. The magnetic tug triggered the electricity coursing through him again.

Need for her incredible shakti surged.

No.

The impulse grew the closer his hand moved to the mark. He gazed at her face, her eyes squeezed shut, and he was overcome with an irresistible urge to touch her wound. Unable to resist any longer, he brushed his fingertips over the injured area.

She hissed through her teeth. Her eyes snapped open, meeting his gaze before she shut them again.

A spark flared inside him, and he had to fight against a dark instinct and desire to plunge his finger inside her, pierce her heart, and finish her off.

"Yes. You can have it. You can take it." The voice was faint, yet it urged him on.

118

Sweat broke out on his forehead with the effort to keep himself in check. He sensed the foreign darkness oozing through her veins and mixing with her blood. The purple poison flowed under her pale skin, smothering her light, her spirit.

"Take it. Take it all."

He clenched his jaw and ground his teeth with the effort, fighting the draw, the wish to heed the cold voice inside his head.

Her essence flickered beneath his finger. He could almost touch it, take it.

No.

The Four would, so why shouldn't he?

Wind blew through the room from nowhere, carrying a scent of dew on fresh spring grass. Breathless, he studied her face again. All the moments they'd shared since he first saw her across that snowy meadow raced through his mind. Warmth and something more, heavier, flooded him, remembering her bravery at their first meeting, stepping up and breaking the ice and tension between them all. She'd brimmed with shining light that poured from her at the mention of visiting the pyramids, and every time she laughed.

Studying her now, weakened and injured on the outside but with more power than he could imagine on the inside, tears built behind his eyes, stinging as he held them in. His hand shook with his emotions. The hideous desire to take her spark and her life faded. The urge to save her and protect her grew. A tear broke past his control.

His electricity sparked, and his glow shone under her skin. He struggled to keep it soft and gentle.

This will work. It must.

Guiding his purifying sparks, he followed the black veins. She glowed from within, and he erased the darkness.

She squeezed her eyes tighter, her lips peeling back, revealing her gritted teeth. Her breathing shifted into pants then almost hyperventilating gasps.

He tried not to hurt her, but he failed. Guilt shot through him, and he wavered. Was it that hesitation—that realization that turned the tide?

Because the darkness in her blood pushed forward. He went cold. The ground he gained was lost, and the pulsing and pumping poison covered his power, forcing it out.

The poison crept toward the wound, and he had to snatch his finger away to avoid contact.

She slumped.

Don't give up.

He braced her shoulder against the sofa with his left hand and cupped his right hand over the mark. She flinched, then stilled.

"I'm sorry," he panted. "I don't know what to say except hold on." He dragged at the poison with forceful suction, using his air to pull it out.

From the strength he used, she arched off the couch.

Yes, yes.

The dark veins were receding. *It's working.*

Her eyes flew open, and she gasped when the last of the poison faded and disappeared. Her skin was pale and perfect.

Grunting with the effort and control it took, he withdrew his hand and sat on his heels with a huff, drawing dark purple vapor out in a small cloud. It left the mark the same way steam escaped a kettle.

It worked. Her veins were clean of the inky poison.

Thank—

Unlike steam, the cloud didn't dissipate in the air.

It pulsed and twitched.

What? No.

It surged for him. It happened too fast. He breathed it in, and it moved into his lungs.

"No," she cried out, reaching up.

It was the last thing he heard.

Chapter Eighteen

Mere's terror made no sound. *No.*

Aron twitched once, and the poison flowed through him to pool in his eyes, making them wholly black. His pupils grew until nothing remained but hollow, empty darkness. The eyes of a demon. She couldn't move.

He cocked his head toward her—an animal—a hungry predator. Chills rolled through her, and she shifted, leaning away, trying not to alert him to her retreat.

Crawling forward in one swift, smooth motion, he moved as if he were the air he commanded until he hovered above her. His black eyes bored into her, but there was nothing there. Whatever loomed over her was no longer Aron.

She couldn't look away, terrified it would break the spell holding him back. Afraid if she broke eye contact, he would lunge. She was frozen with terror, a prey in the jaws of a great beast, so she held still.

He tilted his head and inhaled deeply, brushing his face in her hair, then hovering close to her neck. His warm breath on her skin sent prickles through her.

She stiffened. *Help.*

Fight, Guppy.

A static rumble, almost a growl, came from him, and ice raced through her. *Now.* She thrust her hand out, hitting his chest and pushing him away from her.

The electric spark that came with their contact since their meeting hit her again, but now the light, pleasurable, tingling zap was one hundredfold. Her hand burned, and he hissed and recoiled.

His eyes swirled black and gray before returning to his normal color, except now his expression showed all the horror she'd just lived. A moment ago, he was something else.

He surged to his feet, backing away. His mouth open and his eyes wide—hands up, begging for forgiveness.

Sitting up and shifting to the edge of the couch, she wrapped her arms around her head, and the sobs broke free.

"I—I don't—I'm so sorry, Mere." He left the house.

Her sobs subsided seconds later. A soft buzzing fog covered her and muffled her senses just the way she needed it to. After the terror of him almost ripping her throat out with his teeth, a slight euphoric, almost drunk haze came over her. Maybe his light, then air, had truly cured and cleansed her.

But what happened when he breathed in that vapor? Perhaps he was right when he said it was sentient, whatever it was.

Dizzy, she dropped her head to the couch pillow. *I'm so tired of all this. I don't want to do it anymore.* Unbelievably, she passed out right there.

Yet, even asleep, she sensed he was near. Something in her recognized him even while sleeping. Maybe it was their power greeting each other on an elemental level. And despite what occurred, crazy and stupid as it was, she didn't think she was in true danger or at risk from him—well, except maybe when he was possessed by Order mist.

She opened her eyes. Though she could've sworn he'd been standing close, he was a few feet away, watching her.

He turned. "I'm sorry—"

She tried to sit up. "It's okay."

He halted mid-step. "What? No, it isn't. I don't know what the hell just happened. I had no control over myself. I was going to hurt you."

"Do you still feel that way?" Her exhaustion pulled at her. She craved sleep.

"No, whatever that was is gone." He faced her. "Your touch burned it out of me; that's the only way I can explain it. What was always gentle and good before was totally different. But I returned to myself." His expression was expectant.

Hmm. Like how he brought me out of that vision loop the Four caused when they met the first time? Her exhale was heavy. She didn't have the energy to relieve his guilt right now. "It seems like we cured each other. The poison and mist are gone. You're no longer a risk to me."

"We can't be sure," he said.

Oh, come on, please. Just one break so I can rest.

She should care more. But she was having a hard time with that. Perhaps she was just too tired. "Then what do I do? What can we do? According to Avia, if I leave your side, everyone dies. So, regardless of the risks, I must stay with you."

His mask was in place. "What did she see?"

She shut her eyes, still fighting sleep's heavy pull. "She didn't tell me anything other than to warn me I had to stay with you. I'm going to rest now, okay?"

"Okay." He hesitated then went outside.

She let the buzzing in her mind lull her.

A voice stirred her. She was so, so tired, and maybe she just hovered in that place between asleep and awake.

What?

Pay attention.

She *was* in a dream, floating above the world, looking down on herself. With her arms raised, she stood before a giant tidal wave, larger than a mountain, racing toward her.

An enormous hole grew in an underground cavern. Ivy floated in the center, her arms stretched out and her head thrown back in a silent scream.

Mere's mind struggled to follow the trail while more pictures came, melded, overlapped, and overtook the others.

Asha held her arms up in the air, facing an erupting, exploding volcano, but when she turned around, she had become *her*, Mere, not Asha. Mere winked.

Shooting through a wave, she rode her scratched-up old surfboard, competing for a plastic, gold-painted statue.

But that never happened.

Just the favorite fantasy from her youth. Though she wanted it more than anything, she'd never been allowed to compete with her friends in those surf competitions.

In the next scene, she swam in the crystal-clear water of Koh Tao, Thailand's diving paradise, surrounded by schools of fish in multi-colored magnificence. That memory was from a holiday she took with her parents when she was ten.

She laughed and sobbed at the same time. Her laugh changed to a wail, then to screaming again, then to slow, heart-rending sobs.

The land she walked on was barren and dusty.

Where am I?

She glanced down.

What the hell?

An animal skin covered her body, and she carried strange satchels on her shoulders.

What? When was this?

The vast ground around her heaved and rolled as if a bomb exploded deep underground. The world cracked open, and the giant canyon was a wound... *A scar.*

A spinning mass of inky sparks materialized before her, forming a man in hooded robes standing before her in a dark cell. He spoke to her. *The scars on this earth are proof of what I say.*

Scars? Am I going to die?

Yes.

Soon?

Yes.

Blissful darkness swirled in. *Finally.*

He'd returned. She sensed him again.

"What did you say?" he asked.

What?

She had to fight to wake up. "Did I say something?"

"Yes, just now. Were you sleeping? I'm sorry for disturbing you."

"What did I say?" she asked, sitting up but groggy.

"'You said scars on the earth are proof of what I say."

"I did?" She frowned, lying down. "That other Order Master, Heath, Miles's brother, said it while I was at the Order. Why? Does it mean something to you?"

"Scars on the Earth? Not metaphors but actual places?" He ran his fingers through his hair. "Yes, maybe. Scenes of damage from past sisters. It makes sense."

"He came to my cell, said we are raw elements personified, that we shift the balance the Order provides, and that we have caused the deaths of hundreds of thousands. Our power has scarred the earth or something."

Aron raised his eyebrows. "But if they're actual places…"

"I think I dreamt of Asha near a volcano and Ivy in a cavern." She shifted to sit up but gave up.

"I saw something similar." His face tightened, the muscles in his jaw dancing. Is he hiding something?

Probably.

Who cares?

Guppy?

"Let's call Avia and the others, tell them I'm cured, and ask her if she knows anything about scars on the earth." Breathless from her effort, she tried again and sat up, now reaching for her sweater. She looked down. The veins were indeed gone, and the wound was starting to heal. Pink, healing, healthy skin replaced the dark, ruined flesh.

As she blew out some pants, some more of the lingering pain eased. Aron's light had burned so intensely. She'd never hurt that way before.

Avia answered after the first ring.

"What do you know about the scars?" Aron asked.

"How did it go?" Avia asked.

His gaze snapped to Mere.

She said, "Well, I think." For some reason, she didn't want to explain what happened to Aron after the poison left her and entered him. "The veins are gone, and my injury's starting to heal. Do you know anything about scars?"

"What did you see?" Avia asked.

"Clay and Asha at Pompeii, I think. Cole and Ivy in a gorge or canyon," Aron said. "Mere saw the same without prompting."

"I saw the same thing," Avia said.

"Why didn't you tell us?" Mere asked, slumping against the couch.

"I don't trust my visions, so I'm thankful to have both of you as confirmation."

She hadn't expected Avia to admit an insecurity or weakness. It was progress. She wasn't sure of what, but regardless, it was something good.

"Rio, grab the archive scrolls," Avia said, then paused. "Please."

"They're in the bag," he called from a distance. Was he in another room? Banished by Avia?

"Throw on the video chat," Aron said. He brought the phone and sat beside Mere. She worked harder than she wanted not to flinch or move away.

With a tightness around his eyes, he stood up and held out the phone to her so she could hold it for them both. She took it.

She had a view of Avia and Rio's hotel ceiling before Rio's face appeared. He winked into the camera then spun it to point at Avia, who was arranging various scrolls and parchment. Rio rolled his eyes comically.

Mere would've smiled if she weren't so tired.

"Feeling better?" Rio asked into the phone.

"Yes," she said.

"Well, that's fantastic." He grinned, and now she did smile.

Avia took a fragile scroll, checking the corners then peering at one with a design bordering the text and what could have been ink smears before flipping it over and doing the same on the reverse side.

Her face revealed nothing, but she passed the other scrolls to Rio at the table and flattened the one she'd studied on the surface. Setting a book at a corner and splitting a set of salt and pepper shakers to place one on each corner, Rio handed her a sheathed knife from…somewhere. She took it and set it on the last corner.

Avia studied the document. Silence. There were long seconds of quiet as her gaze roved over the scroll.

Rio pointed the camera at himself. "If you were here, you'd hear gears grinding—she's thinking so hard." He aimed the phone at the scroll, and Aron stepped beside Mere.

She stiffened and offered the phone for him to take it. He froze then moved to the edge of the couch, giving her even more space.

His face showed nothing, but then he gave her a small encouraging smile as if to say *it's okay.*

She turned her attention to the call. "What are you doing?"

"It's a puzzle," Aron said, just as Avia pointed.

She picked it up and started to fold it gently into an origami-like design Mere couldn't follow. Eventually, the scroll was transformed into a small square, but on the front, drawings and text fragments formed a small symbol.

"No way." Rio laughed.

Aron leaned forward without getting in her sphere. "That's an ancient symbol of the Order."

"And there are numbers scrawled around the symbol," Rio said, reaching for it.

Avia rotated the scroll, studying it further. "Coordinates for each element." Her expression was almost wonder.

Rio scribbled down the coordinates for each element.

Avia handed the folded scroll to him. "We need to investigate these locations."

Mere tilted the phone with their video chat so Aron could see it too. Rio grabbed another phone from the table.

He has two phones, too? Mere laughed.

Aron looked at her, and his expression was…*off.*

He's wondering why you're laughing, fool.

"Wait, wait, here, fire." Rio brought his phone to the screen. "It's Pompeii."

"Weren't we supposed to go there?" Mere asked.

"Asha and Clay were going to go, but they went to the Order instead," Aron said.

"Earth's coordinates are inside the Grand Canyon," Rio added.

"Where's water's scar?" Aron asked.

"In the sea off Portugal. Air's also in the water but inside the Bermuda Triangle." Rio smiled and wiggled his eyebrows at Avia.

Mere didn't miss Aron flinch and freeze. A heavy, fearful energy rolled off him.

What's that about?

Ask him.

Later. Too tired.

Rio took the paper with the coordinates. "I assume we're all going?"

"As soon as possible," Avia said.

"Right. I'll call the others." Rio stepped away, dialing.

126

Avia picked up the phone and whispered, "Are you okay?" She hesitated, then, "Can you do this?"

"Do I have a choice?" Mere sensed Aron's flinch this time because her focus was on Avia's face. Irritation surged through her. "You're wondering if I can handle one more adventure? The answer is yes. I'm fine. The sooner, the better, right? They'll be coming after us?"

"Yes," she said.

"So, we're off to Portugal, and you guys are going to Bermuda?"

"Affirmative," Rio shouted from somewhere behind Avia.

"Great, you guys work it out. I want to rest now." Mere stood, handed the phone to Aron, and headed for the bedroom.

She flopped onto the bed. Her eyes were closed before she could get under the covers.

At least the poison's gone.

Chapter Nineteen

Dragging his gaze from the road, Aron glanced at Mere. Her eyes were shut.

Too much was happening all at once. He'd reached aerashakti with no clue how. Unable to resist, he'd made love to Mere, and his feelings about that were overtaking his rational brain. She'd seen him and his brothers as the Four. He'd seen it himself in that nightmare and, if he was being honest with himself, in a recent vision or two.

His desire to do her harm while he'd been trying to cure her had been overwhelming. But then the poison in her blood had behaved as if it were sentient, the same way it had in the tub. It went after him, and it possessed him. He thought having no control over his feelings for her was frightening. What happened after he pulled the poison from her was another level of terror that could never happen again.

Now they were going to Portugal—to search for a scar in the water. That strange moment in the kitchen came back to him. In the trance, he'd been frantic in the dark water, searching for someone—for her.

Prickles crawled along his skin, and the vision came on quickly. *No.*

She stood upon the Grand Chamber dais. Her dark veins had reached her face, leading to her black, fathomless eyes.

But it worked. I healed her.

Like all the previous visions plaguing him, he hoped this one was wrong.

He'd let her rest. She looked peaceful, and he was grateful for that.

Without opening her eyes, she broke the silence. "How much farther? I haven't been this body-mind-and-soul tired since my test." She yawned. "Whatever you did to me drained me."

"Not much longer to the airport. What did you say about your test?"

"My test for aquashakti. The worst day of my life." She shifted then settled. "I failed."

"I doubt that, Mere. I've seen you in action."

"That's not what I mean. Father Austen said the same thing. He assured me I passed. But how? I still don't understand. *Everyone* died…except me. It was a test of my power, in my element, and everyone I loved died. Yet I still achieved aquashakti? I'll never call it a pass." She rubbed her eyes.

His gaze was drawn to her. "Our elements are pure energy, raw natural force. Yours and your sisters especially. What are lives in the path of that?"

"My family," she snapped, and when she glanced at him, her eyes were blue fire. She leaned her head against the window.

"I'm sorry. I wasn't thinking." *Be careful with her.* She's endured so much. "Talking might help?"

But her breathing had slowed.

"Mere?" he whispered.

She'd fallen asleep. With her wide-open persona and trusting nature, would she have confided how her test had occurred?

He and his brothers had endured the Order's vicious tests every year, but the way she spoke, she'd only had one. At the Order, Master Miles had concocted torturous trials they hoped would trigger the brothers' full abilities.

They failed every time. Except for that one year, Aron almost emptied a lake. The year Rio drowned.

It happened on the eve of their thirteenth birthday. Unlike most normal, happy children, Aron and his brother's birthdays were never a celebration. No, instead, they used the day to take them, even as children, to the brink of death. They were dragged from their beds every year since they could walk.

The memory was so vivid, it came alive in his memory. He blinked, and there they were, his brothers—young, skinny, and frightened…

That misty winter morning, waiting on the rocky beach. Sleep deprivation and hunger were just part of the annual rite of passage.

For the previous forty-eight hours, they'd worked behind the Curtain. The Masters whispered to each other on the grassy hill above the slope to the lake.

"One hour left, and we've seen nothing," Master Miles shouted. "Prepare…."

For the final, they drowned Rio, buried Clay, burned Cole, and locked Aron in an airless box he called the coffin. Constructed from reinforced glass and iron, it was no bigger than a travel trunk and unbreakable. Even as he aged, the coffin remained the same size. The confined space affected him more than the impending suffocation.

He'd come to the edge of death every time. Master Miles believed that threatening the brothers' lives might trigger their ascension to shakti.

It hadn't worked yet.

Soldiers buckled them into straitjackets, trapped them in their elements, and left them to fight for their lives. The restraints prevented himfrom clawing at his neck while he suffocated, but it also stopped him from fighting back. The frustrated rage and useless battle from being bound that way sent him spiraling. He would take the cuts and scars in exchange for the use of his arms every time.

It never mattered to anyone what he wanted.

Master Miles glowered. "Rio, get going. Paul will handle the weights and the retrieval. Aron, get in the box; Clay, in the pit. Cole, come with me. I will conduct your test."

Cole's knees buckled when the stone-faced soldiers approached. They dragged him across the beach toward Master Miles.

Aron clenched his fists, watching them take him.

Cole's tests were the worst, and he lived in terror of them.

If the soldiers sealed Aron in his box before Miles tossed the match, he wouldn't have to hear Cole's screams while he burned—unlike Clay, who heard them every time. Clay once told Aron he may be the only one whose test wasn't fatal, and he carried guilt for that, but the suffering he dealt with while Cole screamed was hard for him to bear.

The soldiers pushed Aron into the coffin and snapped the airtight box shut. Being locked inside that stagnant silence was a ritual of torture. First appeared the sweat he couldn't wipe away, followed by short gasps for air, then muscle cramps. A thick cloak was thrown over the box. Darkness was a blessing. At least they couldn't witness his panic or humiliation.

He slammed into the glass and kicked its walls, but as always, it stayed whole. Being bound by the unbreakable straps drove him mad.

Within the coffin, Death came for an annual visit. Dressing in shadow, he arrived at the door and knocked. The final barrier opened wider each year, and Aron struggled against Death's looming, luring invitation to join him.

But really, who could go gently into that?

The air thinned, Aron's head ached, throbbed, and he sucked in the last oxygen molecules. Stars flashed; the blur faded. Death had arrived.

The box shifted. Aron's face hit the beach, and he gulped sweet, fresh air into his lungs.

While he was unstrapped from the straitjacket, he scanned the beach for Cole. Panting, he squinted while his eyes slowly adjusted to the glare.

Cole was always gone by the time Aron escaped the box. One day—he hoped—when he emerged, Cole would be there, unburned, his test passed and triumphant.

130

But it never happened.

Aron rose onto weak legs to scan for the boat bobbing and rocking on the choppy waves. If he suffocated, for sure Rio drowned. Father Paul sat at the motor, his head bowed.

Rio had been under too long. The lake shifted and surged.

The soldiers pulled Clay from the pit and dumped him beside Aron. His straitjacket was unbuckled and discarded.

Clay grabbed the cloak of a soldier walking past. "Rio needs to be brought up now!"

The zombie stepped away with his head down and continued his march to the Masters and other generals.

Aron raised his arms and waved to get Father Paul's attention. His training kept him silent, but the urge to call out built like pressure behind a kink in a tangled hose.

Whipping his head around, he noted the Masters behind him were oblivious. They still discussed the trials.

Clay got to his feet. "Why aren't they signaling to Father Paul?"

Rage filled Aron, the unfamiliar emotion counter to his regular, neutral demeanor, but anger was alive and grew into a violent storm.

"He's been under too long, Clay." He stiffened, then fell to his knees. "He won't make it."

Calling the air, he focused his power outward. The basin rocked, but it wasn't him.

Rio.

His brother panicked while he drowned.

Facing his palms out, Aron sent all his aeravyr toward the lake. The wind roared, and he aimed all that ferocity, formed from rage and terror, outward. Waves switched their natural direction, rushing from land rather than toward it. The tide rolled, crawling away from his wind and air. Paul and his boat capsized, and Aron didn't spare him another thought.

"Yes, Aron," Clay gasped from behind.

Aron struggled, his hands trembling, but he sent more of everything he had to shove it all away from Rio. The water surged over the beach at the other end, like tipping a glass, pouring its contents over the edge. He didn't care. Nothing lay beyond; they were behind the Curtain.

The reversing tide revealed Rio unmoving among weeds on muddy sediment, a thrashing wall rising behind him. Sweat beading all over his body, Aron clenched, flexing every muscle—

"Run, Clay, hurry!"

Clay was already sprinting for Rio, looking at the walls of air and wind, holding back a flood. Aron's wind helped Clay run faster, and he almost flew there.

"You're almost there." Aron sent his words to Clay. "I can't— much longer. Hurry." Aron prayed Clay would get to Rio and return in time. "Faster!"

He squeezed his eyes shut—stretching his strength.

"I've got him." Clay threw Rio over his shoulder and ran for the beach.

With his arms out, Aron trembled, and his muscles strained with the last of his strength. Clay was too slow, moving against the wind. But he was strong and fought his way…almost there.

Aron's aeravyr stuttered and waned. The air wall he'd built quivered before the churning flood overpowered it, and he released everything. The lake raced toward him, returning to where it belonged, surging over the banks. The flood swept Clay up, running with Rio in his arms, past Aron, who was also caught up. Aron crawled to his brothers while the water dissipated. Rio's skin was gray. He had no pulse, and he wasn't breathing.

Clay dropped next to Rio's still form and began CPR. He pumped Rio's chest to start his heart.

Rio was too still. He didn't move.

"Come on," Clay whispered. "One, two, three, come on!"

Aron gripped Rio's arm and sent air into his lungs. They were full of liquid, but he managed a tiny bubble. He expanded it, and a thin stream trickled from his mouth and nostrils. Squeezing his eyes, Aron filled Rio's lungs with more air and drew it out. In again and out. He breathed for his brother while Clay pressed on his chest, pumping his heart.

After what seemed like forever, Rio still hadn't moved. "It's not working—" Clay said.

"Don't—" Aron snapped, fear and rage pulsing through him and at his fingertips. He gripped the straitjacket, lifting Rio's shoulders off the ground. "Damn it, Rio! Breathe!"

Electricity crackled in the air and rushed from Aron as he prepared to unleash his rage upon the Masters.

A breath in the atmosphere, then Aron swallowed all his grief and rage and lowered Rio to the sand. He'd kill Father Paul if he wasn't already dead.

But slow, and too quiet, Rio breathed.

Movement… His eyelids fluttered. Life returned to his body.

Yes.

He groaned and opened his eyes. Relief blasted into Aron.

Thank you.

Clay grinned, helped Rio sit up, and unbuckled the straitjacket for him.

Brushing his hair with a shaking hand, Rio's expression was haunted. "Thanks, man." His voice was hoarse and breathless. "I hoped I was getting better at holding my breath. But thanks for being there."

Clay slapped him on the shoulder. "You scared the crap out of us, bro."

"Finally, one of you has come close," Master Heath said. "Well done, Aron. Now, you are all free to help Cole with his burns."

Because they healed better together.

Clay pulled Rio to his feet, "Do you need me to carry you?"

"Hell no." Rio's laugh was shaky, but he put some weight on Clay's shoulder, and they headed to their quarters.

The Masters had witnessed something new. The brothers achieved more if one of them was under serious threat.

Aron shuddered at what they'd do with that information.

Not that it mattered. They never passed.

They suffered terror, torture, and agony for what?

Nothing.

He blinked the memory away. Mere slept against the door, awash in sunbeams streaming in the window. Swinging his gaze to the road, he hitched his breath; the quick vision flashed in his head, but what he saw hit him in the gut. *Mere had black eyes and veins on her face. He stared at their joined hands—his with black, hanging sleeves and pale skin.*

No.

He stared at her. They had to be gone. He couldn't see any veins now. When she woke, he would ask her to check her wound.

Chapter Twenty

The car's motion had lulled Mere to sleep…again, where she thrashed against the inevitable.

Please, no. Not now.

There was no fighting this; she couldn't protect herself, for who had control over their dreams?

Her failures and weaknesses always haunted her in her sleep. The vicious nightmare played on a horrible, continuous loop. Every time she closed her eyes, she relived the tragedy—the worst day of her life.

The day of my test.

There was never any awareness that she was in a dream to distance or buffer herself from the events. She could never stop it, change it, or wake herself up. The events replayed as if it were the first time. The heartbreak and tragedy felt real, the way it had the day her world flipped upside down.

It always started the same way.

No…

Please…

Mere pulled herself onto the surfboard, straddling it, then sitting up. Energy hummed through her until she almost vibrated with it. Blinking against the blinding sunlight, she grinned at the horizon.

"Another perfect day." But today was more than that; it was special.

Her twelfth birthday. She brushed back her hair and used the elastic around her wrist to wrap it in a bun on top of her head. Slow waves tickled her legs, leaving droplets that dried on her tanned skin.

She grew up as any typical, coastal Australian baby, swimming and surfing, spending more time in the waves than out. Her family lived on the continent's southwestern tip, blessed with the mighty Indian Ocean as her front yard.

Her element was her first love. She loved everything about it, from the delightful, joyful butterflies to the soul-crushing fear of its strength.

Within the ocean's salty depths, she came alive. Her heart would beat stronger; her thoughts would grow sharper. She ruled it all.

Puffing up with pride, she relished how her gift made her unique and powerful. And didn't all little girls want to be powerful?

Her gift for surfing ensured her popularity among the other kids, but unlike her, they were allowed to compete in the surf competitions. It secretly drove her nuts that she wasn't allowed to show off. She was a superhero, but she had to maintain her cover and stay under the radar.

Be yourself, be true to who you are, applied to everyone except her. After years of arguing, she finally accepted Father Austen's wishes and focused on training instead. She had to do something with all her competitive impulses, so she moved on to become the most super, superhero ever.

Unsatisfied until she exhausted herself, she worked hard to hone her skills. She'd mastered all the stages of training: increase and control her element, create steady currents in the most turbulent tides, and even heat or freeze it. Now, it was time for the new phase—to call it from nothing. To draw moisture from the air and expand it to fill a glass was her most challenging task.

Every night at bedtime, she tried to fill that empty glass. So far, she hadn't conjured a drop.

Though Father Austen warned her it might not be possible, she prayed he was wrong.

Enough. Today was a big day.

She let the current carry her to shore. Picking up the board, she jogged toward the house where music and cheerful voices emanated. The party was already in full swing, with kids of all ages running around the yard, squealing as they danced to music from the inevitable drum circle.

She scoffed with a satisfied grin. They were dorks, but they were family. They loved her, and she them.

Her parents always combined her birthday with their annual family reunion, though the term 'family' was a bit of a stretch. Most of the guests were her parents' hippie friends from the old days when they communed together in India. She had at least twenty aunts, uncles, and more cousins than they could keep contained.

Tents started to pop up in the yard two days ago. She was too excited to care how much chaos they caused or how they limited her precious bath time.

Hurrying inside, it took more than a moment for her eyes to adjust to the dim light. More family members swarmed the kitchen and buzzed around piles of fruits and vegetables.

Ah, nuts. She groaned while guilt pushed against her excitement. Her parents always put so much effort into these parties. She couldn't get ready without helping, at least a bit.

She gave herself a mental slap and dove in to slice their garden-grown cucumbers and tomatoes, finishing the massive tub of Greek salad.

Her mother's blue eyes sparkled in the chaotic kitchen. "Thanks, birthday girl." As always, her mom wore her blonde hair in a long braid.

"Sure, Mom. What else can I do?"

"You can get the cooler, and let Marina and Joy know we'll be there in an hour."

An hour later, the group caravanned to the docks to board a houseboat they'd rented for the party. Mere's best friends, Marina and Joy, waited on the pier. The two blonde, blue-eyed girls hugged Mere, and they bustled onboard.

"Have fun, girls," Mom shouted after them, and they scurried up to the top deck.

When the boat launched from the dock, towing two jet skis and a ski boat, it headed for a calm bay. Mere's excitement bubbled over. Leaning against the rail, she let the wind whip her hair and mist her face with sea spray. She looked forward to their day on the ocean.

Everyone swam, barbecued, and rode the jet skis during the party. Marina and Joy convinced Mere to sneak a couple of beers from the fridge. They agreed it tasted gross, but the dizzy heads and jelly legs from the buzz were fun.

As the day wore on, tired kids grew cranky, and the darkness approached. It took ages to collect everyone from the beach and get the final headcount. Uncle Tom, fearing the late fees, took the wheel, steering them to the docks at full speed.

Staring out the window, Mere watched the white foam on the midnight waves while they motored across the water. Marina and Joy, sitting across from her on the couch, giggled at her uncle's jokes.

A soft breath whispered in the air and blew through the open door and windows... It wasn't a sound one heard in nature.

Surging from the night, a yacht, without proper lighting, blasted its horn and cut across their bow, nearly crashing into them.

Uncle Tom hesitated, then cranked the wheel with a fast jerk— too sharp. The boat's bow, weighed down by her mingling family, dipped under the yacht's deep wake. He accelerated over the swell, but the awkward vessel tipped over.

No!

The ocean swamped the decks and dragged the houseboat under. Her world froze for the count of one, two, three heartbeats—just three seconds plus one more breath.

Time was nothing.

She heard nothing. Saw nothing. Felt nothing.

Then her world cracked open, erupting into chaos and screaming. Time snapped back from slow motion to fast forward.

In seconds, tragedy swallowed her whole sun-shiny life.

Searching among the thrashing bodies, she could see as clearly

136

underwater as she could on land.

Mom? Dad?

Family and friends clamored for an escape they'd never find. Like a coin tossed into a fountain, the boat wouldn't stop until it touched the ocean floor. Panic pumped into her heart with each frantic beat.

Wake up. Wake up! This isn't happening!

Do something, you idiot!

She forced her power out. It stuttered, then waned.

What? No?

Trying again, her strength flailed and fizzled. Too weak, she couldn't stop the boat from sinking. She couldn't do anything.

Do not give up, you useless guppy!

"M-mom?"

Within the flailing panic, Mere succumbed to her own. Everyone needed her to help, but she couldn't. How? Who? What should I do?

"D-dad?"

Chaos slowed as the boat filled. From frantic and sharp to calm and soft, limbs and bodies swished and rolled in a tragic ballet.

White flowers on blue fabric—her mom's dress. Mere shoved off from the wall, swimming for her mother. Her eight-year-old cousin Mabel floundered, wide-eyed, in front of her.

Mere's lungs strained, and her heart seized. Gripping Mabel's hand, she towed the terrified child behind her. A jerk tugged Mere. She fought against the current, but it yanked her. How could a current be so strong inside the sinking boat?

Mabel's fingers slackened. Unable to look, Mere knew her sweet little cousin was gone.

Help?

Shutting her eyes so she wouldn't see anymore, she stopped swimming against the current and released Mabel's hand.

The current towed her out the houseboat's open doors, pushing her up as the boat sank, carrying everyone she loved into the dark.

Her lungs strained, and her heart seized. She fought against the current, but it dragged her up.

Rising fast and bursting from the surface, she screamed out her useless grief. The calm, quiet ocean showed no evidence that anything had happened.

Alone in the open, black depths, far from shore, she was torn between sheer terror and full-soul grief.

Help.

A series of shocks ripped through her body; sparks blinked around her like twinkling phosphorescence before speeding across the open sea.

Silence shivered in the air.

A new current jerked her away from the shore, and she allowed it to take her wherever it chose, praying it would take her under, to her family.

They're gone. Everyone. It's all my fault. Why am I so weak? I couldn't do anything.

She spun in her frantic thoughts. Pain and pressure crushed her chest. She didn't want to go on.

Giving in and giving up, she threw her head back, bellowing her grief and rage to the sky…but wait…where did the stars go?

The stars had disappeared.

She swiveled.

No, not disappeared, a great wave, big enough to break off a chunk of the continent, rose so high it blocked the night sky.

Racing to her, the noise grew into a roar, muffling the faint siren from shore—a tsunami warning.

And in that brief second, she was okay with it—happy even. She pictured her loving mother and her sweet dad.

Mom, I'm sorry. Dad, I love you.

As the monstrous wave raced closer, she swelled with anger, fear, and grief.

Then, brighter than a lighthouse spotlight, understanding flashed blinding—not only was the wave alive, but it was hers. It was her anger, fear, and grief that created it. She recognized it all in the monster coming for her.

Do something!

She rose with lifted arms until she hovered above the surface, only her toes remained submerged, and screamed her anguish again. Something cold and sharp but still malleable unfurled deep inside, filling her with strength and resolve.

The wave halted.

Its sheer size and raw destructive force were her anger and grief. But it had stopped moving forward while holding its shape.

Impossible. A wave was motion.

Stretching her fingers toward the beast, she touched chaos, grief, and fury, reflecting her inner turmoil.

She shattered, and her tears flowed free.

The wave waited for her command, and she brushed it with her fingertips. Every desire urged her to let it go and unleash it as a testament to her loss.

The wave bowed before her, begging for permission to decimate, but she reined her red-eyed, frothing fury back.

Will my power even work?

You stopped this wave.

It stopped by itself.

No. You stopped it.

Opening herself, Mere let her essence flow out to meet the surging wave towering far above her. Within her, her spark rolled like a soft tide—calm on the surface with fathomless strength below.

She must stop it. It was the right thing to do. And so, she did.

The stalled tsunami obeyed and shivered before it collapsed into a submissive ripple.

The churning tides stilled. The stars were visible again, and other than the siren in the distance, the night was quiet.

Breathe; it's over.

You did it.

Did what? Lost everyone? Mom. Dad.

Salty tears streamed down to mix with the sea as she swam to shore.

Hours later, the sun lightened the sky, and she dragged herself onto the beach and collapsed. The wet sand cushioned her head while the gentle surf lapped against her body. She let her sobs shake her until the sun rose higher in the sky.

"Mere?" Father Austen was the only person left in her world.

She struggled to stand on her weak legs, stumbling into his open arms.

"My dear, what happened? They've been searching for you."

"They're dead. They're all dead. The houseboat—" She broke down again. "Joy, Marina—their parents. It's all my fault."

"Mere, of course, you couldn't have stopped it. It was an accident—a horrible tragedy."

"It happened in the water. That's my power!" She returned to the tide to dip her fingers in the foamy waves. Even though the ocean had taken everyone, she still loved it. Her element was part of who she was and always would be. "I swear I will never be powerless again." Zinging, sparks and energy, sped from her hands into the tide.

A dark shape appeared on the horizon, moving fast toward the beach. The boat—her family's tomb—scraped along the sand where it stopped on the beach.

Whether from the exertion or the sight of the arm hanging from the houseboat window, bright stars flashed before her eyes, and she passed out.

That night, when she closed her swollen, cried-out eyes, without even thinking about it, her glass overflowed, covering her bedside table and spilling onto the floor.

Mere jerked awake. Aron glanced over. It was dark outside the car window. "Where are we?"

"Just arriving at the airport."

Great.

She groaned. "I don't feel—"

"I need you to check if the mark is still healing."

She flipped open the visor, and the little mirror lit up, casting a rich orange glow. Tugging her sweater down, she gasped. "Wow, it's almost gone."

Her relief was fleeting because she was still so tired.

His jaw clenched.

"I'm fine," she said. "I'm just— Your light burned up all my energy. Or your air sucked it out."

After driving into the airport parking lot and swinging into a stall, he parked before turning to her. His expression was hard but also curious.

She shook herself, curling her hands into fists on her thighs. "I'm okay. Let's go."

Chapter Twenty-One

Aron left the airport at Mere's side, scanning the area on their casual stroll to the taxi line. Nothing suspicious, no obvious ambushes or mysterious vehicles. The Order had been quiet.

How have they not found us yet?

Relax.

Mere had also been quiet, barely speaking during the flight.

Let her recover. Give her space.

When she'd told Aron a ghoul wearing his face tortured her, something he couldn't or wouldn't identify shriveled and died inside him.

He'd wanted distance from her, a wall between them, and yet when a valid reason for it had arrived, when she'd gaped at him with such fear, like he was a monster, all he wanted was to tear down that wall, draw her in, and hold her. Comfort her and prove it wasn't him—take that fear of him away.

She cocked her head to him. "Are we going to the coordinates?"

"It's late. We should wait until tomorrow." His smile was one he'd used many times. It wasn't real, but it convinced everyone. She slept during most of the trip: car and flight. "Let's get a hotel."

The cab took them to a hotel. Once they were settled in a decent suite, he pulled out the room service menu and waved it before her.

Room service would perk them both up. She'd told him she loved it, and this place was supposed to have outstanding food.

Her smile was false. She went along with the plans he and the others made, giving little input, just agreement.

Give her a break.

It had been a lot for everyone, but she'd suffered the most. She'd been collateral damage twice now. Aside from that, their dynamic had changed. They'd slept together, then she'd run from him.

For good reason.

Now, whatever was between them was fragile. *Tenuous.* And all he wanted was her trust.

Be light and supportive. Try to calm and soothe. Remember your role in Egypt. She'd been at ease even after the Four had attacked them. Shit, she'd tried and almost succeeded in seducing him.

He winked at her before scanning the menu then handed it to her. "What do you want? Craving anything?"

When she turned, he was surprised to see how pale she was, with dark purple stains under her eyes. "Do they have burgers?"

His smile was false. "Yes, and they sound good."

Her smile was a flicker. "Perfect, with cheese, please. And maybe a beer?"

"Are you okay?"

"I don't know. I'm just a bit…I don't know."

"Sit, I'll order."

He hung up the phone. She was on the couch, her eyes shut, but from her soft, too shallow breathing that lacked any rhythm, she wasn't asleep.

"It won't be long," he said, his voice soft.

The vision of hollow-eyed Mere flashed in his mind again. Black veins covered her face as she stood with the Four.

"Something's wrong. I can feel it," he said.

"What could be wrong?" she responded in a monotonous tone. "Other than four frightening, immortal beings hunting us, excited for our sacrifice. Or being captured and tortured by one of those beings wearing the face and using the voice of the man I was falling in love with." Her eyes snapped open. An expression of horror flashed. "I didn't mean that."

"Which part?"

She bit her bottom lip. "The love part, of course."

Ice chilled his veins. That hurt more than he wanted to admit.

"I know it wasn't you, but you must understand it *was* you.

The ache in his chest grew. "I do understand, and I'm so sorry."

She shrugged and sent him another flicker of a smile.

"Mere?" He sat beside her on the couch.

She flinched away.

Fuck.

"I'm sorry," they both said at the same time.

"You have nothing to be sorry for," he said, halting.

"And neither do you.'

The cord between them tugged at him, but he pulled back. Her reaction to his approach had been more cold water in his blood. While *she* was willing to try to move past her torment and what she'd seen, she was afraid of him.

Silence pounded like a drum. "Why don't you take a bath or shower before dinner? It might revive you."

She shrugged. "No. It's okay. I'll wait."

Her eyelids slid shut again, and he took out his vibrating phone. The connection between them grew tighter. It became a forceful tugging now.

Get a grip.

The others were checking in. Everyone had arrived, and they

were pausing as he and Mere were. Perhaps her sisters were also apprehensive about what they would discover at these scars.

A knock at the door.

Room service.

The young man set up the cart and gratefully received his tip, bowing to them before he exited. Aron removed the lids covering their cheeseburgers. He passed one to her so she could eat on the couch.

"Thank you." Her voice was almost hushed.

He dragged the desk chair over so he could eat close but still give her enough space for her comfort level.

After both admitted their burgers were excellent, they ate without speaking. He was much hungrier than he'd realized. The soup, from over a day ago, was the last thing they ate.

She also wolfed her burger down, and they grinned at each other as they finished every French fry on their plates.

Her smile sent a spear of light into his aching chest, soothing it slightly. He hadn't seen a genuine smile from her since she'd watched the lightning after they'd made love. A spark shot through him at the memory of her body underneath him, and he had to bite back a groan. Desire was a stalking beast within. He tried not to remember the intensity of that moment.

Reaching for her plate, he forced a gentle smile, and she held it out, a small reciprocating smile–

His finger brushed hers…

Her face…

No.

Fuck. No!

Her frozen smile fell. "What?"

Black veins covered her. They'd spread and reached her jaw now.

They vanished when he jerked his finger away, and their connection broke.

How?

"What? I can see from your expression…" she said.

"Umm." Panic roared and spun, a tornado inside him.

How? Was it the contact? Could it be? "I want to give you your space, but I just touched your finger."

"It's okay," she said, misunderstanding his fear for something else.

"No, it's not."

"What does that mean?" she asked, her voice still too flat.

"May I touch you again?"

"Uhh?" Her hesitation broke his heart.

"Just your finger, and only for a second."

Confusion etched on her face, but she pointed at him. He grazed the tip of her finger with his, and sparks exploded under his skin at the contact. Horror followed when the dark veins returned to almost cover her face. *Fuck.*

He'd pray if he believed.

"What? How?" Her voice carried her panic, and she grasped at his hand until she had it, her fingers entwined in his, staring at the veins on her hand and arm.

"I'm sorry."

"Why are you sorry?" she snapped. "They were gone. But now they're worse?" She dropped his hand as if it were covered in slime.

"I don't think they were gone…just hiding."

"Hiding?"

He'd never heard such a tone from her. "I'm not sure," he said, brushing his twitching, empty hand through his hair. "They were invisible until we—"

"I get it," she said, rising. "Excuse me."

He stood up and stepped away, giving her the space to move past him. She took the phone he'd given her, went into the bedroom, and shut the door.

He grabbed his other phone and called Clay.

~ * ~

Mere sat on the bed.

Gripping the phone, she stared at the wall. Coming in here, Aron would think she was calling Avia, but she wasn't going to. She needed to be alone to absorb everything.

He'd cured her. She'd been positive. She'd felt cleaner…

For a second. For only—.

Then the exhaustion had hit, and she'd been unable to sit up or keep her eyes open.

Rising slowly, she moved in a daze to the full-length mirror and tugged down her sweater. Her chest was free of the mark and veins, but she'd just seen them on her skin.

How long before they can feel me? How long before my power is completely gone?

Her eyes flashed solid black. She recoiled from her terrifying reflection. A buzzing grew from faint to louder then cleared to an ominous voice.

Soon.

That voice… It echoed in her mind. It wasn't the usual voice in her head. It was darker, slower, and laced with fury. She couldn't even say if it was a man's or a woman's; it was so frightening. She revolted.

What is happening to me?

The mark is growing stronger.

In the mirror, her eyes were black.

You can't stop it, the frightening voice said.

That voice wasn't hers. *Stop what?*

Your death.

Foul poison spread vile sickness in her blood, flooding her. It was mixing with her, thick in her veins, but it was also in her head, behind her eyes, in her throat, becoming one with her, and coating her power.

Whatever the mark or the poison was, it had woken up.

A distant hum, like buzzing wasps, *grew louder* as a swirling midnight mist *grew larger* in her head. The mist and buzz spun and gnawed at her thoughts.

"Soon."

What is that?

But the buzzing mist consumed her, and she forgot what had her fists clenched tight against her legs.

She followed the urge to walk to the door—opened it a crack. He was on the patio. On the phone.

She didn't care what he said or what he was doing. But she appraised him.

"Soon."

She shut the door and almost floated to the mirror.

Her eyes were demonic. Frightening.

Help! Get out of me.

She blinked, rubbed her eyes, shook her head. Tears poured over her eyelids, flowing faster than tears should. Her sob escaped, and she wrapped her arms around herself, struggling to keep it in. To be quiet. If Aron heard her, he'd come in.

The slow daze faded to life's sharpness and normal speed. Her eyes were blue again.

Fuck.

I'm so screwed. Heading for the bathroom was an automatic response to her fear. Always had been. Have a shower or a bath. Heal.

Glaring at the tub and stretching her hand out to it, she called water. Nothing…but…pain.

Searing, white-hot agony. Her legs gave out, and she collapsed to the floor. The burn in her chest was so severe that she couldn't make a sound.

Exhaustion ruled her even as she lay in a heap, her fingers like talons flexing and clawing the air just above her invisible wound.

She would've wailed to the sky, but it was too much effort. The pain and exhaustion warred in her chest.

I don't want to do this anymore. I can't.

You don't have a choice.

I don't want to be scared, to hurt, anymore.

You have to keep going, Guppy.

I don't want to.

Rolling to get to her hands and knees, she managed to stand and leave the bathroom. Too frightened of what might happen if she took a bath, she wouldn't even attempt it.

Another bolt of rage fired within her but made no impact. They did this. *The Order did this to me. They made me frightened of my element. They can only control me with magic and possession.*

Because it was possession, the slow taking over of her soul. She'd disappear or fade away. They would find her. They could be on their way right now. The Four would use her to hunt the others.

She laid down. Madness joined her in her sleep, tainting her nightmare with new and chaotic fears.

~ * ~

Aron ended his call. No one had any answers. Short of trying the fifth element, none of them had any idea of how they could help Mere. They couldn't risk that because they'd draw the Four by just being together.

Avia had mentioned that the shadings he and Mere took at the pyramid could reference the scars.

So, Aron pulled the papers from his bag, spread them on the table, and studied them.

Master Miles had sent them there after all; therefore, the carvings must show critical information.

Aron hadn't shared what he'd seen in the cave with anyone. He told himself there wasn't time, but honestly, he didn't know why he'd kept it quiet. Between Mere's capture, his aerashakti, and her mark, it just hadn't been important.

But now...

If those drawings referenced the scars they were visiting, he had to take another look.

Thinking back, he'd been so anxious, though he hadn't wanted to admit it to her. The confined tomb had affected him and muffled his senses.

As he made a rubbing of the tablet in the dark, Mere's camera flash illuminated the image and triggered something. His breathing hitched in the confinement, and he swiveled his thoughts to the job. But the image... His senses dulled, and a distant ring grew louder. The pictures whipped by too fast. He could catch flashes here and there, but his brain couldn't keep up.

Shackles chained the sisters to altars formed from the Grand Chamber floor, where they awaited sacrifice. Mere lay atop the onyx surface, her body still. Swords were piled on the black obsidian floor, with blood everywhere. Cole and Clay lay on an obsidian floor next to a strange altar, with their eyes wide open but unblinking.

Flash. Her camera blinded Aron again.

Scenes of the sisters charging forward, stabbing into the Four just as they morphed into him and his brothers. Then Avia, with solid white eyes, stepped over Mere's dead body to plunge an Order sword into Rio's chest, but he wore a long black robe.

Flash.

Mere, with eyes of solid black, killed Clay, Asha, Cole, and Ivy.
Flash.

Another vision, another future. This time Asha burned Clay to ash, then turned on her sisters.

Over and over, too many of Aron's visions were unacceptable possibilities.

An unknown voice echoed around him. "Your enemies will be stronger. They will defeat you and destroy our world."

Too distracted by the visions and the pyramid's tomb-like ambiance, Aron failed to notice the shooter's approach—he'd failed when it mattered most.

Not until Mere's voice echoed inside the small cave had he snapped out of his trance. The vision's blur blocked a clear view of the cave entrance, and an Order dart hit him in the thigh just as she fell.

When he woke, she was gone.

He shook off the memory of finding her missing and the frightening futures he saw before his power had matured. The vision of Mere standing cloaked in black with matching eyes and dark veins, returned. He'd seen her marked before she'd been taken and before his aerashakti.

Tugging hard at his hair to sting his scalp, he hoped the pain helped him shake off the building fear.

Focus. You can't help if you're losing it.

The ancient carvings weren't difficult to interpret. The first one appeared to be a rough image of a woman under many large swirling lines—possibly a wave or an ocean if he had to guess.

Studying the image, cold prickled his skin. Three women laid at the feet of one. From the placement and depictions of the three women's contorted bodies, they had to be dead.

Water.

Another carving showed a similar scene, more precise than the last. It wasn't just a mountain, as he first suspected. It was an erupting volcano. Three bodies lay at one woman's feet. The standing woman raised her arms in the air with a circular hoop around her body.

Fire.

A strange humming grew from the silence in his head.

The main subject in the following image lay upon three women's bodies under a lightning-filled sky. And rather than the circular hoop as the others had, a beam stretched from the woman's body into the sky.

Air.

In the next image, a woman floated in the center of a massive orb with a large crack stretching up. The hoop around her body broke the world.

Earth.

Shit. Avia was right.

Aron picked up the last shading—the one that had him so enthralled…and distracted.

Four women held hands, united against four hooded figures. Beams connected the women to the hooded Four. The eight stood upon rubble.

A pit roared open low in his gut.

This is a future prediction, while the others are records of the past.

148

Chapter Twenty-Two
Ivy and Cole

Ivy asked Cole to drive their rental car when they'd picked up the obnoxious SUV at the airport. It was enormous.

Miles was well enough to be left alone; besides, he'd said he had preparations to make. From Cole's narrowed eyes and clenched jaw, he'd disapproved of Miles's vague statement, but they had their job to do, so they left him.

Mere was still marked. And they had no answers. So, now, they were all going to specific locations that were supposed to give them some new insight. Or…why were they doing this?

An advantage. That was what Asha hoped for, and Ivy could agree that any potential advantage was worth exploring. Sure. But there was so much happening, so many questions, with everything moving too fast to grasp *anything*. Mere. Mere must be suffering…

Focus, Ivy.

Mere was at the front of her mind, of course, but until they found something, there was nothing to do. So she crushed the image of a tortured, unconscious Mere, and locked it in the diamond box inside her with all the other crap that tended to come forward and mess with her concentration. Compartmentalize. Worrying about Mere now wouldn't help them find whatever was supposed to be at the Grand Canyon. *That* was their mission.

But getting a smile out of Cole was Ivy's side mission.

So, here they were on their way to the Grand Canyon, and she'd asked Cole to drive so she could study, question, and gain more information about him, his brothers, and the Order. And maybe she would finally spy some of his unguarded moments.

Of the four brothers, he was the most withdrawn, quiet, and intense…

Face it; he's plain old broody.

But she wasn't put off. Despite his many attempts to ignore and avoid her, she caught him often. He moved around her as the moon to her planet's orbit, drawn to her involuntarily.

And his gaze. His stare.

She wouldn't have to look up to know he watched her. Often, she'd catch him with a smoldering look that boiled her blood. He'd shift his attention after a puzzled expression crossed his face. As if, like his movements, he was unaware of what he'd been doing.

There was tension in the vehicle, but it was the good kind, and along with the comfortable silence, she was at ease. No awkwardness lay between them, maybe because thick, imaginary strands of electricity connected them. Heat and invisible sparks raced with her blood and covered her skin.

He was distracted while he drove, but she could study him freely.

And, oh boy, did she.

The brothers were all handsome. But Cole was a masterpiece, a villain of classic literature or canvas. The chiseled face that had yet to crack a genuine smile in her presence, the dark black eyes she swore flashed with fire before he broke his smoldering gaze away from her.

"What is it?" His low, raspy voice caused her toes to curl in her hiking boots.

Just the sound caused a physical reaction that would have frightened her with its intensity if it hadn't been so exciting.

Yes, things were really bad. Considering the latest developments, they may not survive the next few days. It was awful to think about, but she and her sisters had lived longer than the previous sisters.

Or so they were told. So, if this was all the life she had, she'd take all the flavor from it and savor it as much as she could.

She'd much rather be with her sisters, but that was impossible, so camping with the most beautiful man she'd ever seen was a pretty sweet second option. If they found something to save them, well, that would be better.

Cole's gaze shifted to her, catching her studying him. How would she get him to crack? She'd been described as kind, stoic, brave, strong. Sure, they're wonderful words. Descriptive and positive. Funny wasn't one of them. "I don't have any good jokes, do you?"

"Jokes?" he asked.

Geez, what his voice did to her was nuts. "Something to lighten the mood."

"You think a joke is going to help with that?" he asked.

"Maybe not." She tried not to grin at his effort to create the cloud over his head again.

Okay. It wasn't the right time to think about smiling; that was asking too much. Maybe she should be satisfied with just getting him to talk.

"What do you think we'll find?" he asked.

All right, so he's starting a conversation. "I don't know, but hopefully something big—important—game-changing."

He licked his bottom lip then bit the corner.

Heat exploded through her at that small action. *Shit.* But he was thinking—she'd learned that much from her days of study. "What?" she asked.

He turned from the road, meeting her gaze, but he said nothing. An unfamiliar hardness was in his expression.

She frowned. "What aren't you telling me?"

His focus returned to the road. "There is nothing I'm not telling you."

"That's obviously a lie."

His jaw clenched. "You're calling me a liar?"

"Yes. We don't know anything. We are following you blindly, and you have the nerve to say there is nothing you're not telling me?"

"Fine, Ivy. What should I tell you?"

Her name on his lips, coming from that low rasping voice, had her reigning in her over-the-top physical response. *Down girl.* "Anything. Please give me any reason to trust you. Something to calm my fears."

His gaze swung, and the intensity of his expression hitched her breathing. "Do you still think you have something to fear from me?"

She attempted a shrug, but the weight of his inspection singed her and kept her shoulders from rising.

He glanced at her once more; this time, his gaze went to her lips, her mouth. "First and foremost, we both know you can kick my ass...easily. Even if I was powerful like Asha, which I'm not, I could never burn you."

Ivy swallowed. She wasn't sure if it was because rock was fireproof or because he couldn't hurt her, but either one was a nice thing for him to admit.

"What more do you want than what I'm already doing? My brothers and I have split up to protect you. Our strength has always been in unity, but we have sacrificed that to help you. We've turned on our past and put ourselves at risk for you. That doesn't earn your trust?"

She scoffed. "And why are you doing that, Cole? What could make you betray the Order and the Four for women you just met?"

His grip worked the steering wheel. "We were raised to fight you to the death. The second I saw you and realized you were the ones they meant, I knew we were on the wrong side."

There was something about the way he said *the second I saw you.* "So, in an instant decision, you risked everything and betrayed them?"

"Yes."

She swallowed when his gaze hit hers, the impact harder than a rock to the head. Stars swirled around his blurring image, and she drowned in his expression.

"We're almost there." He checked his satellite phone. "We'll have to take our own trail to reach the coordinates. How are you at rock climbing, if needed?"

"I'm earth," she said with a raised eyebrow.

"Right." The corners of his mouth curved up ever so slightly. "Just checking."

There. A smile. I got one. She cheered. It was only a sliver, but she counted it because it accompanied a blast of humor or joy from him.

After they stashed the car, she chose a starting point far away from the tourist areas, and they began their descent.

Thanks to her manipulations, the trek to the Grand Canyon floor took them just over six hours of hiking without stopping. Because they chose a sealed-off and abandoned area of the canyon, she created an easy slope to the bottom.

Mesmerized, hiking in wonder, she reveled in the beauty of this kind of nature while the heat of Cole's gaze between her shoulder blades urged her on in the best possible way.

From behind her, he said, "We'll reach the bottom just before dark."

His rough voice rolled over her and triggered her alert mode. She turned. His wary expression and rigid gait meant he anticipated something.

What?

Whatever we're here for, maybe?

"Good thing we geared up at the mountaineering place then."

He'd waved away Avia's money at the checkout, paying for everything. Not that it mattered to her. But it was sweet of him, nonetheless.

The sun fell behind the canyon wall and painted the sky in reds, oranges, and pinks striped across the thin wedge of sky above them. They walked on. Her toes ached in her new, unbroken hiking boots.

When she touched the canyon floor, a ripple of anxiety shot from her sore feet up to her splitting head. A second later, excitement vanished, and tension replaced it.

The sunset had darkened to twilight, stretching every shadow into eerie, cloaked figures as they hiked along the canyon floor. Trudging on, her legs almost jelly from extensive exertion, she sensed warmth underfoot.

"The coordinates are ahead." His voice came from so far behind her. How far ahead was she? Why were her boots getting so hot?

No…not her boots, the ground.

With each step, her feet became heavier, like a lead weight until the earth sucked at her. The ground wanted to drag her under.

Okay, this isn't normal, even for me.

"Do you feel that?" she asked, glancing over her shoulder. A strobe flashed across her vision, from a bright white light that washed everything out to pitch-black darkness, and her heart jerked before it stopped. "I think I'm going to be sick."

What's happening?

Everything shuddered within her, and earth's constant, quiet muffle in her head roared so loud it drowned out any sound or thought.

The world shifted, and she fell...

What's happening?

Opening her eyes was too hard. A weight pressed on her, crushing her chest. "I feel strange." She managed to squeak as her rolling stomach accompanied her pounding head in a symphony of sickness.

Bright daylight glowed against her shut eyelids, and she blinked and gaped at the blasting sun and the clear blue sky.

What the hell? Where am I?

"You must go," a voice said.

She dropped her gaze from the sky to search her sister Mere's sapphire blue eyes. But it wasn't Mere. Though they were identical, some unknown knowledge told her she wasn't Mere.

"She's right. Please. You must."

Avia?

Whipping her head around, Ivy gaped. The woman who spoke was a younger version of Avia—dressed in furs.

What the—? What is happening?

On a dusty plain, Ivy stood before younger versions of her sisters from another time.

What am I seeing?

"Go, they are coming. You must." It was the one like Mere who spoke. "This is never truly goodbye."

"I cannot leave you to fight them alone," Ivy said, blinking away the sting of unshed tears. Was this her in the past? It had to be.

"One of us must survive," the past Avia said. "It's the only way."

"Yes," Mere said.

"Not me," Ivy said. "One of you—"

"You are earth," the past Mere snapped.

A ghost in a machine, Ivy was separate and powerless to control anything. She could only watch as a mute witness.

"We could—" she began.

"There's no time," Avia answered. "We must fight for you."

"Quick, before it's too late," the past Asha said, flames dancing on her hands.

Silence fell across the land, vibrating through Ivy's body.

As the ground began to shake, they all screamed, "Go."

The air crackled with sparks and dark energy. Four hooded gods materialized before them.

Ivy stomped the ground, and it cracked and opened. Dropping below the surface, the earth crumbled under her feet in a tunnel-like chute straight down.

Why am I leaving? They needed to fight together. She wasn't sure if the thoughts she heard were hers or belonged to the one she inhabited.

Darkness pulsed along with a crunching, grinding cacophony as she fell, moving fast underground.

Tears blurred her vision. Her heart hammered then stuttered.

I'm sorry.

Chaotic movement shifted around her. Rock and soil raced up, and she descended faster. She was in free fall.

Deep underground, she stopped tunneling and expanded her space into a large cavern. Her sisters still battled above. If they touched the ground, she was connected to them—always.

Raising her arms above her, she spoke to the earth, her element, herself. "You have cradled me and given me more strength than any single soul deserves. You live and speak in vibrations. My terrashakti comes from you, and I ask you now to carry it to my sisters in their time of need."

She knelt on ancient stone, and with palms pressed flat in front of her, the warmth, so close to the planet's core, traveled into her. The breathing, humming earth was a conduit. She pushed all her thunderous power into the ground to send it up to her sisters.

It lit the earth and moved, but icy awareness blew like wind through her hair, and she gasped, falling forward, just catching herself before her face met the stone.

Piercing ice-cold water splashed into her, though she stayed dry.

No!

Water's aquashakti joined her earth terrashakti. Water coated her inner strength and swished into her cracks and grooves, softening her solid hold, moving her, shifting her, a mudslide, loose and unstable.

Just as she grasped what it meant, scorching heat roared within her and warmed the icy water.

The raw elements that were her sisters had traveled to their still-living sisters after they died.

Fire added flame and fury to the pressure already built inside. Too hot—too cold, burning and freezing from the inside out, Ivy couldn't take the agony of the elements battling... Was air still to come? She couldn't fight alone.

Just after pyroshakti joined her, aerashakti zapped her with lightning.

It was too much.

She blazed and bulged, stretching to contain the churning, battling elements. Despite the pain and pressure, she held on. She had to.

The earth trembled. Every cell inside her burned, stretched, and throbbed. Enveloped by rock and stone, she wept. Tears sizzled to steam on her hot skin. Though all the power pounded and stretched her and would inevitably destroy her, she refused to let go of any of it. Even if it might have saved her, she no longer wanted to be saved.

She had her sisters' shakti because they were dead.

The earth soothed her in its embrace with one last quiver and squeeze, almost a hug, before it released her. Fire and lightning burst from her, and the force blasted the rock around her to crumble and break away.

With the elements' escape, a shockwave blasted from her, and she hung, floating underground in the center of the giant cavern while it broke apart. The four elements swirled in chaos, pulsed, exploding from her, incinerated her far below the earth's surface, and cracked the world open with its force.

The roaring wind calmed and stilled. Bright, white light darkened to gray...then black.

Dark.

The silence throbbed.

She was nothing but energy, earth, creation, and destruction.

I am earth.

Terrashakti surged inside her, so strong she was the entire planet. And with a thought, she could crack it open like an egg.

Zooming out, shrinking, and encasing earth inside a human vessel.

I am Ivy.

"Yes, but you are so much more."

Who said that?

The voice was hers and not hers, many overlapping just out of synch, creating an eerie echo.

She opened her eyes and looked upon herself. A crowd of replicas of her. Many reflections. "We are more than reflections. We are you. We are your past, and you are the last of us."

The last?

"The power and balance must be protected. Our time has run out. You must succeed. You must *share* and *succeed,* or all will be lost."

Chapter Twenty-Three

Cole scanned the canyon's upper walls. They'd finally reached the bottom. Tourists didn't come here, and because they couldn't hike up in the dark, he would have to share the small tent with Ivy.

It was going to be…difficult to sleep beside her.

Ahead, her steps slowed, and he was instantly alert. Each step took her longer to place.

"The coordinates are just ahead," he said, hoping to encourage her. She must be getting tired. He'd been ready to drop an hour ago, but she wanted to get to the bottom.

She stopped ahead. A ripple or a shudder rolled along the ground beneath his feet. But there was no movement of the earth. It was power.

What did she do?

Her flashlight pointed ahead; she glanced over her shoulder, and he flinched. Shocked by her eyes, they were solid white voids with no color at all, he squinted—doubting what he saw.

"Do you feel that?" she asked. Her voice carried an echo, a low possessed sound that tickled the hair to rise on his arms.

The silent canyon mocked his fear.

He'd frozen, but when she jolted and tilted, he surged forward in two strides, catching her before she hit the ground. She was as hard as stone.

"Ivy?"

Terror filled him. She didn't blink but stared unseeing into the darkening sky above.

Lost for what to do, he shook her gently. Panic joined his fear, and they fought over what he should do.

She breathed, at least. But she was rigid. He shuddered, trying not to think of what her cold, unbending body reminded him of.

That cabin, after he'd been tested. He'd been forced to burn it to the ground in an extra test of strength. After he had failed to ignite it on his own, he'd used a lighter to start the fire. When the flames had licked at the roof, he forced his pyrovyr out, using all the rage inside him, and rendered it to ash in seconds.

The next day, he went searching. He still couldn't be sure what compelled him to go back, but he did, and when he walked around, he noticed things: utensils among the coal and ash, a small, blackened bed, toys.

It had been Clay who found Cole there, kneeling in ash and digging like an animal. Clay always sought Cole out before and after the

Masters took him to work.

Cole read Clay's dark expression.

They'd lied. He'd been told it was an empty cabin.

Clay went to the center of what had once been the kitchen and touched the floor, opening it.

In the basement were the bodies. He sensed them.

Cole's eyes had stung with his restrained emotions while he carried the bodies of the mother and twin girls, no more than six years old, out of the cellar. They'd hidden. The mother held them as they asphyxiated. He'd never forgotten the feel of the dead.

As Ivy felt now.

Her eyes were bright white and empty. Helpless, he gazed to the sky. Cold and lifeless, her chest rose with her breaths, and he counted every one.

What could have been hours later, for time had meant nothing, she jerked in his arms, and her warmth returned, softening her.

Thank you.

He cradled her, his chin pressed against her forehead. "Ivy! Come on."

Her brow furrowed.

Did she hear me?

She shut her white eyes. Relief flooded him. Those empty voids in her beautiful face had been frightening—an avenging angel, beautiful but terrifying.

She blinked and opened her eyes.

What's happening?

He was about to lose it. "Ivy," he roared. Gabbing his phone with one hand while his other arm cradled her in his lap, panic pummeled him.

But then she moved her hand…

And touched him—her fingers, then her soft palm on his cheek.

He stiffened. The movement was so out of the blue that it seared him to his core. He froze even while she sent heat through his blood, warming him in a way his pyrovyr never had.

His fire burned, but she heated.

She stroked his cheek with her thumb. The feather caress shivered into him, following the path his fire had just taken to his center—his cold, dark, empty heart. An ember flared inside him, and he lowered his gaze to her face.

Green eyes, filled with something he couldn't read, gazed at him.

Relief prickled his skin, and he dropped the forgotten phone, wrapped his arms around her, and dragged her to him. Still sprawled across his lap, she hugged him.

158

With his face buried in her neck and taking long breaths of her—jasmine, lemon, and a hint of pine–he flared hotter.

She tightened her grip on him.

Tilting back, he met her gaze.

She watched him. She hypnotized him, and with a jolt, he realized his lips were a breath from hers.

"Cole." His name was a whisper from her lips.

Shutting his eyes, he scraped together all his self-control. He had to stop this, but she was quicker. She lifted her chin and brushed her lips over his.

Flames exploded through him at the light contact.

No. Don't do this.

But he slid his hand to her throat, weaving his fingers into her silken hair. Gripping her nape, he had to relax his fingers to be gentle. The fire inside scorched him, and he bent over her. Her soft lips on his stretched something inside him to the breaking point, and with her gentle moan, he snapped. Need roared and overtook him.

She arched into him, her passion taking her as it seized him at the same time, and the kiss grew more urgent. Her lips and mouth sent waves of hunger, igniting him.

They shifted together, their arms around each other until they knelt, never breaking the kiss. His hands were in her hair, on her jaw, and at her throat.

She moaned. And he blinked.

Stop this.

He tried to, but just as she pressed her body to his, he slid his hand down her spine to graze her perfect backside. Unable to help himself, he stroked her then pulled her in.

Stop this now.

This was stupid. He was on dangerous ground.

Shit.

He clenched his teeth.

Get a grip. Stop now.

He broke away, panting. The primal desire she awakened in him shook him to his core. He turned his focus away for breath, wrangling and gathering himself together, then rolled from his knees to stand in a swift but fluid motion and offered his hand.

Her gaze searched his face. Her swollen lips were parted in surprise, her hair tousled from his fingers. He'd never known such longing before. His need was almost a physical force pushing him.

Fingers shaking, she grasped his hand and let him help her up.

"Are you okay?" he asked, genuinely concerned. "What

happened?”

She blushed, and he squinted and stepped away. Had there ever been someone as beautiful as her?

“I was in the past,” she murmured.

He strode to where he’d dropped his pack and unclasped the water bottle. He brought it over and passed it to her.

Holding his gaze, she took the bottle, his arm stretched out to avoid close contact.

“I’ll set up the tent if you want to rest.” He braved a peek at her.

She studied him, her eyes still wide, her lips still kiss-swollen.

Shit.

How was he going to keep his hands off her when she looked at him like that?

Chapter Twenty-Four

Ivy didn't know why Cole was upset.

That frightening vision had been terrible. But when she returned to the world, he'd been holding her with that expression, and she'd reached for him.

Desire wasn't something she had much experience with, but she was very aware that what he evoked in her was on a different level. It had swept over her, and she'd acted.

When they kissed, time stopped. The earth held its breath, and scalding need filled her. She'd been compelled, and yet even with that awareness, she hadn't wanted to stop. Then he came to his senses. Her disappointment had been almost as powerful as her passion.

Taking a drink of the crisp, cold water, she attempted to relax while he expertly set up the tent.

When he stood, job complete, the air between them thickened into a tractor beam. His eyes flashed with flames, and he came toward her. The warm weight thrumming inside her increased with each step he drew closer. A longing but pleasurable throb rolled through her.

Shit. This is wild. He's just a man.

Her hormones acted as if she was starving, and this man was an all-you-can-eat buffet…at the Ritz.

"Are you sure you're okay?" he asked. His voice did that thing to her, melting her into her soft liquid.

Easy.

Why?

Why, exactly?

This could be her last chance to be with a man. In a good way. And though he acted like he didn't, she had a feeling he wanted her, too. Just the way a glance made her physically react had to mean something.

He stopped you.

He wants to know what happened.

She gazed at the night sky. "It's unnecessary, but a campfire would be nice, right? For ambiance, since we're camping."

He agreed, and she waved her hand. A circle of stones rose from the ground, and a pile of sagebrush appeared in the center. "Great," she said. "I may be earth, but I love a cozy campfire." Her cheeks warmed; thank goodness it was still pretty dark.

The stars were so bright they could have been floating at the edge of outer space.

He flicked his lighter and snapped his finger. A spark jumped to the sagebrush and whooshed into a perfect-sized campfire.

She grinned, and when she raised her gaze, he wore a gentle smile. It fell as their gazes met.

Ouch.

"What happened?" he asked.

She shoved away the feelings shaking inside her at the question, his voice. "I saw the past. Too far in the past. I can't be exactly sure when, but furry clothing was involved."

His eyebrows rose. The way he watched her—her insides were a churning mess.

"I was an earth sister from a long time ago. I was with my sisters. They wanted me to run because the Four were coming. I don't—why would I ever leave them? But I did. I ran." Shame was an uncomfortable tightness in her chest.

He said nothing, just continued to listen, his expression seared into her.

"I was underground, and water hit me inside." She touched her chest. "I knew the battle above had taken my water sister. Then fire joined me, and finally, air. My sisters' shakti and their elements came to me when they died."

Now, he did react. His eyes narrowed. "You had your sisters' powers?"

"Well, it wasn't me. It was the earth sister of the past. But yes, she did, for a short time. It was too much for her, though. She exploded underground, creating the Grand Canyon, cracking the earth. I suppose you could say she scarred it."

He blinked long and slow. "The force that would have taken."

"If she created *this*, then, and we get stronger every time, what could I do now? What could any of us do now? We have to call the others and tell them what I saw."

He picked up his phone.

"If something like that happens now— It was a warning. If one of us dies and we're not together? I should never have left my sisters, but here I am, still apart from them. Because if we stay together…"

"They'll find you." He clenched his jaw. "I'm sorry about that. I can't imagine growing up without them and then, after only one meeting, having to leave them."

He showed her his phone. No signal. Fine. It could wait until tomorrow.

His understanding and supportive words were surprising. She appreciated them. Under the broody, sexy dude, his moral strength was high. "I'm okay. Maybe. I think I'll go to sleep. That…was intense."

162

He met her stare. "You take the tent."

"You're not—"

He looked at the unbelievable, star-scattered sky. "I can sleep out here."

"We can share the tent. If you want?"

He swung his gaze to the flames. "I don't think that's a good idea."

"Why not?"

"After what I just—what happened, we shouldn't," he said.

Moving to stand in his eye line, forcing herself to be brave, she said, "After what just happened, we definitely should."

"Ivy—" He crossed his arms, but his fists were white-knuckled. His silence was infuriating.

"You don't want me." Her stomach became an empty pit. "I'm sorry. I thought—I—."

He averted his gaze. "It's not that—I want—but—"

Her heart sank.

"How can we trust this level of desire? This phony match-up with us all. It's too suspicious." As he gestured to her, his hand trembled.

"So what? Do you think it will hurt us? It's no big deal," she lied. "It's just sex."

He squinted, his dark eyes almost slits while he faced the fire. "Yes, I think it could hurt us both. I'm beginning to care for you, Ivy…very much."

She frowned. "I can see how much you'd hate that." Though her stomach gave a small flip at his confession, cold chilled the heat that had just roared through her.

"You don't understand," he snapped.

"Then explain it to me. If this is my last chance to be with a man, I hoped it would be with someone who might care for me and whom I actually wanted." She shrugged, aware the warmth in her cheeks gave away her false bravado.

He went still, but more fire flashed in his eyes.

She met his gaze.

His eyes were stone. "I'm sorry." The tone of his whisper raised goosebumps along her skin and neck. "What do you mean by that?"

"Oh." She shrugged, brushing off his reaction. "Nothing," she lied.

He narrowed his eyes at her in a perusing squint that had her squirming.

She wasn't experienced and was fine with that. Her scattered sexual encounters had left her…unsatisfied. So, it had been an easy decision not to pursue them further. It wasn't worth it.

But this—this thing with Cole was something different. Her body was overruling everything else, and she wanted to listen. With time running out, she *would* listen.

There was something essential and eternal between them; whether it was artificial or manipulated or fucking fate, she wanted to experience whatever it was with him. Because he would be different, he would make her feel what all the poets and artists did. Or she hoped he would.

"This won't be your last opportunity," he said with ice in his deep, rasping tone but fire and ferocity in his eyes.

She wasn't one for denial. "You don't need to protect me. We're running out of time—"

He took two steps and halted so abruptly that he swayed, almost touching her. The fire danced behind him, and his gaze lowered to her mouth.

He raised his hands out, a breath from taking her shoulders. "Okay? Don't say that."

She warmed at his concerned display, but… "Come on, Cole. Do you believe my sisters and I can survive this?"

His face hardened. "You don't?"

She shrugged. *No.* "You have to admit that the odds aren't in our favor. I wish I could, but for some reason, I can't fool myself. I expect to die, and it will be soon. Even if we do fight and we hit the Four, we cause no damage. They are gods according to the Order." The heaviness and foreboding destiny that covered everything was accompanied by such an unearthly desire with beauty all around her, colorful and alive. It had to mean she was on the precipice, right?

He slid his hand to her neck. "I've wanted you since the first second I saw you, Ivy. You've become my curse."

His lips covered hers, and stars exploded behind her closed lids. Pleasure rocked her. Everything else forgotten, she gave in to their kiss. Trembling, passion quaked her to her core. He pulled away.

When she opened her passion-heavy lids, his gaze was scalding. No one had ever looked at her like that–like he wanted to devour her. She swallowed a lump constricting her throat.

He moved his lips to the edge of her ear. "The Order took someone I cared for once."

His words were a whisper but filled with such pain she gasped, and ice crackled through her, chilling her passion. She put her hand on his chest as if she could heal the pain he carried in his heart.

"Her only crime was being with me."

She sagged. It made so much sense: his clear desire yet his forced rejection.

"I cared for her, so they burned her at the stake in front of me."

Ivy's knees buckled. "Cole—"

His arm was instantly around her waist, catching and bringing her up against him. He was solid and warm.

"The Grand Master taunted me. Telling me to save her if I could." His words were quiet. His lips were a breath from her ear. She shivered, and his mouth brushed her skin.

Their embrace was comfort but also fierce protection. He held her like a treasure.

"She screamed for me to help her, but my hands were chained. I still hear her screams every night when I shut my eyes. The Grand Master believed that if I wanted it enough, I could stop the fire with my mind without my hands. At my level, it was impossible."

He relaxed his arm and shifted so he could meet her gaze. He tilted his forehead to rest against hers. "I wouldn't survive it if they did that to you. I'm already too…invested."

"Cole—" Her voice broke, and she held onto him for a whole other reason than her passion of a second ago. He opened his eyes, and his grief cooled her further. She only wanted to comfort him. Taking his hand, she led him into the tent. She continued to hold his hand. They fell asleep side-by-side with their fingers interlocked.

She stretched the next morning in the stuffy tent. He wasn't with her, so she sat up, searching around.

She pressed her fingers to her lips. Had she imagined their kiss? She wouldn't be surprised if it had just been a dream; it had been so good.

But as the sleep fog faded, she remembered the kiss in all its unholy glory and purred at the memory, then cringed. She'd wanted to ravish him last night, and with the mention of his heartbreaking past, he'd put a crashing stop to it.

His grief, she couldn't imagine it, but she wanted to help him. Ease his sorrow. He needed a friend, but after he'd laid beside her, hand in his, she'd passed out almost instantly.

Damn.

Pulling on her boots, she slipped from the tent, and Cole was shirtless in the sunrise's morning glow. *Damn…*

He stood at the campfire, making…

Coffee.

"Good morning," he said, a bit stiffly, but who could blame him?

She sat on the rock beside him. The fresh morning was pure peace. And though they were still in trouble, lots of it, she let herself appreciate the beauty and serenity of the setting.

"Everyone has probably visited their element's scar or will today," she said.

"What should we do? It's a bit early to call."

No news was good news, so she thought about his question.

"What?" he asked. "Your face lit up there for a second."

She smiled. "There is a place—I love. If you're up for it, I would love to share it with you. Since we have all this fancy new camping equipment."

"I'm intrigued."

"Wait until you see it. I hope you don't mind remote."

His gaze met hers, and those damn toes of hers curled into nubs.

Chapter Twenty-Five
Asha and Clay

Scanning the landscape as they approached Pompeii, Asha shifted, unable to find comfort. "What do you think we'll find?"

"Not sure. Hopefully, that advantage you were talking about," Clay said.

She pressed her lips together and pursed them to the side. "More like hoping for."

Miles had wanted them to go to Pompeii before, but they'd gone to the Order instead. It had been the right choice because they were nearby when Mere was taken. When they broke in, Asha had learned that her sisters hadn't seen the Order until they crossed the threshold. She could see past the Curtain because she'd been to the Order before.

Then Mere had been taken prisoner. Asha gritted her teeth. She still had trouble thinking of Mere in that place…burning. Her water sister had been cooking in that cell. Then they'd poisoned her, taking her over and corrupting her power.

Fucking, assholes!

Flames crackled and rolled over Asha's clenched fists.

"You okay, kid?" Clay's deep voice rumbled into her with seismic impact, igniting her and transforming her anger into something different.

"Yes," she said.

Though her sisters had been hopeful, she had a different gut feeling or instinct, and she couldn't deny her dread that whatever they learned would be unwelcome.

But there they were, at Pompeii,

Mount Vesuvius, their destination, resembled a giant barnacle on the rocky terrain. Once, long ago, the enormous crater spewed enough lava and rock to destroy a civilization, but now it slept peacefully. Pompeii, its nearby cities and settlements once thrived there until that fateful day the volcano erupted, encasing everything in ash.

Clay drove their rental car into the tourist attraction parking lot as the sun began to set.

"So, I suppose any treasure we're supposed to find will be up there, and we'll be hiking," he said.

"Yep, let's go." She smiled, adjusting her pack to hide her sword, and together, they bypassed the security barriers.

She paused and scanned behind her. The sunset painted the sky pink and orange. An itchy pressure along her spine made her uneasy but also prodded her up the slope, a marching toy soldier with a cranked key in her back. *Automatic.*

Up and up, higher and higher.

"Hey, do you know where you're going?" he asked.

"No, but there's a pull, and I'm just letting it lead me." She could only describe the sensation as intention. It was a physical draw; maybe it was instinct.

The hair on her arms rose, and her skin tingled.

A dry, dusty shrub covered an opening in the rock wall before her. Her legs quivered. Adrenaline filled her body and urged her forward.

Oh, hello, Adrenaline.... Welcome, my old friend. Thank you for finally joining the party.

Battle instincts primed, warning her something was about to happen. *But what?*

She flipped on her flashlight.

This is where I'm meant to be.

Beyond the twiggy branches was a crack wide enough to slip through.

"A cave," he said.

She jumped, so absorbed in her thoughts she'd forgotten Clay was there.

So much for battle instincts. Wake up.

Called by an unknown draw, she went in and scanned the confined space. A shadow on the far wall disguised a tunnel leading to the center of the dormant volcano. She scuffled along until it opened to a large cavern. Her fingers were unsteady, but she raised them to the wall.

The second she touched the stone, fire flared and filled the cave but snuffed out instantly.

Darkness pulsed in and clouded her vision. The cave spun around her. Unable to fight unconsciousness, her mind swept away.

She stood in a cave but looked out from another's eyes. Was this the same cave?

Where am I? What's happening?

Studying a speck of ash on her midnight armor, her cloak slid over her shoulder. The veins on her hand were black against her pale skin.

Strange. Two soldiers waited behind her, but her Master, also their commander, stood at her side. The three prisoners, bound and gagged, cowered at the rear of the cave.

What am I seeing?

Asha recognized her sisters, but the pyroshakti she inhabited did not. She couldn't voice her confusion because her Master hadn't allowed it. Something was wrong inside her. But she caught fragments of her host's darting thoughts… It had only been days since the soldiers in black caught her, but their control over her was quick and complete. She'd become a shell under the whim of the Master beside her.

With dread, she knew what was coming. Even when the Master nudged her arm, urging her on, she couldn't do it. She tilted her head to him. He read the unasked question and bowed his head in the affirmative. They must be destroyed, and she must be the one to do it.

No. She wouldn't.

She couldn't.

Don't listen.

He stood in front of her, brushed a lock of ruby-red hair behind her ear, and leaned in. "Do it now." His command was a harsh whisper.

With strange dark lines on her hands, she rubbed them together and formed a perfect sphere of spinning flames, lifting it to eye level. Pausing at her reflection in the commander's shining armor, she saw her face…the harsh black veins, and her eyes…her eyes were solid onyx voids, haunted and empty.

Don't do it. You idiot. They're your sisters! You can't!

Asha screamed at herself from her living prison, despite that this was the past and she couldn't change anything. But she couldn't stop herself. She was pure, helpless fury.

The other soldiers waited motionless, with their features obscured by shadow.

The glowing orb still floated above her hand. She paused, turning her head to the Master.

He gripped her arm hard. "Now," he growled.

The pyroshakti sister of the past released the orb. She sent it to cover the women as hot and fast as her power let her, but there was no easy death from fire.

No.

Asha wailed in rage, grief, and helplessness, forced to watch her horrifying history.

Spinning away from floating ash, her sisters, she faced the Master. Shivering and frozen to the bone, she rejected what she'd done. Her soul revolted at her actions.

Sneering, the Master spun his staff, removed a sheath, revealing a menacing iron point, and stabbed it upward, piercing iron armor with little resistance into her chest in one swift motion.

The agony was as sharp and severe as her shock. Pressure and pain paused while she gazed at the weapon. It took one, two, three seconds before the fury caught up with her surprise and bubbled low inside her.

Icy wind swept into her, chilling her rage, but she didn't fall, and she didn't die.

Like a battering ram to her soul, the impact of her sisters' elements crashed into her. Still impaled on the Master's sharpened staff, she arched, and her head fell back. Water rocked her with a rough tide, but she was rooted in strength and connection. Their combined shakti swirled, stretching and fighting the poison that leashed her.

With a grunt, she doubled over. The power intensified, growing. The earth rumbled and rolled beneath her feet, but she stood steady and one with it. Lightning bolts shocked her, but it wasn't an attack. They ignited her. Water warmed and cooled. Together, earth, air, and water melted the poison's control away. Her blocked pyroshakti stirred back to life, returned to her control.

And with it, the fire sister of the past awoke.

Frost covered her, spreading along the weapon, speeding toward the Master's hand. His narrowed eyes widened before he released it.

Ice spread through her, but it carried more than relief. The frost thickened as it crawled over the staff, and with the force of shifting glaciers, the iron shattered. The fallen shards tinkled, hitting the cave floor–the sweet sound of bells in the quiet cave.

Her injury seared and froze, closing. She laughed. Not a joyful sound of happiness but a bitter acceptance that she was still alive and would fight for the time to take her revenge.

The three men gaped at her. The Master retreated a step, but his growing fear fed her.

As if he'd thrown gasoline on a spark, her power, free at last, unleashed. Her anger exploded into raging fury. Before he could flee, she sent flames rushing along the ground toward the Master, where it split into two lines and encircled him. A fiery wall rose, crackling above his head.

The elements battled, ramming too hard inside her.

Hold on.

And kill them.

Yes.

Eager for face-to-face vengeance, she approached the circle. The inferno was a warm tickle on her skin as she walked into it.

The sparks and minds of her sisters melded with her own.

She stood before her Master—her betrayer—as he crouched.

"Stand," she growled at him.

He struggled to his feet with a whimper.

Brimming with vicious intent, her glee grew with his terror.

170

"They were my family. You made me *kill* them. I know them now—feel them. They're with me. They forgive me. And because of them—*for* them—*with* them, I'm going to kill you." Her voice was a quiet hiss.

"Mercy," he begged.

Again, she laughed without joy—an empty, hollow sound. "You believe you can kill me then beg for mercy? There is none for you or anyone else."

Awareness dawned on his face. He wouldn't survive. But arrogance never accepts defeat readily, so he swung his wide gaze around the cave, searching desperately for an escape.

The chaos surged then banked in agreement; they could pause while she took her revenge. She clenched, flexing her muscles, every ounce of her will to keep going.

The pyroshakti carried her desire and vengeance. Behind her, the blazing wall shrank and crawled toward her, up her legs, and over her. Veiled in fire, she reached for him.

He had nowhere to flee. Taking in his rapid breathing, wild eyes, and rigid body, she fed on his fear. He screamed, and she drew in the sound, gritting her teeth and gripping him at the elbows. His knees buckled, but she propped him up, hugging him while burning, enveloping them in a final embrace.

"Goodbye, *Master*," she whispered in his ear.

Smoke curled out of his mouth. Charred skin snaked its way up past his collar, and his flesh split in bloody cracks—crimson lava beneath black, volcanic rock.

Slowly, so slowly…she wouldn't kill him too quickly. This man would suffer all the pain and terror she could cause.

Burn.

Roaring in her head drowned everything out, and as she shut her eyes, a vision flashed—her Master in garish priest's robes from another place and time. He stood before a crowd of villagers. Her sisters were dead—sacrificed and tied to posts in the background.

Anger surged anew, and she set herself free. Bright white, she ignited and incinerated the Master in an instant.

Dropping her arms, she blew off the floating ash remains while his screams still echoed in the cave.

The two soldiers, who'd remained transfixed, turned and fled.

A smirk shifted her lips at the thrill of the hunt, and she followed them. Flames filled the cave, exploding from the entrance with her exit. She sent her rage over the steep, rocky slope, and it unrolled in a scorching red carpet and overtook the running soldiers.

More of the Order army waited below. A huge force spread

across the mountain slope.

She almost pitied the monsters.

Almost.

Volcanic lava flowed just below a thin, delicate crust. She longed to raze the world, release it all, and devour everything in a testament to her vengeance.

I've got nothing left.

The ground was hers because the earth was hers, and she cracked open massive crevasses and fractures, trapping the enemy. Lava sprayed up in a geyser. The sky rained fire onto the black-armored soldiers. Using earth's shakti, she struck down the mighty force of five hundred in seconds.

As she began her descent, electricity crackled in the air. Four hooded men materialized in her path.

She didn't know who or what they were, but what they intended was evident, and she readied for their attack.

Prickles rose on her skin. She froze.

What's happening?

Fight.

But she couldn't move. Image after image, over and over, showed women and girls sacrificed and killed.

No.

Why?

The frightening visions stopped, releasing her, but the shakti raging within were too much. She couldn't move. Her sisters' powers were too much for her body. If she opened her mouth, the raw strength would tear her apart with its release. The roiling cacophony increased beyond her ability to contain it. How could anyone have or hold this much elemental energy?

The chaos built with each second, rising into a crescendo.

It would be so easy to let go. To end it all.

But she couldn't stop fighting. She had been doing so for as long as she had memory.

Her confusion, rage, and relentless courage were all she had left. She'd drag these monsters to hell so they could burn with her.

Cracks, spider-webbed out from her feet. Explosions erupted around her—the earth was flame. Even though she suffered, she kept going.

The Four, arrogant in their ascent, charged her. She braced for the Four's fatal blows while she blasted them with air.

They halted and turned their hooded heads together.

Clenching, fighting to remain whole, she combusted. Her sparks ignited the Four's robes, crawling up until they were wholly burning. Asha gawked at the Four. *What?*

Some silent command must have passed between them, for engulfed, they charged with their blades aimed at her chest.

She snarled at the faceless hoods and released herself. The power obeyed its own master now. She couldn't stop it. Raising her arms, she let the elements burst free. A white shockwave erupted from her, obliterating the Four into dark mist.

Her mind stalled. A tornado caught her within it and spun her fast—no up, no down—everything was harsh wind and chaos crashing around her.

A breath later, the spinning stopped. The howling calmed. She was neither alive nor dead, but she hovered above the land she'd destroyed.

The planet lurched, molten rock exploded from the volcano, and ash plumes darkened the sky. Silence lasted an ominous beat before beacon-like flames shot high into the sky and illuminated the land. It was hell breaking through its containment and spreading to cover the world. She witnessed the obliteration of Pompeii—the destruction she'd caused.

She watched with no eyes—heard with no ears—she was the burning and magma, the ember and ash. *I am the spark.*

The spitting, screaming volcano churned and spewed its rage before death took her away. I am destruction and death…I am heat.

I am Fire.

Opening her eyes because she now had them, she stood on charred earth. Her body housed her consciousness once more. Nothing lived around her. Everything was black and smoking. The air itself was charred and clogged with ash.

This is my power.

This is me.

Death.

Tears stung then filled her eyes.

Listen. Without you, there is no life. You are light, heat, warmth, and sun, as well as destruction and death.

She stood before herself—echoes of herself, her form, and voice. *Your torment is over. You cannot be at peace without acknowledging your balance. All of nature's elements have positive and negative associations. You cook; you purify. Peace is yours if you can understand and accept this.*

How would she ever come to terms with her element? Betraying and killing her sisters?

You will. You must.

She blinked.

Not only had she caused one of history's worst natural disasters, but she, or a past version of herself, had killed her sisters.

Oh, fuck... No. She blinked and was in the cave once more. Clay squeezed her wrist, taking her pulse.

She retracted her arm from his grip as she struggled to her feet. "I'm fine."

His eyes were strained, and his lips pressed in a tight line.

He moved up, but she sidestepped his approach. Clenching his jaw, he raised his hands. "Whoa, hey. Are you okay, kid?"

The nickname he'd given her because he'd been impressed by her Billy-the-Kid-worthy speed-draw warmed her after the shock of what she'd just witnessed.

The expression he gave her was something she'd never seen before. He was shaken.

So was she.

She shut her eyes under the impact of all she'd seen hitting and cracking her. Biting her lip to hold back the stinging tears, she pulled out her phone. "We need to call Mere. She's not the first they've marked."

Chapter Twenty-Six

Avia and Rio

Avia sat rigid in the old steel fishing boat's passenger seat. She refused to admit the fear pounding through her since Aron had called to say he'd failed, but it was all over her, all around her. If she spoke or dropped her practiced avoidance, she feared she might break apart. And right now, her control was all she had.

The sun nudged the horizon when Rio, scanning the calm waves, eased off the throttle, and the boat slowed. "It's getting late. This isn't smart."

Avia ignored him, her gaze locked on the darkening horizon.

"Hey? Avia? Are we really going for the *Bermuda Triangle* now? We should find a bay to anchor in. Go in the morning."

The images spun inside her mind, too fast and awful. She clenched her eyes shut and said nothing.

"The coordinates are still a way off," he said and slowed the boat to idle on the calm water.

She sensed him move. He squatted in front of her. His hand on her shoulder sent warmth into her cold body, but she flinched away.

"Hey, it's okay. She's going to be okay."

Avia would have scoffed at Rio's statement, but her mind was racing. *What would they find? Mere. Ivy. Asha. What would happen to them all?*

"No, she won't. None of us will be."

"What?" he snapped. His voice carried a strain she hadn't heard from him before. Not quite anger, but not the ease with which he usually spoke.

Avia mentally smacked herself and met his gaze. "Even if we survive this, we aren't all going to be okay. Mere was tortured." She hadn't told Rio what Mere had seen about them hurting her. Not yet. She didn't want to…for some reason.

He dropped his head.

She tucked wisps of her hair behind her ear. "I'm not sure people ever fully recover from that kind of treatment."

"You're right." His eyes were gentle.

She had to shift her gaze. His bright, blue eyes always flashed to his dead ones. She hated that. It happened too often when she met her sisters' eyes too. Since that first morning with them all in the cave after the battle in her meadow.

"But warriors don't fret over what's destined for them," he

continued. "They're born to face battles head-on. Whether she believes it or not, Mere's a warrior. You all are," he proclaimed with unwavering conviction.

Avia would have smiled if she had the ability, almost encouraged by his words. "She's far stronger than she believes. The strongest of us all in many ways. She doesn't—wait, stop." She froze. *What the*— Pain lanced her head. "It's too late. We're here."

She clenched her eyes shut. The visions came too fast, but not fast enough to miss every horrible detail. So much blood. Death. The brothers. Her sisters. The world.

She covered her head with her hands, trying to block it out.

Oh—no!

She snapped her head up, her gaze fixed on Rio. Something between a growl and a cry escaped her throat. Panic slammed into her with so much force she folded forward and collapsed, her hands hitting the cabin floor. Panting, she struggled to see and hear.

The wind picked up around the boat.

Is that me?

"Avia? What's happening?" He knelt before her. His face doubled, tripled, then blurred beyond recognition.

She had to calm down. The boat began to rock and sway.

She forced herself to breathe against the jarring pain in her head. "I can feel…"

She'd had headaches before, but this was far, far more. Something was trying to claw and tear into her skull, and it was coming from outside—from all around.

The air.

"Oh, shit." Rio's voice sounded faint as if he'd moved away, but he still stood beside her, staring at the horizon.

"Do you see that?" His voice came out low and slow.

She couldn't turn her head. If she did, the pressure would split her skull open. She forced herself to face him, but she could only shift…in…increments. Everything blurred, and her body—her *being*, her *soul*—stuttered. Raising her hand, she watched it flicker, vanishing and reappearing in a frantic, chaotic rhythm of light and dark. Swallowing hard, she struggled to see where Rio pointed. She blinked a long, slow drop of her eyelids.

A night sky, full of billowing charcoal-colored clouds, waited ahead. But it wasn't the building storm that had him so freaked out; it was that the storm lay behind a true but invisible line. Lightning, wind, and rain thrashed beyond that barrier while they bobbed on soft waves, carrying them toward it.

The scars carried their own power, and she was at the mercy of it.

"The triangle," he said. "Unbelievable."

She could only blink.

He faced her. "Hey, what's happening?"

He'll turn around if you don't convince him you're fine. You've come this far. We don't have time to return. Face whatever it is now. This has to be a break. This has to give us a chance. It has to.

She managed to speak without screaming aloud. "Yes, we have to go in there."

She used the air to carry her words on a breath to him while barely forming the words.

"Perhaps we should wait until…" He cranked the wheel, trying to steer out of the current. He accelerated away, but the boat's engine was useless in this storm, and it dragged them in.

Passing into the storm, rain pelted the old fishing boat's windows and roof. A wave of nausea hit her, and she bent, unable to grasp her head for fear of even shifting a hair and triggering the amount of raw pain it would cause.

Under the clouds, the cabin dimmed, and though a storm raged outside, everything was sluggish.

The air was thicker and heavier than it should have been. She stared out the window as a thousand lightning bolts hit the water at once.

Impossible.

Earth-shattering thunder cracked just above them. Her vision vibrated, flashed white, then nothing.

The wind blew strong, whipping her hair. Light blasted her eyes. She stood on rocky terrain, no longer on a boat but on a mountain peak. Four shadowy figures stood before her.

She held a soft, small hand and recognized Mere's touch, but she was on the ground, and blood dripped from the corner of her mouth. Her wide, white eyes flickered shut. One of the hooded wraiths removed the sword that pierced her useless metal armor.

He pointed the glowing weapon at Avia, coated and dripping with her beloved sister's blood.

Avia gasped, collapsing at the waist as fury and pain tore her into sharp shards, taking her breath away. Ivy and Asha lay together, their arms linked but unmoving.

"Avia!"

Rio's voice broke through what she'd just seen. Their boat was being tossed around in a surging storm. The sky was dark, and she was rocked violently by the boat's thrashing, spinning movement.

What?

Her vision stuttered, and she was in sunshine on the mountain jutting from water so clear it was transparent leagues deep. As flocks of birds flew across a cloudless sky, vast schools of sea life swam below.

No water like this exists.

Gasping, she clutched her chest. Pyroshakti and terrashakti battled with her aerashakti. She vibrated with too much chaos. It fought to be free, but it was all she had left of her sisters; she wouldn't let it go.

Night flashed, overlapping the light. Like someone was flicking the lights on and off, but the light-switch controlled day and night.

What is happening?

"We have to get out of here," he shouted at her, sea spray splashing the salt-stained windows of the spinning boat. "I can't calm the water. This isn't natural."

She swung her gaze to the window, but it was gone. They were in the bright light.

She felt her sisters in their sparks, and they gave her their strength to fight on. Lightning filled the sky, the bolts reaching toward her as if she were a beacon atop the mountain. She released her water sister's hand and raised hers overhead, touching the thousands of flashing points the instant they converged on her, called to her hands.

She wouldn't be able to contain it all, but she waited for the last element to join her and bring her to an end. Her sisters' shakti would eventually take her away from here to join them.

Soothing, cool water poured into Avia.

They were gone. But not– They were with her, inside her. Fire brought ferocious heat and flame. Earth was solid, rooted strength. Water transformed into racing movement and adaptability, and air bound it together with understanding and stability.

As water calmed the storm raging within her, her sisters' sparks rolled into a cocoon of air and reached a calm, soft balance. The power curled in waves and spun in tornadoes, guiding them to meld and coexist instead of fight.

She was each spark and sister. One last sob escaped her for water. Bowing, stiffer than stone to her vile enemies for earth, she grinned with the feral glee of her fierce pyro sister, and finally, she let out a fighting roar for herself. She was one with them in balance and harmony, complete, whole, and strong.

The Four stood before her, their weapons pulsing with a purple glow, but she turned her palms out, blasting white light at them, containing them.

Yes.

She had them. They twitched and twisted in strange contortions.

This is it. I can—

The night crashed in around her. Rio was at the wheel, fighting for control of their vessel. His knuckles were white on the steering wheel—his lips tight, jaw clenched.

My sisters.

Blinding sunshine blasted her eyes, and with a garbled gasp, a staff thrust out of her chest, stabbed from behind.

No.

Lightning continued to charge her, raining on her. She screamed in rage and pain, and the Four evaporated into mist.

Dropping her hands, she grasped the pointed staff, so sharp it cut. Blood stained her hands. She turned her head to see behind her, struggling to stay on her feet.

The man released his disguised weapon and circled her, studying her. She didn't know where *he* came from. He was familiar and not. Evil waves radiated from him. "You were almost there," the dark-haired, purple-eyed man whispered, almost mocking her.

She recognized that face, but no, that made no sense.

His voice was low and rumbled into her so violently, it shifted her being. He touched her cheek in a disgustingly intimate gesture. Though there was no pain, waves of nausea flooded her. *I know you.*

He brushed his thumb along her lower lip, then brought it up to study, smeared with the blood from her mouth. His eyes widened. Meeting her gaze, he licked his finger.

"Closer than I imagined." The purple of his eyes flashed and glowed. "Do you know me?" he asked.

Yes.

Gulping, then sputtering, she sprayed blood onto his face. He flinched.

She gritted her teeth and managed to push the heavy staff out her back before she collapsed to her knees, gasping and wheezing.

The robed man grinned. "I'll be waiting for you."

Kneeling on the thrashing boat, Rio met Avia's gaze. "Avia, what's happening? Stay with me? Where are you hurt? Avia!"

The bright light returned, and the Four stood as statues behind the man with purple eyes, stuttering and flashing in and out of existence.

The sky flickered to dark.

She was on the boat deck. Rio knelt above her and pressed her chest. "What the hell happened?" His voice was loud over the wind.

His hands were red, wet. *Was that blood?*

The sun blinded her, but the combined shakti of her sisters pulsed within her. She was on her back, staring at the sky. Energy from below spread into her body. The stab wound throbbed, and water swirled, replacing her lost blood, and frost spanned and connected severed veins and arteries, while her terrashakti healed her torn flesh, knitting it together, like magic. She slowed and calmed her breathing. Her body healed with her sisters' shakti. She'd survive this and get her revenge.

A soothing hum played in her head as she drew strength from the earth, air, sun, and sea around her. The buzzing hum became angry. The sound of swarming insects grew louder and louder. She tried to shake off the annoyance, blinking her eyes to the blue sky, but a dark, living cloud hovered above her.

No.

"Tear her apart." The words were in her head and out. In her ears and all around her. *He* had commanded them.

Avia raised her hands to protect herself, but the mist dove and covered her. She couldn't stop herself from inhaling it or it entering her injury. She screamed, and tears poured from her eyes.

Power struck and fought inside her. The balance was gone, and the roaring, tearing fight resumed. She arched off the ground, and violet-tinted light blasted from her chest to beam into the bright sky.

She couldn't hold on. With the building pressure, it was only seconds before she'd explode, and there was no fear or sadness, only a desire to see her sisters. The beacon stuttered, then a shockwave blew from Avia and traveled up the beam, blasting a hole in the atmosphere… A rip in time and space, a tear opened low in the midday sky to bright pinpoint stars in the endless dark space beyond.

The pitch-black void poured through the tear, bringing bright, distant stars floating within the flood and into her world.

Foreign space mixed and melded with the air around her, spinning, shoving, stretching the distorted atmosphere. Everything vibrated at an unbearable frequency…until it snapped to stillness.

But that was unnatural; the air and water moved in heavy waves with too much gravity in some places and not enough in others. It was no longer an earthly place but the location of her death. The aerashakti scar formed the Bermuda Triangle.

The beacon burned her, rebounding and spreading into her to blast out her mouth and nose until she disintegrated into nothing.

Avia jerked up. She'd been lying on the floor with Rio gripping her shoulder, watching her warily.

The water was calmer now.

"What happened?" she asked.

"I was able to get us out. A moment of calm, and I steered us out."

There was blood on his hands.

"What happened?" she repeated, staring at them.

Why was he bleeding?

"It's your blood, not mine, but I can't find an injury. You seized on the deck, and blood started leaking from your mouth and pooled on your chest."

She covered her head with her hands.

What was that?

She searched for the visions, and they came as they always did.

No.

Nothing had changed. She'd risked everything and gained—no, no, no. When her sisters found her in Switzerland, and her memories of them returned, those visions came back too. Nothing ever changed.

Rio, Cole, Clay, and Aron, their faces beneath the dark hoods of the Order robes. Her three sisters lying dead on an obsidian floor–the same one she'd seen in the Grand Chamber.

Ivy and Mere showed up at her cabin in Switzerland, and Avia's worst nightmare was resurrected. The hell she'd believed gone, averted by her actions at a young age, laid out once more as clear as if she read it in a book.

She had three sisters, who were strangers, and they were going to die.

She wrenched her mind from the heartbreaking image of Rio's lifeless eyes, in one of her many visions, to his very alive ones watching her now.

"I'm fine," she said, mastering herself and inspecting the blood on her clothes. "I just need a minute."

Rio sat on his heels; his head bowed. "Did you have a vision?"

"I'm not sure what that was."

Chapter Twenty-Seven

Mere and Aron

Blinking against the blasting sunshine, Mere shielded her eyes under the vast blue sky. The sway beneath her, along with the scents of the sea…

Sickness roiled in her, but she was never seasick. This was something else.

The rather fancy boat was a rental Aron had arranged at the dock at Ponta Delgada.

Her spark flickered in answer to the gentle bob and sway of the waves, letting her know it was there and strong, but she couldn't use it.

His lips quivered into a shaky smile. He raised his sunglasses and met her gaze.

"How much farther?" she asked.

"Just a few minutes."

Still so exhausted and now sick, the intensity and foreboding of what might be coming overwhelmed her. She prayed they found answers soon.

He readjusted his sunglasses, but even the dark lenses couldn't hide the wary glint in his eyes and the tension in his shoulders.

"What do you think we'll find?" She searched the water.

"I wish I knew. We need to be careful. Stay together…" Aron's words trailed off, almost distracted, but his rigid posture and scowl proved he was anything but.

The magic of the open bay called to her. She'd prefer to be in the water, sliding among the currents and spinning with the waves. But what if those strange living cords returned?

Her legs quivered as if they were rubber. She stumbled over to sit on the cushioned seat and face the rear of the boat. The wake's hypnotic flow and foam drew her gaze, soothing her with its continuity.

Okay, so she was scared. After what happened in the bath, a larger part of her than she wanted to admit feared what would happen if she went in.

Rage surged inside her, hotter than fire.

They made me fear water.

Breathe.

The orange sky darkened to blood, then died…becoming starlight on sable before Aron eased off the throttle.

Can you feel it?

The water tugged, urged, covered her—

What's that?

Panic rocked her, slamming into her with full force. Choking on a breath, she bent forward, her anger dissolved under panic's violent impact.

Something's here…waiting for me.

Mere's chest constricted, and her heart stuttered. She struggled to breathe past the heavy pressure. "We need to go, Aron."

No.

"It hurts." She grasped at her chest, digging and scratching, trying to release the growing pressure and pain.

Stars flashed before her eyes. Darkness pulsed at the edge of her vision. "I don't like this. I want to go back."

The thumping in her head grew into a shriek loud enough to silence the boat's hum.

What's happening?

"Please—"

They'd stopped moving. The engine was quiet. Adrenaline flooded her, twitching her muscles.

"Please?" she choked out.

"Mere?" His muffled voice came from far away like a distant echo.

Agony blasted into her chest and heart and forced the air from her lungs.

"Are you okay? Mere? Mere?" Aron's voice faded.

"You will die, but not yet. When we are through with you, you will greet death gratefully."

The mocking voice was Aron's, yet it came from her mind.

"What did you say?"

The laughter in her head grew until it screamed and cackled. *Help.* Aron… He stood now… His current expression of concern was just another convincing mask. His true face was apathy.

Yet something big was about to happen. It was in the sky, the water. The heavy air, the weight of her soul…it was all over.

This is it. Should I say goodbye?

He reached for her…

Muscles stiffened, and she froze in a blind panic. She held up her hand, halting his approach.

Voices yelled so loud her head was going to explode. Terror spiked, but she managed to stand and shake her head once before her vision flashed white. Bracing herself against the rail, panting with the effort to control what she couldn't, she leaned forward…

Fresh, cool seawater surrounded her, jarring her.

What happened?

She was in the water and sinking.

Did I fall?

Did I jump? The water dragged her down as if a ten-ton weight was strapped to her ankles. The descent was too fast. She couldn't stop or even slow the plummet.

Too deep.

It's over. I'm dead.

It doesn't matter now.

The cold, dark water yanked her down. She'd never make it to the surface before her air ran out.

But it was okay. This was how she wanted to die. No sacrifice. No fear or violence—peaceful—just to drown in her element. Let it take her.

She could hold her breath longer than maybe anyone on the planet, but she couldn't breathe underwater. She'd frequently tried to as a child but never accomplished the feat.

Her feet touched the ocean floor, and a sharp pulse radiated from her chest, sending an electric current to force its way through black, thickened veins, burning her hot, though the dark water was colder than ice.

Chapter Twenty-Eight

Darker than night, Mere was blind in the water, but it moved with strong, rushing currents. The water swirled around her until it vanished— She breathed air.

Air?

This can't be happening.

Voices. Not hers. Not inside her head. People were speaking. Sun warmed her skin.

Underwater? Impossible.

Blinking, then blasted by light, she squinted in the glare.

Am I dead? Where am I?

What's happening?

The scene in front of her wasn't real. It couldn't be.

She was inside the scar's memory and seeing through a past aquashakti sister's eyes.

White cobblestoned ground met light blue ocean under a pristine sky.

Laughter surrounded her, and it stirred her heart to flutter with boundless joy. It was familiar, but she couldn't place it.

Who's that?

Searching around—

No way.

The laugh came from Avia, not *her sister* Avia, but a past version of her. There was far too much light and joy in this laughing woman to be Mere's sister. Avia played with a group of children, blowing their toy ships along a thin channel-like aqueduct.

A familiar, sweet scent tickled Mere's senses and triggered pleasant and peaceful sensations. Serenity flooded each color, sound, and inch of the scene.

Flashing red caught her attention, standing out against the white background.

Oh my–

Asha.

Or someone who could've been her twin, carried a young girl with bright, crimson hair, aged around three or four, across the white marble courtyard. Grinning, she nuzzled the child's neck before setting her on her chubby little legs. With those limbs already in motion, and a wooden toy sailboat clutched in her hands, the girl bolted off to join the other children.

Mere searched for Ivy.

She must be here somewhere, too.

Surrounded by beautiful architecture with columns that reminded her of ancient Greece, one who was identical to Ivy spoke to a crowd in the courtyard. The circular channels and canals within the white city resembled a scene Plato once described.

Atlantis?

Could it truly be?

In her dreams, Mere couldn't have conjured a more beautiful island and seascape. Her sisters lived here with others. It appeared they had children, and they seemed happy.

A giant statue of four women with linked arms stood in the marble courtyard. The resemblance to Mere and her sisters was easy enough to recognize.

Joining Avia and the children gathered at the water's edge to race their toy boats, Mere pointed her fingers at the water to send mini whirlpools spinning in the gentle current. The children squealed and laughed, delighted as they begged their boats to avoid the small spinning traps and cheered for their friends' boats to capsize.

She had no control over her body. Though she was *kind of* herself, she couldn't affect anything. Trapped inside—a silent witness to inevitable horror.

No matter how idyllic this scene appeared, the peace wouldn't last. Atlantis was just a myth. As she now understood, like Asha was probably discovering too, Pompeii as well as Atlantis no longer existed.

Prickles on her neck had her searching behind her. She scanned the horizon.

Salty wind brushed her skin, and the sweet scent soured to foul. Smells of seaweed and decayed flesh tainted the air. Putrid wind sailed into the square, overturned the toy boats, and fluttered her hair.

The one who was Ivy stopped speaking. A hush fell in the courtyard as an electrical charge seared through Mere, triggering her adrenaline. Her sisters sensed it, too, for they turned their faces to the sea. The sharp, whistled alarm from Ivy froze everything else for a breath. The children stopped their play, their smiles falling—

Then, the clamor of bells shattered the pause. The children ran to their parents. A dark-haired man picked up the little girl with red hair, the one Asha had been carrying…

She lifted her hand in farewell. Even without seeing her face, her grief and sadness flowed into Mere from across the square.

More bells sounded in the distance, joining the chorus as the alarm spread across the island. People everywhere raced for the canal.

They're coming.

Lightning flashed in the sunny sky, striking the marble statue behind her, the huge bolt cracking it down the middle.

A flaming boulder soared over their heads and crashed into the statue, shattering it into rubble. A second one hurtled toward them from nowhere. Calling a powerful geyser to spray up from the sea, Mere knocked it off course and forced it into the ocean.

Yes.

A hundred more meteors filled the sky.

No!

"It's okay." Asha was beside her with a hesitant smile and tears still in her eyes. But their lifetime bond of joy, sisterhood, and survival passed between them with one glance.

Aching pain pulsed and constricted Mere's chest. They stood together, prepared to fight and defend, while Avia and Ivy ushered their people into the boats tied to the outer canal.

Scanning the water where the attack had come from, Mere raised huge ocean spouts to catch the flaming rocks. Hands up and moving fast, Asha managed to shift every meteor into the hissing water, sending billowing clouds of steam toward them.

Steam covered the empty square, creating a scene of ominous, muffled silence in the building anticipation. Minutes after the lightning first hit their statue, the city was deserted. Every citizen had boarded the boats, heading for the open sea. Avia filled their sails using wind, and Mere urged the current and tide to carry them away as fast as dried leaves on a rushing river.

With their job of evacuating the people complete, Ivy and Avia joined Mere and Asha. They searched across the water from the arched entrance to their city.

Where are they?

Lightning forked in the midday sky, and Mere flinched as a bolt struck where the statue once stood.

The Four appeared before them from a cloud of black buzzing mist.

"Connect," Asha cried out.

Fire roared around them in a protective wall. The sisters linked arms and held their palms out.

Hundreds of lightning bolts fired from the sky. Avia formed an air shield.

The world slowed to half speed.

No.

Asha's warning cry was too late, and a single bolt hit Ivy, burning a gaping hole through her chest and out her back before Avia's shield finished closing. Mere's breath caught, and she choked.

No!

Spinning inside a whirlpool of grief and rage, Mere forced the ocean to rise and roll away from the island.

"Hold on." Asha helped Ivy, taking her hand and squeezing it.

The ground lurched and vibrated with Ivy's shudders as blood leaked from under her and trickled from her mouth, pooling on the white stone. Unable to hold her head up, she rested her cheek on the smooth ground.

Ivy's dying.

The ground rocked harder. Black mist swarmed in front of Asha.

No.

The four cloaked gods materialized from the cloud with their swords drawn and stabbed four blades into Asha as she knelt over her dying sister. She arched, and red mist sprayed across the white marble.

Mere and Avia screamed together.

The Four withdrew their glowing swords. Asha fell sideways— dead before she hit the ground.

No. Stop. Please, stop this.

The Four circled Ivy, who still struggled on the ground, now stretching her fingers for Asha's too-still body, anguish in her cries. Her arm trembled as she raised it in useless defense. With no mercy, the Four plunged their swords into her, and her head fell, her arm dropped.

No, no, no.

Tears blurred the past Mere's vision, but furious rage focused her mind. She summoned the water and called all its incredible expanse. With their peoples' boats long gone, she dragged the water to her.

The ocean sensed her grief and her anger and responded.

It rose.

It swayed.

It crawled. She took the raw, churning destructive mass, brought it in, and sent it out. The sea sped away from the city to build even more strength before she called for its return.

Time slowed.

Fire scorched her and burned inside her. Water flowed as always, but now a spark as bright and hot as a burning star joined her. It stoked her temper as well as her strength. She'd gained Asha's fire.

Asha is dead.

Ivy is dead.

They're not your sisters, Guppy. They're past sisters.

Lunging forward, Avia shot lightning bolts at the Four. The bolts hit their targets, sparking the Four's robes. Flames ignited, rolling up and spreading over them.

Pressure pounded inside Mere, and a thick, solid connection anchored her to the marble below her feet. A quiver and soft roll underneath her—warmth and a pulse. The Earth breathed and lived, and awakened for her. She understood. It was Ivy's terrashakti.

Avia's eyes, just spinning silver, were now white as she grabbed Mere's hand. Together, they surged and blasted fire, earth, air, and water. The fifth element exploded from their chests at once. With their dead sisters' sparks within them, they could call the beam of light, also called the Quintessence.

White light blasted from Mere, warming her and filling her with a flicker of hope—a second later, her hope shattered.

Lightning filled the sky. A single bolt slowed and stretched for Avia. As if attracted to her own source of lightning, every bolt in the sky connected as the flashing beacon struck her, ripping her away.

No.

Unable to scream, cry out, or breathe, the demons rushed forward, blurring with speed, and stabbed Avia the second before she hit the ground.

No. Please, no.

Tears filled Mere's eyes and released, ran free in rivers. "My sisters."

It's just you now.

There's no hope.

Everything shuddered to a stop.

I'm alone.

Ten thousand volts of electricity zapped her. The force knocked her forward with the internal impact. It wasn't just pain; it was power. It wasn't another attack. The zaps hadn't come from *them.*

Air. Avia.

A lump of grief stuck in Mere's throat. Air joined the earth, fire, and water waging inside her.

Fight! All her sisters yelled at once.

I can't. It's my turn to die.

As her sisters' sparks brawled within her, Mere gazed at the building wave in the distance, just holding herself together. Too much pain, too much noise, too much—

Please, hurry.

The island's one mountain exploded behind her, sending a beacon of fire shooting into the sky. Raging air spun into a tornado in the courtyard, but she stayed rooted to the ground.

Her wave drew water from the sea's darkest depths, forcing it to climb high toward the heavens as it sped for the island.

The Four hadn't killed her yet, and she'd take them…everything with her.

Raw energy battled inside, and she couldn't hold it in. If she didn't release the power, it would destroy her.

It would destroy her anyway.

Her fury and agony grew to an impossible climax. The Four vanished into mist then reappeared behind her with raised swords. She spun, and using Ivy's and Asha's earth and fire, she threw flaming rocks at them. "You will not take me too!"

The rocks collided with her targets, and robes billowed in flame before dissipating.

She fell to her knees.

Let it go.

There was nothing left anyway. Her sisters were gone.

Make them pay.

With only seconds left, the wave crested above, and the volcano exploded—Mere's physical body couldn't hold on; her skin stretched…

Hold on! Fight! her sisters commanded.

Mere awaited the water's approach with a fierce grin.

The Four surrounded her.

My sisters, I'll be with you.

Hold on!

They drew their swords.

White flashed over her vision as a shockwave obliterated her and the Four, forming a giant crater in the ocean, forcing the water away to join the wave already on its way. A swell, larger than the earth had ever seen, crashed over what remained of her island, dragging it under and crushing Atlantis within its cold embrace.

Chapter Twenty-Nine

From nothing and nowhere, Atlantis sank as Mere died. She'd absorbed her sisters' elements, and her body, unable to contain the force, was torn apart with her death. Light faded as the vision shook.

I destroyed Atlantis. I wiped it from the world.

Silence. Darkness lived, breathed, and crawled—closing in around her. The black would swallow any glimmer, any spark.

But I'm still here waiting for something.

All was quiet in the void as if nothing existed but her mind. The end.

Is this death?

What else could it be?

If this was indeed death, it was a shapeless, weightless night but still conscious.

It's horrific. Do I have eyes? Ears? A body?

Maybe she existed just as a pure mind or thought.

But I think, therefore, I am? Am I?

To hang or float, suspended alone in this nothingness forever?

Hell wasn't fire as faith taught. Hell was seeping black, strangling nothing, suffocating emptiness.

Wait.

Shhh...

Solid, heavy weight pressed against her in the dark. A presence.

Someone's here. Or something.

The unknown entity could've been a mile away or just in front, but it loomed all around her.

I need light.

And lightning flashed, illuminating the darkness. Shadows billowed and grew—something roamed in the gray mist. Something *was* with her.

A purple bolt flew toward her, and though she had no physical body, it burned her chest.

A ripple washed over her in fading light and—

Mere.

It was her voice—but it carried echoes as if many spoke as one.

She opened her eyes.

I have eyes now?

Standing in the bright square where she'd just died, a crowd of women stood before her—a sea of faces...of her face.

And they spoke as one. "You are far stronger and braver than you believe. You carry guilt you should not. Release it. You must stop running and stand your ground. You must fight. If you do not, none of you will survive, and all will be lost."

As one, their gazes lifted to the sky. Then they snapped to her, all eyes solid white. Their open mouths screamed at once, *"Wake up now."*

Water crashed over Mere, rolling her along the ocean floor, the pressure almost crushing her.

Go!

Swim up. Now!

A powerful current dragged her up, but something stopped her, yanked her back.

No.

She bent to tear off what must be seaweed tangled around her leg but recoiled in horror. Wasted air escaped her in a useless stream of bubbles, for her underwater scream made no sound.

Not a sea plant—a *nightmare*.

A decomposed man gripped her ankle with his pale, putrid hand. His jaw hung slack and peeling. Foggy gray eyes condemned her with their silent accusation. Rags, similar to the garments of Atlantis, clung to his bloated, rotting corpse.

With some unforeseen knowledge, she understood he was a victim of Atlantis... *My victim.*

They hadn't all escaped. Or the destruction was just too vast.

Kicking away as her air waned, the skeletal hand wouldn't let go. If she couldn't escape, she'd drown.

I'm too deep.

The sand rippled.

No. No.

A thousand hands clawed, dragging themselves from their loose sand graves, and reached for her.

The dead of Atlantis climbed from the ocean floor, searching for revenge against the one who killed them.

Too many bodies to count scrambled over each other to hold her there until she drowned. Dead, white faces accused her.

No...no...no.

Among the dead were Asha, Avia, and Ivy.

Grief squeezed Mere's aching chest.

Shutting her eyes to block out the horror, she waited for death to take her.

No. Fight.

It's too late.

No, Guppy! You are stronger than this.

The voices were louder now, not just her voice, but all the water sisters of the past. All her sisters shouted at her.

We are life and death. We are nature—neither good nor bad. We are power. We can both create and destroy. Our power can be used for good or evil. There is nothing weaker than giving up, and you are not weak! Do not let them win!

You are Water!

I am Water!

You must fight!

Yes.

The past sacrifices played before her on a loop, some horrific historical record. Thousands of women and girls were sacrificed because of the Order's jealousy and impotence.

You must be strong.

Yes.

Tired of fear, of guilt and regret, she raged. The pain and anger of generations murdered filled her. Stirred her… Burned her…

I will fight.

All those times she'd forced herself past her limit while training to increase her stamina played in her mind—and how, even now, she wasn't fully aware of how far she could go.

The nosebleeds, the seizures. Her mother, resting a wet cloth on her forehead, then gently dabbing the dried blood at her nose with a corner—

You tried so hard to save her. But you couldn't save any of them. And you've never truly tried since. But you must now. Nothing's stopping you.

Yes. Mere had given up. Worked hard until a point and then—

No more. I will go into battle; we will destroy the Order.

I will fight!

Searing hot water blasted her in the chest as hard as a firehose. She absorbed the water, drawing it inside, triggering soothing energy to course in her veins. Relief was instant. The pain she'd carried since she woke in Avia's vehicle vanished. The water cleansed her.

Yes.

Thank you.

This place healed her.

The sand was settled. No more zombies. As if they'd never been.

But she was still underwater.

So deep…

Go!

A current stronger than the one that carried her to the ocean floor yanked her up, and she shot toward the surface. Dark water grew lighter.

I'm still too far.

Urging the water to carry her faster, she kicked her legs feebly as her lungs burned for air.

Come on. Hold on.

The icy water warmed as the current carried her higher. She would never make it.

Hold on.

Images of Ivy, Avia…Asha. Their courage…their strength…

Yes.

No.

Mere's lungs strained and convulsed when her air ran out. She couldn't help it. She breathed the saltwater inside; she couldn't stop herself. Her mouth opened, and water poured in, choking her.

Everything glowed bright white as if she'd stared into the sun too long. Was she still moving up? A shock zapped her. The light faded to black.

I'm…healed.

Myself.

~ * ~

Aron took another breath and dove. The water was too dark to see anything.

Don't give up!

He surfaced for more air and went under over and over, stretching each breath to last as long as he could. Darting his eyes around, he searched for her, afraid and losing hope.

She'd been under way too long. The panic gripping his chest squeezed the last air from his lungs.

Surging up for a breath then diving under the thrashing tide, he reached out blindly, praying to gods he didn't worship to help him.

She's gone. No one could survive this— No.

Refusing to admit the only possible truth, he surged from the water, gasping.

Go again.

It happened just as he'd seen in that vision in the haunted kitchen.

Don't give up.

He swam, blind in the black water. Grasping, hoping to touch her, find her. Praying for the cord that connected them to bring her to him.

Inhaling, preparing for another submersion, he froze as the water around him stilled. He bobbed in a small, calm pond within a raging ocean… Then he spotted her.

She floated on her back in the center of the calm water.

He flushed with fire as he propelled himself toward her, grabbing her shoulder. Towing her over to the boat, he dragged her limp body onboard.

"Mere, wake up. Mere!" Running his hand over her, he searched for air, even a tiny bubble somewhere in her lungs.

Oh, shit. No!

There was too much water. He tilted her head, sealed their lips together, and blew precious air into her.

Come on.

He pumped on her chest, scanning, pressing in rhythm. Water trickled from her mouth. He blew air into her mouth and lungs.

Connected to the air, he forced it inside her, he made it flow in and out of her lungs, breathing for her.

She was cold, limp…lifeless.

Please, Mere.

Uncalled sparks formed on his hand, and light spread out, covering her. The shock caused her to jerk and bow, arching off the deck.

He kept urging the air in and out of her lungs. "Come on. *Come on.*"

Open your eyes.

His chest was on fire, his vision blurring with tears.

No. No.

Don't leave me.

He moved the air in and out in a gentle rhythm, even with his raging panic. The sparks gathered unbidden and shocked her as if they were reaching for her, fighting for her of their will. She arched off the boat deck, and as she dropped…*Yes! Yes—she is there.*

A cough.

Yes.

A breath.

Yes.

Panting, he collapsed beside her. Her breathing, though shallow, was even.

Thank you.

Brushing her hair away from her closed eyes, he grazed then cupped her damp, chilled, and beautifully, perfectly pale cheek. The dark, infected veins were gone.

His chest ached, and he exhaled long. Relief. She was finally, truly healed.

"Now, please open your eyes," he whispered, letting the air carry his voice to her ears and put all his power into his intention.

Chapter Thirty

Gone because of me.

Mere witnessed it—was part of it—caused it.

Atlantis, or a similar utopian society, existed once, but she destroyed it. Annihilated an entire civilization.

Breathe.

Because of her, Atlantis lay buried on the ocean floor.

The Four failed to achieve a sacrifice they sought—

But also…

I'm healed.

Not only was the constant pain, heaviness, and exhaustion gone, but her hopelessness and terror were replaced by focus and determination. The mark had faded. Its power extinguished. By accepting her fate and facing what she must do, the water had cleansed her.

Open your eyes.

The wind caressed her face with salted air, and she blinked. The night sky had more stars than she'd ever seen.

Wow.

"Mere…" Her name was a prayer. Aron bent over her, his usually dark charcoal irises were silver, spinning like tiny tornados. He cupped her cheek.

Searching his expression, she wondered how she could ever think he'd be the one who hurt her.

Order trickery aside, he couldn't be evil. Her spark reveled in his. They were part of their own balance.

He shut his eyes, resting his forehead to hers. His relief was a physical caress that sent desire crashing over her in a tidal wave. She stopped him from retreating by placing her cold hand on his shoulder.

He stilled for a breath, then opened his eyes. The gray had darkened, the color still spinning. The muscle in his jaw ticked. The warmth in his eyes turned from gentle concern to scorching.

Saltwater still on her lips, she had to kiss him—to taste him.

I almost drowned, or did I drown?

As if reading her mind, he cocked his head, questions in his expression.

She smiled, giving silent permission that she wanted this, and he understood. He angled over but stopped, his lips a breath from hers. Fathomless longing pumped and throbbed within her.

His gaze rose from her lips to meet her eyes. "I love you, Mere.

I thought I'd lost you. I won't lose you. I can't."

Swallowing past the lump that obstructed her throat, his words rolled over her on a tingling sound wave. Before she could react to the reaction his words caused, he erased the gap and crushed her lips in a soul-shattering kiss. Their mouths fused; fire exploded through her.

Oh, yes.

She combusted and melted into lava when he slanted his lips across hers to take their kiss deeper. She was overcome. While he'd kissed her before, he'd been holding back. Electricity sparked into her. His tongue swept between her parting lips, and she forgot everything but him, the pressure of his mouth on hers, his body along hers.

He broke the contact and hauled his soaking sweater over his head. She sat up, tugging at her wet sweater clinging to her. He, kneeling before her, came to her much-needed aid, helped disentangle her, and yanked the sweater off.

His gaze dropped to her chest.

She hesitated but glanced down. Only a healthy scar where the mark had been remained. His finger trembled as he brushed the shiny pink skin. No dark veins appeared.

She grinned, and light filled her. How long had it been since she'd been so free? She wanted to laugh—laugh! Years, if she was being honest. It wasn't just the mark that was healed.

She smiled, but it fell at his expression. Pure hunger radiated from him. White flashed in his dark eyes, and without breaking eye contact, she unclasped her bra, and let it slide off.

Ever so slowly, his gaze shifted from her eyes to her breasts. He swallowed. "You are perfect." He almost growled the words, and they touched her, her breasts tingling at the vibrations that could have been fingers rolling over her nipples.

Biting her lip, fire sped in her veins, scorching her even though she was soaking wet on the boat deck. The cord between them tugged her, trying to drag her to him, and she gazed at her chest to see if an actual bond stretched from her to him.

He went so still that she snapped her gaze to his and froze. They were pure lust and desire, and her body churned and quaked with anticipation.

Oh, yes.

He didn't breathe for a heartbeat. When she reached for him, he lunged for her. One hand covered her breast, and the other went from her throat around her neck, combing through her hair to cup her head. He covered her mouth in a soul-altering kiss. Her toes curled, and her moan was primal.

198

Rocking into her, his arms prevented any impact from the deck, but she was on her back, him settling between her legs, all in one fluid, incredibly hot movement.

"Aron," she sighed.

She'd never wanted anything more than him inside her, taking her hard and fast. Oh, he wanted her, too. If there'd been any doubt— none after that kiss. She writhed under him and went for his belt.

The way he paused, pulling back, and smiled, that curve of his lips, was so hot, she melted.

Yes, oh, yes.

"Aron," she moaned, desperate for more.

And he obliged. He skimmed strong fingers over her, grazing along the side of her breast on the way to her hip, causing her to flinch into him.

Please.

He kissed the scar on her chest. Then he licked and nipped a path down.

He drove her mad with his slow ministrations.

A sound that could have been purr or growl escaped him, either way it was animalistic, and it pushed her closer to the edge. But when he licked her, then blew hot air across her peaking nipple, her hips jumped.

All thoughts vanished. She clenched and thrummed with a pounding ache when he took the tip of her breast into his mouth. "Oh, yes."

A rolling growl was his only answer, and his teeth gently grazed her, followed by a long, slow lick. While he lavished one breast then the other with his mouth, he stroked his hand from her hip along her stomach.

She was dying for him, but he was stretching out the pleasurable agony.

Slipping his hand into her pants, he grazed her. She quivered from his gentle brush. He pulled the thin lace fabric of her underwear aside and slowly slid one finger along her center while he took her nipple in his mouth, flicking his tongue, then sucking.

She arched in an uncontrolled thrust and grabbed at him, almost sobbing with desire. How long could she bear this exquisite torture? She wouldn't be able to take this much longer. Had anyone ever died of lust? Because she just might be the first.

With a last roll of her nipple between his teeth, she almost squealed.

Fuck.

He rose, lips swollen, to retake her mouth. She opened for him.

His tongue swept in, and his teasing, tentative finger plunged into her.

She cried out from the sheer euphoria of it.

"Tell me what you want," he said while he kissed her.

Panting, she thrust, using her thighs to try to draw him into her. "I want you. All of you, now. I've never wanted anything more."

His finger swirled inside her, stroking in and out. Tracing small circles just inside her—his thumb pressed that spot.

The hunger grew, the pressure built, and she was on the verge. Just as she hovered on the edge, he lowered his lips to her breast and nipped lightly, then flicked her nipple with his tongue.

"Oh, yes!" She fell over the cliff, her body spasming and releasing as her orgasm pulsed on and on.

When he kissed her again, she spiraled into unreached and unexplored depths of what sensation was.

Enough is enough. It was his turn.

She wanted him to have half of what he'd just made her feel. Her wet pants and underwear were too restrictive. She sat up tugging off her clinging clothes, watching him from inside her passion fog.

He knelt in his wet jeans, his gaze unmoving but burning.

Unclothed, it was time to make him as naked. She reached for him, but he crawled toward her, stopping her. She reclined, her breath hitching at his expression.

Hovering above her, his eyes seared every inch of her.

Fuck.

Sliding her hand from his hard chest to his open pants to encircle him, he flinched at the contact.

In an instant, the slow rhythm of their interaction transformed into a frenzy of desire. She surged into him, the urgency between them intensifying with each passing second. His arm encircled her instinctively, but she wasn't content with mere proximity. With a deft movement, she maneuvered him until she was seated, and she straddled him, seizing control with irresistible passion.

She tugged his pants off.

There.

Taking him in her hand, she relished him, stroking him—

"Mere–" His voice was low and guttural. "I want you now. Trust me. We will have time for all that later."

She climbed on top him, placing her hands on his chest. "I love you too."

Shifting, she slid over him, locking their gazes, then sank onto him, groaning as fireworks exploded behind her eyes, and her being sighed at the completeness of it.

"Mere," he said her name between clenched teeth.

Straddling him, with him buried inside her, was the most delicious excitement, and her body acted on its own. The water churned, rocking the boat as her pace and passion increased.

He gripped her hips and rocked with her. The primal urge was so intense and building she had to shut her eyes.

Tilting her hips and abandoning herself to the rhythm, he matched her perfectly.

Spray misted over them, and she was only vaguely aware of geysers blasting all around the boat. Allowing the sensations to take over, to drive her, climbing faster and higher, they were one storm of wind and rain. Together. The pent-up release that built with the power of Atlantis, of her death and rebirth. All of it grew and stretched beneath her skin.

Yes.

Like the water bursting from the dark ocean's surface, she exploded, crying out, her echo carrying over the surging water. She dropped her head, her fingertips digging into his chest as she panted and shook from the force of her climax.

Grinning at her, he cupped her face, then in a blur of movement, rotated them until she was below him, and he was between her legs.

Oh, fuck, yes.

Wearing that soul-crushing grin, he kissed her then entered her in one smooth motion.

She flexed around him.

He was perfect.

Sliding out then in, she met each thrust, rocking together, hard and fast. They were frantic but in rhythm until more raw, primal pleasure roared through her, and they climbed to their mutual shattering release.

Whoa.

Together, they thrummed and panted in each other's arms, basking as their mutual ecstasy subsided.

The boat rocked on the residual waves as they lay entwined, their breathing slowing. A shining phosphorescent glow surrounded their boat, creating a magical light in the night.

She smiled, and the act filled her with sunshine.

Finally.

His genuine smile in return was the added shove she needed to reach true joy. It had been too long since she experienced anything that resembled happiness.

Enjoy it while you can.

She snorted.

No shit.

Chapter Thirty-One

Aron never imagined the levels of ecstasy he'd just experienced were possible. He laid on the boat deck with Mere resting in his arms. This woman, his enemy, his death, had become everything...his love...his life.

Finally, he understood the foolish things people did for love. It made sense because he was now one of those hapless fools.

Searching ahead in his mind, he couldn't find any more images of Mere cloaked or marked.

She's cured.

But...

But he did see other options now. It seemed he and his brothers would still become the Four, and the sisters would suffer then die at their hands, for the Order always wins.

Always.

No.

He'd been wrong before and prayed he was wrong now.

"Are you okay?" he asked, studying her.

The innocent enthusiasm that had once radiated from her face had returned, but it was different. The light in her had dimmed. Her bounce had slowed. But she seemed whole—at peace.

"Yes, I think so. Thank you for everything you did to help me."

Pleasure aftershocks still tingled inside him. He glanced down. A pink scar marred the flesh where the wound in her chest had been. But it was healed.

"What happened out there?" he asked. "I dove in after you. I lost you for a long time."

"I'm not sure. It must have been some scar magic. But Aron, Atlantis–or something like it–once existed here, and I destroyed it."

"Atlantis?"

She frowned. "We are stronger than any of the previous sisters, but a past water sister destroyed Atlantis more than 2000 years ago. If we keep getting stronger, what are we capable of now?"

"Mere."

She held up a hand in a *wait* signal and a gesture of supplication. "Honestly, I don't want to think too much about that right now." And her spreading grin shone bright as the sun after eternal darkness.

Big, fat raindrops landed on the boat's wooden deck, and resembling an ancient goddess, she stood, raised her hands, and let the rain wash over her.

Joining her, he twirled her into him. In that instant, he understood completeness… They danced with lazy smiles, silent under the glowing, lightning-filled night sky. As they moved, their rain-soaked bodies pressed against each other, ignited their passion again.

Standing on her tiptoes, she whispered in his ear, "Can we *please* do that again?"

Her words were thrilling enough, but when he caught the excited twinkle in her turquoise eyes and the mischievous joy in her expression, he unraveled. He couldn't stop his full grin.

How was she so resilient?

Was it the aquashakti? Damn, it had to be because Rio was also resilient as hell.

Lifting her, she laughed and looped her arms around his neck before meeting his lips in a searing kiss. Her laugh sent tickles following his earlier tingles. Her lips set him on fire.

Dude, you're done for.

He carried her to the small cabin in the boat's bow.

Who cares?

~ * ~

Ecstasy pulsed inside Mere, tension building. Aron settled her on the bunk, and she trembled when he sat beside her, his gaze drinking her in. She touched his jaw and kissed him gently. To relish his soft lips on hers.

He let her set the pace and that allowance stoked her passion from tentative to off the charts. She couldn't maintain her control with this man any longer.

Her blood rushed, and he mumbled her name.

"Yes, Aron," she pleaded.

Shifting, he dragged her hips closer.

Yes.

She gripped his shoulders, and he laid her on the bed, his burning gaze roaming across her while he hovered above her. He kissed her, and with the contact, everything but the two of them disappeared. She ran her hands over his shoulders, stroked his jaw with her thumbs, then combed her fingers through his hair, succumbing to his mouth.

She wanted much more, and she wanted it now. Her soul rejoiced in a toe-tingling response, and she would *absolutely* give in to this never-ending, eon-spanning-life-and-death passion.

Holding above her, he teased her with caresses, strokes, licks, and kisses until she couldn't take it. The pleasure was too intense, and his slow pace only increased her desire to incredible heights.

Ready, more than ready, she begged. "Aron, please?"

"Not yet, my love. I want to take my time."

His words sent her over the edge. She had to bite her lip to keep from crying out as ecstasy rocked her. If he saw it took just his words and attention to drive her to orgasm, he might grow too arrogant.

She clamped her eyes shut.

Oh, yes.

Returning to earth, she was ready to launch again when he ran his fingers over her stomach to her hip where he drew lazy circles on her hot skin. Blowing a warm breath over her breast, she groaned, but when he blew an icy breath a second later, she cried out with something more than desire.

Arching against him, she begged him to make love to her. "Aron," she pleaded, but he cut her off with his mouth.

The passion in his kiss liquefied her as he slid his hand between her legs and grazed her with impossible-to-handle tenderness.

She flooded with heat and became liquid.

His mouth singed her, and he kissed down over her curves…going…

No.

Oh my—shit.

Yes.

His warm breath on her skin sparked her heart to beat like a drum. She was the tide. His mouth covered her—drank her in.

How can pleasure be this intense? She drowned in pure sensation.

"Aron," she moaned.

Help.

He spread her legs wider and flicked his tongue.

Oh, my—fuck... Yes. She wove her hands into his thick hair as his tongue stroked her. If she thought she'd experienced pleasure before, she was wrong. It all paled compared to this. Her incoherent words and long moan made no sense. But when his tongue dipped inside her, her body acted alone, bucking embarrassingly. His deep chuckle was pure sex, and it did her in.

She burned, pulsed, and exploded, sending her spinning in a whirlpool of incoherent ecstasy.

Lightning flashed in his dark eyes when he rose and slid along her, in between her open legs.

He took her hands and entwined his fingers with hers over her head. Pressing her into the soft mattress and clenching their hands, she gasped as he entered and filled her.

The completeness was another plane of existence, peace, and

perfect balance. Their connection was woven within the fibers of her very essence.

Where did I end, and he begin? Who cares? It didn't matter. We're together.

"I love you, Mere," he said softly against her ear.

"I love you, Aron," she whispered.

They breathed as one, keeping still, both holding the pause—she basked in feeling the fusion of their hearts and their souls.

She ached with the need to move, but because of the intimacy and pleasure of their joining, she didn't want to be the one to break the longing, loving, rightness.

So, they broke it together, and their slow, gentle rhythm set her on fire.

Yes, oh hell, yes.

Even in such a terrified state for her, her sisters, her body urged her on. She loved this man; this magical, incredible, dangerous man.

His charcoal eyes swirled with silver, and lightning flashed in his pupils.

Her blood sped in her veins.

In sync, they climbed in ecstasy, hovering at the edge, then cried out and tumbled over at the same time. She whirled as pleasure thrummed on and on.

Entwined, they lay, panting in rhythm. A bright light glowed, and she glanced down.

What the...?

Lightning sparked into a web across her. It tickled...but the lightshow still unnerved her.

"Aron?" Her voice broke.

He raised his head from where it nestled in her neck.

Startled, she flinched. Except for the forks of lightning in each one, his eyes were almost solid black.

He shut his eyes, and the lightning vanished. Blinking, his dark pupils were circled by silver.

A chill froze her. "Are you okay?"

"Yes." His voice was a breath. "Are you okay?"

She swallowed before she said, "Yes."

~ * ~

Mere waited on the sun-drenched street while Aron returned the boat to the rental dock. Approaching her now, he scanned the area as he walked. Though his appearance was relaxed, she was pretty sure he wasn't.

But she was.

I'm free. Free of that poison and darkness.

She glanced at the horizon as he stopped beside her. "What's next?"

"Up to you. The mark is gone," she said.

The purple ooze was gone, too. And just to ensure all was well, she called a film of water to cover her. She voiced her relief with a hum.

"Do you want to get a room tonight?" he asked.

She wanted to. His expression, the pleasant ache inside her; she *really* wanted to. "Why not?"

His smile flipped a light on inside her. "I'll get us a car."

Under an hour later, she sat in the passenger seat of the rental—whole again. Alive. Warmth flowed strong as a river in her veins.

"How are you feeling?" His tone communicated a lot in one question.

She smiled. "So much better. Thank you." She sat up.

The Rua du Paim, the highway out of Ponta Delgada, was bordered by a barren, desert-like landscape. It was quiet, with only a few cars coming and going.

"You've been through so much."

Yes, and though she was free, the Order would still be coming for her and her sisters. The brothers. Aron. The Four.

Her chest thumped. Panic swept over her, and she choked.

"Can you st-stop for a minute? Please." She squeezed the words out between gritted teeth, breathing fast.

He swerved to the shoulder, his gaze on her. "Slower. In and out."

She reined in her panting and eased air past the pressure on her chest. "I need a minute. It's just panic. Not real." Getting out, she braced against the door, drawing in long, breaths that were wheezing, and not getting enough…

He joined her and touched her in a gesture of support. Her chest opened up, and rich, delicious air flowed in.

Pull yourself together, Guppy. You're not alone. You have your sisters. Aron is here. You'll be okay. You're better now.

She followed his gaze to the view. The beaches were packed. Bobbing boats dotted the harbor.

Smiling, he put his arm around her shoulder. Her panic subsided at his contact. The casual but loving action tugged at her chest.

Pressing her palms into her eyes, she groaned. "Do you have any idea how confusing and frightening this all is?"

"Yes."

"Will they be able to tell if the mark is healed?" she asked.

"I don't know," he answered.

She doubted he would know, but she had to ask. "Why did they mark me?"

He tilted his head. "Control you and your power, and you can't fight them. You become another weapon in their arsenal. The mark would've taken you over. "

"How do we stop them?" She didn't like the fear in her voice.

He drew her in a bit more. "I still believe the fifth element is the key."

She furrowed her brow. "But it didn't work."

"It was the first time we tried it. There must be some way the four elements in balance can help. The beam of light was a life-altering weapon. Maybe it will take all eight of us. Master Miles said the only way to defeat the Order is for all of us to reach full power."

With the mark gone, she was lighter, cleaner…ready.

And it was true. Her soul-shivering terror of the Order was less somehow. Yes, she was frightened, but she was filled with the desire to fight, not run, not hide. Aron had brought her back from darkness and fought so hard for her—with her. "Aron?"

"Mm?"

She didn't want to destroy his peace. Her peace. "What I saw you do to me—in that cell—I'm not sure. But I think it means something more—"

He stiffened. "I know."

She started. "You do?"

"I have seen it, too, but I believe we can change it—"

She had to hear him say it. "What? What are you still hiding from me?"

"I think the Order plans to…*somehow*…make me and my brothers into the Four."

She shivered with cold ice. "So, you do know."

"I don't *know* anything."

Her temper flared. "Semantics."

"Yes, maybe. But as I said, things are always changing. I don't *know* anything."

"Shit, Aron. Why haven't you told me everything?"

"I've witnessed many dark paths where we are the Four."

The ice in her veins turned to fire. "Many?"

A muscle ticked in his jaw. "I haven't told my brothers."

"Why not?" For some reason, that made her feel the tiniest bit better. "Two reasons. One, I hope we can stop it, and two, I don't want to tell them I've had visions of us as soulless ghouls hurting the women we love…"

She choked at the emotion in his face, but he shut his eyes and dropped his head.

Her gaze drifted ahead to the sparkling water so far off on the horizon. "Do you think Avia knows?"

"Wouldn't she have told you?"

She frowned. "I'm not sure. For the same reasons, you didn't. Or maybe she hasn't seen it."

"She's seen it," he said matter-of-factly.

She had to agree. When she confronted Avia about Aron and the brothers being the Four, there was something in her denial. It was as if Avia had been waiting for that reveal, that accusation.

"We'll find a way." He caressed Mere's cheek, sending her heated blood rushing through her veins with a familiar tingle. Thrilled and heartbroken at the same time, his touch was the comfort she craved.

Choking on a sob, she was whole again, but her emotions were still divided.

His thumb brushed her skin in a slow arc. "Are you really okay?"

"I feel like myself again."

As crazy as I am…

And always will be, Guppy.

Chapter Thirty-Two

Mere couldn't ignore the longing refiring between them, just standing against the car on the side of the road. Aron brought around his arm, which he'd laid across her shoulder, bringing her against his chest. Both hot lust and incredible comfort filled her at the same time. Bending his head, he kissed her. Desire pulled ahead, rippling low inside her.

With her face tilted up, he wrapped her in a warm hug as he kissed her.

The wind whispered and rushed past them, covering the landscape in muffled silence.

He tensed mid-kiss.

What now?

She leaned back to search his eyes for answers, but he stared past her at something behind them, off the road.

No. Please no.

His lips brushed her forehead as he lifted his gaze over her head. His warm lips chilled from passion's flame to ice. Vapor puffed from his lips with his breath as if he were on a frozen mountain peak and not on a hot desert road. Just as his lips had, his body grew colder.

She tried to move, but he didn't relax his hold.

"Aron, let go." She struggled, twisting to see what he was staring at.

No.

The Order.

They'd found them. Order soldiers lined the slope below the…road? There was no road—just a grassy hill.

What? Where's the road?

So jarred by the sight, her heart tripped.

The air sparked between the two sides. The pause lasted more than three seconds.

Scanning the army, her stomach clenched, and her legs swayed at the sudden change in the landscape behind them.

What happened here?

She searched beyond the army across the empty land. Everything was gone. "Aron, what's going on? Where did everything go?"

He said nothing, squeezing her with urgency.

All traces of humanity vanished. No city, roads, buildings, or power lines. The port town of Ponta Delgada had disappeared.

A low voice pierced the eerie stillness. "What do we have here?"

It sent prickles along her skin. She tried again to get out of

Aron's icy embrace. "Aron, what's the matter with you?"

With a shock of horror that pulsed over her, prickling skin, she saw his *black* eyes.

Not the dark passion of widened pupils and spinning charcoal irises. His eyes were…empty.

The way they'd been when the poison from her mark had gone into him.

No. Not now. Please, no.

Her hand against his chest didn't work the way it had before. He stood stiff, cold. She wanted to scream, but she had to hold it together and figure this out. Would the shocks and horrors ever end…for her…for any of them?

The man slowly walked toward them from the head of the army. He wore Order robes, but with the hood off, his dark hair and almost glowing violet eye were visible.

Aron's gaze was locked on him.

The man from the forest.

She froze, and the dark power rippling off him slammed into her.

Oh shit.

"Aron," she shouted. "Let me go."

Lighting flashed in the pitch black of his eyes. His cold arms vibrated around her, growing looser.

"Bring her," that chilling voice called from behind her.

No.

Aron twitched, though he didn't move.

"Aron, please," she begged.

His gaze didn't waiver as he dealt with some internal struggle. There was a chaotic rhythm to his vibrations, and once he relaxed, she sucked in her breath fast and dropped, twisting out of his hold.

Rising and stepping away and out of his reach, she faced the man strolling forward.

But he stopped when she freed herself. His causal air vanished.

She shot a giant icicle toward him. It came so fast, with no effort.

The man who had to be a Master whipped around, his cloak swirling, and he shattered the ice shard with a staff that appeared from nowhere.

Firing off three larger, stronger icicles, he shattered each one as if they were barely morning frost.

Who was this Merlin mother fu—?

The soldiers fired hundreds of darts into the sky…

No.

They rained…

The man with the violet eyes slammed his staff into the ground. A large crack spread, racing toward her. The darts or the crack? The crack widened as it sped faster toward her.

No.

She sent another three giant icicles at the man and dove to the side, rolling away from the crack with her arms covering her head to protect from the darts…that didn't come.

They stopped mid-air and fell. She jumped up and spun. Aron stood behind her with his arms up, holding off the darts, his eyes still black. Unable to catch them all, the ones that escaped his shield impaled him.

Going to his knees, he took his shield with him.

No. Aron.

Stinging tears filled her eyes. She couldn't take a breath past the lump obstructing her throat and spreading into her chest, constricting her. But in her need to stay focused on the Master and army, she grasped onto the fact the bullets were the tranquilizer darts the Order used to take her alive. They wouldn't kill Aron.

He's okay. He has to be.

Her heart thumped in the silence that pulsed between them. She was left alone to stand against a Master and his army.

Be brave.

There were so many of them, and this man was far scarier than the other Master she met.

This is no man.

Come on, Gup.

She shoved all her fear and weakness to run out of her until she was emptied of it.

"How did you break the mark?" The man slammed his staff on the ground. The army marched forward a step.

She flinched but scowled at him, "Who are you? You're different from the others."

A flicker of annoyance crossed his face. "I'm Master Iacomus."

She couldn't believe he'd paused and answered her. "Really?" She tilted her head and pursed her lips in an over-the-top doubtful expression. "You seem like *more* than a Master, even a Grand Master from what I've seen."

He had a look of distaste, but he lowered his staff from a menacing arc to rest by his side at ease. "And you're the water element."

She gave him a mock bow. "Tell me about the mark and why it tried to kill me, and I will tell you how I broke it."

His frown was hard. "It tried to kill you? Explain."

212

"I'll just say I almost drowned because of it."

"You are the water element, are you not?" he asked, impatience in his tone. "And you're alive."

"So?" she said, confused. "Aron said he sensed a sentient desire to kill."

"Ahh, yes. Aron would feel that, I suppose. And it's fortunate for us both that it didn't succeed."

She bared her teeth, a brand-new expression for her, but the level of rage and hatred was also unusual.

The slightest tilt of his lips gave away his pleasure at her reaction. "Your mark was caused by the Four, correct?"

She gritted her teeth at the memory of that thing's finger inside her, stabbing her heart.

"That is not the only way to mark someone, but it is…effective. One of the Four marked you with a fragment of his soul."

Soul?

She had to fight to stay standing. That voice. Was it one of them?

"That intent Aron sensed is the sole desire of the Four and the Order. It's doubtful you would have been killed. On the edge perhaps, and mistakes have been made when there is enough hate involved, though we have waited too long for any errors…" His purple eyes flared. "How did you break it?"

"I touched the scar." She pointed to the empty bay. "Out there."

"I see. So, the scars have healing abilities. I wondered. It's a shame. We did have you. You were ours and almost ready to gather your sisters and come to us. But since you broke the mark, I am here, forced to seek you out and fetch you myself." He slammed his staff down once more, and the army took another step forward.

Her anger rocked, lapping and spilling over her dam. "*Yours? How* dare *you?*" Clenching her hands into fists, she yelled at the frightening man. She carried the voices of her past sisters with her, their courage, their pain filling her.

Fear and rage battled.

Then he grinned.

And yeah, rage… won.

His fucking smile snapped her control. It was every leering, handsy, abusive asshole. It was pure dominance, misogyny, and violence. But she wouldn't let this beast walk away with that smirk on his face. No fucking way.

Fight. Now.

Yes.

Her emotional dam bulged and sprayed as she leapt from anger to red-hot fury. "For centuries, you have hunted us, stolen our power, taken our lives! It is our turn. This time, *we* will end you!"

It's all you now.

I can do this.

Yes, Guppy!

"*I* will end you."

The army took another step.

"*You* will end me?" He snarled. "You are nothing. Another weak, useless vessel, too fragile to hold such power. It will be ours. *You* will be ours."

She wouldn't falter this time. They wouldn't take her. Only death could stop her now.

Summoning her aquashakti, she connected to the water in the bay. There were no swimmers, no engines, no boats of any kind. Wherever she was, behind the Curtain, or whatever, there were no innocent casualties to risk.

She reached toward the open, empty sea.

Bring it in. Wash these fuckers away.

Using every tensed muscle to strengthen her connection to the water, it responded and crawled across the empty land. She wrestled and dragged it toward them, building mass as it moved. Iacomus's eyes flickered. The air crackled. The sky darkened, and the Order soldiers charged on some silent, unseen command.

Shields up.

Calling her element to stretch across the landscape between her and the army, she froze it. The giant wall instantly appeared and blocked the army.

It's so easy.

Reaching far out to sea, scooping all the water her power would allow, she emptied the bay. Adding everything she could to the giant wave, she called the water to come faster.

She ran to Aron, forming an ice shield to cover them in a dome, praying the ice was thick enough to withstand the water and big enough to hold the air they required.

Protect us.

Connected to the massive wave, she forced it to sweep the land. The army had nowhere to go.

Bringing the wave crashing down with a thunderous onslaught onto the dome, she cringed at the black shapes slamming into their barrier, but it held.

Sweat covered her. Blood that started with a trickle now poured out her nose as she diverted the water around their shelter to prolong its

214

durability, but her unending power was draining. Stars danced before her eyes, even as she stretched herself to the limit. Reaching for Aron, maybe…

As soon as she touched him, his spark flared and filled her with strength. Light air rippled over her, and her energy refilled. Even unconscious, he helped her.

The water flooded the valley, pounding the hill with enough force to ensure all the soldiers were either drowned or pulverized. But she fought on…

Just a little longer.

But it took too much... Her vision shook, and her muscles ached with the tension. She'd reached her limit.

You can let go.

No, I have to—

It's okay. You can stop.

The water snapped from her control as she released it, allowing it to return to where it belonged. The ice dome vanished into steam, and she stood.

Wait…what?

She swayed and dropped beside Aron's unconscious form.

There were bodies everywhere. Not Order soldiers. Human bodies.

No Order soldiers at all.

They were people, families…children.

Victims.

No. No. No.

She became liquid. Red and black bursts snapped over her eyes like lenses—open and shut. Roaring filled her head.

It didn't happen.

"What have you done, Mere?" Iacomus asked, his voice penetrating her mind.

It's not real.

"This is a trick," she whispered.

I didn't do this.

Her head thumped. She couldn't breathe. A scream built in her head, piercing until her eardrums bulged to the brink. Covering her ears did nothing because the sound was inside her head.

Stop. Please stop.

The anguish was too much.

The din lowered and cleared to voices.

Accusations.

A thousand, a million victims' cries flooded her mind.

"You killed me."

Voice upon voice, too many—

"Stop!" Red and black bursts still covered her vision, and she couldn't absorb—Covering her head, she screamed.

Another flash. The houseboat filled with water, dropping below the surface. She spun, helpless and frantic under the chaos and drowning water—all the people, her friends, her mom and dad.

No, no.

The slow, undulating rhythm of the bodies bumping into each other sped up, jerking forward fast.

Atlantis folded under the force of a giant wave. More bodies rising from the sea, decomposing and angry.

"It's not real. It's not real. Please," she cried.

I killed them all.

You did not. Pull it together. You're past this. Get up, Mere. Get up!

Chapter Thirty-Three

Mere's scream pierced the muffled darkness and charged Aron with adrenaline and purpose. The sound reached right into him and squeezed his heart. Stirring on the ground, he forced his mind to clear, shaking off the dark, then the fog.

Before he opened his eyes, he sensed they were behind the Curtain. Unlike Mere, he was a frequent visitor. *The testing grounds.*

The last thing he heard was the quiet swish of the Curtain, and his mind was no longer his own.

And Mere. He'd pinned her too hard while she'd struggled in his arms. Watching the darts descend, he'd barely managed to force his hands out, to fight the hold just enough to stop them from reaching her.

Fighting the haze, he stood. Slow, but he was under his own—

Wait, what happened here?

Bodies…everywhere.

This isn't real.

He spun, searching for Mere. *No.*

Her cries had stopped, but she sat rocking, her hands over her ears and, his heart cracked. *Shit.* She stared at the body of a small child.

He was at her side in one stride. "This isn't real, Mere. Don't believe it."

"Bring her; let's go," a cold voice said.

The automatic reaction to obey swept over him, and Aron grasped Mere's arm.

No.

Stop. He blindly obeyed. How's this possible? Who is this man? *What's happening?*

He couldn't fight the order and pulled her arm harder. That familiar zing to his chest lit his soul and burned fire along the invisible cord connecting them. He dropped his gaze to follow her tears. Every molecule in him tensed at her sorrow, her confusion.

He stroked her upper arms with his thumb before releasing her. Her grief broke him. Of course, she'd believe this illusion. He'd believed it, too, until he remembered where they were. She was too gentle and good, and she carried too much. He stood and faced this new player in their epic game of battle and survival.

"I don't know you," he shouted.

Was this the Grand Master's replacement? If so, he was far more monstrous than his predecessor.

"I am Master Iacomus. Bring her."

The urge to follow compelled him to listen to this man, to *obey*. How? Why? Was he marked? *Enslaved?* He reached for her.

No!

Don't do it. Fight it.

Closing his eyes, his visions came clear and fast. Image after image of Mere in terror, suffering. Everything he feared for her displayed before his eyes. What the Order had done to him and his brothers over the years, what he couldn't let them do to her. What they'd already done. He couldn't let her bear anymore.

Heat burned through him, followed by a cracking icy chill as if breaking a severe fever. Sweat beaded over him. Tears welled in his eyes, and he relaxed his hand.

She hadn't even noticed what he'd almost done. The Master's illusion had worked. He'd knocked her out of the fight without landing a blow against her.

He brushed his lips over her brow and spun to the Master. There was no connection to the Order, no foggy obedience. Aron's mind was clear of any allegiance, and he wouldn't straddle the line anymore. It was easy now—time he made a real choice.

Raised and trained to hunt her, use her, and sacrifice her; instead, he'd fallen in love with her. It happened to Clay and Asha. Would Rio and Cole follow?

Though Aron fought the destiny of it, how could he? His fate wasn't to fight Mere but to love her and fight *with* her. He'd never be able to kill her or her sisters.

And he wouldn't let the Order do it either.

They belonged together. She belonged with him, beside him. He wanted her heart. He wanted all of her. They were two halves of the same whole.

Calling his aerashakti, he shot lightning bolts from his hands toward the Master.

Iacomus scowled, watching the bolts join and cover him in a net. It lasted seconds before it disappeared.

"You will regret your betrayal." He lifted his staff above his head and swung it in a circle.

"No." *He's calling the Four.*

Aron's power was too slow to stop him.

The Master's upright arm halted on its descent. Jerking and twitching, his mouth dropped open, he made a gagging noise that became a scream then a high-pitched wail. It froze Aron's bones until they were heavy with ice.

He turned. Standing behind him, Mere stretched her arms toward the Master, her palms open, her blue eyes dark spinning whirlpools.

The Master bled from his mouth, nose, and eyes. Crimson beads formed on his skin, then ran down his face in streams. His cry echoed across the empty land, he twitched until his cry cut off—severed. He whipped his head to the side, cocked—listening.

A beat of silence pounded in Aron's ears, air whooshed by, and the invisible Curtain swept open and closed.

They were in the real world. The air, the hum, the people, it all returned.

The bodies were gone. The Master disappeared. Mere stood still as stone, she stared wide-eyed at the empty ground.

Shit.

He had to make sure she understood it had been an illusion. "It wasn't real," he said. "It was a trick."

She lifted her head, and her expression winded him.

"Listen to me, Mere. They're all capable of persuasive trickery and illusions. Those people weren't real. The land was empty. No people behind the Curtain."

Covering her face with her palms, she dug her fingertips into her scalp.

"Mere."

"After what I did to Atlantis? How could I do it? All those people."

"Not people. No. They weren't real."

Breaking and bending, she snapped, "What's real? How can I know? Destiny, truth—trance, or nightmare. What is real—"

"Mere…" He took her face between his hands, and her rigid body bowed. "I love you. That's real. Your sisters are fighting. That's real. You are powerful and strong. No matter what, I will fight with you until we win this. That is real."

"I love you too—"

His clenched body relaxed.

"—but I'm not sure I trust you," she said.

"I promise I will prove my loyalty to you and your sisters. You have nothing to fear from me."

"That's not true. I have everything to fear from you," she whispered.

"Destinies can change," he said.

Her face tilted up. "How?"

He touched her cheek, and she didn't move away. Her gaze flickered to his, full of strength and vulnerability, joy and horror, love and grief. An urgency to keep her beside him and never let her stray too far, not for possession but for the desire to be together, to fight with her, to learn and love everything about her, overwhelmed him.

"We keep fighting." Like a chilling wind, the vision blew into his mind and struck him.

Cole stood with Ivy before the Four. They were alone. The Master whom Mere had just fought was there. No. How?

Where are they?

Mere flinched when he accidentally squeezed her too hard.

He released her arms. "Sorry."

Her eyes exposed her trepidation at his unintended reaction.

"We have to find Ivy and Cole. Please, call Avia, now," Aron managed to get out between his clenched teeth. He had to hold onto the vision, searching for any hints or clues of where they were.

Before the vision faded, he glimpsed snow-tipped mountains and pine trees, with the roaring of water. They weren't in Arizona anymore.

Mere took out her phone and dialed. "What did you see?"

"It's Cole and Ivy. The Four found them. And that Master was there."

"Master Iacomus? Do you know him?" Mere asked while the call rang.

She switched on the speaker and held it between them. Avia answered at the other end. "Aron?" Her voice was urgent. "Ivy and Cole."

"I saw it too. Where are they?" Aron tilted his head toward the car and they both walked.

"Rio is on with Clay," Avia said. "He has gotten better at locating people, and he should find Cole fast. Get to an airport."

"Did you try them?" Mere asked.

"They aren't answering." Avia's voice was sharp.

Aron wrapped his arm around Mere, drawing her in and holding onto her. "We're on our way. Send word when Clay locates them."

Chapter Thirty-Four
Ivy and Cole

Shivering, Ivy had to turn away so Cole wouldn't see her fighting so hard not to smile.

His lips were a thin line and…blue.

Brooding had never seen this level of brood.

He's embarrassed.

After arriving in Vancouver, they'd flown to the small airport on Haida Gwaii, and after hours on the small boat navigating the archipelago, there'd been a mishap.

Attempting to be chivalrous and help her into the canoe they would use for the final leg of the journey, she startled Cole, and they both ended up in the water.

Everything. Soaked.

It wouldn't have been such a big deal if they hadn't lost their phones. They were out of touch.

He didn't like it. She didn't either.

But there were no tech stores around to replace the phones, and though they both agreed they must stay in contact, they had traveled too far.

One of the villagers from the dock, who'd be returning, said they would send messages for them and bring a replacement phone, but it would take at least two days.

After the extended and hottest stare-down of her life, they decided to stay. The others would panic, maybe, but Clay would be able to find them if there were an emergency.

Who else would find them out here?

It was her refuge. It was a damn shame it was so difficult to get to. Or maybe that was *why* it was her special place despite the past. The small island was extreme, raw, rugged, nature. Nowhere in the world did her element thrive more than it did when she was here.

The island, one of many homes to the Haida people, was the most beautiful place on Earth.

"This place is spectacular," Cole admitted, despite being wet and freezing.

She grinned at his undeniable reverence. "Right?"

Once a logging camp, it was transformed into the survivalist type operation she'd been sent to as a girl. That camp only lasted one year because of the tragedy. Perhaps it was her fault, and maybe it was for the best that it had closed, and the island forgotten. The giant boulder split down the center, and lying on either side of the plateau was the only evidence of what had occurred. And now, years later, the island remained empty.

The old crumbling structure would be acceptable to stay in, but Ivy wanted to camp on the earth and under the stars.

The building had multiple bunk rooms, a large mess hall, and a kitchen from the 1800s. It was built on the plateau, and the rest of the island was rock and forest, surrounded by swelling, crashing ocean. The small tributary, only accessible by canoe during high tide, was the one way to her private escape. The elders had passed that knowledge on to very few.

Most people used helicopters, if the wind wasn't too rowdy. Being locked in by weather was expected, so what might take two days could easily stretch into two weeks or even three before the weather broke enough to get someone there.

The isolation was part of the reason there was no longer a camp still running. Summer was a little easier, but not much.

Cole had an expression of wonder as they approached a tree, her favorite gnarly, Emily Carr, Arbutus tree.

Squawking drew her gaze to a lower branch. " Check out that trickster." Ivy smiled.

The corner of Cole's mouth rose in a crooked, slanted smile. Though only half went up, the light reached his eyes, and for an instant, she was struck by his beauty.

Wow.

"This place has a pulse," he said, lengthening his strides to catch up and walk beside her.

She grinned. The other side of his mouth joined the first. *Yes. I got it. Now, that's what I've been waiting for—a full-on smile.*

"Let's set up camp. I want to show you how we fish here." Joy filled her to almost overflowing.

She was home. Not in the same way a house was, but the place her soul could rest and play. She'd known it the instant she stepped on the island, and though it was the location of a great tragedy in her life, she still relished it and made it *her place.*

And Cole was here with her. Excitement zinged inside her.

~ * ~

Cole struggled to keep a grip on himself. Yes, he'd fallen into the ocean, and being the totally smooth soldier he *wasn't,* he'd dragged Ivy in with him.

He'd yelped from the bite of the cold water, but at least he'd shrieked underwater, and she hadn't heard. But when he surfaced, she'd laughed.

Light shone from her, switched on the minute they landed on the tiny island in the northern Pacific Ocean.

"Where should I set the fire?" he asked because she clearly had a plan, and he wanted to respect that.

Her mouth quirked to the side. "Where do you think?" She spun in a circle. "Maybe over there? Then we can stare at the view."

Flames crackled seconds later, and she gravitated to its warmth. He unpacked all his clothes, laying them out to dry. He took the clothes she passed to him and laid them on the rock circle she'd provided.

They stood on opposite sides of the circle. Through the flickering flames between them, he watched her start to take off her wet clothes.

Oh.

He urged the flames to climb higher and block her from view before a hint of her glorious skin showed. Last night, he'd had to work hard to put the brakes on their world cracking passion.

She said she wanted him, and though he burned for her, he couldn't take that step. Just kissing her had taken him over, proving they couldn't go any further.

He removed his wet clothes and laid them out.

The flames grew and danced, crackling and popping in the gray cloud-covered afternoon. They stood naked on either side of the inferno, and it seemed oddly fitting in the setting. A pagan god and goddess basking in nature's wild, untamed elements.

When their clothes were dry and back on, she led him to the logging camp. "I stashed some supplies here."

She went inside and came out with a trunk.

"Any phones in there?" he asked.

She laughed. "No, but I've got these." She dragged out a bunch of nets. "We can drag these nets to catch some fish."

Thankfully she hadn't handed him a spear—nets he could handle.

They spent the late afternoon fishing and talking. Thanks to her skill, they'd caught a bounty and cooked and dined on the tiny beach.

The sun having eased its rotund form below the horizon, he extinguished their beach fire. She led the way to their camp.

"I'll take you up the cliffs tomorrow," she said. "The view is the most magical in the whole world."

"I look forward to it," he said, his voice almost a whisper.

She was sorting their gear when a boat's shrill motor broke through the roaring tide and whipping wind.

They faced the shore. A speed boat speared for the beach fast.

He spotted a flash of red. "Is that Asha? What are they doing here?"

Ivy strode to the edge of the plateau.

"They'll never make it." When the last word left his mouth, the crashing ocean calmed to unnatural stillness, and the boat slipped into the thin crack between the cliff edges to scrape along the rocks.

And indeed, Asha jumped out, sprinting for them, with Clay, Rio, and Avia on her heels.

What are they doing here?

A minute later, they reached the top. Asha gave Cole a silent bow of her head in greeting, running past him to Ivy.

"Are you okay?" she asked.

He glanced over his shoulder, and Ivy had Asha wrapped in a hug. Clay appeared over the plateau's edge next.

"What are you doing here?" Cole asked, walking over to meet him.

Avia and Rio were the last to appear. "Aron and Mere will be here soon," Rio said, scanning the area. "They're bringing a different vessel. We thought, considering how difficult it would be to arrive, the more options for escape, the better."

"What's happened?" Cole asked Clay.

"Avia and Aron saw the Four. They found you here and…"

"They aren't here." It was a statement. But Clay turned his confusion to Avia.

Her brow was furrowed. "I saw them."

"Here they come."

Cole froze, but Rio meant Aron and Mere, and seconds later she bolted up the slope, Aron striding behind her. Mere bowed her head at Cole also on her way past him straight into grinning Ivy's open arms.

Chapter Thirty-Five

Absorbing the peace and comfort she'd missed during their separation, Mere snuggled into Ivy's embrace like a warm blanket. An absent peace flowed into her even with the looming dread.

"Are you okay?" Ivy asked.

"I am. I'm healed. It was the scar. Are you okay?" Mere asked, searching behind her for Aron.

"Yes," Ivy said. "Why are you all here?"

We made it in time. Ivy's here and safe.

"I saw the Four," Avia said.

"So did Aron," Mere blurted.

Rio stared at Avia. "If we split up now, maybe we can evade them."

"Let's go," Avia said. "It's a trap. They're coming—" Her words cut off as the world thrummed and jerked beneath their feet. The tide surged so hard that it sent spray far and wide enough to cover them in salty mist.

"They're here," Cole said.

"Let's go," Clay shouted.

The ground shifted and rocked again.

The Four.

Aron and Clay ripped open the bags they carried and grabbed weapons.

"We have to fight," Asha yelled. "We can kill these bastards."

"No," Avia and Aron both shouted.

Shit.

"As strong as we are," Avia said. "We're not strong enough to defeat them. We can't win here."

"Everyone," Rio barked from Avia's side. "To the boats."

Clay tugged Asha's arm. "We have to split up. Let's go."

"I'm not going anywhere without them. We'll have to fight," Asha snapped.

"Shit, Asha, you can't all go together," he snarled.

"We need her," Aron said softly, gripping Clay's shoulder. "Without Asha, we have no chance."

"Right," Asha said.

Squeezing her sisters' hands, Mere drew strength and energy—flowing from them and rushing into her—then passed it back.

"We'll have to fight them. It's too late. There's no running anymore," Aron called.

Asha set the tops of trees around the plateau ablaze turning them into giant standing torches. Avia filled the sky with forked lightning. With their combined power lighting the grounds, the night flashed and vibrated with orange and silver strobes.

The grounds, now illuminated, crawled with hundreds of Order soldiers running up the beach and over the grounds, swarming toward them like ants to their hill. Mere's stomach clenched.

Here we go.

Pops and cracks sounded in the sky. Aron shifted to cover Mere, and his brothers shielded her sisters. The ground lurched harder, throwing her off balance.

The air prickled.

They're here.

The Four materialized from spinning black mist with their arms up. Mere flew backward through the air and landed twenty feet away as if hit with an invisible battering ram. Her connection with her sisters was severed.

Hitting the ground hard, Mere was winded as the air whooshed out of her. Where were they? Where were her sisters? She got to her feet. They'd been scattered.

You've got this.

Fight.

And she did.

She raised her hands, and two giant icicles, six feet long, stretched from her palms and flew fast for the Four, two more right behind the first ones, but they soared through her targets without any impact.

"Get to Asha," Ivy shouted at Clay.

The ground lurched so hard Mere fell, unable to keep her balance. On the rolling ground, she flipped onto her back and gazed at the fireball meteors and lightning bolts crowding the sky.

Get up!

She jumped to her feet.

Avia's lightning blew rows of soldiers away… *At least they went down.*

…but they kept coming. So, Mere blasted the next, on and on.

A hand on her shoulder shoved her to the ground. Aron pushed his hands out to catch the onslaught of power coming from the Four. His air shield stopped the attack, but he struggled to hold off the second wave.

"Get behind me," he gritted out.

Clawing at the grass, she got to her feet. Spreading her hands out, she called waves of giant icicles to spear from the ground. They impaled line after line of soldiers.

But more kept coming.

White light flashed beside her, and Avia soared backward, crashing into the building behind them. Bullets filled the air, but Avia used her wind to direct them off course. The bullets were large and strange.

Mere squinted, but her vision shook with the earth. They weren't bullets but darts.

They still hope to take us alive.

She called more ice spears to stab another row of soldiers. Many of them still alive struggled, but her ice kept them immobile. Some vanished into purple mist.

Good. Keep going.

The long, broken windows in the dilapidated lodge behind Avia blew out in a glass cloud. Thousands of shimmering, grime-covered shards hovered a beat, then speared for her unprotected back.

No.

"Avia, behind you," Mere shouted.

Glass swarmed and circled in a cyclone around her. Her blood sprayed out in a circular red mist.

No.

Rio, who'd been helping his brothers hold off the soldiers, lowered his gun, swinging it on its strap behind him, and ran into the glass tornado. His water power surrounded them in a frothing pillar, knocking the glass away. When he dropped his power, Avia clung to him.

There's no doubt about it. Rio's with us.

No matter what the Order planned, the brothers were fighting them. Cole stood in front of Ivy while she conducted the trees in an orchestra of impaling instruments, stabbing and sweeping masses of soldiers away. But they kept up their assault, and the Four continued their attack. She was outside her body while the battle raged around her.

Their defenses wouldn't hold much longer. The more power they expelled, the quicker they drained. They needed to cause some damage or flee.

Asha's flames transformed into a huge, sharp, burning sword before she swung at the lines of soldiers, decapitating them by the dozens, knocking them off the plateau, and clearing the beach of everyone.

Asha grinned. "Whoa. That's new."

Her eyes spun red flames as she sent more blankets of fire racing out as if unrolling a carpet. Flames surrounded the Four, crawled closer…

Asha's flame met Mere's flooded ground, and steam rose in a billowing wall between the sides. The Four's flames shot from the clouds like blasts from an invisible dragon, scorching the sky. Mere doused each attack, but even while the wind roared around her, the steam and smoke obscured her vision, and she lost her sisters. Aron was near, but where were the others? The clouds surrounding her blinked white and orange with strobing attacks.

"Watch the perimeter," Rio shouted, but it sounded far away. "They're still coming."

One of the brothers was shooting, maybe two.

From behind, icy wind blasted past Mere and blew the steam away, clearing the scene.

The Four had separated her from her sisters. They each stood at one of the four directional positions—North, East, South, and West. The Four waited, grouped in the center, each facing one of them. The brothers, fiercely guarding her sisters from behind, fought the soldiers, using guns and power to hold them off. Mere thought of that Order symbol Avia had found by folding the scroll. The way they stood could have been a copy of that symbol.

No!

She darted to the right, but a lightning bolt hit the ground at her feet. Flames covered the space to her left. There was no escape or way to connect to her sisters.

Because of what she'd experienced at the scar, there was a doomed familiarity about this while everything slowed to a humming crawl. She recognized the feeling of fulfilled destiny and enormity in the final instant before her sacrifice.

Please. No.

Under Avia's glowing lightning, the many bolts cast a bright stuttering light over the scene.

Ivy had tears shining in her eyes. "It's not the end for us, right? We'll be together?"

Avia resembled some beautiful melancholy ghost with her white hair blowing around her. She stood unnaturally still and stared at the ghoul before her.

Eyes spinning red, Asha bared her teeth, swiveling her head, awaiting the next attack. Leaping to the left, she teetered before jumping in the opposite direction as the ground broke away. Black, jagged obsidian rose, blocking her from retreating in the other direction.

"Do not give up," Asha yelled and surrounded the Four with flames. "Come on, you guys, fight! Don't let these assholes take us!

Don't let them win!" She blasted a stream of fire through the ghost before her.

"Mere," Aron snapped, taking her hand and spinning her. "Come on! You are not in this fight, but you have to be. You are strong. We can't do this without you. Be ruthless. Be vicious!"

Her eyes widened.

"You can do this. If not for yourself, do it for them."

The one before Ivy blurred with speed as he raced forward and grasped her around the throat—the fear in her eyes... *No.*

No.

Fury, buried so deep, bubbled and rose. Growing as it sped for the surface from the ocean floor.

Fight! For your sisters! For yourself!

Anger and rage filled her with more power, and Mere responded to that rage. Monstrous fury. Asha was right. So was Aron. If this was her end, Mere would take as many as she could with her.

The blood of the sisters, generation after generation, murdered at the hands of these monsters. Take your revenge.

Still holding her arm in a vise, Aron's black pupils spun in a midnight tornado. "Kill these bastards. You can do it. I've seen your power, Mere. Fight!"

Yes. Now, before it's too late.

Chapter Thirty-Six

Fight!

With Aron's touch fueling her, Mere shot her water to cover the ghoul holding Ivy. She used her aquashakti to surround it in a cocoon of swirling current and froze it. As the ice spread, she forced spears to shoot inward from the outside, and Ivy was free. She shuffled to Cole, who helped her rise and tucked her beside him with his arm around her waist.

Connected to Cole, Ivy threw her arms up to clasp together above her head as hundreds of huge thorn-covered vines shot from the swampy earth and covered her assailant.

Mere spun to where Clay had joined Asha, gripping her shoulder. Her flaming spear ignited and covered the one in front of her.

Avia and Rio stood back-to-back, touching. He shot at the soldiers while all the lightning in the sky connected and blasted the demon before her. With the brothers connected to them, they could do damage to the Four.

Mere's arms tingled as she clenched her fingers and threw her hands to the sky. Water surged from the ground surrounding the Four. They blurred and rippled within the still water, and she froze it, hoping to hold them there.

Asha swung away from the Four to help Clay with the surging soldiers, burning away another wave with her flames.

Catching the movement from the corner of her eye, Mere's ice shield was too late. The rocks flying for Asha were too fast, and—

Oh—

No.

Rocks pummeled Asha, one snapping her head forward with an audible crack. She crumpled, but the sound alerted Clay, who caught her and lowered her slowly.

The night's orange glow vanished with Asha's power.

Ivy sprinted for Asha.

Avia lit the sky. Rio and Cole continued to fight off the soldiers. With gentle hands, Clay rolled Asha over. Ivy dropped beside them with her head bent in concentration, her expression grim, her face pale.

Keep them safe. Protect them.

Avia, Rio, and Cole covered their rear to hold the army off.

Blood trickled from Asha's mouth and her left ear.

When Ivy's gaze met Mere's, it said it all. Asha was *not* okay.

Asha's moan was weak, but she fought to stand, to keep going. Because it was *Asha*, and she did not stop—ever. She panted. "Help me up."

Clay, with eyes hard, wrapped her arm around his neck and stood, holding her around her waist, keeping her up and steady.

Loud cracking drew their attention to where the Four had stood. The ice crumbled, but they weren't within. They'd vanished.

Mere's skin prickled. They were still close. Asha raised her shaking hand and more flames erupted in the trees, lighting the dark in a dancing orange glow.

There.

The Four waited, shielded from within the forest border.

The soldiers halted their advance, and the rocking earth stilled. An ominous silence covered the land.

"We need the fifth element," Ivy shouted.

"I can't do it," Avia said.

"We don't have a choice. We're getting creamed." Ivy speared a baseball bat-sized vine to split and impale two gunmen.

Asha unrolled more blankets of flames to burn the army.

"The scar healed me," Mere said to Avia. "Maybe you can do it now, and it will work if we try."

"Avia," Aron yelled, firing lighting into the mass of soldiers. "You must try. If it fails, I'll be here, but you are far stronger than I am. We need *you.*"

Facing the Four shielded in the trees, Mere joined hands with her sisters.

Focus, fight.

As soon as they connected, their combined shakti flowed into Mere.

Yes.

Her aquashakti swelled, but Avia wrenched her hand away. Mere held on. Some primal instinct took over her, swirling with energy yet refusing to release Avia's hand.

A thread of electricity coursed along the chain into Mere and zapped Avia hard enough she had to drop her hand.

No.

With their connection severed, their building power waned then vanished.

Help. Aron?

And he was there. He spun from guarding her and took her hand. Mere's spark responded instantly to his. He was the air in their balanced elements. He stood for Avia.

We're together. We're on the same side.

Energy raced into her with such force her head whipped back, and euphoria filled her. With Aron, there was *more*—more strength, more precision. Before, the electricity was a nightlight; now, it was a lighthouse. A white light beamed from her and struck one of the Four, holding it still.

Another beam blasted from Aron, holding another one. Asha had to lean on Clay to stand upright, but she contained another one with a beam from her chest.

Ivy's light connected, and the chain was complete. The fifth element surged without a barrier or block.

Love, peace, harmony, and balance.

With Aron's help, they'd trapped the Four. They floated off the ground, surrounded by a halo of their divine white light.

But nothing happened.

"Rio, Cole," Clay snapped. "Heads up! The trees, more soldiers—coming in!"

Rio and Cole continued shooting at the swarm, but they couldn't fight the Four and the Order's army at the same time. They couldn't hold this forever.

"What do we do?" Mere called to her sisters. "It's not working,"

"I'm draining," Aron shouted, and his beam stuttered and died. Then Asha's and finally Ivy's lights went out, too.

But Mere's was strong. They were all connected, and she could touch the sparks inside them. "Don't let go." With the element's sparks still in the chain, she could hold the fifth element... *Alone.*

Her one beam imprisoned the Four, and as her strength drained, faster than water through a net, she hung on. *She had them.* It justified every minute of her intense training. She wasn't weak. She was *fucking powerful.*

Yes, Guppy. Yes.

She allowed herself one second of triumph.

All those times she strained herself, used her element for too long, and fought until she lost consciousness would pay off if she could hold on now. "What do we do?"

Hollow, bitter laughter shivered over her.

Aron's laugh.

Prickles raised the hair on her arms.

"Oh, Mere." Aron's false voice floated across the lawn. "We had no idea how powerful you were."

Aron, who stood beside her, holding her hand—squeezed it harder, twitching.

Of course, it wasn't Aron who spoke. One of the Four used his voice to toy with her.

"We enjoyed your time with us—we hoped you'd join us."

It's not Aron. Remember their tricks.

"Holy shit," Rio gasped. "Guys—"

The Four's hoods were up, though now, rather than the black voids, the brothers' faces stared at them.

Aron's spark faded.

No.

Squeezing his hand, she couldn't connect to his power. Air was gone, and without it, her beam flickered out. The brothers stopped fighting, too shocked by their copies before them. The Four's trick had worked. Aron's evil laughter covered her in a sticky film.

She screamed her fury and frustration. "Fuck you! Why won't you bastards die?" Her dam groaned and cracked further, the feeble construction straining while the surging water rocked, spraying, leaking, and pouring over the top. "Aron, please try."

"Is that what you saw?" He couldn't tear his gaze from his dark counterpart.

"It's not you." Mere said. "Please, that thing isn't you. You're here with me. You can't let them do this. It will be the end of us—help us." She tugged him, but he refused to meet her eyes.

The shooting stopped. A shroud fell around them, over them. All the soldiers stilled on an unheard command.

Guns lowered, and a shape emerged from the trees. She swallowed the lump in her throat.

No.

"It's time," Iacomus's voice sounded from all directions. "Take them now."

She swayed but locked her knees to stay upright.

Addressing Aron, Iacomus said, "I had to witness it for myself, but yes, it's time. We can take them now."

"No," Avia wailed. Her voice—her face was white, her eyes wide.

Iacomus glared at her with his eyes but smirked with his mouth, bowing. He whipped his head to the brothers. "Let's go," his bellowed command ringing through his tone.

With the battle paused and the night quiet, the air pulsed with energy. Silence froze the scene. It had weight, and it smothered Mere.

Breathe.

But her breath strangled her.

His face shifting, Iacomus bared his teeth. "I said now!"

Pressure grew, and the seconds ticked by like minutes. His expression was venom and hate. He dropped his head, and his hood slid down, covering his face.

Mere searched for Aron behind her. His eyes were squeezed shut, his posture rigid.

"He's doing something to the ground," Ivy shouted, but her words didn't connect fast enough in Mere's mind.

Purple mist with glowing threads spread from his feet and crawled over the grass in a complex spider web design.

"We have to get out of here." Avia's quiet words floated to her almost as if she whispered them from right beside her.

There was no way to hide from those purple wisps. They swirled and climbed toward her legs, her sisters', all of them.

"We're going to lose them." Avia's voice was quiet but clear, and far more anxious than it had ever sounded.

Mere backed away, bumping into Aron, who stood frozen, watching it approach with horror on his face.

Crackling energy sparked under her feet, and the mist thinned, receding, and disappeared. Was Avia doing this? Aron? Ivy?

Doesn't matter. Fight, now.

Kill him.

Yes.

Calling her aquashakti, Mere connected to the water in Iacomus's body.

But the Four appeared in front of her, blocking Iacomus from her view.

Conjuring more giant icicles, she sent them at the Four.

Asha rolled out more fire-blankets, racing toward them, covering everything. Then stepping away from Clay and drawing her sword from her back, Asha swung it in front of her in one smooth motion and charged at Iacomus.

A shot rang out…so loud…so sudden, and stark in the flashing, burning, soaking night, bulging the thin membrane in her ears. A faint ring and hiss were all she could hear beyond the muffled hum, drowning out all other sound.

Asha jerked and fell.

"Asha!" Clay dove for her, and his shout knocked the air from Mere's lungs.

Help her.

Blood, dark as the rubies on her sword pooled between her fingers even as she clasped her shoulder. Clay covered Asha's hand with his and added pressure to the wound to slow the bleeding.

"Cole," Clay roared.

Mere couldn't break her locked gaze. Asha's life seeped through

Clay and Asha's interlocked fingers.

The sight of it reminded Mere of what she saw in Atlantis. Asha dead and bleeding on the white cobblestones, her eyes open but lifeless. Then Ivy, lying in a sea of red next to her. And Avia…

Stop it.

Eyes black and vacant, Cole stood behind Ivy, his arm across her neck and his gun to her head.

"What the hell are you doing?" Clay yelled.

Slow and steady, Cole raised his gun, aiming at Avia, but Rio seized her arm and twirled her like a dancer out of the bullet's path and crashing into him. Moving with her spin, Rio covered her then shoved her behind him.

What's happening?

So pale, her black eyes spinning with fire, Asha managed to get up.

How could she even stand, let alone fight?

A head injury and a gunshot wound?

She fought for them all.

Get in there. Help her.

Ivy struggled, but Cole gripped her around the neck, squeezing and choking her.

"No," Mere yelled.

He's killing her.

"Stop," Asha shouted.

Kill him.

Searching for the water in Cole's body the same way she had with Master Iacomus, Mere called her power. Heat seared from the healing scar on her chest, and the Four all charged her. She balked.

As one, they reached for her—Aron jumped in front, blocking them. "Don't help me. Stop Cole! He's killing her."

But her pleas were too late. Ivy slumped, her eyes fluttered shut, and her hands dropped.

No.

She's unconscious. She passed out.

But a familiar shudder rolled through the earth, a sad, pleading breath, then silence covered the grounds once more.

No one breathed… Nothing moved.

One, two, three.

The living earth choked, then gasped.

"No! Ivy!" she cried, and Asha cried out too.

No. Please no. It can't be.

New power grew, unfurled, and pushed at Mere's skin, quaking from inside her.

This can't be happening.

I have her terrashakti.

The familiar sensation of a foreign element growing inside her shattered her heart. She'd gained earth's element and understood what it meant, for she'd experienced it before.

Rooted and robust, steady and solid, Ivy's tremendous power erupted inside her.

Does it mean?

Yes, Guppy.

No. It can't.

Ivy's gone.

Avia and Asha stepped forward from nowhere, flanking her. Her sisters' primal rage coursed within the earth, connecting them.

Within seconds, her heart and soul's purpose shifted from fear and grief to rage and revenge, and it overwhelmed her. She sensed air and fire at her sides, but she *was* earth now as she was water.

Connected through the soil, her sisters' shakti pulsed with hers, and together they glared at Cole. She moved, breathed, and thought as one with her sisters, but there was something more—a dormant presence within her awakening.

Heavy silence swelled in the air. Her sisters were with her, one with her, sharing one mind. Was it Ivy who bridged the gap between them? Or was it the force of their combined grief and rage?

A voice of unity and balance spoke within Mere. *What is this strange awareness flowing between us, uniting us as one? And why now?*

Deep in the recesses of her mind, a fog moved toward the front. A spinning, white mist that spiraled and jumped. It ignited her blood even while it confused her with its soft buzzing noise.

A misty white veil fell before her eyes.

We will fight.

"Yes," the Master snarled from somewhere in the shadows.

The Four appeared, blocking her view of Cole and Ivy. An obstacle between her and her target.

"Take them," Iacomus said.

Everyone heard the command in his tone, but Mere heard something more—the demand to just take her like she was nothing, an object to pick up and *take*, as they have since the beginning, to take her the way they take everything…the way they took her, tortured her, and marked her. The way they took Ivy—

The rage that overcame her she shared with her sisters, but also the sisters of the past. With Ivy's terrashakti, there was so much more now. Every woman hurt and victimized, tortured and murdered, their tears and their power joined her. Their fury built on history, all the women sacrificed for these monsters, the tilted scales, the no hope, no future, bullshit of it all thrummed inside her. It pounded, it punched, it ripped and tore. And joined as one with her sisters, Mere was finally ready.

With a crack loud enough to shake the world, surging, churning water, rocking and slamming against its containment, exploded, breaking down her dam. The mighty force blasted stone and rebar, concrete and brick, and all her willpower to dust. Blind fury, unlike anything she'd ever suffered before, roared free… The force of all her emotions—kept locked away all her life—released.

Unleashed!

What did he say? That she was too weak a vessel for such power?

Fuck that…

Let's finish this.

…and with her sisters, with Ivy's terrashakti, she attacked.

Chapter Thirty-Seven

Aron clenched his teeth as stark panic shocked into him.

Still as stone, Mere stood side-by-side with Asha and Avia. Like powered-down robots, they waited frozen, their chins low but their wide white eyes vacant and locked on Cole.

Holy sh—

"Yes," Iacomus growled. "Take them."

His words were a trigger, and Avia, Asha, and Mere reacted. Avia spun to the army of thousands around the plateau's edge, the slope, and the beach, just lifting their feet to resume their charge. With her hands out, she sent flashing light from each of her fingers to blast every single one through the center of their forehead, connecting them in a brilliant spiderweb. In seconds, not one soldier remained.

"Fuck," Rio uttered in an awed tone.

Mere, her eyes white, threw out her hands, and ice spears roughly eight feet long and four feet wide in diameter erupted from the mud, impaling each of the Four.

He gasped. *How? How could she do this now? There was no connection with him, and yet she was able to strike the Four.*

Asha called a boulder from underground. Though her focus was locked on the Four in front of her, she set the rock ablaze and sent it flying into the forest behind her, where the Master had stood.

But he'd vanished.

Then, together, the sisters faced the Four.

The dark ghouls seemed to flicker and stutter, almost panicking in the face of the sister's display.

Before, they could barely connect or hit the Four. Now, their attacks landed, the Four were taking their blows, revealing the sisters' savage new power and strength.

Mere called four more giant ice spears at once. Each one struck its mark, and so she sent almost twenty more.

Aron watched the black robes rippling with the impact.

Yes. It's working.

"No," Iacomus shouted. "Stop them!"

Flinching at the command, Aron took an automatic step toward Mere.

No.

You beat this.

Help them.

Breaking his focus from the sisters because they had their battle under control, he had to get Ivy away from Cole. Cole's eyes were darker than a starless midnight sky. Aron shuddered.

But…wait… Yes!

Ivy was alive. Barely. She breathed, and though her breaths were shallow, she lived. "Let her go, Cole. You can't do this."

Cole's demonic black eyes were transfixed, following the sisters' attack.

Mere sped forward with Asha and Avia on either side, fighting in a silent coordinated attack. Asha blew a spark from her hands into an inferno that stretched, coiling and growing. In the same way, her fire was a sword, cutting and slicing with flames before; now, it became an enormous dragon.

The dragon emerged from the blaze, roared, spread broad burning wings, and whipped its long tail, rising into the sky. Every living being watched the beast, following the horror. It climbed higher, then rolled over itself and dove, opening its huge jaws, blasting the Four.

Avia must have made the dragon spin fast, creating a raging, flaming tornado around the Four.

Aron had never seen anything like it.

The sisters spun and fought. Avia threw out shields, protecting Asha and Mere, and they hammered the Four. Mere sprinted from Asha's side, splashing through the flooded grass and drawing Aron's attention. He watched, unable to breathe, while she skimmed atop a wave of her making, speeding behind the Four to shoot her ice spears into their backs.

They bent forward, taking the impact.

Yes.

"Get Ivy," Rio shouted.

The sisters advanced, and the Four dark demons retreated. He stood rigid. The sisters blurred with speed, leaping forward, each grabbing one of the hooded monsters. *They move in unison.*

But he had to help. He stepped up to assist Rio and Clay, who stood before Cole. With nothing but darkness in his eyes, Cole raised his gun, aiming it at Aron.

"Are you going to shoot me too, *brother*?" Aron asked.

The hesitation was all he required, and with a roar from Clay, Aron and his brothers charged at Cole.

Fire rose in a burning shield, but Aron ran straight into it and hit a solid wall. A blast shocked him and sent him flying backward.

"Come, Cole. It's time we departed." Iacomus's voice was cold and promised more would come…

Purple roiling mist crawled from the Master's staff, billowing up and covering him, Cole, and Ivy. "No!" Clay sprinted for them.

Aron blew the mist away.

But they were gone.

No.

Rushing to Mere, Aron stopped short as each sister lunged, grabbing one of the ghouls. The one in Mere's grasp twitched then rolled and flowed like liquid, the one Asha gripped burst into flames, and the one Avia had turned into opaque vapor. It was a reversal of what had happened at Avia's cabin when the Four first appeared and somehow transformed them into their raw elements. The fourth slipped below ground and rose again behind the sisters, drawing his sword.

"No," Aron shouted. His brothers joined him, and he raced for it, but a shockwave blew over them and knocked them down.

Jumping to his feet, Aron swiveled, searching for them.

Gone. The Four had retreated.

Again.

Mere, Asha, and Avia stood alone, their arms lowering at the same slow, even pace.

The night was quiet and still.

In the silence, Aron moved to Mere and studied her rigid stance. How they fought in synch was incredible, and their dominance over the Four? How? What did it mean? Aron met his brothers' questioning expressions. Clay and Rio went to Asha and Avia.

A vibration rippled under his feet, and Mere swayed. Aron was already there waiting to catch her.

Avia and Asha dropped in the same instant into Rio and Clay's arms. Meeting his brother's now grave expressions, they were as unnerved by the sisters' coordinated display as he was.

Lifting Mere, Aron sensed her breath and couldn't help it. He crushed her to him, bringing her in, and inhaling her scent of fresh spring rain, wild frost, and the briny mischief of the sea.

With a soft moan, she blinked away the white covering her eyes.

"Ivy's de—dead." Her voice was a whisper, and she choked the words out. Blood poured from her nose and dripped from her ears.

"No. She's alive. I could feel her breathing."

Her eyes widened, her lips forming an 'oh.' "Help Asha," she whispered before she passed out.

~ * ~

Ivy.

Snapping her eyes open, Mere took in her surroundings. She lay on a filthy old mattress on a broken bunk.

Asha.

She sat up then bolted from the room and into another—red-soaked clothes were everywhere, and blood pooled on the floor.

No.

The scene was horror. Asha lay on a large picnic table with Clay and Aron bent over her, performing surgery. Standing with Rio close beside her, Avia watched the operation.

Stay calm. Don't get in their way.

Cole.

He'd shot Asha in the shoulder.

Why's there so much?

The bullet clinked in the bowl Clay dropped it into. He began stitching up the hole. For all their terror of the Four, a bullet could kill them faster and more easily than anything supernatural or power related.

Aron passed Clay a bandage.

"H—how is she?" Mere choked on the words.

Avia didn't break her focus from the operation.

"Let me see," Clay said.

Aron shone a flashlight and lifted a corner of the bandage he pressed to her head.

Bile rose, and Mere's stomach lurched. Through the parted, damp, hair, there was a dark crack in her skull, and loose flap of her scalp. "A-Aron?"

"It's okay. She'll be okay." He remained focused on Asha even while he comforted Mere.

He's lying.

Gray lips blended with pale skin. Tearing her gaze away, searching for a distraction, Mere approached Avia. Her face was cut, and her clothes were soaked with red Mere took Avia's hand and led her to the couch while Avia kept her silver eyes locked on Asha.

"They've got it for now. We can't do anything while they work, so let's fix you up." She sounded weak. She rummaged around in one of the many first aid kits and found cotton swabs and peroxide.

Mere poured the peroxide into the bottle's lid, dipped the swabs in, and brushed them across the gashes on Avia's cheek.

"Aron said Ivy was breathing," Mere said.

Avia didn't respond.

"I was earth. I had her terrashakti, like at the scar. At Atlantis. But it happened after…she died…"

Avia broke her gaze from Asha, but she didn't meet Mere's eyes. "I can't feel earth. I don't have it anymore. Do you?"

"No." Mere fought her stinging tears.

"Aron's right. Ivy's alive. I don't why her power came to us, but she gave us what we needed at the right time to fight. Right now, I'm more worried about Asha.”

“Why? What’s—”

Avia flinched, not from the peroxide Mere rubbed into her wounds but from what she witnessed on the table behind them.

Mere swung her gaze to see. Jerking on the table, Asha coughed, spraying red mist from her mouth.

“Aron,” Clay barked.

“I’m clear.”

No.

Avia jumped up, pointing at Asha, who rose two feet off the table. Her body seized, and fresh blood poured from her wounds. Avia’s air carried Asha floating aloft until she was still once more.

Clay bowed his head, and Avia lowered her to the table.

He and Aron went to work instantly. Avia sat on the couch, more robotic than Mere had ever seen.

“We can’t stay here. They’ll regroup,” Rio said, standing on the other side of the rotting couch.

“We can’t go anywhere until she’s stable,” Clay snapped.

“I have to get to your other cuts,” Mere told Avia.

She refused to leave the room, but she allowed Mere to tear her pants, accessing the damage to her legs. Jeans had given her at least some protection from the glass tornado. Her head, torso, and arms suffered most of the damage.

Rio helped Mere by stitching up some of Avia’s worst cuts. She didn’t stir once after she raised Asha off the table—not even a flinch from the needle Rio used to sew her wounds. By the time they were done, seventeen bandages covered Avia from head to toe.

Ignoring Rio’s offers of help, Avia slipped her ruined sweater on herself.

“Where will we go?” Mere asked.

“Anywhere but here,” Aron said. “We’ll leave when it’s safe to move Asha. For now, we can take shifts watching and resting.”

“We have some time,” Avia said, eyes wide and unblinking. “They have Ivy. She’s enough for now.”

“What does that mean?” The matter-of-fact statement filled Mere with dread.

“They won’t kill her.” Avia frowned. “They need us alive.”

“They’ll hurt her or mark her. We have to get her now.”

“Ivy is tough,” Avia said.

“But—”

“We will go for her soon,” Avia said.

“Why did Cole do it?” Mere asked.

"It wasn't him," Clay growled from where he worked. "It was something in the ground. Ivy stopped it, but she couldn't stop it all."

"He was under some kind of compulsion—" Rio's expression was harder than Mere had ever seen it. "His eyes—he had to be. He wouldn't have done that to Ivy—us. Did you feel it?"

Rio's grief and fear for his brother was in his heavy, solemn expression.

"I did. It *was* compulsion," Aron said, without stopping his work on Asha.

"I did too—" Clay said. "But I was more focused on Asha than what that bastard was doing." He glanced up at Aron. "That purple mist. It never reached us. But it took Cole and Ivy. She kept it off us."

"I had to fight it," Rio said.

"It was the same compulsion that Master wielded behind the Curtain, near Ponta Delgada," Aron said. "I fought it—"

"The spell was so strong. I broke it. But I still worry—" Aron said.

She shuddered. Aron's cold, black, unreachable eyes. His icy grip on her arms.

"Of course, you worry," she said. "But as you said to me once. We can only continue to fight."

He glanced up now and met her eyes as he spoke to them all. "I have seen their plans," Aron said carefully.

"You have?" Rio asked.

"You're not going to like it."

"What?" Clay grumbled, still working. He dabbed a stained shirt or blouse to soak up Asha's blood at the edge of her wound.

"I had a vision, or more accurately, a number of visions, where the Order will succeed in their plan of turning us into the Four."

Silence poured into the room and filled every crack and corner.

"No way," Rio snapped, breaking the heavy, angry spell.

"That's impossible," Clay said.

Rio surged to his feet and began pacing. "Impossible! Impossible?" His cold scoff carried no humor. "Yes, but so is half of what we deal with every single day." He spun to Aron. "Are you sure of this?"

"Not sure of anything."

"And you?" Rio's gaze hardened on Avia, an expression that Mere had never seen on Rio's face. "I suppose you've known all this but kept it to yourself."

Avia lifted her chin, ignoring him, and stared at Mere. "Asha—?" Her voice broke; she sounded frightened. "How could she have kept fighting the way she did with such an injury?”

“She’s strong. She needs to *keep* fighting.” Mere swayed as exhaustion covered her and pushed her down. “Ivy, too.”

Avia’s gasp shoved all the air out of Mere’s lungs. Her sister was off the couch in a blur.

No longer tethered to the earth, Mere buckled.

“No, no, Asha. No.” Clay’s voice said enough. Something slammed the table. Mere assumed Clay’s fist because she refused to turn around.

I can’t.

Mere glanced up and met Aron’s eyes. They were pure sorrow.

“Move,” Avia barked at Clay. There was emotion in her command…more than she’d heard from her air sister…ever.

Ignoring Avia, Clay wept over Asha’s pale, motionless body.

Asha can’t be dead. I would feel her—. But I don’t have fire.

Not yet.

Shut up!

His hands clasped together, Clay pressed on Asha’s chest, blowing air into her mouth and lungs.

He could heal like Ivy. He could heal…

“One, two, three.” After thirty fast pumps, he breathed twice for Asha.

He refused to give up.

The room was quiet except for the steady count to thirty, then two breaths. Blood from Asha’s mouth stained his lips red. Seconds ticked by, stretching out too long. No one made a sound or moved except for Clay.

He eventually slowed, shutting his eyes, and pressed his lips to her forehead, his tears falling to her face.

“Wait,” Aron said. “Quiet.”

Clay’s hand was on her chest, the other on her cheek, and his devastated expression broke into a grin. “That’s right, kid, you fucking fight! You kick death’s ass.” He dropped his forehead to rest against hers. Laughing and sobbing as more tears fell onto Asha’s cheek.

“Yes,” Avia sighed, bending to Asha. She took Asha’s hand, and a smile lit her face—a true smile.

And wow.

It was possibly Avia’s first genuine smile since Mere met her air sister.

So, that’s what breathtaking means.

She was luminous. Light radiated out of her and her silver eyes shone like moonbeams. Mere gravitated toward Avia.

"She's breathing," Avia said.

Asha breathed. She lived.

Standing straight, his hands still on her, soaked in sweat, Clay said. "Her pulse is strong, but I don't understand, I thought she was gone."

"Who cares, man?" Rio grinned.

The touch of Clay's lips to Asha's forehead was so gentle Mere's heart shattered. More tears welled in Clay's eyes, and he managed a small smile and a clipped head bow. "I removed the bullet and managed to stop the bleeding. She can't lose any more. Her head injury is our biggest concern—the seizure was not a good sign. She could be out for a bit. But, yes, she made it."

"I've had seizures," Mere said. "If I use too much power, sometimes I run out of juice and react badly."

"I wish that was the problem. The seizure is from the head trauma." Pale, Clay paused. "Though the skull is fractured," he gulped now, his throat moving, "It's the brain swelling I'm most worried about."

Mere swayed, but she gripped the couch to stay steady.

Aron was beside her, his hand a feather graze on her shoulder. "Your nose is bleeding, Mere. You should rest."

The warmth from his touch soothed her but also emphasized her exhaustion.

"Come with me." His voice was only for her.

She couldn't stay on her feet much longer anyway, so she let Aron's touch guide her out of the room. Though she wasn't injured, she was drained, and her brain must have grown too big for her skull.

In the dark room, he unrolled a sleeping bag and laid it on the mattress. She flopped onto the bunk. A blur of his body stood in the doorway before he shut the door.

Blood dripped from her nose and ears, wetting the old musty pillow beneath her head. Her eyes fluttered.

I went way past my limit.

No, duh.

Asha.

Ivy...

Chapter Thirty-Eight

Mere opened her eyes, and her mind-fog spread to her vision. She couldn't focus. Her head was too heavy.

Where am I?

"Mere?"

Aron's voice was warm, and she flushed with heat.

"Did I wake you?"

More than unfocused, she couldn't see him in the dark, but she didn't have to. "No, I was just…"

"I wanted to talk to you." He paused and took a breath. "That thing…it was an exact copy of me. It even had my voice."

Her chest ached at his words, and she sat up. "Yes, but—"

"That's what you saw hurting you?" His voice held more than just fear; there was disbelief, grief, and anger.

"Aron—I—"

"I never imagined…they would be that…realistic." His denial was understandable, but the hurt in his voice called for comfort and reassurance.

"It wasn't you. You were holding my hand—another one of the Order's tricks. Remember?"

He wasn't the monster who'd hurt her but the man she fell for the first time they met…

But *deep* down, rolling behind her repairing dam with all her darkest nightmares, fears, and regrets, was the suspicion that the Order had a way to control the brothers. Cole had just demonstrated that. That knowledge was a drop of distrust inside her sea of boundless love. It provided a measure of doubt her fickle heart sorely needed. *Avia and Aron both had visions of the brothers as the Four.*

That didn't change her love for him.

Still in darkness, he sat beside her on the bunk. "Everything they told us was a lie." She could barely make out his expression, but his voice evoked honest vulnerability. "What if they've played us this whole time?"

"I don't have an answer," she said. "What happened to Cole is what happened to you, right?"

Aron dropped his head. "Yes, I think so."

She found his hand. "Do you know what it is?" If she expected open honesty, she must offer it in return.

"No. There was a compulsion to obey."

She bit her lip. "Do you think that it comes from the same power

246

as the mark? How did it compare to when you breathed in that mist?"

He squeezed her hand. "The same."

Her stomach rolled with potent nausea and dread. "I learned something about the mark." She swallowed. How was she going to tell him? "Iacomus said it's a fragment of one of the Four's soul."

He stiffened. "What— How?" He paused. "What came over me was inhuman hate and darkness."

His sigh chilled her. "It was like a much more potent version of a hold that has always been there, and I'm only aware of it because I broke it."

"Do you think that compulsion can come back?" she asked.

He cupped her hand between both of his. "I don't know. I wish I did."

Even with his horrible confession, she warmed at his honesty. He was giving her information that would frighten her, lessen her trust, heighten her fear, and yet he gave it to her.

He was a good man and had broken the obedience and control the Order had over him.

She leaned into him. "I'm with you, Aron."

"I'm with you too, Mere." His arm going round her, and his gentle squeeze melted her. "Ever since Avia's field in Switzerland, I've been drawn to you—connected to you. I was suspicious at first, but I understand now. You're my other half; you balance me, and I'll fight with you until the end."

"I'll fight with *you* until the end." She glanced at the door. "How is she?"

"Clay's with her. Her head is healing."

Mere understood what he didn't say. Though they healed well, she was still unconscious.

A bit shaky, Mere climbed from the bunk. She froze as she swayed, holding onto the bed frame to stay upright.

Sparks flared, joined, and wrapped his hand in pulsing light. "Holy shit, what happened?" he asked. "You're covered in—"

Her legs crumpled, but his muscled arm wrapped around her waist to hold her up. Gripping her wrist and studying his watch, he counted her pulse.

She touched the caked, dried crust under her nose and glanced at the bed.

What?

The pillow, sleeping bag, and mattress were red. Her shirt was soaked.

How?

"This happens sometimes, though not to this extent." Her whisper sounded hoarse. "I don't think I've ever used that much power before."

Frowning, he released her wrist. "Your pulse is weak, but it's okay."

"I need to get cleaned up."

"Let me help," he said, easing her to sit on the bed. "I'll get you a bath ready."

"A bath? Here?"

"I'll see what I can do."

He marched into what had been a bathroom, and after a scraping sound, he was back a minute later. "There is a tub of sorts and even an old candle. What do you think?"

She smiled when he bent taking her into his arms. "I can walk. I'm not some damsel—"

"I'm aware," he said. Tucking her against his warm body, he carried her into the bathroom. She couldn't stop the snort at what was clearly a horse's water trough. The candlelight flickered casting the room in dim dancing shadows.

"I tipped it out and cleaned it of debris and spiders."

"Aww, thanks." And she meant it. "That's sweet." She snapped her fingers, calling hot water to fill the large tub, and smiled when it came without hesitation.

"Before you ask me to leave, it's best I stay in case you faint. You lost more than a pint or two." He winked, adding teasing lightness to his tone.

She couldn't stop her spreading grin, but his fell when he reached for her shirt.

She swallowed, almost choking on what his expression did to her.

His fingers hovered millimeters from the fabric, giving her time to retreat, swat his hand away, or say no. But she wasn't going to deny his help when he was offering it.

When he brushed her skin with rough, strong fingers, she jumped. He studied her face, and took the shirt, drew it over her head, and dropped it in the sink.

The blood-splattered jeans took a minute to peel off and kick aside before he slipped off her bra and underwear.

Lightning flashed in his eyes.

His expression scorched her… And she melted from it.

Breathless, she asked, "Could you help me get in?

Shivers wracked her. It could be the way he watched her or from

248

the blood loss—pretty sure it was the former.

Stepping up behind her, he took her left hand and placed his right on her waist. If she arched her back, she'd rub her bottom against him.

Electric shocks sparked between them, sending a tingle to curl her toes.

Her foot, hovering in the air, about to get into the trough, she paused and glanced over her shoulder. "You're not going to electrocute me if I get in here, are you?"

"No." Though there was humor in his voice; it sounded huskier than usual.

She stepped in, released his hand, and sunk into blissful heat. The water caressed her, warmed and healed her.

He turned. "I'll be right back. Don't faint."

She giggled. "Then don't be long," she whispered, semi-confident he would hear as he left the room. In the peace and solitude, she slid under the surface, submerging. The heat covered her.

Your fight is far from over.

I know. But not now, okay?

When she came up, he was back, and he had a bar of soap and… "What is that?"

"A T-shirt."

"What? Who's?"

"Mine. I thought you might want to scrub, and I don't think there's a clean piece of cloth left around here. I have one towel, and that's for when you get out."

Smiling, she took it. With hands and shirt lathered, she scrubbed her shoulders, neck, and face.

He reclined, folding his arms across his chest, his gaze on her. The long, weathered counter took his weight. His gaze followed her every movement. She sank under, came up, and soaped the T-shirt a second time.

"Let me help you." He took the soap and shirt from her and knelt beside the tub.

He plunged the shirt into the tub, and she gasped, becoming acutely aware of his hands as they entered the water. Each swish of his fingers was a velvet stroke across her skin.

Oh, shit.

Adding the soap in his other hand, each sweep and twirl of his fingers was a maestro's motion, conducting the music of her body.

Removing the shirt and squeezing the excess water out, she cursed his hand's absence and longed for his touch. But he gently scrubbed the warm, soapy fabric down her neck and shoulders.

The soap smelled divine, and he lathered it into her hair. Blood-tinted suds sloughed off his hands, floating on the water like fluffy pink clouds, too pretty a color to come from violence and soap. He brought out a small bucket from beside the tub, and with a glance at her, she understood his wordless action. She filled the pail with warm water.

He tilted her chin up and poured the water over her head to rinse the suds away.

Fresh and clean, she stood, and he unfolded the towel and wrapped it around her. Swinging her from the tub, he carried her into the bunk room, sitting her on a clean sleeping bag.

"Another sleeping bag?" she asked.

"This is Ivy's."

Just the mention of her sister's name had Mere's heartbeat ratcheting up in fear. "They'll hurt her."

He sat beside her. "Avia's right. I believe she'll be okay…for a bit."

Mere swallowed the lump in her throat.

He stroked small circles over the center of her palm. "As okay as anyone could be as their prisoner. But they won't kill her." He stood, turning. "I'll find you some clothes."

"Wait, just a second…please."

He halted on his path to the door.

She cleared her throat. "You aren't what the Order wants you to be or what they trained you to be. Though I'm still not sure what the Order will do and what role you and your brothers will play, I trust your intentions. I believe you're with me."

Their bond was undeniable. He'd completed the chain of their combined shakti. What little she understood of the fifth element, his ability to represent air in place of Avia must mean something. How could someone who intended evil balance them the way he did?

And why wasn't Avia able to complete the chain? Mere would ask her about that…soon.

He walked back to sit next to her. And peace trickled in, bringing comfort just with his presence. He raised his fingers, brushing them along her jaw.

"I trust you, Aron, even with the fear of what may still happen hanging over us. I won't run or hide. I'm with you." She cupped his jaw with hesitant fingers.

Shutting his eyes, he leaned his face into her touch.

She shifted forward, ignoring the towel when it slipped lower.

But he didn't close the gap.

Boldly, she pressed her lips to his, and the familiar shock zapped her tired limbs.

Then he moved, and their mouths fused in a soft, slow kiss so romantic she doubted she'd be the same afterward.

He parted his lips and kissed her with such tenderness, her eyes stung with uncalled tears.

She wanted more, but there was something wonderfully sweet and yet epic in the way they just kissed. Such a vulnerable display, the love and intensity in it swept her away—powerful enough to create a planet or destroy it—save humankind or *erase* it.

He stroked her jaw. "I love you, Mere."

"I love you, Aron." She could've wept at the emotion she witnessed in his expression.

He stroked her cheek. "You take my breath away. You're the strongest, bravest person I've ever met. I'm in awe. You have my respect, my commitment, my love. We will win this fight. I promise you."

Now, she did weep but turned away to hide her fresh tears.

Damn, his sweet words.

How could she feel this good with everything still so wrong? She'd been so scared and alone…

Ivy and Asha are in danger. We all are. And always will be.

Take the joy when you can.

I want to live. For as long as I can.

"You should get more rest," he said. The concern just warmed her more.

"I must check on Asha," she said, slipping from the bed.

He gave her a mysterious smile and looked at the towel she'd left on the bed.

She grinned, "I suppose I need clothes."

He found some, and Mere had to admit she preferred Asha's cargo pants and T-shirt to Avia's fancier and more restrictive attire. Dressing, she was surprised to notice her stores had refilled.

She couldn't help a small surge of guilt when she and Aron walked to the living room together, and everyone was awake and waiting.

Clay sat at the table with his gaze locked on Asha. He didn't blink when they entered.

Mere swallowed the knot in her throat.

"Good, I'm glad you're up," Rio said. "We should go."

"Yes, we have to get Ivy," she said. "She can't stay there."

"Don't worry, we'll get her. She's strong," Avia said. "Asha's well enough to travel."

"Avia? That Master—did you see something about him?" Mere remembered him from the road watching them and Avia's panic during the battle.

Avia's expression was the same unreadable mask it always was. "Yes, that was Father James, my handler. And my shock was because I could have sworn I killed him on my twelfth birthday."

Silence fell and crackled.

Mere's shock crashed into her in a tidal wave. *How? What? Avia?*

Rio's blue eyes darkened until they were almost black. "What?"

No kidding or lightness were in that tone of his, and for a split-second, Mere saw the underneath, darker side of Rio, that she hadn't thought existed.

Everyone has a dark side, Guppy. Everyone.

"I will fill you in on the way," Avia said. "But we need to go. Now. Things are shifting and changing too fast."

Mere glanced at Clay, but he didn't meet her gaze. "I wouldn't risk Asha if I disagreed."

Avia, pale and wide-eyed, shot to her feet. "We have to hurry," she shouted with enough urgency in her voice that Mere's heartbeat picked up its pace.

They left in the two boats, and when they hit the mainland, they'd split up and head for the Order—separately—so they wouldn't see them coming.

Mere took in the beauty and ferocity of Ivy's favorite, perfect island. The burned, black spindly, forest, scorched cliff faces, and the crumbling, smashed-out structure...

I was once destroyed and broken—like that.

No more, Guppy. You're a shark, now. Leave it behind, in the past. Carry on, go forward.

I'll never be powerless again.

About the Author

Courtney Shepard lives on Salt Spring Island on the beautiful coast of British Columbia. As a writer and lover of fantasy, her days are filled with wonder as well as writing. Courtney writes fantasy where love is dangerous, magic is messy, and fate always has a twist. The Unbalanced series is a passion project that began years ago.

Website/Blog URL: http://www.unbalancedseries.com/
Twitter: https://twitter.com/CAShepard76
Facebook: https://www.facebook.com/unbalancedseries
Instagram: @courtneyshepardwrites
TikTok: @courtneyshepardwrites

Unbalanced

Every generation four sisters with power over earth, air, fire, and water are born to fight against a fanatical, secret faith. The Order exists only to sacrifice the sisters for their power. With each success their strength and control grows. They have never failed, for their rule depends on it. The sisters, separated at birth, are unaware of what hunts them...but they are coming.

A handsome stranger discovers Asha in hiding and swears allegiance to her cause. She falls for him; though he is not who he says he is. Betrayed and imprisoned inside the Order, Asha is without her power for the first time in her life. As the war heats up haunting secrets and true motivations are revealed, but the sisters must unite and override their instincts and trust the untrustworthy if they are to fight their terrifying destiny.

Chapter One

Asha sat inside her tent, sweat beading on her forehead as she waited for her summons. It had taken days to trek through the jungle, each step too slow, with thick, wet foliage tangling and straining to obstruct every inch of their progress. She'd helped the men hacking at it with machetes in the relentless rain, venting her frustration, but her efforts did nothing for their pace. Being forced to cut through the thick jungle to avoid roadblocks and any heavily guarded side trails pissed her off. It wasn't worth it when they could have taken the roadblocks easily.

But stealth won out over speed, and they'd finally arrived after dark to set up camp five miles beyond the base's perimeter. Her rain soured spirits sweetened as the sky cleared, and the insects chirped and buzzed like soothing music in the quiet jungle.

Father Sean opened the flap and crouched in. "Okay, they've returned. It's time to go. Remember, no survivors."

"Yes, sir." She brushed a loose lock of hair from her eyes and gave him a mock salute. He scowled at her and backed out, barking orders to the men. She grinned. It was so easy to antagonize him, especially before a mission. He was wound particularly tight tonight.

She crawled out and stood, stretching before pulling on her black, knit toque and tucking her ponytail up inside. Her hair tended to stand out even on the darkest night, but with a hat and dressed in black jeans and a black T-shirt she blended well.

Staring up, she took a deep breath as she studied the stars of the now clear, night sky. The stars always comforted her but in a melancholy way as if the distance was too great, and it prevented a full connection. They burned so brightly against the pitch, but combined with the jungle symphony, they were even more magnificent. Picking up the machine gun propped against her tent, she walked toward the trail. Eight of their hired guns slithered over to join her. "Halt," Father Sean barked. "Not yet. You're not going with Asha. She'll do this phase alone."

Whenever Father Sean added new men to their team, they were surprised, if not shocked, by his reliance on her. She was his number one and their sexist minds balked at the idea she could do such an important, large-scale job alone.

Was it because she was a girl, or because she was sixteen? Probably both. But she didn't really care. She always worked alone; others were merely support, called in for clean up after her role was done.

On cue, eight pairs of eyes gave her the customary up and down evaluation. *Eww, gross.* She rolled her shoulders back, hiding her disgust, and returned their roving glances. She flashed her sassiest, most sarcastic wink and puckered her lips to blow a kiss.

"Asha, go."

She spun, smirking, and jogged into the jungle, jumping and dodging, cutting her way silently through the underbrush. The jungle thinned and her mind hummed as she approached her target. She slowed, coming upon the huge, stone wall. It rose before her and surrounded the rebel compound. Crouching low, she studied it without a clue how old it was. Ancient. It was definitely ancient. The rebels may have taken the structure, but they hadn't built it.

Crumbled rock littered the base; moss, and vines wove their way up the stone barricade. It had obviously faced its share of attacks over the years, but it remained strong and impenetrable. Regardless of its numerous scars, it endured. She liked that.

Until tonight...

She didn't like that. It was historical. The walls were twenty feet thick, the diameter just under a mile. Guards walked high above, carrying machine guns and scanning the jungle for movement. She took note of where the jungle was dense and grew closest to the wall and then slipped back under cover as a guard passed on the upper level. The rough dirt road led to the only entrance, a huge, swinging gate large enough for trucks to enter.

She crept forward, drawing air deep into her lungs, and faced the gate, her machine gun resting heavy on her back between her shoulder blades. Her gaze followed the figure above. She drew her silencer-equipped pistol from her thigh holster. A muffled pop and the guard spun and fell a few feet to her right, dead before he hit the ground.

Quickly now.

She slipped the gun back as familiar tingling rolled through her. On her third breath, she called her power.

Bright orange flashed in the dark, and she grinned as delight bubbled inside her. She sent the flames, burning with unnatural ferocity, racing to the gate where they exploded then surged, engulfing the entrance. Instantly, the thick reinforced gate blackened and crumbled to ash, leaving a gaping hole. Someone shouted from inside the base, and she slipped back into the jungle and out of sight.

Her fire rolled like a tidal wave through the base while she waited safely outside, letting it do its work. The plans remained fresh in her head, and she could send the flames without looking.

She left her hiding spot and climbed through the burning gate to ensure all the guns and drugs, *and rebels* had been destroyed. From just inside, she scanned the entire layout. The four main buildings were burning ahead, just visible through the smoke. A muffled scream still echoed over the haze, and she clenched her fists, fighting to block out the horrifying sound. She dragged her feet forward.

Don't close your eyes; stay alert just a bit longer.

She finished off the remaining buildings by sending more trails racing along the ground. The flames hit their mark and exploded, lighting the jungle. It would be hours before the buzzing and ringing in her ears subsided completely. A lone rebel made a break and scurried along the wall before her fire swept up and overtook him.

She surveyed the compound, fighting to stay on her feet. Drained, her body was heavy, sluggish, and rubbery. Thankfully it was done. After the booms, the clean-up crew would already be heading her way. She turned to go, but a glint in the ash and soot caught her eye from one of the blackened jeeps beside her.

With a glance around and guilt creeping over her shoulders for her grave-robbing impulse, she pulled a sword from under its charred owner. Asha laughed aloud, gripping the golden handle, sparkling with diamonds and rubies. It depicted a fire-breathing dragon, beautifully crafted and winding around the hilt to protect the wielder's grip. The jewels were vivid fire, and though flashy and rather ridiculous, she loved it.

Testing the sword, she rolled it over, admiring the sparkle. It fit her hand but was far too big to wear around her waist. She'd never trained with a sword, but holding it, she was fiercer, stronger. Everyone carried guns these days, and though it didn't really make sense to use a sword, with this newfound beauty she didn't care. It called to her, like a natural extension of her arm, and she looked forward to using it. She was confident she'd master it after some dedicated practice. One last glance across the compound for any rebels she'd have to finish off and another flash flickered. She squinted; she could see clearly through the smoke, but her eyes must be mistaken…wrong. Two small, charred bicycles leaned against monkey bars and a set of swings. One of those hollow metal structures that would wobble and jump the moment you swung three feet off the ground. They were black and charred with chips of red paint peeking out.

Her blood froze in her veins as she sprinted to the first building. She reached the door in seconds and kicked it in. A dark opening, smoke, and…

Overturned beds littered the rooms with burned bodies and broken machines amongst the blackened rubble. She gagged from the smell of cooked and burnt flesh.

A hospital?

Asha ran to the next building, kicking at the blackened wall. It crumbled inward revealing a scene from her most unimaginable nightmare. The bodies were much smaller there, children and infants, maybe thirty, crushed and burned.

I'm not seeing this. I didn't do this.

Not real. Their intelligence recon should have shown children, and the satellite photos would have shown the playground. Their sources had failed them. Shock clouded her vision turning it white, buzzing swelled in her ears. *No.*

The sound increased, expanding inside her head to near splitting. She gasped past her shallow breath, trying to get more air, but could only drag in thin wisps. Oh God, the panic was coming—the heavy weight squeezed her chest. She struggled to breathe.

I am a monster, slaughtering babies and children.

Her brain failed, short-circuiting and firing futilely inside her head. Rage and panic consumed her as the fire had consumed the compound. She didn't have to look down at her hands to know the flames were spreading, climbing up her arms and covering her entire body. Drained to the point of fainting, with her swelling panic came an adrenaline-fueled power boost.

A sliver of fear sliced through the chaos raging inside her. She hadn't lost control in years, and it would be bad…very bad. Her heart pounded against her chest, and her vision spun. Power flooded her and built. Her fury flared inside like the roaring, jeweled dragon adorning her sword, but she couldn't contain it. Her rage clawed to be free. As she dropped her head back, the shock wave burst from her body, obliterating the compound to ash. Her vision spun, but she fought, clinging to consciousness.

No… Hold on.

Darkness closed into black, and she fell back into the ash-filled crater.

~ * ~

Ringing buzzed in Asha's ears, sounding so far away but growing louder. Helicopter rotors coming closer. She groaned, rolling and grasping her throbbing head. A dart plunged into the ground an inch from her face, raising ash in a cloud. She jolted up, naked and dusted with gray soot. Even her boots had burned away. She squinted against the glaring sun.

How long had she been out? Where was she?

This couldn't be the jungle, not even scorched tree trunks remained on the blackened, flattened wasteland. She couldn't fully grasp the range. It resembled the aftermath of an atomic blast. All evidence of her crime had been erased.

What have you done?

Father Sean leaned out of his helicopter above, harnessed in and aiming his second shot. Heat bubbled, and she clenched her body until she shook. The weapon in his hand said it all. He was handling her.

No way, not this time.

With narrowed eyes and a teeth-baring snarl, she leapt to her feet. He'd used the tranquilizer before, but never when she wasn't in full panic mode. This was the aftermath, and he was familiar enough with her power to recognize when she was spent, yet he was still taking precautions.

She threw her hands into the air, her fingers stretching for her target and drawing her power. Fire shot out in a weak stream, but the helicopter veered away, and her flame failed to cover the distance. She tried again, but it traveled only half as far.

Please. She searched for a spark in helicopter's engine as it retreated.

"Come back, you coward!" She was out of juice. Her power was gone for the next hour or two.

She looked down at the sword, buried in ash, the rubies sparkling bright beneath the gray dust. Grasping it, Asha sprinted over the burned, blackened ground while scanning the horizon for the jungle. The blast perimeter was visible in the distance, and she pumped her legs harder. Their camp lay safe beyond but was littered with debris and covered in more ash.

Father Sean had taken the weapons but left their tents. Her hands still shook, and her stomach rolled as she yanked on jeans and another black hoodie. There was no way he would just sit back and allow her to escape. He would be after her even now. She craned her neck back, searching the trees for snipers waiting to contain her. It wouldn't be the first time.

With her gear on her back, she shook herself to clear her mind. *One step at a time. Stay focused on the next step, nothing more.* She urged her legs to move and jogged along the rough trail they'd carved out the night before.

Coming up on the military road, she ran parallel with it until she spotted the first roadblock.

The three boys were distracted, playing a card game with bullets and cigarettes for their currency. As boy soldiers do, they were dressed up like Rambo, complete with the tough-guy scowls only teens can master so well. But she could see those sad, devastated eyes, with no innocence left.

Goddammit, sometimes life was really unfair. She drew her gun and whispered curses for what she had to do then crept from the jungle. They continued their game as she took position. She cleared her throat, and they froze, all reaching for their forgotten guns.

"No!" Asha shouted halting them.

She gestured for them to sit and hold their hands in front of them. The scowls never left the boys' faces as she restrained them with plastic zip ties and covered their mouths with tape. Taking their guns and tossing them into the jeep, she climbed into the front seat. Keys hung from the ignition. *Perfect.*

The boys' eyes widened, and she turned her head just a moment too late. A man, most likely the boys' handler, lunged from the bushes.

Before she could draw her gun or even duck away, he'd grasped her by the hair and slammed her head into the steering wheel. Her nose crunched and broke as he smashed her face again. Blood meant nothing, but the blurring tears could get her killed in an instant. He yanked her head back again until her neck strained. Metal flashed before her. *Knife.*

He swung it around, and like the beat of a steady drum, time slowed on two counts. He was going to cut her throat. Still too drained to use her power, she wished her panic would rise and bring fire rushing back, but her emotions were never more calm or stable than during a fight. *Soldier mode.*

She thrust out her palm, and the knife clattered to the jeep's dash. Grasping the thick forearm still tangled in her hair, she jerked it forward and pulled his elbow down over her shoulder. The pleasing crack was followed by his muffled grunt and her release. Time kicked back in but moving too fast now, like a runaway roller coaster, a spinning merry-go-round. She twisted and kicked out. Macabre shivers of glee tickled through her at the sound of more crunching bones when her feet connected with his face. Blood spurted from his nose, and he crumpled in a heap. She leapt from the jeep and landed on the ground before he could rise.

His knife gone, he aimed a pistol, but her boot clipped it, knocking it away as he squeezed the trigger.

Too late. She jumped, stretching back into a handspring, dodging the bullet's unknown trajectory. Landing unscathed, she launched forward, her vision brimming red and teeth grinding, and kicked him in the balls. She spun, catching his face with a roundhouse kick, and he fell back.

She crouched and slammed his head into the ground. He was disgusting, repulsive, and evil, and she had no qualms about her actions. Putting scum like this to death was going to be a pleasure.

Warm blood splattered her face and poured through her fingers, but she carried on until she expelled her guilt and fury, and the roaring stopped, and her vision cleared. She sat back for three panting breaths.

Back in the driver's seat, adrenaline pulsed. She shook and jerked but paused before reaching for the keys. She took the knife from the dash and tossed it beside the boy closest to her.

His brows rose over eyes as wide as sand dollars, and though his friends' expressions were hooded and suspicious, he could've been smiling under the tape covering his mouth. She gave him a wink, started the jeep, and sped down the dirt road.

Get it here:
www.unbalancedseries.com